THE SEA GARDEN

Present Day, On the Mediterranean island of Porquerolles off the French coast, landscape designer Ellie Brooke has accepted a commission to restore an abandoned garden. The fine house and surrounding estate overlook the glittering sea but the longer Ellie spends there, the more she senses darkness.

WWII, Two very different women have their lives irrevocably changed: Iris, a junior intelligence officer in London, and Marthe, a blind girl who left her farmstead to work in the lavender fields who is being drawn into the heart of a Resistance cell operating in Nazi-occupied Provence. As secret messages are passed and planes land by moonlight, danger comes ever closer...

THE
SEA GARDEN

by

Deborah Lawrenson

Magna Large Print Books
Long Preston, North Yorkshire,
BD23 4ND, England.

British Library Cataloguing in Publication Data.

Lawrenson, Deborah
The sea garden.

A catalogue record of this book is
available from the British Library

ISBN   978-0-7505-4121-3

First published in Great Britain in 2014 by Orion Books,
an imprint of The Orion Publishing Group Ltd.

Published in Large Print 2015 by arrangement with
Orion Publishing Group

Magna Large Print is an imprint of Library Magna Books Ltd.

Printed and bound in Great Britain by
T.J. (International) Ltd., Cornwall, PL28 8RW

There comes a murmur from the shore,
And in the place two fair streams are,
Drawn from the purple hills afar,
Drawn down unto the restless sea.
The hills whose flowers ne'er fed the bee,
The shore no ship has ever seen,
Still beaten by the billows green,
Whose murmur comes unceasingly
Unto the place for which I cry.

–WILLIAM MORRIS, A Garden by the Sea

BOOK I

The Sea Garden

1

The Crossing

Sunday, 2 June 2013

The island lay in wait, a smudge of land across the water.

From the port at La Tour Fondue, the crossing to Porquerolles would take only fifteen minutes.

Ellie Brooke put her face up to the sun, absorbing the heat. On the deck of the ferry, where she had a prime seat, there were few other passengers this late in the afternoon.

The young man had his back to the curve of the deck rail, facing her. It was his T-shirt that drew her attention: the lead singer of a heavy metal band thrust a tongue out from the boy's chest, an image that invited reaction but succeeded only in making its thin, blond bearer appear innocuous in comparison.

The engines thrummed and the boat nosed out into sea glitter and salt spray, then powered up to full speed. The island was already sharpening into focus when the young man climbed over the deck rail, spread both arms and then let himself slip down the side of the ferry, a silent movement so quick and so unexpected that Ellie was not the only passenger to admit that she had at first doubted her own eyes. No splash was heard in the

11

churning water close to the hull.

Perhaps their shouts to the crew were seconds too late, the choking of the ferry's engine not fast enough. The young man had gone over the edge too close to the bow to have had any chance of swimming away safely. As soon as he hit the water he would have been sucked under and pulled towards the propellers, it was said later.

In the moments immediately afterwards, though, in the calm as the engine noise died and the ferry drifted, it seemed quite possible that he would be fished out spluttering, shrinking with embarrassment at the gangling weakness of his limbs, the idiocy of his stunt. Someone threw a life belt.

On deck, more passengers emerged from the cabin to lean over the rail, asking why the ferry had stopped. They were drawn to one another, wanting to help but frightened of getting in the way as the crew set about a rescue procedure.

Ellie did not speak French well enough to understand much of what they were saying, but it was clear that the middle-aged couple with a small yappy dog, the man carrying a briefcase, and the elderly woman were united in their furious incomprehension of the young man's actions. The man with the briefcase was particularly vocal, and his tirade sounded like condemnation. A man in a panama hat and loose white shirt hung slightly back, making no comment.

'Did you see what happened?' she asked him in English, hoping he would understand.

'Yes.'

'One moment he was fine. It didn't look as if

anything was wrong. The next he was gone.'

'It's terrible.'

'Was it an accident, or–'

'He climbed over.'

There were shouts from the water, but they were not cries for help.

'Don't look,' said the man.

She turned away. Bright sunlit sails slid across the sapphire sea. A small aircraft cut across the sky.

Waves slapped against the port side of the ferry. A dinghy was quickly joined by a police launch. Shouting cut through the buzz of the crew's electronic communications. Falling cadences of conversation on deck marked the transition from irritation with the delay to understanding. The fear felt by all was primitive: the oldest sea story of all, the soul lost overboard.

A hundred years ago the ferry boat had been summoned to the mainland by smoke signal – the fire of resinous leaves and twigs lit in a brazier outside the café at the end of the Presqu'île de Giens, she remembered. It was the kind of detail she enjoyed, culled from the reading she had done in preparation for the trip. Now, within minutes, invisible modern signals brought the emergency services.

Ellie stood up and went over to the rail. Not for the first time, she wondered why she had come.

As it was, her arrival on the island was bound up with more immediate questions from the harbourmaster and two male police officers who boarded the ferry when it docked. Her first impressions of

13

Porquerolles' fabled beauty were shot through with shock and a sense of waste. Oleanders and palms waved a subtropical greeting from the quayside, while the passengers were asked to give their names and contact details and to make statements before disembarkation. What had she noticed about the young man? Had he spoken to anyone? Had he seemed agitated, nervous? It seemed trite to reply that she'd paid more attention to the vulgarity of his T-shirt than to the person wearing it.

She showed Lieutenant Franck Meunier where she had been sitting on deck, and approximately where he had been standing.

'Did he shout as he fell?' The police officer was all sharp eyes, buzz-cut hair and controlled strength. Not as young, close up, as he seemed when he came aboard. His English was good, though heavily accented.

'No. At least, I didn't hear him say anything.'

'Was he sweating, perhaps – had he taken drugs? Did you see his eyes?'

'I wasn't close enough to see. I don't know.'

The white and steel needles of the marina extended out to the ferry dock. A warm breeze rang with clinks of metal rigging. This shore felt far more foreign than the one they had left, as if the sea voyage had crossed much more than the few miles of the strait.

'Where are you staying on the island?'

'A hotel on the Place d'Armes.'

'Which one?'

She pulled a piece of paper out of her shoulder bag and handed it over, uncertain of the pronunciation.

'L'Oustaou des Palmiers,' read the officer.

She nodded.

'You are on holiday?'

'No. Business.'

He frowned, rubbing at his crew cut. His head looked newly shorn. 'What business?'

'I am a garden designer. I'm coming here to look at a garden tomorrow and meet a prospective client.'

Had she been less driven to prove herself, she might have turned the job down months before, on the grounds of impracticability. Any number of garden designers and landscape architects were better qualified to take on the restoration of a garden on a Mediterranean island; someone who – unlike her – already knew the terrain and was experienced in the dry heat, rocky soil and exoticism of the Riviera would have been the obvious choice. But spring in England had been dismal, a fleeting glimmer of sun in March and gone by April; the subsequent weeks of grey skies and rain had been unbearable. It was the simplest of urges that had brought her this far, on the journey up to London and beyond, the flight to Hyères: the need for heat and the light. Of course she was curious about the job too, and lured by the flattering terms of the invitation.

'Who is this client?'

'Laurent de Fayols. At the Domaine de Fayols.'

Lieutenant Meunier considered this, then looked back through his notes. 'When did you first see the man go to the deck rail?'

For what seemed like hours, pinned down on the motionless ferry, Ellie gave answers that could

15

offer nothing in the way of insight and could save no one. From the dock she could see pale beaches and low, verdant hills berried with red roofs. The fort above the harbour punched up a fist of stone through green trees. The sun was dazzling.

Finally she was allowed to go. She wiped a hand over her forehead and consulted the information and a map outside the tourist office on the quai. 'Average temperature for June, 20 degrees Celsius,' she read. It was only the beginning of June, and almost seven o'clock in the evening, yet it felt hotter. She set off wearily towards the Place d'Armes. The wheels of her travel bag, weighted by a laptop, a box file of sketches and photocopied material from old books, scraped along behind her.

It was a wide, dusty square dominated by a church with a distinctly Spanish look. Three sides were edged with eucalyptus and the canopies of restaurants and shops. She made her way round, moving slowly from pool to pool of harsh light and shadow towards what looked like a hotel at the far end. It was not the Oustaou des Palmiers. Nor were any of the other establishments – the apartment entrances or art galleries, the souvenir shops, or the bar that looked as if it would be crowded later, outside which a jazz guitarist now practised. She walked on past fruit stalls stacked with watermelons, apples, strawberries, bananas, pineapples, until she was back almost where she started. It was only then that she saw she had missed the hotel by a few metres when she arrived at the square. The sign was hidden under a red canopy and succulent green creepers that shaded tables laid outside for dinner.

Inside, the reception desk was a cramped counter under the stairs.

'I'm Jean-Luc,' said a young man who looked like a student dressed for the beach, shirt hanging open to expose a smooth, bare chest. He handed over the keys without consulting any paperwork. 'Anything you need, you can come and find me.'

Mercifully he asked nothing about her journey.

'And there is a message for you,' said Jean-Luc. He smiled and looked around vaguely in the small space behind the desk, as if he knew he had put it somewhere. 'Ah!' He seized on an envelope and handed it over.

'Thank you.'

'I will take you up.'

He picked up her bag as if it contained only air, bounded upstairs.

The room was better than she'd imagined, with simple decor and a harbour view. Jean-Luc bounced across the room – he walked in that elastic way of the young and very fit – to show her the air-conditioning control and compact bathroom. When he'd gone, she threw open the windows and stood for a while, trying to reconcile what had just happened with the pleasure boats swaying at anchor and, beyond, the sea of scudding white sails. Slipping her shoes off, she padded across bare polished floorboards.

She looked around for the envelope she'd been given and found it on the dressing table. Her name was written in ink, the hand bold yet elegant. It was a long time since she'd received a message written in fountain pen. Or any handwritten message. It all added to the feeling that she had stepped back in time on this island. She slid out the card. Her hands were still trembling slightly.

'I am very glad you have arrived safely,' she read. 'I look forward to seeing you at the Domaine de Fayols tomorrow morning. I will send transport for you at ten o'clock. Enjoy your first evening on our lovely island.

'Cordialement, Laurent de Fayols.'

What had made him do it, the boy in the T-shirt – what disturbance in the mind, or sickness, or terrible event had induced him to go over the edge, and so quietly? Had he intended to kill himself, or only to attract attention?

There could be no comfort in solitary thoughts in a single hotel room. She put her camera into her shoulder bag and headed outside. A rough concrete road led away from the main square and crumbled into dust that sifted into her open shoes as she walked through pines and Mexican cypress tall enough to deaden any sounds.

Even in her darkest moments she had never con-sidered suicide. Not even in the agonizing weeks after Dan died, when she was struggling to process the loss. Her business was life: the nurturing of plants and the innate optimism involved in plan-ning gardens that would not grow to meet her vision for years, decades even. It had been hard, but she had turned her grief into determination. Self-reliance, too. She had simply worked harder, investing in life. But perhaps other people could find neither the strength nor their own versions of

18

her beech avenues and sculpted borders to watch over.

Where the path split, the beach was signposted: Plage d'Argent. The scent of pines, intensified by a dense heat, mingled with the unmistakably salty tang of the shore. Dan would have loved it: Porquerolles, the island of the ten forts. As a dedicated army man, he had been fascinated by any kind of military history. A tear escaped. He's gone, Ellie told herself for the thousandth time. Let him go. She had to let herself go too, push herself out into the unknown.

The sea nibbled at bone-white sand. She stood alone, lost in thought, where shallow ripples nudged shells into lace patterns across the beach.

2

The Domaine

Monday, 3 June

In the morning sun, the Place d'Armes was an empty white expanse. Activity was confined to the shops and cafés under the trees. Ellie bought a guidebook and a large-scale map from the nearest *tabac* and sat on a low wall in the shade to open out the map. When she couldn't locate the Domaine de Fayols immediately, an unwarranted spike of panic rose. But there it was, marked on the southern rim of the island, close to a cove and

19

a lighthouse. Until then she'd had only the word of Laurent de Fayols that the place would exist when she arrived.

By ten o'clock she was waiting outside the hotel. No cars were permitted on the island, and most people who passed were on bicycles: dented, clicking, cumbersome machines of uncertain vintage, used by countless people on countless holidays. The only alternative was a horse-drawn cart. Ellie watched as the driver jumped down and ran inside the hotel. Minutes later he came out with Jean-Luc, who waved her over.

'This will transport you to the Domaine de Fayols.'

The driver pulled her up into the seat next to him, his work-callused hand rough against hers as they touched, then he tutted and murmured to the elderly black horse, brushing its flank gently with the whip. They set off, swaying high above the road. The wheels winnowed up puffs of dust that trailed the cart as it jolted along the track. Ellie clutched her bag and folders tightly.

Neither of them spoke. The driver kept his eyes ahead. Scrubby evergreen bushes released a strong scent of resin and honey; forests of pine gave way to gentle south-facing vineyards disturbed only by the ululation of early summer cicadas. Sitting up tall on the seat, she craned around eagerly to see what plants thrived naturally.

It was a wild and romantic place, Laurent de Fayols had written, the whole island once bought as a wedding gift to his wife by a man who had made his fortune in the silver mines of Mexico. One of three small specks in the Mediterranean

20

known as the Golden Isles, after the oranges, lemons and grapefruit that glowed like lamps in their citrus groves.

There were few reference works in English that offered information beyond superficial facts about the island, and those she had managed to find were old. The best had been published in 1880, by a journalist called Adolphe Smith. Ellie had been struck by the loveliness of his 'description of the most Southern Point of the French Riviera':

The island is divided into seven ranges of small hills, and in the numerous valleys thus created are walks sheltered from every wind, where the umbrella pines throw their deep shade over the path and mingle their balsamic odour with the scent of the thyme, myrtle and the tamarisk.

She inhaled deeply.

They turned off the track and up a drive spiked by Italian cypress. Soon the driveway opened onto a turning circle in front of the house. Inside the circle, in front of the house, stood a venerable olive tree surrounded by a bed of lavender. On either side of the house, towering pines, eucalyptus and more cypresses stood guard.

'*Ici, la Domaine,*' said the driver.

'*Merci.*'

Ellie accepted his chapped hand, and climbed down. The facade of the house was rendered in pale terracotta with butterfly-blue shutters. It was a substantial property, three storeys high, under a traditional tile roof. Sculpted clouds of box hedge in galvanised planters lined the steps to the front door.

She had hardly started to take it all in when her host emerged, advancing down the shallow stone steps with his hand extended. Laurent de Fayols must have been in his sixties, not particularly tall but slim and elegant, with deep brown eyes that she knew at once would be persuasive.

'Come in, come in, my dear Miss Brooke – and welcome! At last you will be able to see for yourself what we've been speaking about.'

There was no doubting his enthusiasm. His tanned face looked young behind designer sunglasses that he pushed onto the top of his head. Despite the heat, he had slung a jaunty yellow pullover across his shoulders.

'I can't wait.'

He led her into the house, across a hallway and through the centre of the house. A few moments of relative darkness, and they emerged on a wide terrace of pale stone. The sharpness of the sun made her blink, then her eyes adjusted to a glistening panorama of sky and sea framed by palms and parasol pines.

Ellie went straight to the balustrade. The flat area immediately below was broken up into a formal pattern of beds containing oleander and more clipped clouds of box, a southern imitation of the grand parterres of aristocratic chateaux. A rose garden beyond was the first in a series of gardens created on descending levels, apparently linked by a magnificently overgrown wisteria. Dense lines of cypress hid any farther areas from view, including the memorial garden that was her special brief. As a whole, the garden was charming, luxuriant, but – from a professional point of view – dilapidated.

'A great deal of work needed, *non?*' said Laurent.

She relaxed a little. At least he was under no illusions. And his command of English was even better than she remembered from his phone calls.

'Now, you will take coffee with me? Come!'

She found it hard to draw her eyes away from the exquisite vista. The light brought semi-tropical flowers into keen focus: spiked and veined and pulsing with life.

Laurent de Fayols led her along the terrace and around the corner. He had the brisk walk of the older man who takes pride in his fitness.

'This is west-facing,' he said. 'We sit here in the evening.'

Flaking pillars formed a wide loggia, an inviting spot. One wall was smothered by jasmine. On a table sat a coffee pot, cups, a jug of iced water and an untidy pile of papers weighted down by several old books with metal clasps.

'And you can still see the sea!' She wanted to swim there, immediately – she had a childlike surge of excitement at the sight of water so clear the rocks at the foot of the cliffs looked like clumps of turquoise flowers growing on the seabed.

'Yes, the position is perfectly chosen. That's the Calanque de l'Indienne down there. And this is the book I told you about on the telephone.'

With an effort, she returned her attention to her host. He pushed a tome the size of an atlas towards her across the table. The leather binding was scuffed, but the marbled endpapers were a

23

startlingly vibrant red with no sign of damage. It was a photograph album full of foxed images of the garden – and of its makers. The figures pictured flanking the dark arches and horticultural opulence were dressed in heavy clothes that seemed to deny the heat and the density of the humidity. Here and there were blank pages between which botanical specimens had been pressed long ago; flowers that in life had once been extravagantly scented and vibrantly coloured were flattened and bleached on the page. Yet the shapes of these brown, crisped flowers – the canna lily, the agapanthus, the rose – spoke of succulence.

She accepted the small gold-rimmed cup of coffee that Laurent handed her.

'It's going to be quite a challenge.'

'I would not trust anyone who claimed this was an easy job.'

He came round the table and stood next to her. 'This is the memorial garden just after it was laid out in 1947, in memory of Dr Louis de Fayols' – he turned to the right page with an ivory letter opener – 'and here it is in bloom for the first time in 1948, though obviously the Italian cypresses are still small and the boxwood has yet to establish. But this shows very clearly the spaces in the planting.'

It was a formal garden designed around a *bassin* edged in stone, a rectangular pool captured as a sheet of black in the photograph. A carved stone bench of Italianate design was placed at one narrow end. At the other stood two lichened statues, one that might have been Venus, the other Mercury, to judge from the wings on his ankles. A large stone urn was placed in each corner of the garden. No flowers had yet been planted.

'Typical of its time,' she mused. 'So many of the grand gardens were created when the Riviera was populated by rich foreigners – who wanted outdoor temples to wealth and the imagination.'

'I know you have the sensitivity to do this.'

It was not the first time Laurent de Fayols had invoked her sensitivity. She took note. Sometimes when clients spoke about her qualities, they were really speaking about themselves.

'You have a sense of history, too,' he went on. 'You respect that.'

'If you mean the Chelsea garden,' she said, knowing full well that he did, 'that was very different. It was a modern impression of an era, not historical fact – a stage set, if you like.'

The exhibition garden she had designed for the Chelsea Flower Show, gold-medal-winning and much admired in the media, had brought in more business than she could take on, and a host of misconceptions.

'Of course. You know I'm not looking for you to reproduce that. It was the small details in War Garden that spoke to me. The gramophone. The woman's jacket hanging on the spade in the tiny vegetable patch. The crinkled photograph of the soldier, and the man's cigarette case left as a keepsake.'

She'd opened her mouth to protest when he preempted her. 'I know. That is not garden design, it is more ... a piece of theatre. But trust me, I saw that you were the person I had been looking for. Young, with fresh ideas.'

25

'Well, it's a question of understanding the period, doing the right research.' And it was true, she did enjoy that aspect. 'I have been poring over old books in the British Library for references, but there are very few. The best I've found is a description of the island's indigenous plants in a Victorian travel account.'

It didn't amount to much, but it had probably been *Delphinium requienii*, *Genista linifolia* and *Cistus porquerollensis* that lured her here to discuss the commission.

He was looking out at the garden, where exotic tree ferns unfurled like frozen green fountains on a path down to the shore. Impossible to guess what he was thinking. The sea breeze lifted tendrils of jasmine. So close to the sea, the scent was intoxicating: a heady blend of salt and musky sweetness. Ellie felt a wave of conviction that it was all possible. The restoration of the memorial garden could be achieved, the realignment of the great archways and evergreen walls, the reinvigoration of the rose garden.

Laurent leafed through a few more pages of photographs and stopped at one that revealed a doorway cut into a hedge, edged by topiary of a monumental triumphal arch.

'That is spectacular,' said Ellie.

'It stands at the southern end of the memorial garden. It wasn't yet made in the first photograph.'

'Is it still there?'

'The remains of it – very damaged now, but I can show you the place.'

'I'm curious to know what's on the other side of the arch. It draws the eye in and makes the visitor

26

want to walk through.'

He tapped his nose, then winked. 'Now you are interested, yes?'

She gave him a smile, feeling that they were beginning to connect.

This was the aim of an initial meeting with a potential client: to understand exactly what he hoped to achieve. The garden designer – like an architect – was the practical means of bringing the client's imagination to life. For that to happen, there had to be an understanding based on a clear sense of the pictures in his mind; but also, and perhaps trickier, there had to be a personal relationship. The connection between designer and client was crucial to the success of any project, and the lack of it very often a precursor to failure.

Laurent led the way back to the terrace. 'After you,' he said when they reached the first of two wide stone staircases down into the formal parterre. Closer up, the box hedging clipped into interlocking patches was brown and patchy.

Through the rose garden, the path ran straight ahead to the mass of mauve wisteria, now past its best. At ground level, Ellie could see now that it formed a tunnel leading deeper into the garden, gnarled trunks growing over a long wooden frame that was rotten in places. At the end was a green space the size of a large room, walled by a hedge of clipped myrtle. From all sides white trumpets of datura hung down, smelling faintly of coffee.

'I've never seen such a display,' said Ellie.

'My mother planted them many years ago. Moonflowers.'

'Also known as devil's trumpet.'

27

'Angel's trumpet, too. Or so she told me.'

One garden opened from another in a series of secret rooms. Stone steps were made treacherous by creeping ivy. As they walked on, rotting leaves seeped from unexpectedly dank corners. The temperature dropped. There were no more flowers.

'And this is the memorial garden.'

It was a temple of darkest evergreen, scattered with an artless arrangement of broken pillars and statuary. The statues of Venus and Mercury were bigger than life-size. Mercury no longer had wings on his ankles, only tumours of lichen.

'That's astonishing ... like ruins left by the Greeks or Romans.'

'The doctor was a great classicist. Some of the wells we have here were sunk by the Greeks and then forgotten under the scrub. He was very proud of reviving them.'

The water in the stone *bassin* was a black mirror, then silver as she went closer. Its magnetic stillness drew her in.

'Tell me more about the doctor – he was your father, grandfather? – and how he came to the island.'

'My father's uncle, in fact.' He stared out again, as if picturing the old man in the grounds of his estate. 'You know already that Porquerolles has a long military history?'

She nodded. 'The island of ten forts, a strategic defence for the south coast of France.'

'Used for centuries as a retreat for old soldiers and army convalescents. During the Crimean War, it was a hospital camp for wounded soldiers, and there was an orphanage there for many years for the children of the fallen.

'A hundred years ago, M Fournier, the man who bought Porquerolles with the fortune he made in the silver mines of Mexico, began all kinds of agricultural enterprises. He planted the first vineyard. But he wanted to be a benefactor too. He kept open the convalescent centre and brought his own doctor to run it. When Fournier died in 1935, leaving a widow and seven children, the presence of the doctor was all the more important for her peace of mind. The Domaine was built as one of the farms for the Fournier estate, but the widow Fournier set it aside for the doctor and his family.'

'Is it still part of the estate?'

'No, it was bought by the doctor after Fournier died.'

'It's a huge house – did he have a large family?'

'Two sons.'

He hesitated.

'Your father's cousins, then ... did neither of them want to take on the Domaine?'

'Both were killed in the war.'

Ellie pressed her eyes closed. 'That's awful, I'm sorry...' It was a feeble response, but she never knew what to say, how to put her feelings into words to a stranger. What could anyone say? 'But this garden commemorates the doctor, not the sons?'

'That's right.'

'So who was responsible for creating it?'

'My father. And the man who had been the head gardener here in the golden era before the war. Both of them wanting to honour the past in their different ways. When my parents took over the property, it was in a terrible state. The island was occupied during the war, and all the Porquerollais and French were evacuated. First the Italians, then the Germans. They showed no respect, none at all. The islanders came back to find their houses plundered or blown up, furniture reduced to matchwood. Boats had been destroyed, vines pulled up, citrus trees scythed to stumps ... it took a long time to restore and redress the balance.'

Ellie shivered. No wonder; she was standing in deep shade. She rubbed her arms and moved towards the few rays of sun that penetrated the overhang.

'Here is the doorway and arch in the photograph.'

It had once been cut with precision. Now the yew hedging was half dead. A cavelike hole gaped where the doorway had once been, and the dark pillars of cypress seemed to hide something behind them rather than stand guard, as they did elsewhere.

Ellie stooped and pushed through.

The grounds ran down to the sea, through wind-twisted pines, crumbling rocks and the unexpectedly lush green of the bushes and trees that held fast to every scrap of earth. On a cliff to her right was the lighthouse. Now she understood the way the house sat on its land, with the open sea to the south and the rocky bay of the Calanque de l'Indienne to the south-west.

The warmth poured over her like hot water. The wide blue sky and lustrous sea were all light and space. For a few heady seconds she felt a sense of freedom more intense than she had ever experienced.

They walked back slowly towards the house.

The sunlight could not quite dispel the difference in atmosphere now that she had seen the interior of the garden. It was as if a dark underside had been revealed that changed the cast of the whole property. But the whimsy of it, the way the eye was drawn down through every vista, the inventiveness, the fairy-tale quality, the melancholy of the lost gardens – it all excited her.

A summer dining room, shaded by a vigorous vine, had been created at the far end of the terrace. One long wall, perhaps the wall of the kitchen garden, was roughly washed with yellow ochre. A row of kumquat trees stood in glossy black pots, tiny orange fruit trembling in dark foliage.

Laurent pulled out a chair for her. The table was set for two.

A thin woman of about fifty came out to serve them. Silver threads shone in her black hair, pulled back severely with a large bar clip.

'Is Mme de Fayols not joining us, Jeanne?'

'She sends her apologies, monsieur.'

'I thought you said your wife would be in Paris,' said Ellie, conversationally.

'My mother.'

A muted clatter of lid and serving spoons.

'Is she unwell?' he asked in French, turning to Jeanne.

'No more than usual.'

At least that was what Ellie thought they said. Jeanne served a delicate tart of tomato and caramelised onion. A leaf salad with light tangy dressing. Grilled crayfish. She left the table.

'My mother will be disappointed not to be able to meet you straight away. But there will be plenty of other opportunities. Now, eat! Some wine? Water?'

Ellie took a small glass of rosé.

As they ate, her mood lifted again. She found herself warming to him, and to his enthusiasm. She sensed a dash of mischief. His wife lived mainly in Paris, he told her, close to her spiritual home of fine clothes and the arts, trips to the opera on the arm of a young walker, light lunches beneath crystal chandeliers. It was clear the arrangement suited them both. Ellie assumed that Laurent would have his own attachments in the south.

'This property is my passion,' he said, as if reading her mind disconcertingly accurately. 'If I have a mistress, she is here.'

He took a sip of wine and dabbed the corners of his mouth with a starched white napkin. 'So ... tell me what more I can do to persuade you to accept the commission.'

'I'd like to walk in the garden alone this afternoon. I want to get a sense of the place, and to think about how the new parts and the restoration might work. Perhaps just look at the other plants, in the shade as well as the sun, to understand how it all fits together. Then I will do some preliminary drawings to scale.

'Also, I need to work out what irrigation is available. I'm assuming there is, or has been in the past, some kind of watering system. Everything is possible, of course, but with a job like this we have to start at the beginning, and the first investment may be to put in new irrigation pipes. We could spend a fortune on a library of the right plants, but without water we would lose them as soon as they go into the ground.'

He waved away that concern. 'There is a source linked to a channel under the first myrtle hedge. It's never been a problem before. I can send someone down to show you. Now, I must attend to some other matters. You are welcome to spend as long as you like here.'

The first task was to survey the site and take precise measurements. Then she photographed the memorial garden from every angle. Close to the house she found a ladder that she propped behind the hedge and climbed to achieve a view of the whole area. She downloaded the photos onto her laptop and began to make a series of loose sketches by hand on tracing paper.

Her instincts were to respect the set pieces of the garden – the central stone pool, the high green walls, the position of the statues, the grand exit – but to soften the hard edges with planting that added a modern depth. It was important to stay to see how the sun set over the land, to walk up the hill and look down, considering which plants and colour schemes would be most effective.

Hours passed. Ellie made templates for more sketches and then lost herself in the garden. Now that she was on her own, undistracted, the grounds seemed so much larger than they had only a few hours before. Absorbed in her work, she felt calm. Was one of the attractions of garden design the imposition of order on an unruly natural world? If so, there was plenty to engage her here. As ever, once the client had left her to her own devices she could see more clearly.

The sound of footsteps approaching startled her. Someone had come into the maze of garden rooms. Anticipating the employee Laurent de Fayols had said would show her the water source, she was already smiling as she turned around. She waited, then called out, 'Hello? I'm in here!'

No one answered.

She walked over to the remains of the grand topiary arch, lured by the perfection of the view: the sea; the clouds of umbrella pines and cistus, with its evening fragrance of warm amber; the artful framing of the lighthouse. She was so quietly transfixed that when a bird cawed above she turned, too abruptly.

A jab of pain; a deep scratch to her arm oozed blood. She looked around. One struggling bloom of palest pink in the ragged green doorway revealed an old shoot of rose studded with vicious thorns.

The sun was setting behind a line of trees; it cast a great bird's wing halfway across the field when she finally headed back towards the house. In the warm shade of the first enclosed garden, the datura plants were already releasing pulses of their heady night scent. The coffee aroma of earlier was now a burnt chocolate and earthy spice smell that would deepen with the night. Ellie felt a burning sensation in her nose, like mustard.

She met no one. The prosaic accoutrements of the garden – the lengths of hosepipe, ladders, wheelbarrow, rakes and rolls of twine – were left scattered along the way like clues to a treasure hunt.

The terrace was empty, too. She crossed into the semi-darkness of the sitting room. A flicker of movement drew her eye to a row of display cabinets to her left as she passed. Rows of exotic butterflies and moths were pinned fast to the velvet backdrops, their exuberant wings as regimented and inert in death as they would have been chaotic and fluttering in life. Ellie paused by their fragile corpses and felt a surge of irrational fear.

She rationalised it as the after-effects of what had happened on the crossing. In recent months her grief for Dan had lost some of its rawness; now it had broken wide again. If she were to be honest, she had felt on edge since she arrived on the island.

A fire was burning in the grate under a stone mantel. Who would want a fire in early summer? But she saw now that it was the reflections of this fire that had made the flickering movement on the glass-fronted cabinets. She stood still for a few moments, disconcerted by her own over-reaction, wondering where to look for Laurent, whether to go into the hall and call out.

After the searing sun of the morning, followed by the enclosed dark shade of the garden in the afternoon, the light in this immense room pooled around set pieces of furniture. In front of the fireplace stood an armchair, a side table and an antique sofa. Beyond was a baby grand piano illuminated by a standard lamp. A painting was lit by an overhead light bar that spilled polished gold across a console table.

A tap-tap-tapping echoed on stone.

Ellie started.

'*Qui est là?*'

A very old woman was standing in the doorway, propped on a cane. Her breath came in waves of exertion, a sound like the sea breaking on the shore and receding.

'It's... I'm... Ellie Brooke – the garden designer.'

The woman tapped her way to the armchair by the fire. She was thin to the point of emaciation; the legs that took her across the room and lowered her tentatively into her seat were sticklike as a crane's. She waved away Ellie's offer of help.

Settled at last, she propped the walking cane against the side table. It had a striking horn handle, curving to a point.

'I thought you were long gone,' said the woman in English. Only the mouth moved; the rest of her frail body was a statue.

'I didn't realise it was so late.'

'You gave me a fright. Come closer.'

Ellie approached.

'Be so kind as to put that light on.'

There was a lamp on the table. Ellie reached under the shade and found the switch. The illumination burst between them. Ellie found herself staring intently at the deeply lined face in front of her. The eyebrows were pencilled arcs, very nearly hairless.

'Come back into the light where I can see you.'

36

She narrowed her eyes as Ellie did as she asked. Ellie felt the examination, every inch of it. The breath, too close, was dry and powdery with a sweet violet note that did not quite mask the rotten whisper of dental decay. Ellie resisted the impulse to pull back.

Mme de Fayols – for there was no doubt that was who she was – gave her a hard look, seemed to start to say something and then decided against it. A clock ticked loudly, and the fire cracked and popped.

'How will you get back to the mainland?'

'I don't need to, actually – I'm staying at a hotel.'

'Back to the village, then.'

Ellie hadn't thought.

Mme de Fayols extended an eagle's claw from her sleeve and rang a tiny bell.

The housekeeper came at a brisk trot. They conferred rapidly.

'Jeanne's husband will take you back.'

'Is M de Fayols here? I should thank him.'

'No, he is gone,' said Jeanne.

'Oh. Well, good night, then,' Ellie offered.

The response was a dismissive raise of the hand. There was no sign of Laurent on the way out. At the front door, Ellie wondered whether the horse and cart would be brought round again. But the driver who had collected her that morning roared up on a quad bike, pulling a small trailer in which two people could sit.

She climbed in, greeting him, but although he acknowledged her thanks, he remained as taciturn as ever.

The noise of the engine cut crudely through the

37

tranquil evening. They passed pale sandy tracks, some that disappeared intriguingly into pine forest, others that reached down to the sea. Gradually the grey-blue outline of the mainland melted into the twilight.

The police officer from the ferry was sitting at one of the outside tables at the hotel. He was drinking a glass of wine and reading the newspaper. Ellie nodded to him in recognition, but it was only when he stood up and indicated the seat beside him that she realised he had been waiting for her.

'I have to ask you some more questions about the mortal incident,' said Lieutenant Meunier, without any preamble beyond a cursory inquiry after her day. 'The prosecutor at the Port of Toulon has requested more information.'

She was tired, in need of a shower and beginning to feel hungry. 'All right.'

Meunier was as bright-eyed and bushy-tailed as before. 'You may have seen in the evening newspaper that the dead man has been named. Florian Creys, nineteen years old. A student from Strasbourg.'

'I haven't seen the newspaper.'

'The journalist spoke to some of the passengers who were on the ferry. One of them now says that the dead man may have been pushed.'

'I don't think that can be right. He was standing alone.'

'The witness says that he was standing with a man wearing a straw hat.'

'That is not what I saw. But I was not looking at the young man all the time.'

The lieutenant squared his broad sportsman's shoulders. 'So it could be possible that he was pushed.'

'That's not what I said. I am sure that I saw him climb over the rail and go over the side. He was alone then, but I suppose he might have been standing next to someone before that.'

'You were looking at him at the exact moment he went over?'

Ellie fiddled with the pendant around her neck, then stopped as soon as she realised what she was doing. 'He was in my field of vision. I wasn't staring at him, but he was part of the picture in front of me.'

'You are certain of this?'

'Well, as certain as I can be.'

Under close questioning, however, the picture in her mind did not seem as robust as it had been. She judged it unwise to say so. Best to go with her instincts that her memory was true.

'Did you see a man on the deck wearing a straw hat?'

'Yes ... there was a man in a panama hat.'

'Did you see him standing close to the deceased man?'

'No.'

'At no time?'

'No.'

'Did you speak to the man wearing the hat?'

'Actually ... yes. I did.'

'What did you say?'

'I can't remember. No, wait ... I think I asked him whether he had seen what just happened. He said he had – he had seen.'

39

'And then?'

'He told me not to look.'

'What did he mean when he said that?'

'I thought he meant that something terrible was now visible in the water. Something that I wouldn't want to see.'

Meunier wrote it down. 'Do you know who this man is?'

'I only saw him on the boat.'

'Describe him.'

Ellie gazed past the policeman, feeling oddly detached from the tables and chairs under the red awning and the sparse sandy square that she recognised now as an old military parade ground. The Place d'Armes – of course.

'He was quite tall – about six inches ... sorry, er ... fifteen centimetres taller than I am. Dark hair, dark eyes, olive skin. Good-looking. Late thirties, early forties, that kind of age.'

'Nationality?'

'French, I assumed. Didn't you interview him?'

He ignored her question. 'Did you notice anything else about this man?'

She shook her head. 'He wore a loose white shirt, stylish in a very casual way. That's all. I wasn't really concentrating on him at the time.'

Meunier pushed his card across the table. 'If you see him again, please call me as soon as you can.'

She had intended to eat a quick supper and spend the rest of the evening working on her preliminary sketches. But once up in her room, she lay on the bed, exhausted. How could someone say that Florian Creys was pushed when she was certain he

40

had been standing alone? Why hadn't the police interviewed the man in the panama hat while they were all still on the ferry? She tried to remember if she had seen him after he told her not to look at the water. Remembering the shouts from below made her shudder. She was looking away, as he had urged her, concentrating fiercely on the sailing boats in the distance, not quite able to subdue the horrors her imagination was producing. She did not speak to him again. Whether he was still on deck after the ferry restarted, she could not recall. In that case, he probably was not.

And if someone was saying that Florian Creys was pushed – he had definitely not been pushed, unless her memory was completely false – had that person also told the police that the man in the hat was responsible?

She shut her eyes, trying to still her mind. But the gardens provided the next wave of questions. Could she work with Laurent de Fayols? Was he as affable as he seemed; were his expectations realistic? Why hadn't he employed a French de-signer? If she accepted the job, would she be able to give effective instructions to the landscape contractors; would they be able to source the right plants? Then there was the encounter with Mme de Fayols. What was it about the old woman and that firelit room that had made her so uneasy?

Ellie pictured the dark yew garden room and felt its green walls closing in. She trusted her instincts, and was unsettled by the implications.

Inevitably her thoughts turned back to Dan, thoughts she failed to avoid. What were you sup-posed to do when someone you had been closer to

41

than anyone in the world was no longer part of your life? When his absence was ever-present in empty seats and the cold, wide space in the bed, in the phone calls that went unmade, the observations unsaid and the landscapes unshared? Two years since he passed away, and his loss seemed harder than ever to deal with.

He had come into her life with the force of an accident, and left it with equal abruptness. Four years together. Not nearly long enough.

She hadn't been looking for anyone like Dan, wouldn't have known where to start looking, but when he stopped his car – stopped dead – in front of hers and ran off into the crowds on the pavement, she had no choice but to stop too, preferably before the bonnet of her VW went any farther into the boot of his Audi. She was late as it was for a meeting with a man called Ivell, an expert in rare British plants; Dan was only just in time to save the life of a man who was having a heart attack in the middle of Chichester High Street.

Ellie watched as Dan ripped open the man's coat and began to pump his chest, while a knot of helpless passers-by formed. 'Call an ambulance,' he shouted. Her mobile was already in her hand.

He was an army medic, a surgeon, he told her as they swapped insurance details.

'Hardwired for decisive action,' she said, trying not to flirt and failing. At least the patient was coming round as the paramedics arrived.

Dan grinned. 'We're a bit reckless with the machinery when we have to be. Sorry.'

Hers were not the only admiring glances, Ellie

42

noticed. He was tall and blond, with a loosely confident stance.

'Can I buy you a coffee to apologise?' he asked.

'That would be great – oh, but I can't, I'm late as it is. It's work, and–'

'It's important, I understand.'

He was wearing a soft flannel shirt, the shade of a cornflower, which she would come to know as his favourite. Darker blue eyes crinkled in amusement.

'You've got my number,' she said.

Two months later, they moved into the cottage near Arundel together.

She twisted the ring on her finger. Rubies and seed pearls, bought in the Lanes in Brighton for her thirtieth birthday. She wore it always, along with the pearl pendant.

Even now she could hardly bear to hear the news from Afghanistan, the terrible roll call of the dead that would not stop. The dread had been ever-present that she would hear his name one day. When the Afghan shell hit the yard outside the hospital at Camp Bastion, he was coming off duty, having saved three lives on the operating table. Captain Dan Wensley, with his contagious good humour, the hair that always stuck up in odd places and the startling blue eyes, the mouth that always seemed on the point of a smile and could kiss her like no other, the broad shoulders and the manner that asserted without words that he was in charge and you would be safe with him. His life was taken in an instant. A freak incident. They happened, and they blasted the heart of families, relationships, normal life. There were still times when she felt only half alive, either too sensitive or too numbed to feel normal.

She woke at two in the morning, unable to understand where she was or why she was lying down in her work clothes. Something was wrong, but she didn't know what it was – then consciousness formed, followed by the same old heart-shiver and the leaden dread.

Dan. The boy on the boat. The garden. She was shaking slightly, just a tremor. At six o'clock she gave up on the idea of more sleep and went for a run. It was only when she was passing the empty reception cubbyhole that it occurred to her the main door would be locked and she might not be able to get out without calling someone. But it opened easily when she tried the handle.

The air was pleasantly fresh as she broke into a jog, map in hand. On the Pointe de Lequin, twenty minutes east along the coastal path, she stopped, allowed her heart rate to fall as she surveyed the strait. The hills of the mainland were sharply defined in the way the world can look after disrupted sleep. Somewhere close by was the eighteenth-century Batterine de Lequin and, farther round the headland, the Fort de l'Alycastre, built under Richelieu – two of the ten forts left that formed a defensive front along the rocky north coast against the island's many invaders over the centuries.

She resumed her run, pushing herself harder.

3

The Lighthouse

Tuesday, 4 June

Ellie ate breakfast outside the hotel under the red awning, concentrating on the pleasures of perfect flaky croissants and greengage jam with strong, rich coffee.

After the run, she felt more positive about both herself and the garden commission. Five days was a reasonable time to assess the plot and the landscape and the scale of the job at the Domaine de Fayols, and to present a professional folder of preliminary sketches; whether it was long enough to get the measure of Laurent de Fayols, she wasn't so sure.

The air was already hot and close. She stuffed a swimsuit into her bag along with her notebook and papers and marched down towards the harbour and the cycle hire shop. The machine they offered her had five simple gears and a comfortably well-used saddle. She nodded, pleased to have a measure of independence from the unpredictable modes of transport offered by the de Fayols estate.

A wide path led out of the village, past signs to beaches she had still not visited. She took the long way round, wanting to see more of the west side of the island and to work out exactly how the Domaine de Fayols sat in the landscape. The bicycle tyres crunched on small sandy stones as she followed the trail between green oak and pines: the Aleppo and the parasol pine. She spotted an *arbutus*, a strawberry tree, and pulled off the path to have a closer look.

On the south-western side of the island the path opened out into a small bay, reinforced by jagged rocks. All seemed at peace. It was too early in the year for tourist hordes; here was freedom from the modern world, for a while at least. There was a timelessness about being on an island so small that it seemed closed in on itself; the sense of being adrift, not quite connected to the rest of the world.

She pedalled along the coast path to the Calanque de l'Indienne. It was a small bay rather than a cliff inlet. On the west side was the lighthouse; on the other, the house at the Domaine de Fayols rose above the trees and green terraces of its garden. Ellie dismounted. Small brown crickets scattered as she walked the bike across tough grass.

On the sea below a boat was tied up by the end of a steep path; the turquoise water was so clear that the hull was fully visible over the pale ghosts of submerged rock.

From here, trees screened the high dark hedges that surrounded the memorial garden and the other outdoor rooms. Those gardens still puzzled her: the sense that they were the wrong structures in the wrong place persisted. Why would anyone have wanted to enclose gardens in this place of wide horizons in the first place? It didn't make

46

sense, but perhaps she was overthinking. Perhaps there was no reason, or it was deliberately counter-intuitive. Perhaps not until the reconstruction began would the answers become obvious. She had only the faded photographs to work from, and they were like looking into tarnished mirrors.

Some of the sculptural elements clearly held some past meaning, plotting the line back to the past and the doctor's passion for ancient history. But surely that could have been achieved more naturally in more open spaces, like the classical temples built on hillsides surrounded by light and air? If it had been left to her to create from scratch, she might well have chosen the same site above the sea, but the design would have embraced the elements and announced itself proudly. As it was, the memorial garden was hidden away like a secret to be protected.

She made a few notes, a quick sketch of an arch that might frame rather than block the sea view, while alluding to the heavy original. When she looked up again, a man was watching her from the de Fayols side of the bay.

It might have been Laurent, so she waved. He did not respond.

The lighthouse was set on a great solid base, like a chimney rising from a bunker. What looked elegantly well proportioned when framed by the arch of the memorial garden was a monumental structure closer up.

Ellie pushed the bicycle towards it. Birds shrieked from high trees, among them the Wasp-eater, the Thin-Beak and the Stormy Petrel, ac-

47

cording to the guidebook. Giant fennel plants, showstoppers of the plant kingdom, offered globes composed of hundreds of yellow flowers; the towering stalks of these relatives of the hemlock contained a resin that could sicken grazing livestock and even kill. There was no sign of livestock here.

She walked around two sides of the lighthouse before she saw the door. The handle was rusty, but it opened easily.

Inside was a tiny museum – or rather, as there were few display cases but a considerable number of photographs and framed information sheets on the walls, a simple room offering a potted history of the lighthouse.

Ellie reached instinctively for her notebook, already scanning the walls for a complementary mirror view across the bay to the Domaine de Fayols.

The largest photograph was garlanded with a draped French flag with a plaque bearing the date 22 August 1944. It showed the lighthouse dirty and run-down. To the left of this was a poster-size photograph, with a bilingual caption, of Senegalese troops led by General Magnan, breaching the beach defences to liberate the island under covering fire from American marines in their corvettes. To the right was another large photograph, of a line of islanders walking into the Place d'Armes led by the Abbé le Cuziat. According to the caption, they broke spontaneously into a rendition of 'La Marseillaise', the song echoing in the still air as the stout abbot hurried to the bell tower from which he raised the tricolour. Several houses on the left side of the square, as well as the beautiful Fournier house known as Le Château, were still smouldering in the wake of the departing Germans.

On a glass-topped table in front of these was a large, open ledger filled with rows of dates and figures, open to August 1944. A pair of well-worn gloves was attributed to Henri Rousset, the guardian of the lighthouse and recipient of the cross of the Legion d'Honneur in recognition of his heroic wartime actions.

Ellie spent a few more minutes looking around but found no connections to the Domaine across the bay. She pulled the door closed after her and walked slowly to the edge of the cliff.

Patchy rock and scrub stretched out in the sun like old animals that were losing their fur. She almost tripped over a tall stone, so dazzling was the light. She looked down at her feet and saw that the stone had been placed deliberately by the path. Sunk into it was a lead plaque that read:

Angelo, bel Angelo Gabriel
Se tu non festi un angelo
Non vole resti in Ciel
Chanson

The sun pulsed ever warmer on her skin. Ellie stared down with a sudden sense of joy, which just as quickly dissipated, as if she had been on the brink of some profound understanding that fled from any scrutiny. It was the thought of war, she rationalised, like the death of the boy on the ferry. Everything led back to Dan. The loss and terror was the same, whether that war raged within the

49

pages of picture books, fought with chariots and winged horses and pomegranate seeds against the dark powers of the underworld, or with cannon-balls sent from ships to Napoleonic forts on islands, or in the searing deserts of Helmand.

She wished she believed in silent communication, in delicate signs that some spirits still burned, but she did not.

Yet something made her look back, up at the lighthouse lamp, and the words came into her head: *the light of the world.* The thought caught her by surprise. She had never been particularly religious, even less so after Dan.

The man was standing quite still, studying her.

He was about ten metres away, maybe less. His hands were pushed deep into the pockets of baggy trousers. It was hard to make out his features in the glare of the late-morning sun. Her first thought was that he had something to do with the lighthouse, that he had come to ask her whether she wanted to make a donation to the home-made museum. She opened her mouth to give a tentative '*Bonjour*' but replaced it with a weak smile when he backed away. His retreat was curiously mocking, his palms held up in apology. She felt stupid, as if she had made some groundless accusation.

She looked away. Could he be the man she had waved to across the bay? She tried to recapture the scene in her mind, but it refused to materialise.

When she looked up a moment later, he had gone.

'I had another idea last night. It came to me after

50

you left,' said Laurent de Fayols. 'What do you think about a garden landscaped to be seen from the air?'

They were in a book-lined library, mercifully cool and softly lit after the harsh morning sun over the sea. Her photographs and sketches of the memorial garden were spread across a table.

'It would be a piece of fun, with a serious purpose,' Laurent went on, obviously enthused. 'You have heard, I imagine, of Jacques Simon? No? OK, so since the early 1990s he was involved with what they call land art. Jacques Simon planted fields so that their designs and pictures could be visible from the air. Mainly these fields were on land close to airports, so they came into view when the planes took off and landed.'

This was so different from what they had previously discussed that she was at a loss. 'You think you might want to try a design like that here?'

'There are many pleasure flights around here – it might even be a clever way of getting publicity for the wine we make.'

Ellie hesitated, feeling blindsided. He seized on her bewilderment to usher her out of the room, onto the terrace and down into the grounds. 'Come, come! You'll see what I mean.'

Instead of taking the wisteria walkway towards the memorial garden, he led her through orchards of apricots, peaches, nectarines and almonds, trying to explain his vision for this set piece as they approached the vineyard.

It would have to be cleverly done, she thought, with reliable plants, but why not? If it was done well, it would be the talking point of the garden,

51

and would generate good publicity for her as well as the vineyards at the Domaine de Fayols. It would be a unique, modern creation. As a commission it had some distinct advantages over the historical restoration.

'All right... I'm just thinking out loud here... If you want to dream up the kind of picture you'd like, then I'm very happy to discuss the practicalities, how it might be achieved. You want this as an alternative to the memorial restoration?'

'No, in addition, of course. I'm not sure yet how I want it to look. It's just the beginning of an idea at the moment, you understand.'

'Of course.'

As she looked up, a small plane passed overhead. A white scratch opened across the dense blue of the sky.

'Gardens have always been about history and symbolism,' said Laurent. 'The earthly paradise, the enclosed retreat from a cruel outside world.'

'I agree. That's the fascinating dimension–'

'I knew you would see it that way!'

'But' – she struggled to find a way of putting it diplomatically – 'this is completely new ... not at all what I was prepared for.' Only a day into the project, and Laurent was already revealing himself to be one of those maddeningly indecisive clients who constantly change their minds.

'But I believe in you, Miss Brooke. I have no doubt that you could achieve anything you wanted. And it is not impossible, is it?'

She pulled a face. 'It can certainly be done,' she said when she saw how optimistic he was. So it could be, though it would require considerable extra work. 'Can you describe what you have in mind?'

He rattled off ideas. He took her through the types of vines planted on the estate: *monistel, grenache, queue-de-renard, clairette-pointu, cinsault, rosé d'Aramon.* He proposed they taste the wines; she could study the subtle differences in their colour; it would be an amusement that she would enjoy.

But before they even reached the vineyard, Laurent veered off on yet another path. 'Come, I want to show you what remains of the Greek wells... That part of the estate opens up some most interesting possibilities...'

She left that afternoon with an aching head. Whenever she had tried to discuss the memorial restoration, Laurent had quickly reverted to his new agenda, to advertise the vineyard from the air. His vision involved a river of red and pink to represent the abundant flow of wine. An interesting idea, but Ellie had to consider the practicalities. Rivers of lavender had been done. Waves of red, though – planted with what? Roses, pelargoniums, dark red oleanders? The best designs were all about patterns and playfulness, though there was a line between creative ingenuity and silly excess. And what about the labour-intense maintenance each year, and the poor longevity of such a scheme? Even a river of lavender would only last for a decade or so without careful tending.

Close to the most north-westerly point of the island, the wooded path sloped gently to meet the tideless sea. The beach was empty. She swam at last in the sea, feeling herself revive in water that slipped around her limbs like satin sheets.

Birds pecked at the shoreline. At one point someone else came down to the sand, then a dog ran past. The next time she looked back, both dog and owner had gone.

Her arms felt strong as she made for the rocks at the arm of the bay. The water was so clear it was like a discovery of a silent new world of cave entrances and subterranean flowers. A deeper dive, and she would be able to touch the bed. A few kicks, and she went down. She was almost there when, from nowhere, the thought welled up that she might never make it up again. She stroked harder, watching her own pale arms draw closer to a constellation of starfish, a night sky above a coral garden.

A dull pain in her chest intensified. The water darkened all around her, and she panicked. If she didn't act now, she would lose consciousness. She turned back, in a sunlight-shattering, froth-churning, choking rush for the surface. As she broke the water, the thought came to her: you nearly drowned.

She splashed to the nearest rock and held on, panting, blinking the salt from her eyes. She was fine. How ridiculous. Nothing was wrong. Yet the feeling persisted, hardening into an image of her own body on the seabed, the only movement from her hair waving slowly like weeds.

To prove her vitality, she swam crawl and backstroke until the sky was catching fire.

Shops and restaurants lined the harbour water-front like a string of amber beads in the gathering night. To the whicker of bicycles moving past, returning sailors leapt from their yachts and shouted greetings and gathered to relay news of the day's winds and triumphs.

Ellie parked the bicycle outside the hire shop.

'You want again for tomorrow?' asked the proprietor.

'Yes, please.'

'You have a nice time?'

'Very nice, thank you.'

She realised she was relieved to be among other people – people who were not scrutinising her – and to have a friendly, inconsequential exchange. Back in her room at the Oustaou, she checked the messages on her mobile as her laptop powered up. There were a couple of messages; she called the office first.

Her business partner, Sarah – the May of Brooks May – picked up on the second ring. 'At last! I've been trying to get hold of you, and it kept going straight through to voicemail.' It was reassuring to hear Sarah's voice, to visualise the red curls bobbing as she tried to do six tasks with her spare hand, still at the office attached to the nursery just outside Chichester.

'I was with the client most of the day.'

'So how's it going?'

'Well ... not straightforward, but it's a stunning place. All sea and sky and light – except for the site of the restoration, unfortunately. But there's plenty of scope. It could be sensational.'

'But?'

'But...' How could she explain? 'There's no "but". The amount of work the client's talking about is a bit overwhelming – more than just the memorial garden. There's a lot to be done to the gardens leading into it.'

Sarah's silence on the line seemed to question whether it had been a good idea to take this on. But they had rehearsed all the arguments too many times: this was business, a game-changing opportunity to expand internationally.

'You don't always have to be so ... tough, so hard on yourself, Ellie. You can say that it's too much.'

Ellie hesitated, then decided not to tell her business partner about the boy on the boat; reliving it would not help.

'Look, I'll call you in a day or so and let you know how it's working out here. There's a lot of mind-changing and ... I don't know, a bit of a strange vibe. It's not going to be straightforward.'

'What do you mean?'

'Oh, I'm just ... perhaps I'm tired. I can't seem to think.'

'Sure you're all right?'

'Yeah ... I need to do some more research. It could be a huge job for us, a real chance to prove ourselves, but obviously I need to be sure we can deliver.'

'Given the obvious difficulties, perhaps the most practical solution would be to offer some designs and let them arrange construction?'

'You may well be right. But to get full credit we'll need to oversee the whole project. I'm sure it can be done, but it will require some thought.

Perhaps we could think about subcontracting, or sharing the jobs of building and purchasing the plants with an established landscape company on the mainland.'

'Do you want me to come out? The Akehurst job will be finished in the next few days; I could get on a plane.'

'No, it's not worth it. I'll be home myself soon enough. But you might do a bit of research on landscape and garden firms based in Provence that we could approach.'

'But it might be helpful to–'

'No, really, the extra expense... Laurent de Fayols is only paying for one of us to get here. If nothing comes of this, we'll barely cover costs, and the office will be closed in the meantime.'

'If you're sure.'

''Course.'

She didn't go far that evening, eating dinner at one of the tables laid out under the Oustaou's red canopy. No sign of Lieutenant Meunier tonight. She felt the pocket of her jeans. His card was still there.

'You are very serious, thinking all the time,' said Jean-Luc as he placed a platter of Provençal hors d'oeuvres in front of her.

'Yes... Jean-Luc, do you know a man on the island who wears a panama hat, white linen shirt?' Even as she was saying the words, she felt stupid. 'No, forget it. There must be hundreds of men here it could be. I'm–'

'Sooner or later, you meet everyone here.'

He smiled as if he knew why she was asking.

She let him think what he liked. He was right,

though: the Place d'Armes was clearly the beating heart of the island. In the slightly sticky heat, men played *pétanque*. The evening crowd seemed to be mostly families with younger children, and older couples, self-consciously dressing down. The few teenagers were of university age, roaming in well-behaved packs. The atmosphere was the same as any holiday island with good sailing: full of the quietly well-to-do and the bourgeois families, *bon chic, bon genre*, who had been coming here for decades, all meeting each summer, their children growing up together during long days full of healthy activities.

When she had finished her meal, Ellie strolled out among them, people-watching carefully. She lingered at the many ice-cream shops so as not to look conspicuous walking round and round the square. They sold extraordinary flavours: lavender, liquorice, apple tart, candied orange, bitter caramel and an unfathomable blue confection labelled 'Stroumph'. She did not try any, nor did she see anyone resembling the man she'd spoken to on the boat.

4

The Restoration

Wednesday, 5 June

She arrived at the Domaine de Fayols by nine
o'clock the next morning, hoping to show
Laurent her preliminary sketches of the memorial
garden and get his reaction.

'He has gone to Paris,' said Jeanne.

'Oh.'

The housekeeper gave a smile as thin as her
body. 'Did he not tell you?'

'No.'

'He left some information for you.'

On the library table was a botanical dictionary
dedicated to the region, on top of which lay a note,
again written with a fountain pen. 'Another idea!
An apothecary garden as part of the memorial?
The doctor experimented with growing the
medicinal plants he needed.'

That was all. No polite excuse or explanation
for his sudden absence. She looked up into a
shaft of sunlight that fizzed with dust motes. In
the brightness Ellie noticed for the first time how
worn most of the furniture was, the faded colours
of the rugs on the tiled floor.

It occurred to her for the first time to question
whether there was enough money to pay for the

restoration job, let alone the daunting new projects Laurent now seemed to envisage. She stared into an enlargement of one of the age-speckled photographs with a rising annoyance. It would not be the first time she had been inveigled into wasting time on what had turned out to be nothing more than a fantasy of self-importance.

This time Ellie recognised the tapping on the stone floors. The sound of waves – breaths in, breaths out – preceded the entrance of Mme de Fayols.

'*Bonjour, madame.*'

The woman waved away her greeting, paused unsteadily and then approached with the irritating inevitability of a wasp to an August picnic.

'After the fire, I had to have someone to live here with me, or that was what the mayor decided when he came down to see me with his deputy and a woman from the commune I had never met. As if they felt I needed to be looked after like a child. It was only a small fire, but it left this room blackened to blazes.'

She rasped a strange laugh at her choice of words. 'It looked worse than it was. The couple who came to look after me covered it over with cheap paint, but I couldn't bear to be in there; the smoke marks didn't take long to break through the thin white skin, so the room was shut up.'

Ellie had no idea what to say.

'That was when Laurent decided to come back from Paris. He had to, for me, don't you see. Good of him, all things considered. But he has to go back now and then, to keep everything on track. We can't expect him to stay here all the time.'

'It's perfectly all right,' said Ellie. Though a hint of his intentions might have been polite.

'He's a gambler, you know, like his father. Sometimes he has a run of luck, other times ... well, let's not dwell on the other times.'

Ellie shook her head.

'You make choices when you're young and you spend the rest of your life paying for them,' continued Mme de Fayols, with the same hard look as the previous evening. She pointed at the note and the open book on the table. 'That's what this is all about. Don't say I'm not being as helpful as I can be.'

It was an odd thing to say. 'Laurent told me the story of the doctor. I can see why you would want to preserve the garden in his memory.'

'There's always a price to be paid.'

'Right... I'm going to take these out with me, see whether there are any traces of the old landscaping.' Ellie shut the book, keen to escape.

'You do that,' said Madame. 'Though you still don't understand, do you?'

'I'm sorry?'

'Nothing. We have to watch out for the past. It can come back to bite us.'

'What do you mean?'

But the old woman only smiled.

The wisteria tunnel and the enclosed green spaces felt comfortably familiar as she wandered down to the memorial garden.

Four stone urns, which had not been there the previous day, stood one at each corner of the *bassin*. Were they the originals? She would have to

61

check. Laurent must have asked the estate gardeners to get them out of storage or move them from another part of the garden. They were planted with lilies, the equivalent of house flowers arranged in vases – they wouldn't take root. Why bother? What a waste, when the grounds were under reconstruction. Were they some kind of message to keep her thoughts on the primary purpose of the garden?

At the head of the pool a stone bench had appeared, too, quite possibly the one from the photograph. It had been broken at some stage and badly repaired. The stone serpent that had once coiled across the front edge was missing its head, and one end of the seat was cracked. It seemed solid enough, though, and useful too. She pulled her laptop and sketchbook out of her bag and sat down. Whether Laurent de Fayols was here or not, he was paying for a week's consultation and would want to see something tangible for his money.

Staring into the green wall, it was easy to lose herself in an imagined version of the garden as it had once been. She drew quickly and scribbled notes on plants and light.

A movement across the pool caught her eye. From her seated position the water gleamed silver. But something had sent ripples across its surface. Curious, she got up and leaned forward, one foot on the stone rim of the *bassin*. From this angle the water was pewter grey. Her reflection was sharp and still.

The outline of a man slid up behind her.

Her heart seemed to jump out of her body. She spun round. 'Yes? Who's that?'

There was no one there.

Dizzy, she looked back at the reflection in the pool. She was alone. She went down on her knees, hands on the edge, to lean over the water. It was a serene, glossy blackness. As she pulled herself away, the shadow of a bird swooped across.

Then she was shaking uncontrollably. She remained sitting on the ground, dazed by her body's reaction. As her fright subsided and she consolidated logical explanations for what she had seemed to see, she was unable to shift the notion that the figure resembled the man who had slunk up behind her at the lighthouse. Stubbornly immune to logic, he took up position in her thoughts, each detail coming more clearly into focus: the assertive stance, the loose clothes, the stillness that somehow constituted a threat. But there was no one there – how could he have been a reflection behind her?

Her back prickled. Now that her imagination was working overtime, she could not shake the feeling of being watched. She let her eyes move from left to right. Apart from a creaking in the trees, all was quiet. She twisted her head slightly but saw no one. A shift of the light through the leaves raked light across the grass.

Unsettled, but cross with herself now, she tried to concentrate on the photographs. Under a magnifying glass she attempted to identify the plants Laurent had in mind for an apothecary's garden.

A shadow fell.

This time the figure did not dematerialise. It was stout, with a well-tended stomach over which blue workman's trousers were hitched. One of the

63

estate workers, surely.

'*Bonjour, monsieur.*'

He wrestled with the possibility of ignoring the niceties, then ingrained politeness won out. '*Bonjour, madame.*'

'Have you come to show me the water source?' she asked, speaking slowly in English. '*La source?*'

'*Non.*'

He looked suspiciously at the photographs, her notes and her breasts. '*Pourquoi vous êtes ici?*'

He launched into a tirade, much of which she could not understand. His accent was thick, and he snarled his way through his piece without looking her in the eye. But she got the gist. He and the other gardeners could not understand why she had been brought in. They could easily do what was required themselves. And Madame had never wanted the old garden restored; she enjoyed its savage dereliction.

His message delivered, he stomped off before she could begin to formulate a reply. Not an emissary sent by Laurent, then – but quite possibly by his mother.

As early as her conscience would allow in late afternoon, and with enough notes and sketches to justify her time, Ellie gathered her things. She was looking forward to finding another swimming cove, to getting back to the friendly ease of the Place d'Armes. She had almost reached the top of the terrace stairs when Jeanne came out to meet her.

'Madame would like you to dine with her this evening.'

Her mind blanked in search of an excuse.

64

'I'll show you up to a room you can use to shower and change.'

'I'm sorry, but I have nothing to change into. All I have are the clothes I'm wearing.'

'Follow me, please.'

They ascended a wide stone staircase. Along a dark corridor, Jeanne opened a door and went ahead to unclasp the shutters. As light came in, Ellie saw that a familiar bag had been placed at the foot of the bed.

'What on earth...?'

'Madame asked me to arrange for your luggage to be brought from the hotel. She felt it would be easier if you stayed here for the remainder of your visit.'

'But–'

'The de Fayols know everyone on the island. It was very easily arranged.'

Ellie shook her head, knowing that she was beaten.

'Dinner is served at eight. Madame will receive you on the terrace at seven thirty for an *apéro*.'

The furniture in the room Jeanne had prepared was dark and heavy: a large wooden wardrobe and a matching chest of drawers, both ornately carved. A massive headboard, also carved to depict some complex scene, loomed over the bed, a small double, raised high off the floor. She tried it with a hand. It felt surprisingly soft. Her spirits rallied slightly.

First, though, she would leave a message for Sarah, to tell her – to tell someone – where she was.

She dug into her shoulder bag for her mobile.

Then scrambled around deeper inside. It was not in her bag.

Heart pounding, she tried to think. Had she put the phone in her bag that morning? Yes, she remembered checking for it. Had she left the bag somewhere at any time? No, surely it had been with her all the time she was at the Domaine. Had she put it down in the village where some opportunist thief had dipped into it?

Her travel bags were there on the floor. But they seemed deflated. She ripped the zip open and saw that half her clothes were missing. Sat back on her heels, head spinning. Then she got up and opened the wardrobe. Her few dresses and clean trousers were inside on padded silk hangers.

In a bathroom across the corridor skulked a huge roll-top bath and a tiled shower. The latter boasted a complicated arrangement of levers and taps that had not been updated for many years. Steam hissed into the room. She reached towards the taps with one outstretched arm, prepared to pull back if the temperature was scalding. But the vapour was freezing cold. Chilled and puzzled, she fiddled with the controls to no effect. In the end she stripped and ducked briefly under the cold stream of water, shivering as she washed quickly.

She was shown into a side room draped in heavy fabric. A pair of ruby glass urns held lighted candles. Reclining on a chaise longue like an ancient odalisque, Mme de Fayols put a finger to a decanter that rested on a mat of fine crochet work.

At this gesture, Jeanne moved forward and poured a purple tincture into a heavy, etched glass,

66

then passed it to Ellie.

'Eau de vie – flavoured with myrtle,' said the old woman. 'Try it!' She watched intently as Ellie raised the glass to her lips. 'Myrtle from the garden. I steep the berries with honey in the local firewater, but the secret ingredient is the flower, added for the final day. Such a pretty white flower it is, drowned in purple for just one day.'

The liqueur tasted of stewed plums. Not un-pleasant, but very strong. It went to Ellie's head after the first sip.

Jeanne moved forward with an oil lamp, casting light over cabinets and ornate display cases full of curiosities. Heavy Chinese antiques, inlaid with mother-of-pearl, stood awkwardly with delicate glass vases and chunks of whalebone engraved with maritime pictures.

The old lady followed Ellie's glances around the room. 'The de Fayols family has lived here for three generations,' she said. 'The doctor was a great collector and traveller. Not only artefacts. Botanical specimens too. Did Laurent tell you there was once an apothecary garden here?'

'Yes, he did. You speak excellent English, madame.'

Each time they had spoken, Mme de Fayols' command of the language had become more fluent.

She gave an unladylike snort of laughter at the compliment. 'I'm not French – I'm British. Or I was, a very long time ago. Just as well you didn't say anything vile to Laurent, all the time thinking I couldn't understand, or had gone deaf or lost my marbles.'

'I wouldn't have,' mumbled Ellie.

'No, I don't suppose you would.' Some private amusement seemed to surge into her lizard eyes.

Now Ellie's ear was attuned to her accent, it seemed less foreign and more of an earlier era. The short vowels of aristocratic speech, rarely heard these days except in old British films and newsreels. 'Orf,' she said, for *off*. 'Said,' for *sad*. It was there, though barely more than an echo.

'Laurent is a very good son. He has had a commendable career in the civil service. Took his degree in *sciences politiques* at the Sorbonne in Paris, followed by one of the great admin schools so beloved of the French of a certain bureaucratic bent. His first wife divorced him, and his second wife is much younger, an arts administrator. Why would she want to give up Paris for a tiny speck of land off the coast? Fine for holidays but not much else. She is serious about her career, and more importantly for a woman, she is taken seriously.

'But when Laurent retired, he felt a pull to the island. And by then I could no longer live here alone.'

This was not quite the story she had told that morning. Then again, the old lady seemed more compos mentis now. Perhaps she had taken some medication that had restored her balance. 'How did you–'

'How did I end up here? That's a very long story.'

Ellie settled, expecting to have to listen for a while, but Jeanne stepped forward.

'Yes, you can get me the telephone now,' said Madame.

68

An old set appeared, its long cord snaking back to the land-line socket. The housekeeper dialled the number.

'Laurent ... the girl is here.'

She handed the receiver to Ellie.

'Hello?'

'Ah, my dear, I offer my apologies. I have been called away on business. Could not be helped, I'm afraid.'

'I see.'

Now she understood the excellence of his English, too.

'Promise me you will wait until my return. I'm sure you will be comfortable at the Domaine.'

'How long will you be?'

'Not long, only a day or so. But we must discuss the plans before you leave. It's never right if it's not done face to face with the drawings, is it?'

'That's true,' Ellie conceded.

'So that's settled then.'

'Well, it's–'

'Excellent. I will see you in a couple of days.'

The line was cut dead, without a goodbye.

Ellie handed it back to Jeanne, who was hovering, expressionless.

Dinner was a desolate affair, served at one end of a long table in a room that felt empty.

A chicken dish was served, but only to Ellie. Mme de Fayols refused a dinner plate for herself, then accepted the positioning of a side plate in front of her, and a sniff at the fricassee in the serving bowl, but waved it away.

'I don't enjoy eating any more,' said Madame.

69

'But you go ahead.' She smiled, either oblivious to Ellie's discomfort or enjoying her small social cruelties. Were they deliberate, or a natural result of being a very old lady in triple isolation: on a private estate, on an island, long adrift from her native land?

Though she was hungry, Ellie tried to eat as if she too disdained the practice.

Mme de Fayols sipped at a glass of white wine. 'You seem very young. You do realise that to create a garden is to work with time, don't you? It's possible for you to understand nature and growth and change and all the ... science business – but those who make gardens to last must understand the past and see into the future.'

Ellie restrained herself from offering the retort she would have liked. 'What was it like when you first arrived here?'

'It was a wild place.'

'I'm trying to imagine how it was ... the formal gardens overgrown? The citrus and olive groves and a lot of scrub, like the garrigue land?'

'Much of it had fallen back into garrigue, yes. But the structure of the formal gardens was well established before the war. The hedges were strong. Then there was the apothecary garden, of course, thanks to the doctor. He began that during the war, I believe, when there was no likelihood of receiving any medical supplies. There was a kitchen garden, naturally.'

'And it was you and your husband who first made the memorial garden?'

The old lady nodded. 'What do you think of it?'

'It's ... intriguing.'

'It has a life of its own, our garden.'

Ellie nodded, trying to indicate that she understood while chewing on a sliver of chicken. Moths butted at the glass of the full-length window, closed to the night garden.

'Oh, you really don't know what I mean. This garden that reflects the misfortunes of others, it pulls you in. It has a hold. It doesn't let you go, even if you have to get away.'

'I'm not sure–' Was she referring to Laurent and his sudden departure?

'The greatest shock is to discover that the person you love is not what he seems. As more evidence emerges, it's hard to see him in the same way. And whatever the circumstances, it's always the small things that give us away.'

Ellie swallowed. Perhaps she wasn't supposed to understand. Mme de Fayols seemed to take pleasure in wrong-footing her.

Her hostess plucked at the slack of her shawl, pulling it tighter around her as if she were cold.

'I think you know all about that, don't you, Miss Brooke?'

Ellie was saved from having to find a response as Jeanne reappeared with a tray, set it down carefully and left the room without a word.

'A cup of tea, Miss Brooke?'

'Actually, that's exactly what I'd like. Yes, please.'

'Good, dark tea. It's the one thing that reminds me of home.'

The only sound was the tea being poured from a porcelain pot. Ellie's thoughts drifted off.

'It's haunted, you know.'

'I'm sorry?'

'It's haunted.'

'What is?'

'The garden. It was where he was shot. Executed.'

'He?'

'The good doctor. Did Laurent not explain?'

'No, he didn't tell me that.'

'Tell me, did you feel anything in the garden – any change in temperature, any sense of being watched?'

'The temperature is always very pleasant. It would be inside those high hedges, even in summer.'

'You didn't answer the important part.'

Ellie looked her in the eye. 'No. Well, apart from ... there was someone, this afternoon.'

'Yes?'

'A man. I took him to be one of the estate staff. He said he was a gardener and that he could have done the work without any help from me. Or words to that effect.'

'Substantial chap, in peasant's blue?'

'That's the one.'

Falteringly, Madame took out a cigarette from a spring-loaded case and fumbled with a slim lighter. The cigarette wobbled wetly on her bottom lip until, after a struggle, it was lit and a thin stream of smoke exhaled.

'That's Picolet. He wouldn't manage the work. Well past it, these days.'

That was rich, coming from a woman of her advanced years.

Madame took another puff in a stagy gesture that might once have been alluring. 'No, I don't mean Picolet.' Exhalation of smoke with a tidal rasp. 'You are either peculiarly unobservant or you are a liar, Miss Brooke. You know exactly what I mean.'

'I'm not sure I do.'

'Do you ever sense spirits around you in certain places?'

'I don't tend to give such things much thought.'

The cigarette smoke coiled between them. 'Ah, what it is to be so sure. Except you're not sure, are you?'

'I don't believe in ghosts, if that's what you're asking.'

'You understand what is meant by haunting, though. How would you account for the phenomena that so many others understand as haunting?'

'I think ... that these phenomena must be a sign of some inner disturbance.' Even as she heard herself saying the words, they seemed to be coming straight from her subconscious. As if she had no idea this was what she really thought. 'Anxiety, stress...' she continued feebly.

'I see. Anxiety could certainly come into it. But more likely to be a result of a haunting rather than a cause, surely?'

Ellie stared at her hands wrapped around the cup. Unease at the turn of the conversation and the way the woman had been able to insinuate herself into her thoughts hardened into an urge to escape.

'You can't run away from everything, you know.'

Ellie tensed. She put down the cup and sat up straighter. 'It's certainly possible to sense a mood

73

in a garden, to read the signals planted there. Gardens can be laid out and planted to capture an atmosphere, just as houses can be furnished and dressed to reflect different tastes and moods. Key pieces, the way light and space are used. In the harsh light of summer here, reds and hard yellows stand out too much – they clash and unsettle the eye and our expectations. It's all about emotional reactions.'

'Ever the practical miss, with her logical explanation.'

Ellie felt drained. Some vital information was seeded in the strange misfire of communications that passed for conversation with the old lady. 'What else is there?'

'Do you believe everything can be explained?'

'Well, if you're talking in general terms, then no. But that is only because we don't yet have the knowledge to understand.'

Mme de Fayols smiled disconcertingly. 'On that at least, we agree.' She took a birdlike sip of tea. 'How long have you been interested in the war, Miss Brooke?'

'I'm ... the Chelsea garden was a commission from a services charity. They came to me with the theme and some of the ideas, and I worked to their brief all the way through.'

The old woman subjected her to a withering assessment. 'You're not very happy, are you?'

Ellie gave her best professional smile. 'I'm fine. What makes you say that? This is a very interesting project.'

There was another long pause.

'I mean in general. Your life hasn't quite worked

out as you hoped.'

Ellie stared back, not trusting herself to remain polite.

'The restoration of the garden was not my idea,' announced the old lady, with some malice. A disparaging expression pulled at the waxy creases of her face. 'But as my son was determined to go ahead, I thought we might as well have the right person to do it. Perhaps I have made a mistake in choosing you.'

'It was you who asked me to come?'

'I am the one who reads the English newspapers.'

'I'm still astonished how many people saw that piece and how many commissions have come from it.'

'But you're out of your depth here.'

'Why do you say that?'

'It's clear to see. I had hoped you wouldn't be, but – well, we can none of us predict exactly what we'll get, can we? Now I hope you understand that I am very tired. I shall say good night now.'

Mme de Fayols struggled slowly to her feet.

Ellie rose too, waiting to see how she could help but unwilling to touch the old lady. Why did you arrange for me to come here, let alone insist I stayed the night, when you don't even seem to like me? Ellie wanted to ask. Each encounter seemed to confirm that Mme de Fayols was suffering from some kind of psychological disorder. Ellie hesitated to attach a label to it, but something was clearly amiss.

'Good night,' she said.

Upstairs Ellie pulled open drawers, knowing that she had not put her phone in any of them, but at a loss to know where else to look.

The second drawer down on the right-hand side of the chest was heavier. She had to jiggle it to slide it out. At first she couldn't make sense of what she saw. Then her blood chilled as the shape seemed to come into focus.

It was a heavy steel revolver, obviously old. Ellie stared at the gun. She reached out instinctively, then pulled her hand back. She must not touch it. Had it been there all the time? Was it loaded?

Carefully she pushed the drawer back in and opened the one on the left. Inside, it too was empty, apart from one item. It was a pillbox with a glass lid. It contained a single tablet.

Through the window she had left ajar to let fresh air into the room, the garden was dark. A violent animal noise rode the darkness and then receded. A wave of sadness broke over her. It was sadness, she reflected, not shock or fear. If the stark presence of the revolver had forced her to confront herself, it revealed nothing to be ashamed of.

Yet was it intended to be a test? If so, it was one that said more about the oddness of the mother and son who had brought her here. Mme de Fayols' voice replayed in her head, along with the sense that she was being mocked. *You're not happy, are you?*

Was it so obvious? And what could she do to hide it? No, she wasn't happy, but she was allowed to be unhappy for a while. It would pass, surely. It had to.

An unspecific pain woke Ellie. For a moment she felt unable to breathe. She put a hand up to her face, and it spread wetness onto her mouth and cheek. She felt for the bedside light switch and gasped as the bed was illuminated. Dark red stains blotched the white sheets.

On the back of her right hand was a wound from which blood was still seeping. A suffocating darkness bore down on her and a rushing noise filled her head. She forced herself to calm down. Somehow she had cut herself. She must have caught her hand on one of the protruding elements of the carved bedhead. She turned over to look, and it was obvious that was what had happened. A goat figure with viciously curving horns was well within reach of her right hand.

She got up slowly, slightly queasily, and ran her hand under the basin tap. There were tissues in her bag, and she wrapped several tightly around the wound. For a while she lay awake in the darkness as the panic subsided.

It was not until the morning that she dared to look in the second drawer again. It was empty. She stared, searching for an explanation in the dusty interior of the chest. She must have dreamt it, she decided; she had been trapped in a nightmare so vivid she was convinced she had been awake.

Her phone was still missing, though.

5

The Historian

Thursday, 6 June

It had been light for hours when Ellie went downstairs. At the foot of the stairs she listened for sounds from the kitchen, but all was quiet. For one odd moment she had the feeling she was the only person in the house. The sensation passed. If there was no one in the kitchen yet, she would make herself a cup of instant coffee.

As she crossed the hall, she looked through the main room to the French doors, closed now. At that precise moment something hit the clear surface with a dull thud. What were the chances of that happening just as she looked in that direction? Shakily, she went over to see what it was. A small black bird was lying on the tiles outside. It must have flown into the glass. The bird had made no sound of distress. It had knocked itself out. Or perhaps it was dead.

Ellie turned away.

There was no one in the kitchen. Surely Jeanne would arrive soon. It didn't feel all that early. She looked at her wrist and saw that she had left her watch upstairs. As she did so, a clock chimed softly. Seven – or was it eight times?

Ellie went back into the hall, then the sitting

room, looking for the clock. As she did so another small bird slammed into the window. It was so quick and so upsetting, especially as the corpse of the first was still twitching, that she felt sick.

Out in the grounds, Ellie was determined to bury her anxieties by thinking about work. She had not yet seen the memorial garden this early, and she should do. Notebook in hand, she mapped the sequence of shadows in the anterooms leading into it and the angle of the sun in the main space.

Sitting on the low stone rim of the *bassin*, she sketched the archway and the precise proportions of the view of the lighthouse and the bay.

At first she thought it was birdsong. Then, when the melody was accompanied by words, she wondered whether one of the gardeners was singing as he worked. Though it was too high for a man's voice, surely. A child of one of the gardeners, then. She strained to get a fix on the source, but could not.

She listened for sounds of activity, but soon the grounds were quiet again. She continued her sketch, looking up quickly and regularly from the page. It was only when she put her pencil back on the paper that the impression formed in her head, as if her mind had only now been able to process the image, however indistinct. Had someone just walked across the view of the sea and through the gap in the arch? She sat completely still and raised her head. She was alone. The once-grand topiary arch rustled in a light breeze that shook loose dead leaves and twigs. The view was uninterrupted.

It was hard not to think about the previous

night's conversation with Mme de Fayols. Her instincts were to dismiss the old lady's assertions about otherworldly sensations as a spiteful game. She seemed to enjoy finding ways to disconcert Ellie. It was pathetic, really; she should feel sorry for her. It occurred to Ellie only then that perhaps she was the one who was mad. Had the strange episodes over the past few days tipped her over the edge? All she was sure of was that she needed to talk to Laurent. But she would not be spending another night at the Domaine while she waited for him to return.

She would do it her way. Ellie cycled the most direct route back to the village and harbour, resolutely keeping her thoughts on normal matters: a late breakfast of coffee and croissants; checking at the hotel to see if anyone had come across her mobile. She was flushed with the effort as she pushed into the wind. When she saw a pay phone on the road leading into the Place d'Armes, she took the chance to use it straight away. Her fingers trembled as she got some coins ready and pressed in the numbers for Laurent de Fayols' office in Paris.

He was not there.

She gave a moan of frustration. Wait – his mobile number was on the first letter he had written her. The letter should be in her bag. She scrabbled. It was. She tried the number twice; each time it prompted a repeating electronic message that she guessed meant the number was out of order.

As she came out of the phone booth, she felt rattled. It was only a short walk to the friendly hotel on the other, corner of the square, but she was grateful for the support of the cycle as she wheeled it. Her legs seemed to be trembling slightly, more than they should for someone as fit as she was.

The Place d'Armes no longer seemed so benevolent. The voices of young children running across the dust sounded from a long way away, as if in an echo chamber. She was gripped by the unpleasant sensation that had begun at the Domaine de Fayols: a profound detachment that placed the world beyond a film of gauze.

The sun was already oppressive, sapping her strength. Yet she knew she needed the safety of crowds. She headed over to a bustling café with tables set out under the eucalyptus trees and propped the cycle against the low stone wall before taking a seat in the shade.

It was frustrating to have come so far, only to find that the job was a dud. But these things happened. She flipped through the pages of her sketchbook. The scrawled notes seemed to jump, and the drawings looked like angry doodles. She pinched the bridge of her nose to dull the pain that had settled behind her eyes.

Her heart sank when the other chair at her table was pulled out.

'Do you mind if I join you?' A man's voice.

'Not at all.' It was an automatic response.

She hardly looked up as he took the seat by her side.

'Are you on your own?' he asked.

'Yes.'

'I can't understand why.'

81

Ellie gazed out at the square and fixed on the trees and the church until the lines began to melt.

'I'm sorry,' he said, when she failed to respond.

'What?'

He remained silent, looking at her. It was impossible not to look back. Eyes deep brown, with vertical frown lines above the nose. Straight eyebrows. The floppy dark hair and olive skin of Roman genes, she thought, though the process of forming impressions seemed to be too heavy for normal brain activity. She scarcely felt capable of any rational thought.

Ellie dropped her eyes to her coffee cup.

She was so close she could see the seams and the weave of his white shirt. Then the fabric seemed to swim in and out of focus. She thought she might be about to faint. The last thing she wanted to do was make conversation with a stranger. On the other hand, if she wasn't well, it felt better somehow to be with someone.

'How are you enjoying the island?' he asked.

She closed her eyes and dug her fingernails into the flesh of her palms. Her head felt thick, as if she had a bad cold.

'Are you all right? I'm sorry. Would you like me to go?'

His concern was real enough. She gathered herself.

'I'm fine.'

There was something her subconscious was trying to tell her. It almost became clear, then receded. The man smelled of tobacco, sweet and not at all unpleasant. The scent hung in the air between them like perfume.

'Do you live here, or are you on holiday?' she asked, the words ringing hollow as she said them.

He was deeply tanned, with beautiful skin for a man, smooth and unlined.

'My family has lived here for many years – many generations.'

'You work here?'

'Oh...' He raised his palms and pulled an expression that said, *Not really*.

'On the mainland, then?'

'No ... I'm here almost all the time. I'm ... a historian, I suppose you would say.'

'I see,' she said, though she didn't. 'What kind of historian?'

'Military history. I specialise in World War Two. And you?'

'I'm a garden designer. I'm doing some preliminary work at a property here.'

He looked over at the waiter, but the man was busy at the bar and didn't see him. It didn't matter, thought Ellie. Actually, it was reassuring that they could sit undisturbed.

The world slowed. She was starting to relax. In fact, it was lovely to sit next to this man. It didn't make sense, but it was as if she had come home after a long journey. Perhaps it was the intense atmosphere at the Domaine de Fayols; it was only upon leaving it that she realised how strange and overwhelming it had been.

He was telling her about the different beaches on the island, and the groves of mandarin and grapefruit that once grew all along the Langoustier road, trees brought from Sicily to start the citrus groves.

83

'It must have been a glorious place to grow up,' she prompted, enjoying hearing him speak.

'It certainly was. During the long, hot days we children found shady hiding places and made encampments, ramshackle affairs. When we roused ourselves from these cocoons, we filled up with apricots from the orchard, then walked for hours down the hill to dip our feet in the sea.

'We judged the time by the sun, tiredness and hunger. When we were parched and covered in dust, we would turn back to the farm.

'We lived in the open air, of course, all summer long. We ate at a long wooden table on the west-facing terrace. Each night the sunset, each night a different composition, in fire colours.'

The way he spoke, she could picture the place exactly.

It was as if all noise and movement had ceased around them. For Ellie, there was a sense of histories large and small unfolding.

'In the winter we hunted, the men and the boys,' he went on.

He didn't much like to hunt, though he learned how to do so effectively with gun and knife. They went after rabbit and pheasant, mainly. But what was the point of using up ammunition, when there was always also the constant risk of a stray bullet hitting a poacher child, of whom there were a surprising number? Better to hunt by night. Easier to track the prey to its resting place and wait, to creep up on a pheasant in the low branches of a tree and rip it from its nest.

'There was always more hunting by moonlight. Not only of game. The fishermen stole grapes at full moon to make their own wine, and it was understood by all that they would. Sometimes you could smell the bouillabaisse they cooked up on camping stoves on the rocks below the vineyards.'

She could see it all, the men with their tin bowls, the shimmer of silver on fish and sea. The cliffs rising steeply.

'If you like history, you should go diving,' he said, his words slipping insidiously inside her thoughts. 'The scuba schools are down at the harbour.'

'I've seen them. But I've never done scuba before.'

'You should learn. There are fabulous dives here – wrecked ships and subterranean cliffs. And there's a plane wreck on the seabed to the south-west beyond the lighthouse. You should ask about it.'

'It sounds very exciting.'

'You don't have to scuba – you can just snorkel. The Domaine de Fayols place is just by the Calanque de l'Indienne – that's as good a place as any to start. The water is so clear you can see right down to the bed in most places. But to make the most of it, you need proper equipment. Perhaps I could give you–'

'What's your name? I never asked.'

He smiled, and then stood up. 'Ah, well ... it's a small place. Perhaps our paths will cross again,' he said.

'Perhaps they will.'

Ellie watched him walk away soundlessly on his canvas shoes. It must have been close to noon, for he had no shadow.

85

Where was he going? She tried to imagine his life on the island: a wife and children, perhaps; a mistress was a distinct possibility. Maybe he was going to see her now, in a house hidden among the pine trees, before returning for an evening with his family. The archetypal Frenchman and his women, his exquisite manners and pragmatic approach to matters of the heart.

His rolled-up sleeves and open-necked shirt, baggy linen trousers and old espadrilles. The panama hat he pulled on as he walked away. By the time she stood up to run after him, he had vanished.

Why hadn't she realised sooner? She should call Lieutenant Meunier. If she hadn't lost her mobile, she would have called him right then and there – wouldn't she?

'Where have you been?'

Mme de Fayols carved the air in the hall with the curved point of the horn handle of her cane. In the dim light her pupils were so huge that her stare was completely black.

'You are supposed to be doing a job here! You have to be here to understand. You can only learn so much from the books and the photographs. The rest you have to feel, sense, absorb. Or have you felt it, and wish you had not?'

Ellie said nothing, determined not to pursue this line of questioning.

'You feel it. I know you feel it.'

A deep breath. 'I went to the village because I needed to do something.'

'But you're here to work!'

'And I have been working on plans for the garden. You can see them if you wish, but you must understand that they are preliminary ideas rather than plans ready for submission.'

A couple of impatient taps from the cane.

'Actually,' said Ellie, 'I've done as much as I can here. Now I need to refine my sketches, which I will do back at the hotel. I'll just collect my things and get on with that as soon as possible.'

Mme de Fayols looked as if she had been slapped in the face.

Ellie found Jeanne in the kitchen. It was an even colder reception than normal. Tersely Ellie told her about her mobile, still missing though Jean-Luc had assured her he would ask all the staff at the hotel.

'So I need to use the telephone here to call Laurent, please.'

The housekeeper indicated the telephone mounted on the kitchen wall. When Ellie rang it, Laurent's mobile was still out of service.

'Are these his numbers when he's away?' she asked, pointing to a list pinned up on the wall. Several numbers clustered around a simple T.

Jeanne nodded.

Two calls rang and rang, and one was answered by a hotel concierge. Laurent de Fayols was not currently in residence.

'Will you be sure to tell him that I'm working back at the Oustaou des Palmiers, please? I'm going upstairs now to collect my bags.'

'I'll come with you.'

It was as if she was not trusted to be alone in any part of the house. Ellie wondered what on earth the old lady had told Jeanne.

Upstairs the lamp in her room was on – and lying sideways on the bedside table. Her small collection of cosmetics was strewn across the floor. Papers were scattered. Some of the larger drawings she had done were ripped to shreds.

'What on earth – what's happened here?'

Jeanne shook her head. 'I have not been in here today. This is how you left it.'

'I absolutely did not,' said Ellie. For the second time that day her vision blurred and she felt faint. The bed was rumpled, as if it had been slept in. She knew she had made it that morning, remembered thinking that she must leave everything perfectly tidy to withstand any checking by Jeanne.

Her camera was on top of the chest of drawers, but switched on, draining power. She gave silent thanks that she had thought to take her laptop with its precious files with her into the garden that morning. There was no damage to the camera, but when she examined it there were no photographs left; they had all been deleted.

'Someone's done this,' she said to Jeanne. She turned to gauge the housekeeper's reaction, but she was no longer there.

Drip. Drip. Drip-drip. It took longer than it should have for Ellie to hear it. The drips sounded as if they were coming from a lazy tap or shower. But the bathroom was down the corridor. She found her travel grip and went over to the wardrobe.

Inside, her clothes were soaking wet. They smelled of the sea.

Drip. Drip.

She surveyed the wreckage. Then with shaking hands she stuffed her things into the grip, wet clothes onto dry. She pulled open drawers and swept out anything that was hers. Luckily it was not much. She glanced round for anything she had missed, hoping irrationally to see her mobile.

The light hit the headboard of the bed at an odd angle. It was only then that she took in what the carved scene depicted. It was a version of the garden with the topiary arch, in which some pagan dance was taking place. A devil's horns, shaved to a point. The cut on her hand throbbed.

She lunged for the door. For a mad instant she half thought it might be locked, but the handle turned easily enough. She almost fell down the stairs with her bags. There would be no horse and trap waiting to take her back. No option but to wheel the cycle with the luggage, even if it meant slow progress.

On a table at the foot of the staircase an hourglass was running. The sand flowed smoothly from one clear bulb into the other. Who had set that, and why?

A door banged.

'Miss Brooke?'

Madame was leaning on Jeanne as she came into the hall from the sitting room.

Ellie felt a trickle of sweat run down the back of her neck. Her heart thudded.

'You can't leave,' said the old lady.

'I'm afraid I have to.'

'What will I tell Laurent?'

'I left messages for him. I will speak to him myself.'

'If you go now...'

If she went now, then what? It would be the end of the French restoration project? Quite probably. There would be no prestige and quite possibly some bad publicity. But she had the terrible feeling that this was the end of something more than just one garden job, over before it had properly started; that events were taking place out of her control, but she had no idea what they might be. She took several deep breaths. Was this how it felt when a nervous breakdown began? Was that what was happening? Stupid, she told herself, you're making it worse by letting these ridiculous thoughts take root.

'I will speak to your son, madame. But after this ... I can't see that I will be able to work here.'

When she got back to England she would take a week off, maybe two. She could relax and let herself recover. It was the incident on the ferry, the forts and the military parade ground, the talk of war and the memorial garden that had combined to bring on this nervous reaction, crisis, whatever it was, and revisit her grief over Dan more painfully than ever.

'I have to go.'

'If you do, it will ruin your career. I will say that you took our money and weren't capable of delivering.'

'I've been paid nothing yet.'

'Apart from your flight and a stay in a hotel. The hotel you had to leave and come here because we were worried about your extravagance, racking up huge bar bills and charging them to our account.'

'But that's not true!'

'Truth is the first casualty of war.'

Ellie shook her head in bewilderment. What was she on about now?

'Furthermore, you attacked me.'

'You know that I did not.'

'Who will the French authorities believe, though? That is the only aspect to concern us.'

'The room I stayed in last night was trashed when I went up just now. My clothes are dripping wet,' Ellie started, then faltered. What was the point? The woman was not well.

'How do I know you haven't done this yourself?'

'Why would I do that?'

'Are you saying there has been a break-in?'

'Well, perhaps there has. My phone has disappeared, but that went yesterday. But it would be a very strange burglar who decided to delete my photos but not take the camera and drench my clothes in seawater... I don't know what kind of vicious game is being played here, but I want nothing to do with it. I've had enough of this craziness!'

Madame swayed, seeming to shrink into decrepitude as the tirade went on. Jeanne frowned and moved towards the old lady protectively. 'We did not do this,' she said.

Ellie wrenched open the main door.

Of course the bicycle was not where she had left it. It was all so predictable that Ellie congratulated herself on guessing as much as she went down the steps. There was nothing to worry about – nothing at all. It was only a malicious game played at the command of a madwoman.

She could walk. The island was so small, no

walk was too far. Without a glance back, she set off. The bag containing her laptop was heavy, and she had to stop frequently to change sides before trudging on. When she came out onto the main track she paused, half expecting to be stopped by a domaine worker in a vehicle. No one appeared. Then she began hoping that a vehicle would miraculously appear and offer her a lift, but that didn't happen either.

As she trudged towards the village, the tension in her shoulders and legs eased a little. To the left of the path, the sea formed strips of sequins. Farther out, it was the darkest blue she'd ever seen.

Much as she had been determined to swim in the Calanque de l'Indienne, it occurred to her that it might be unwise now. As soon as the thought occurred, however, she longed for cold water on her body, that delicious shock on immersion, to float, eyes closed against the sun. She was so close to the *calanque*.

Without further thought, she put down her bags and broke into a jog, slowing only to pick her way down over the rocks to the sea. It was steep, and loose stones made her slip more than once. She was alone. Standing on a flat rock half hidden by a pine, she stripped off down to her underwear and let herself into the water.

She floated on her back, barely moving. She was fine; everything was going to be all right. Beyond the wide inlet, sleek modern boats skimmed across the blue, trailing white ribbons of froth. Too fast, too soulless, she thought; this was a journey to be taken slowly, a transition to be savoured.

The sudden weight on her chest seemed to compress her whole body. She was being both pushed and pulled down. Banks of trees seemed to tower over her, blotting out the sky. At least, she thought they were trees. The shapes were pushing her down. She was underwater now; she could see clusters of bright darting fish, and the pressure in her head was building as the water became colder and bluer and deeper. She could not breathe. Deeper, into black water. Nothing more to see. All was black.

Her head seemed to explode. Then she was in the light again. Her teeth chattered. She was cold, and then hot. Gasping, she found she could stand. She was still in the shallows. Yet she had been drowning. It had been so vivid. What had just happened?

Ellie made it, terrified, to the rock. She hauled herself onto it and tried to slow her inhalations. Gradually a hot, heavy stillness settled over her, and she found the strength to drag herself out of the water.

She had to be rational. It was the only way she could get through this. Had she fainted? Was this anxiety, a kind of panic attack following on from the first time it happened, and worse a second time? Or was there another explanation – an infection caused by that nasty thorn scratch, reopened by the gash from the bedhead? A plant she had come into contact with, maybe ... those hanging bells of datura in the entrance to the garden rooms were witches' weeds, cousins to deadly nightshade and henbane.

The logical progression of thought steadied

93

her. Even so, it was a while before she picked up her bags and started walking again.

Her watch said it was eight o'clock in the evening, but she was not sure how that could be possible. At the Oustaou des Palmiers, Jean-Luc looked surprised to see her, though she was sure she had told him she was coming back. There was a small room she could have. She would have taken a cupboard.

Up in a tiny bathroom in the eaves, she looked in the mirror. A startled wreck stared back, dirt and charcoal smudged across her face and hands and pinched shadows under her eyes.

Kneeling by the bed, she switched on the laptop, praying for a strong Wi-Fi connection. A search, and the answers to some questions, at least, were there at her fingertips. Most parts of the datura were poisonous, and the seductive scent masked toxic hallucinogens. Confusion, delirium and drowsiness were all symptoms of accidental poisoning. Coma, in the worst cases. Agitation and convulsions had also been reported. Muscle weakness. Memory loss.

Some sources claimed datura seeds had been used as a murder weapon, others that it was known in ancient times as a means by which whores might sedate then rob their clients, who would remember nothing.

Most of the cases discussed online concerned the plant's dubious use as a recreational drug. It was slightly worrying – but also made sense – that the trippy, lucid-dream states it induced could recur spontaneously over a period of several days.

Ellie sat back on her heels. It was certainly possible that she had come into contact with the datura in the garden. But she had not ingested the seeds, which accounted for most of the experiences requiring an antidote. She wondered whether she ought to ask Jean-Luc if there was a doctor she could see as a precaution, but actually, now that she was back in the safety of the hotel and in control again, she felt better. Whatever had occurred seemed to have passed. She drank four glasses of water in an attempt to flush out her system and curled up on the bed, desperate for sleep.

6

The Flight

Friday, 7 June

It was a bad night. She woke constantly, feeling either nauseous or thirsty. The waking broke her thoughts into vivid dream fragments: on a low rocky promontory a tower melted on a crag; the ferry was waiting for her; crowds surged up from the quay, but she was searching for the boy in the T-shirt. She kept losing her bags. The man at the lighthouse was watching her, face still hidden. At last she was on the boat, then she was balancing on the rail over the sea, walking it like a tightrope. Falling through blue air, trying and failing to fly.

As early as she could, she called Sarah from the reception desk of the Oustaou des Palmiers. 'It's not working out. I'm sorry. My flight home isn't until tomorrow evening, but I might go back to the mainland and stay in a cheap hotel in Hyères tonight – I'll see how I feel.'

In Sussex, Sarah was eating breakfast, swallowing rapidly. 'What's gone wrong?'

'I'll tell you everything when I get back. But don't waste any time on contacting the landscapers out here. Oh, and I've lost my mobile, so don't worry if I don't pick up.'

'Ugh, what a pain. Lost how?'

'It disappeared while I was at the client's place. Misplaced, stolen, taken as part of the game, I don't know.'

'The *game?*'

'Don't ask. I'll tell you when I get back.'

'Are you sure you're all right?'

Tears threatened to spill over. 'Fine. Just... I just want out of this. It's not what we thought.'

'OK, well... I'll wait to hear from you. Call me when you get to Hyères, yes? And Ellie? It doesn't matter. It's only one job.'

'I know. But thanks.'

'Speak to you later.'

A warm breeze ruffled the palm trees and drew soft clinking sounds from the sailing boats in the marina. Just a few miles away from the Domaine de Fayols, the island seemed a different place, full of light and life, cause for cautious optimism. The previous day was a world away, farther than a few kilometres, longer ago than twenty-four

96

hours. She was relieved to feel relatively normal, if tired and gritty-eyed, as she walked down towards the ferry office to look at the timetables for the crossing back to La Tour Fondue. Perhaps she had been right about the datura, and all that water had done the trick. With a pang of guilt she remembered the hired bicycle. On the way to the ferry she should go into the shop and tell the man that it had been left at the Domaine. He could keep the deposit for his trouble.

On a quayside board the timetable showed crossings so frequent that the return trip would be no more complicated than catching a bus. She could turn up whenever she wanted. There was nothing more to worry about.

Signs advertised pleasure cruises, catamaran trips and visits to the other islands. A row of similar ventures was in healthy competition. Several dive schools offered lessons in using scuba equipment. Pictures of sunken ships interlaced with shoals of subtropical fish were placed as bait by an open door for those who were already qualified to dive and could be enticed on a guided expedition.

'You want scuba dive?' called a student type with long hair and a manner in which flirtatiousness did battle with lassitude. Ellie remembered something.

'Do you dive over the wrecks?'

'Certainly, yes. Many ships on the bed.' He managed to make it sound quite lascivious.

'What about the plane wreck?'

He pulled a puzzled face.

'Aeroplane?' she asked.

'No plane. Only ship.'

'Maybe someone else does that dive trip?'

'No. There is no plane in the sea.'

'Oh. OK ... *merci*.'

'You make a dive to see some ship?'

'Another time, maybe.'

A fishing boat nosed into the harbour, and two men spread out their catches: spiny crab, sea urchins, prawns and squid, as well as less exotic fish. It was surprisingly quiet, so close to the buzz of the village, the crowded marina with its pleasure craft and fishermen, the pastel stucco buildings with their bars and restaurants under red awnings. Porquerolles was an attractive place, no doubt about that. She wondered if she would ever return. Under different circumstances, it would be gorgeous. Now that the past few days at the Domaine de Fayols seemed a world away, she could be objective again. Frankly it was amazing that more approaches from prospective clients weren't a waste of time, wealthy, eccentric, unrealistic and demanding as those who could afford her services often were.

She walked aimlessly, just for some gentle exercise to test her muscle strength. The path to the east rose up through spiny bushes – *griffes de sorcières*, witches' claws, as she now knew from one of Laurent's botanical dictionaries. A few hundred metres farther, pine trees were gnarled and blackened, as if they had been scorched by a forest fire but survived.

Not long now, and she would be off the island. She could leave any time she wanted. The hills behind Le Lavandou on the mainland reared up in reassurance, so close that they seemed no farther than the opposite side of a lake. White sails skipped over the blue, and she watched them, thinking of the man in the billowing shirt, how sweetly serious he was at the café and how he had noticed and helped her when she felt unwell.

She walked on. Then, as if she had summoned him by the power of thought, there he was – or a figure that could easily be him – on the path ahead where it curved round a higher point in the direction of the Cap Medès. Or had seeing him sparked the thought, subconsciously? She began running, but when she emerged from a line of holm oaks, he was nowhere to be seen.

The disappointment she felt was entirely disproportionate. She tried to justify it; as a local there was so much he could explain: whether there had been any other news about Florian Creys, what his background was and why he had slipped off the boat in front of them; the oddness of the de Fayols family and their domaine; what was wrong with Madame, and whether everyone on the island knew she was a lunatic.

If nothing else, she would have liked to run into him once more, anyhow, to say goodbye and thanks. Apart from Jean-Luc at the hotel, he was the only person who had shown her real kindness during the past few days. There had been something about him she found calming.

She skittered to a halt. What was she doing, chasing him like this? Had she lost her mind again? She turned round to start walking back to the Plage de la Courtade. A handful of earth trickled from above, as if the higher ground had been disturbed. She looked up but could see only trees. Her train of thought half forgotten, she turned back the way she came. Her shirt was damp and cold on her back.

'How is your work going on the garden?'
As she reached the harbour, there he was at her shoulder. His battered espadrilles had made not a sound on the concrete runway of the quay.
'Oh! It's you.' Close up, she caught the aroma of old-style French tobacco. 'The garden ... it's not really happening now.'
'Problems?'
'You win some, you lose some.'
'I saw you over at one of the dive places.'
'Yes.'
'Are you going out on a dive?'
'I was just curious.'
He said nothing.
'I asked about the plane wreck, but they didn't know about it.'
Not many people do.'
'I see...'
'It is there, even if most people don't know about it.'
She watched closely as he ran his hand up his right forearm. As the sleeve was pushed back, it revealed a contusion of red scars. 'It was you on the ferry, the day the boy committed suicide, wasn't it?'
'Yes.'
'There's a police lieutenant, Meunier, who wants to talk to you. They're still talking to everyone, trying to get an accurate picture of what happened. I've got his card somewhere.'

'Meunier? OK, no problem. I can find him.'

'Someone is saying the boy was pushed. Did you think he was pushed?'

'No.'

The sea shuddered in the wake of a passing boat, setting off a carillon of metal against mast in the marina.

'The trouble is, the more you try to remember exactly what you saw, the more you begin to doubt yourself.'

'First instincts are normally right.' He fidgeted with a heavy brass cigarette lighter he brought out of his pocket. 'So what happened over at the Domaine de Fayols?'

'I'm not taking the job – I'm going home today.'

'Good.'

'Good? Why do you say that?'

'There is something I want to ask you. Will you walk with me?'

'I still don't know your name.'

'Gabriel.'

'I'm Ellie.'

Slim tree trunks twisted like wrought-iron lattice-work, holding up clouds of acid-green foliage against the sea and sky. From the coastal path, the hills on the mainland were soft purple-brown mounds.

'How exactly did you come to be involved with the Domaine de Fayols in the first place?' Gabriel asked, in a tone that implied she was out of her depth there.

'Laurent de Fayols sent me an email. He'd heard about my work. We spoke on the phone a few times and arranged for me to come over to look at the garden. But then he went off to Paris, and Mme de Fayols informed me that she was the one who'd found out about my work and chosen our firm, yet she has done nothing but undermine me since I arrived. It has all been very strange – and to what purpose?'

'She has a certain reputation.'

'I am very glad to hear that.'

'She is crazy.'

Ellie laughed, and the tension in her shoulders began to release. 'Certifiably ... or was that just a figure of speech?'

He did not reply.

As the trees grew more dense, a brown weave of needles on the path deadened the sound of their footsteps.

'So the memorial garden at the Domaine de Fayols will have to wait to be restored,' he said.

'I'm sure they'll find someone else.'

'I hope so. It's important to preserve it. It's special, the way it brings together the land, the sea and the sky – and the lighthouse.'

'I agree. The view of the lighthouse is integral to the garden.'

'You are very perceptive.'

'I went into the little museum there. I thought perhaps there might be a connection to the Domaine, but if there is, it's not mentioned.'

'Did you see the record book and gloves that belonged to the lighthouse keeper who remained on the island under the Germans during the war?'

'Yes.'

'Henri Rousset refused to join the evacuation,

and the occupiers needed him. He was permitted to stay to operate the lighthouse as normal. A very brave man.'

'I saw the large photograph and the flag,' she said. 'I guessed it must have been something like that.' She shivered involuntarily as it came back to her: the feeling as she stood on the cliff looking up to the beacon that she was on the verge of making some important connection.

Gabriel was quiet for so long that she wondered whether he was going to respond. They climbed farther, following signs for the Fort de l'Alycastre, defenceless now, gnawed back to bare stone by birds and wind. Tufts of sea grass stole up the squat stone walls like a raiding party.

'Rousset put his life at risk to safeguard the lives of thousands of Allied men,' he said. 'Before the Allies landed at Saint-Tropez on the fifteenth of August, 1944, these three Golden Islands had to be neutralised. At the crucial moment, just before the amphibious assault, he disabled the lighthouse beam to confuse the German night defences. Meanwhile, another beam was set up farther along the coast to imitate the Porquerolles lighthouse.'

'How did he know what he had to do?'

'A Resistance agent managed to get out here to tell him. It was risky, but it had to be done. Allied intelligence agents in Marseille wanted to blow up the lighthouse, but bombing it from a plane would have condemned Rousset, a good man who had stayed on the island watching the Germans and waiting for his chance to act, to certain death – and risked the destruction of nearby properties.'

'The Domaine de Fayols,' said Ellie. 'I'm beginning to understand. But how did the Resistance get someone out to an occupied island, in an area that must have been heavily defended?'

'A light aircraft, flying at night.'

'That must have been extremely dangerous.'

'It was.'

'So the plan worked?'

'Up to a point. The objective was achieved. But Rousset was beaten senseless, had his head kicked in by the Germans when they realised they had been tricked. He never properly recovered, nor was able to remember exactly what had happened.'

They had stopped walking. Below was a beach of pebbles where three small boats rocked in the shallows. Even with one hand shading her eyes, Ellie could only see in patches of light and dark.

'But there was someone else who had stayed on the island, surely,' she said. 'The doctor. Louis de Fayols.'

'They told you that, then.'

'Madame de Fayols told me.'

'Yes, during the war the doctor continued to care for the convalescents, mainly Italian soldiers. Most were poor young conscripts who had done very little harm. The doctor felt a responsibility for them. When the Nazis took over, they sent the Italians to prison camps, but they realised the value of having a doctor on the island. He was ordered to stay, effectively a prisoner in his own house. They shot him there, in the grounds, on the night the plane landed.'

'But the Allies were so close, the liberation was

about to begin – why do it then?'

He did not answer.

'I can understand how you became a war historian, trying to make sense of it all.'

He nodded gravely. 'So are you going back to London?' he asked.

She smiled at the assumption. 'Only passing through, but I don't live too far away. Why?'

Gabriel pushed a hand through his hair. 'Would you … consider doing something for me, to help me with my research?'

She was touched by the way he seemed hesitant about asking, this man who was otherwise supremely confident.

'I'll certainly help, if I can.'

'Some of the material I need is in London. The story concerns both France and Great Britain. It occurs to me that if I could find out in advance which archives hold the documents I need, then it would make my job quite a lot easier when I come over to England.'

'Of course. I'm sure I can do that.' It would mean keeping in touch, maybe even meeting up. She felt a smile spreading. 'No problem at all. Tell me what you need to know.'

They found a shady spot and sat down. Ellie made notes as he spoke. It was hard to tell whether his interest in her was romantic or just friendly. They did not touch, even by accident. When he had described the events he was working on, making sure she had enough useful detail, they spoke of other relationships and the difficulty of love disrupted by war. He seemed to understand her need to talk about Dan and, as

105

she did so, it felt for the first time as if she was freeing herself for the possibility of another life.

The afternoon grew hotter. Gabriel leaned back on a tree and closed his eyes. Ellie began a small sketch of him, ready to snap the book shut if he stirred. At last she was living for the moment, seizing the day with an optimism she had not expected to feel again. There no longer seemed any urgency to catch the ferry back to the mainland.

At the hotel there were two messages. One was to call Laurent de Fayols as soon as she got back. She used the landline on the reception desk.

'What's been going on while I was away?'

She would have told him, but he continued without waiting for an answer. 'And you left your phone. Will you come over to get it?'

Reluctantly, she agreed.

The other message was that Lieutenant Meunier was waiting for her in the hotel dining room. Wearied by his persistence, Ellie went to meet him. The door was open, and he filled the space by the window, alert and aware of his power, looking out at the harbour. It was very possible he had seen her with Gabriel.

They greeted each other brusquely.

He was going to ask her whether she had seen the man in the panama hat, she knew it. A question to which he already knew the answer.

'I thought you should know the result of our inquiries into the death of Florian Creys. It cannot have been pleasant for you to have this as part of your introduction to Porquerolles, but perhaps it helps to know. I have come to tell you that Florian

Creys had a history of depression and drug abuse from the age of fourteen. He was diagnosed as schizophrenic a month ago. Last week he walked out of a clinic in Strasbourg and headed south.'

'So ... it was suicide, then?'

'The prosecutor at Toulon seems satisfied that it was.'

Ellie peered at him, the narrowed eyes and bulky shoulders that made the room seem so small around him. 'But you're not satisfied.'

He made an expressive sound with his mouth. 'It probably is so.'

'Very sad.'

Just another sad story of a young man who found he could not deal with the world; he would not be the first or the last, the lieutenant seemed to imply. 'You say that he was standing alone when he climbed over the rail.'

'Yes.'

'You say that there was someone else who saw the same as you – but we cannot find this person.'

Now he was closing in on his point.

'I have seen him again – the man in the panama hat. I saw him today.'

'Where?'

'Here, by the harbour.'

'But you did not call me.'

She sighed. 'I haven't got my phone. I lost it. I gave him your name and told him that you wanted to speak to him. I'm sure he will call you.'

Meunier appraised this information. 'Do you know the name of this man?' He took out his notebook.

'Gabriel. He didn't tell me his surname.'

'You did not ask?'

'Well, no ... he said he was attached to the university at Aix. I was going to google him,' she admitted.

He blew air out of his mouth, shaking his head.

'You could find him that way,' she pointed out.

'And you don't know where I can find him on the island?'

'No ... I'm sorry, I–'

'This is a serious matter involving the death of a young man. In cases like this we have to be sure that all the witness statements support the conclusion. You do understand that?'

She nodded. It seemed to be more about paperwork than anything else.

Against her better judgement, she went back to the Domaine de Fayols. What else could she do? Her mobile held so much information; it felt as if more and more of her life was filed on that phone. Jean-Luc offered to lend her a bicycle from the hotel.

For once the exercise did not calm her mind. The warmth and colour of the landscape had faded. The atmosphere was changing; banks of dark cloud had massed on the horizon; trees whispered in the wind. Was it happening again? Why was it that any connection with the Domaine de Fayols provoked this anxiety?

Dusk was falling early as she pedalled up the drive. The house grew more imposing, its grand facade streaked by the last rays of sunset permitted through the clotting sky. Most of the shutters were closed, and as she looked up, another was pulled shut by an unseen hand, as if the inhabitants were locking themselves in, or securing the house to leave.

Ellie dismounted. She hadn't any time to waste, should have been on the ferry hours ago. She would go in quickly and get out.

The main door was slightly open. Even so, she rang the bell at the side and waited. When no one came after a few minutes, she pushed the door open and entered the hall.

'Hello? Laurent?'

Dance music from the 1940s swelled from somewhere deep inside the house, then stopped. A ticking grew louder, then faded, replaced by a light scratching from one side of the hall, as if mice were invading the wall cavities.

'Hello?'

A faint churchy smell, recent polish perhaps, hinted at order and respectability. She would do everything by the book. It would be foolish to provide the de Fayolses with any reason for finding fault with her professional services. She would not allow them the satisfaction. Returning to the portico, she pulled the door shut and rang the doorbell again, keeping her finger pressed down as she counted to five and released.

The noise continued to ring inside her head, drowning out any other sound.

After a few minutes, a familiar tapping on the flagstones approached the other side of the door and then stopped. Ellie's heart sank. The tapping began again, but was receding now.

It was a few more minutes before the door was opened.

109

'*Bonsoir*,' said Jeanne, no longer bothering to speak in English. '*Venez avec moi.*'

Ellie followed her across the hall.

In the large sitting room the doors to the terrace were half closed. The lamps had been lit. Outside, the taller trees were bending in an increasingly heavy wind.

The *tap-tap-tap* of a cane began again.

Laurent bounded in from the terrace.

'Ah, you're here! I was making sure the boat was moored properly. Better to be safe if there's going to be a storm.'

Relief at seeing him so unperturbed, so *normal*, allowed Ellie to give him a genuine smile. For a moment he was silhouetted against a sickly yellow-grey sky as he moved towards the drinks tray.

'Will you take an aperitif?'

'No, thank you.'

He poured a glass anyway, and held it out. 'A kir made with our own rosé.'

She shook her head, then took it because there were more important issues to settle.

'My phone, do you–'

'Ah, yes.'

He made no move to fetch it, far less explain how it had left her possession. Instead he raised his glass.

'Let's talk. I want to persuade you to accept the commission. Surely you won't go without reconsidering?'

She watched him carefully, holding her glass but not drinking.

'I'm sorry I had to leave for Paris,' he went on. 'But now I'm back, we can resume our work, *non?* While I was on the move I had some good ideas, and there are various details that I think would appeal to you.'

'My week here is up, I'm afraid. I have a flight booked tomorrow, and commissions back home that need my attention.'

'But we can discuss further, at least.'

'Perhaps.' The lies we tell, she thought.

Tap-tap-tap. Ellie's heart sank.

'Maman,' said Laurent.

Mme de Fayols leaned on her cane. Her eyes were hollows in the candlelight. Laurent leapt over in time to steady the sway and led her tenderly to her high-backed armchair.

'You look frightened of me, Miss Brooke,' she said, staring at Ellie. Her head was skull-like.

'No, not at all. I'm tired, that's all.'

Tired of your games, she wanted to convey.

'I tried to tell you, didn't I?'

Ellie forced herself to stand still, though her legs trembled with the urge to run. She looked to Laurent. 'I really can't stay. I just – want to collect my phone. Please.'

But he was in no hurry to indulge her ahead of his mother. She asked for her drink, and he poured a tiny flute of purple liqueur.

'We were like animals hunting at night,' said Madame, still addressing Ellie. 'It was all in-stinct. My instincts have always been acute.'

Ellie stood uneasily rooted to the spot, wonder-ing where she had heard a similar phrase recently. She glanced at Laurent, but he was oblivious.

'We had to spot minute differences,' his mother went on. 'A glimpse, a flicker, a peep, did not

111

carry the same weight as an observation or a stare or even a gaze. We were all deciphering symbols … these traps. But we all see in different ways.

'If you saw someone arrested, you had to pretend not to know them, to have no connection. It was life or death. We were silent and helpless in the countryside, where all the winds have names but none of us could whisper ours. Our names were not our own. Our lives were not our own. Can you understand that?'

Ellie shook her head. She had no idea what the woman was talking about.

'Secrecy was everything. It informed the shame of defeat and underpinned our fears for the future. I am old enough now to be cynical, but even then I knew that we all see things in different ways, even when we are on the same side.'

A clock ticked loudly, though Ellie could not see one in the room.

'You concern me, Miss Brooke. You don't seem to want to know about this, and you need to know it.'

Ellie sighed, looking impatiently to Laurent for help. But he was flipping through one of his books in the same way he had when he was searching for a particular image to show her, fired by another of his big ideas, no doubt. If she wanted her phone, she would have to interrupt.

'I'm sorry to have to–'

'He was a traitor, and she helped him. I hate them both for what they did. It stays with you and poisons what comes after.'

The reedy invective broke with such aggression that at last Laurent seemed concerned. He came over and put his hand on her thin arm. 'Have you taken your pills, Maman?'

'The treacherous Xavier, who left me to fend for myself and betrayed so many others. He threw us to the dogs!' Mme de Fayols spat on the floor.

'Maman–'

As Laurent addressed his mother, Ellie saw the boy he must once have been, the enthusiasms, the eagerness to please, the incomprehension and, ultimately, the ineffectiveness.

Jeanne came in with a tray. Had she been listening outside, judging when to intervene? Was this the subject that marked the tipping into a barely contained madness and the trigger for intervention?

Mme de Fayols waved the housekeeper away imperiously. Her voice was becoming a snarl, shocking from so tiny a person. 'War is brutal, Miss Brooke. It unleashes man's inhumanity, shows a man's true character. And that's why any connection to Xavier had to be treated as suspicious.'

'*Madame, tenez!*' Jeanne held out a glass of water and a small porcelain bowl in which a selection of pills had been arranged.

The handle of the cane cracked down. Glass shattered on the stone floor, accompanied by a howl of fury from the old lady. The housekeeper took a deep breath but said nothing. She turned to go out of the room, presumably to fetch a dustpan and brush.

Laurent bent over his mother, his back blocking her from sight.

'Go. Go as soon as you can,' Jeanne whispered to Ellie as she passed.

'Where's my phone?'

'In the kitchen.'

'Did you take it?' asked Ellie incredulously.

'No! Why would I do that? Madame said she found it in the library.'

'What?' This was beyond exasperating.

'I will bring it now.'

In the flash of light that followed – was the storm finally breaking? – Laurent looked frail as he tried to calm his mother. For the first time, Ellie wondered whether he was more worried than he had seemed. His face, when he looked up, was drained of its colour.

'He's here!' cried Madame.

'Who is, Maman?'

'You brought him,' she said, pointing to Ellie.

'I came on my own. To collect my mobile.'

Madame looked past her, out at the terrace.

A slight movement beyond the doors could have been rain, or leaves or distant lightning.

'The priest came today,' she went on. 'He performed an exorcism. He said there would be no more trouble.'

The tang of incense in the hall. Ellie looked around, half expecting to see some ghostly figure. At last Laurent met her eye. He shook his head. More flashes of light – surely this was lightning – reflected on the polished surface of the table. Through the glass doors the night sky slipped past, riding the wind.

Mme de Fayols rambled incoherently, then screamed. Laurent tried and failed to calm her. Then the cries thinned. She dipped her head. Her bony fingers plucked at the folds of her skirt.

In an instant Ellie felt nothing but sadness for her. Then–

'Oh please, no...'

Mme de Fayols was hardly strong enough to keep the gun level. It shook in her frail grip. Was it the same gun that had been in the drawer upstairs? As if that mattered. She would drop it at any moment. Laurent was quietly making his way behind her chair. A few more seconds, and he would take it from her.

'I'm so sorry,' said Ellie with parched throat. The weapon was no doubt all for show, but she had no intention of taking any risk. 'You're right. I shouldn't have come here. I've obviously upset you, and I didn't mean to. I'm sorry.' The words came out as a kind of sob that did not sound like her.

No response.

Ellie watched her. The rushing in her ears came again. Her muscles were flexed to run, but she was pinned to the ground as if in a bad dream. All I wanted was my bloody phone, she thought.

An explosion of thunder overhead seemed to crack the house open. A second later the room fizzed with an eerie brightness, and the gun fired. Her reaction was pure instinct. In the jolt of light and noise, Ellie ran. At last she was moving, throwing herself forward as fast as she could, out onto the terrace and down the stone stairway.

The garden was black. There was barely any light from the sky – no stars, no moon. The storm clouds were thickly banked. But the day's heat lay heavy on the ground, hotter now than it had been when she arrived, like the updraft of a forest fire. Another bolt of lightning plunged a shaft down into the tree line.

She veered round, trying to keep to the path. It was hard to decide what to do – was it crazy to ride a bicycle in an electric storm? Should she just keep running, or find somewhere to hide until the worst was over? More thunder rumbled overhead.

Her feet were no longer crunching on gravel but springing off grass or soft earth. Somehow she had lost the path. How could she have missed it? She stopped. Her vision was blurred.

She put her hands out. She touched foliage, a dense wall of hedge. She could smell the opulent death scent of the datura. She ran along the length of the dark wall, as if feeling for an answer. Her head felt tight. If she could reorient herself, she could find the long way round the house. Perhaps that would be safer anyway.

A rustle sounded up ahead. She froze. When she moved, she sensed other movements. She was not alone. It was as though she were being tracked.

'Ellie! Stop – come back!' It sounded like Laurent.

She fled, running faster than she had ever run. Lightning cracked – or were those more shots? She ran until her lungs were bursting. The ground was sloping downhill. Her muscles felt so weak she stumbled, but kept going. Ever steeper, the path plunged downward. If she stopped, she would fall. But she knew now where she was.

The sea was ahead, the choppy blackness of the *calanque*.

The lighthouse. Was that a beam of light?

She was jerked backwards. She had been caught.

116

Hands out to push her invisible assailant away, she touched prickly branches. Her shirt had snagged on some small tree or shrub. She pulled away, tearing the fabric. Gasping for breath, she doubled over.

When she came up, she turned slowly, hardly daring to look behind. As far as she could make out, she was alone.

But then the clouds shifted, releasing enough opaque brightness to show dark shapes gaining on her. This time, she would not go back. On and on she scrambled. She was soaked through. When he caught her, his hands were slippery on her arms.

It was Gabriel.

He pulled her close with infinite tenderness. 'It's over now,' he said.

'Madame de Fayols – she tried to kill me!'

'It's all right, it's all right... I've got you. I'm here now.'

'You came to find me? How did you–'

He stroked her hair with a warm hand, easing away the fear. 'Shh ... you don't have to worry about anything. I'm here. Whatever needs to be done, I can help you. You're safe now.'

She let herself fall against him.

They walked away from the garden by the sea. The storm had ceased. The clouds were lifting to reveal a flame-red sky; he held her by the hand. They were bathed in the sunset. A plane soared over-head, and she seemed to be taking flight herself.

'No rush now,' he said. 'We have all the time in the world.'

He was right. That was the moment she felt the

117

past slip away, the longing for a man who was gone, along with the grief that had locked the door to her future. She could still feel the sadness, but it no longer held her down.

In this present hour, there was time for anything to happen, endless time.

So she continued slowly, with Gabriel, the man who understood the power of the past, towards the most westerly point of the island. Dark rocks stood waiting to be sculpted by the wind. Tiny seeds rode the air, waiting to fall and take root. Under the sea, corals formed and pearls hardened. Sap rose and juices fed along the vines. White trumpets flowered, and mandarins and lemons shone like drops of gold in fragrant groves.

BOOK II

The Lavender Field

1

Provence

April 1944

Not a word should be spoken. The scent was the word.

Each week it was the same routine: the girl caught the bus coming down from Digne, no different from any other nineteen-year-old with a job to do. The bus pulled in under the plane trees in the village of Céreste, and she alighted. By a bench where she placed her baskets for a moment, she reached into her shoulder bag for the perfume bottle and carefully dabbed her wrists, applying enough fragrance for it to be unambiguous. Nothing suspicious about this, simply attention to detail; a charming advertisement for the Distillerie Musset, makers of soap and scent. A blue scarf secured her hair; tied around her waist, the lavender-print apron she wore to serve in the shop. Then she picked up her two heavy baskets and made her deliveries: one to the hotel, one to the doctor's surgery and one to the general store. She walked purposefully but would stop for a few minutes to pass the time of day with occasional customers. Then, when her load was lighter, she went on to various houses around and beyond the village and finally arrived at the café.

She would order a small glass of weak wine, and greet the regulars. It was important to acknowledge the Gestapo officers or the Milice at the best tables. She would drink the wine, turn to leave, and then hesitate by the man reading the paper. Sometimes she went over to the Germans to ask if they had any special requests, a present for a girl perhaps. She always gave them a heart-lifting smile, just the right balance of sunny nature and shy innocence, then took a few paces back to the table where the man sat with his newspaper. He was always there, a little unkempt, smudging his glass with dirty hands. Sometimes he read, sometimes he stared into space. They all knew that his spirit had gone. He drank too much. She ignored him, let the scent pass the message. It had warmed now on her skin, thanks to all the walking; her quickened pulse pumped sweet fragrances into the air between them. Lavender: come to the farm. Rose: we have more men to move. Thyme: supplies needed urgently.

She stood at the table, halfway between the counter and the door, making a note of any orders from the men who enjoyed their new powers so much. Smiling pleasantly, though all her instincts told her to spit in their faces.

She glanced up at the clock on the front of the Mairie to check that her watch was correct. Unwise to hang around too long at the roadside bus stop, with the eyes of the men in the café lingering on her. She thanked the café owner, then walked across the road to catch the return bus as the clock hand moved down to show half past three. A nice normal pace, all the way.

2

Wild Violet

1943

When the war lowered the whole of France into blackness, everyone spoke of shadows falling, the dulling of the sun. It seemed to Marthe that she was one of the few who already had the knowledge necessary to survive. She had never seen the occupation of France, but she felt its force pressing down like a meaty pair of hands around the throat; it weakened the breath and weighted the body. On Nazi flags dripping from official buildings, a sinister half-spider sat on a full moon against a background of blood, a sight surely no more peculiar to see than to imagine. Polished black boots rang on cobblestones, stamping authority to the streets, and harsh voices shouted in a language no one understood. The more Marthe heard, the braver it made her: she was no worse off than anyone else as the Germans and the despised Vichy regime tightened their hold on the south.

'Filthy collaborators!'

The insult flew at them like a hissing insect. Mme Musset and Marthe, walking arm in arm down the boulevard des Tilleuls in Manosque, said nothing in response. Marthe felt Madame's grip dig deep into her arm. Their pace picked up, but the older woman made no attempt to refute the accusation.

Marthe allowed herself to be steered along the street to the shop with its own small perfume distillery and soap factory at the rear. There they stopped abruptly. The morning jangle of keys preceded their entry into a calming billow of lavender. Madame opened up the shop, then oversaw Marthe's tasks for the day, providing two young girls to help her. They set to work in the shed at the back, making a fresh batch of rosemary soap.

'Is it true what they say, that we are collaborators?' Marthe finally asked Madame as they stood side by side in the shop putting together an order of *eau de lavande*. It was shaming to admit, even if only to herself, that she had never considered that they might be.

'We are doing the best we can for ourselves.'

'But when people say–'

'It's best to forget whatever you happen to hear.'

'So–'

'We all have to bend with the wind.'

'But–'

'No more questions, my petal.'

'"Nothing is to be feared, it is only to be understood." Do you know who said that?' persisted Marthe. 'Marie Curie, the great scientist – the great *woman* scientist. They told us that, more than once, at school, and I have always believed it.'

'And I cannot disagree. Now, make sure these stoppers are pushed in as tight as can be. I'll not send out leaking bottles.'

Marthe pressed her thumbs harder into the cork until it stuck fast in the glass neck. In the

124

end, she rationalised, bravery came down to faith: faith in the Mussets' kindness and calm authority; faith in the knowledge that waves still broke on the southern shores, that spring buds would unfurl into flower and fruit would ripen.

Throughout the war the Distillerie Musset had continued to manufacture and distribute basic lines of soap and antiseptic cleaning fluids, and small amounts of scent. In most parts of France, a soap made of wood ash and clay was a luxury permitted only to those who had the dirtiest employments. In Provence, where olives still produced oil, and soap could be made from the most basic of local plants, the wartime mix was easily improved; the authorities demanded they continue, allowing Victor Musset to negotiate favourable terms for the supply of any excess.

'What's the alternative?' M Musset always said. 'Without work, we will all starve. With produce, we can at least barter. And if we do not work, what are we? We are dead trees, or fruit that falls unripened. If we have no respect for the land and the crops, respect for the olives and almonds and vines, then we have no respect for ourselves.'

Following their lead in this as in everything, Marthe allowed herself to embrace this comfortingly simple philosophy of life in the foothills close to the great lavender fields on the Valensole plateau. She had already left one home and found another, faced both her fears and then the terrible reality that they were not unfounded. This was the place where, against the odds, the loss of her sight had opened up a world she might never have known without her blindness.

The Mussets were clearly fond of Marthe, and she was so grateful to them for her apprenticeship at the Distillerie Musset that she never thought to question what they told her. They were a second family, and with that came absolute trust and acceptance.

The war had not yet begun when Marthe Lincel went to the perfume factory for the first time. It was a visit organised by the school for the blind in Manosque. If anyone were ever to ask her, she would tell him without hesitation that it was the day that changed her life.

She was eighteen years old, almost ready to leave the school, when she took her first careful steps towards the long table in the blending room at the Distillerie Musset, her hands in the hands of other girls, one in front and one behind. The girls walked in concert down from the school, through gusts of dung from the stables, past the ramparts of the ancient teardrop-shaped town, on past incense from the church and into the tree-lined boulevard des Tilleuls. At the door to the shop, a bell tinkled, and moments later they seemed to enter the very flowering of lavender.

The scent was all around them; it curled and diffused in the air with a sweet warmth and subtlety, then burst with a peppery, musky intensity. The blind girls moved into another room. There they arranged themselves expectantly around a long wooden table, Mme Musset welcomed them and a cork was pulled with a squeaky pop.

'This is pure essence of lavender, grown on the Valensole plateau,' said Madame. 'It is in a glass

126

bottle I am sending around to the right for you all to smell. Be patient, and you will get your turn.'

Other scents followed: rose and mimosa and oil of almond. Now that they felt more relaxed, some of the other girls started being silly, pretending to sniff too hard and claiming the liquid leapt up at them. Marthe remained silent and composed, concentrating hard. Then came the various blends: the lavender and rosemary anti-septic, the orange and clove scent for the house in winter, the liqueur with the tang of juniper that made Marthe unexpectedly homesick for her family's farming hamlet over the hills to the west, where as a child she had been able to see brightness and colours and precise shapes of faces and hills and fruits and flowers.

Afterwards, as the pupils filed past Mme Musset, each nodding her thanks, Marthe found she was speaking before she had even decided to. 'Could I come again, please?'

'You enjoyed this, my petal?'

'Very much, madame. I can't tell you how much.'

The line of girls was pressing into her back now, warm and softly solid.

'I will talk to your teacher.'

The movement of other bodies carried her along past the lilting voice that Marthe could have listened to all day, telling her so much she wanted to know and making sense of the world in a way that she understood instinctively.

'Till the next time, I hope,' said Marthe.

She could not speak on the way back. It was as though her senses had fully opened and the smells of the town were not only distinct but living, complex but delicious puzzles to solve. Waves of vanilla cream from the patisserie danced with iron from the blacksmith's forge. As they waited to cross a road, she picked up powdered sugar and spring woodland.

Voices of young children sang out: 'Gathered today! Wild violets – only a centime a bunch!'

Marthe dropped the hand she was holding and plucked a centime from her pocket.

Mme Delphine Musset, wife of Victor Musset, owner of the small perfume distillery, also held the title of potions manager, which denoted a higher calling than the production of homespun fragrances. She was a mixer of country tonics and medicines. In a more southern, less industrialised country she might have been known as a wise woman, the kind who dispensed natural cures and used her powers with compassion.

She kept her word to Marthe. Over the following months, she arranged for her to come back a couple of hours one afternoon a week. Marthe washed bottles and stirred soap mixtures with the workers in the sheds of the courtyard factory behind the shop. She was there when deliveries of other essences were made from the farm: the grass-green herbs of spring and winter infusions of cardamom and ginger. But in the course of the many tasks there was always time to talk about which aromas combined successfully and why the addition of one could deepen the impact of another; and the more Marthe asked, the more she was allowed to do. When the time came for her to leave school, she had impressed the Mussets enough with her nose for fragrance to be offered an apprenticeship as a scent maker.

The war came, but life in the unoccupied south went on. For the first few years of learning her craft, Marthe lodged in a room of a house belonging to a friend of Mme Musset. It was close to the shop-factory, and her landlady would take Marthe's arm for the five-minute walk along the pavement under the plane trees to her workplace.

When Mme Musset spoke, it was in the true accent of the southern mountains. Every vowel proclaimed her ancestry in these rocky slopes. To Marthe, whose only physical contact with her was the guiding touch of her hands, Mme Musset was a stout person, with a wide, red-cheeked face. It was several years before Marthe was given a description of the strong bony features that gave her a touch of the witch, one of those elderly women in fairy tales who might be good, or might be evil.

'The kind who sets a trap,' said Bénédicte.

By the time Bénédicte told her this, Marthe was engrossed in the alchemy of perfume and the infinite possibilities it offered. Bénédicte, her sister, was fifteen years old, with little experience outside the farming hamlet where they had been brought up. She had loved to read from an early age; Marthe remembered her bent over an illustrated book of folk tales, the grotesque coloured plates showing wild creatures and wilder humans with distorted features, and she understood where this disconcerting image might have sprung from.

'That's not like you, to be unkind,' said Marthe. 'You told me that's what you wanted me to come for, so that I could describe to you what you couldn't see for yourself.'

'That's true. But–'

'I'm not being unkind. I'm doing my best.'

But Marthe felt her certainties fracture. Here was her sister, usually so good-hearted and loyal, speaking out of turn about the Mussets, her saviours. Mme Musset had seen something special in her. She had kept her word, and they had chosen her. More than that, Madame had given her a purpose in life, and a future she could scarcely have imagined but for the lucky chance of a school visit to the distillery.

'And Monsieur Musset, what do you think of him?'

Bénédicte gave a nervous laugh. 'He's the boss, and he acts like one.'

'He can be a bit distant when he's at work. And short-tempered, sometimes, when people make silly mistakes. "He doesn't suffer fools", that's what Madame says. It took me a while to gain his acceptance. But – oh, Bénédicte! – when he is with his family, he is the kindest man. You should hear the terrible jokes, and how affectionate he is to his wife.'

She didn't need her sister to tell her that Victor Musset was a wide tree of a man – Marthe could sense his bulk and hear where the rumble of his voice started deep in his chest. When Marthe offered the Mussets her ideas for new perfumes, he might suggest a touch more refinement, but there was always expansive praise for her efforts. Madame's small sigh after an inhalation told her all was well. But Monsieur's heavy arm came around her narrow shoulders, and she would shine in his encouragement like a star in the firmament. She had had to work hard to earn his approval.

'He works harder than anyone, always on the move all day between the fields and the production line, the shop and the customers. At least three days a week he's out on the road in the old trap delivering the basic lines in soap and cleaning products. He says he likes to do it himself. He loves to eat, and talk and read, too. In the evenings he reads the essays of Montaigne, makes notes and reads aloud from them – so you see he is a man of culture. The pages of his book turn slowly, and his pencil scribbles. You can tell he is thinking deeply.'

Gradually she had relaxed in his company. The Mussets had no children, but there were always people around at their farmhouse up in the hills above Manosque – in many ways spending time there, as she soon did, was like coming home to the farmstead where she grew up. She missed her family, naturally, but what she was learning at the perfume factory was so absorbing that any misgivings or homesickness passed.

'I'll never forget the day Monsieur called me over to the chair where he was reading by the fire. "Here are some words for you, little one, from the wisest man I know," he said. He meant Montaigne, of course. "A straight oar looks bent in the water. What matters is not merely that we see things but how we see them." And ever since then ... well, I've known he is thoughtful of others. He is a good man.'

Bénédicte took her hand and squeezed the fingers affectionately. 'It's obvious you're happy here. Maman and Papa ... it'll make them happy too when I tell them.'

'I am, yes.'

It was true: despite everything, she was happy. Sometimes it was hard to put such an elemental feeling into words. How was it possible to capture in words what the essence spoke for itself?

After her sister's visit, Marthe's head was brimming with new pictures: the fields of lavender at Valensole, all the subtle grades of blue and purple; the way twilight melted them all into one; the precise hues of the liquid distilled from each plant, the shape and colour of the bottles and a new understanding of the surroundings where she was learning her craft. Just as plant variations were bred together to create new hybrids – like the lavandin from the delicate wild lavender – this was what she did with the descriptions her sister had supplied; she grafted them onto the sights she remembered from childhood and re-invigorated them.

Somehow, though, in Marthe's mind the kindly pumpkin face she had given her mentor Mme Musset was always more dominant than the face that could be seen by others. Without sight, you had to understand what was beneath the surface.

Madame was a true and generous person who cared for her. The endearment had come so naturally – 'my petal' – a name not used for anyone else. The deft way she set out the essential oils for Marthe, always in the same order and the same place on the table, spoke silently of encouragement. The thoughtful cleverness in the way Madame had labelled Marthe's first experimental blends by using sealing wax stamped with letters from an old printing set, so that Marthe could identify each one by touch. Later, when the quality of Marthe's nose and invention was becoming more and more apparent, she was permitted to open the tiny vials of more exotic ingredients bought in Marseille before the war – orris root, amber, patchouli – and used drop by precious drop to add distinction to the homely fragrances of the landscape.

When Marthe's widowed landlady decided to close up the house and move to Banon to live with her daughter and grandchildren while her son-in-law was held as a prisoner of war in Germany, Marthe went to live with the Mussets at the farmhouse surrounded by lavender fields, halfway between the plateau and the town.

3

Almond Blossom

1943

The shepherd's body was found up on the steep slopes where the lavender made its last wild clutches at the mountain peak.

Each year the sheep were moved across the high meadows above the lavender fields. Here men still adhered to the old ways: hardy men with gnarled and twisted limbs, as if they had been carved by the same winds as the rock sculptures.

One of them was the shepherd Pineau. Alone under the blue citadel of the sky, he guided his flock from one ancient stone *borie* to the next. All the farmers knew him: old Pineau in his ragged clothes had been part of the landscape when the great surge in lavender growing for the perfume industry had begun, when the Mussets and others began staining the slopes purple. The shepherd was a man who knew every stone and tree of the ridges, a man who seemed part of nature: part mountain, part stream, part animal, living his life by the turn of the seasons, solitary with his sheep, walking from rocky ledge to pasture, valley to plateau, as they fed. He sang as he went, songs that had been sung for centuries.

That summer day in 1943, when small puffs of his flock broke away and drifted in lazy clouds down the hill, the lavender farmers knew something was wrong. In the uplands men and women had always relied on one another. They went up looking for him.

Urgent footsteps on the path, spitting stones, brought the news to the Musset farmhouse that evening. A hammering at the door, and Auguste burst into the kitchen, panting. 'Old Pineau's had it – they got him!'

Auguste Baumel was the Mussets' best supplier, son of the farmer who had planted vast swathes of the new hybrid lavandin on the plateau.

M Musset scraped his chair back. For a moment there was silence. Then Madame flapped into action, fetching glasses, telling him to pull up

134

a chair, pouring from the bottle.

'I went up with a couple of the others to ... check on him. I took my cousin Thierry with me,' said Auguste. Thierry ran a garage in town. Marthe couldn't think what expertise he might have provided up in the fields.

Auguste gulped down a drink, and it made him splutter.

'Take it easy, lad.'

The story spilled out. Looking back, it seemed to Marthe that they had forgotten she was in the corner of the room. She listened intently.

Inside the shepherds' hut, hardly more than a pile of stones with its lone chair and table, Auguste and Thierry found Pineau's tin drinking cup on the floor, abandoned. Outside, under the lone olive tree, the shepherd's last meal was still being devoured by flies and beetles. They called his name, thinking he might be injured, unable to move. They found him a hundred metres away, face down in a stream he had used for drinking and bathing. Blowflies hummed over sweet and sickly flesh.

'We turned him over to be sure,' said Auguste.

'And was it–'

'A shot to the head,' said Auguste. 'They must have found him as he washed his hands before eating.'

Silence.

Marthe didn't dare move, let alone speak. She felt the chill of the spring water as it filled the shepherd's nostrils, the stones pushed into his mouth by the flow. Twice dead, by bullet and by water. She remembered her sister describing the

135

hills and mountains as waves on the sea, and the pictures in her head merged. Marthe told no one, but she had a dread fear of drowning.

M Musset paced the floor, his words coming as fast as Auguste's. 'Every barter is a risk. We put aside our differences for a common cause, but never forget that others have their own agenda. It is no longer possible to assume that any two people understand a situation in the same way or have the same loyalties. The natural order has gone, that is what we know.'

She could make no sense of it.

Perhaps one of them noticed her then, as she sat scarcely breathing in the chair by the window. Whatever prompted them, the two men headed for the door and went out.

Marthe's skin prickled. She wondered whether Madame would say anything, either to them or her, but she only clattered some pans and ran the tap.

The shock of Pineau's murder fused with the aroma of burning onions and garlic as Madame turned away from the stove. Insults in the street and the herbal astringency of rosemary soap. Memory and scent, so closely entwined. It can't have been long after that Arlette came to live with the Mussets, bringing a tin of real ground coffee beans. For years they had drunk only a bitter brew of acorns. The rich coffee fragrance was so intoxicating, so redolent of lost freedom, that it brought a tear to the eye. Rosemary, burnt onion and coffee; the lavender harvest; all combined and gave coherence to Marthe's memory of those

136

precise few weeks in July 1943.

Arlette was Mme Musset's niece, daughter of Madame's sister who lived in Lyon. Her parents ran a drapery shop, but since the Germans had crossed the demarcation line and eradicated the *zone libre*, Lyon was considered as dangerous as Paris. Arlette, nineteen when she moved south, had a smile so wide it could be heard in her speech and made others smile in return. She was resilient and optimistic, and she was going to be an actress one day, though quite how she was going to achieve her dream in Manosque rather than the great city of Lyon wasn't altogether clear.

The first time Marthe heard Arlette's voice, it was singing. The song ended, but even when her chatter took over, it had a musical quality that seemed to brim with confidence and joie de vivre, the words barely able to contain the giggle that might erupt at any moment. Marthe had pulled herself back into the corner of the room, as if she might make herself invisible, fearing disdain from the laughing voice, steeling herself for resentment at her position as a cuckoo in the nest.

But Arlette bounded over to her. 'You must be Marthe – I've been longing to meet you! Aunt Delphine sent me some of your lemon balm scent for my birthday, and do you know, I've had women stop me in the street to ask what it is!'

Marthe could only stutter her thanks for the compliment.

'Your ears must be terribly singed.'

'I beg your pardon?'

'My aunt and uncle talk about you all the time – heaping the praise! Your ears must burn on a

137

regular basis.'

'Well, I – that's very good to know, thank you.'

She might not be sincere, Marthe reminded herself.

But over the following months Arlette proved herself not only enthusiastic but practical and a hard worker too. She rolled up her sleeves to make soap alongside the other employees, as well as helping with the deliveries and going out with Monsieur to drum up more business. At the farm too she took on any job that had to be done.

Along the way she and Marthe became firm friends. The war was horrible, but they both agreed it was never a good idea to worry about anything you couldn't change.

'You can't go around asking "What if?" What is, that's the only thing that matters,' said Arlette.

'I had to learn that lesson too, but it was hard,' admitted Marthe. She had surprised herself by confiding the story of how she became blind to Arlette. How, as her eyesight worsened, she had focused – closely, unbearably closely – on what she could still see and feel: the heliotrope flowers on the slope outside the barn; the meadows; the smooth iron of the banister rail under her hand, the half-moons of stone stairs worn away by centuries of use; the tiles on the floor, which still bore the imprints of dogs' paws like fossils. The passages and steps and rooms of her childhood home were safe in her memory, the bedrock and template of all that came after. And then her parents had sent her away, to a new place she had never seen.

'Tell me. Tell me all of it,' Arlette said. Often

that first summer they lay in a grassy dell by a group of wild plum trees, gorging on crisp fruit.

'I've never told anyone this before.'

But Arlette would wait for her to find the words. The hum of bees in the background intensified the tart honey of the plums as they sucked the stones clean.

And so Marthe would talk. She told how she had been taken to Manosque when she was eleven years old. Her parents explained that they had brought her to a school for girls like her, and then they left her there alone, struck dumb by the realisation that her worst fears had materialised. At the school for the blind everything around her was alien. Had her parents any idea what it felt like to be surrounded by emptiness, swirling and roaring?

'Were you very angry?'

'Yes. For a long time. I threw myself down the stairs once, furious because I didn't know what that stairwell looked like. I hoped my parents would understand and come and fetch me. But they never did.'

'That must have been terrible.'

'It was, but funnily enough it was the start of better times for me. The two girls who found me at the bottom of the stairs and took me to the matron became my good friends. Renée and Elise. They were so kind, but I'd been so wrapped up in my own worries, I hadn't even noticed before that they were there.'

'Friends make all the difference, always. And something good came of your pain.'

'You're right. But it was the fury at my situation

139

that spurred me on. I had to learn how to read a new darkness by using all my senses. I had to identify each sound – think of listening to an orchestra and trying to work out which instruments are playing and in which patterns. I had to interpret the way the air felt on my skin and taste the seasons as they changed. If I thought of myself as anything, it was as a young dog exploring new worlds carried by smell.'

That was why, when they listened to the news on the radio or heard talk about the occupation, Marthe felt no different from the others. She heard what they heard. None of them had seen the events described. The most appalling acts of cruelty and inhuman barbarity were carried out unseen, experienced in absences and abstracts.

As autumn turned to winter that year, they gathered around the wireless each night, forswearing the propaganda of the Vichy government to listen illegally to the BBC broadcasts through storms of interference. From London, patriotic exiles sent out morale-boosting bulletins of Nazi reversals and relayed the stern, growling drama of Churchill's speeches. And messages would come through, snippets of trite-sounding news from the exiles to their compatriots across the Channel, 'The French Speak to the French'.

By then Auguste often joined them for dinner first. He had taken to bringing pamphlets printed by the underground resistance, from which he was keen to read aloud.

'"The Vichy prime minister Pierre Laval is so desperate to keep his deal with the Germans on

140

track, to place France at the right hand of the victor at Europe's top table, that he is sacrificing the country's young men in ridiculously unbalanced numbers: eight young Frenchmen pushed over the borders to work in German factories for each prisoner returned."'

'I tell you, the Germans obviously hold Laval in contempt, but it's as nothing compared to the contempt I feel for the bastard. And as for Maréchal Pétain, don't get me started on that dangerous old fool! What the hell do they think they are doing? It's unbelievable ... *unbelievable!* And people still think that he saved the country once before, in the Great War, so no one can doubt his patriotism! He may have been a patriot once, but he is no patriot now.'

A murmur of agreement went round the table. When the occupation began and the Germans assumed control of the northern half of the country, Pétain told the French people it was a pragmatic arrangement; that the French govern-ment at Vichy was protecting its people in the wider interests of the country. If France cooperated, he claimed, they would emerge stronger, in partnership with Germany, after this war was over.

A bottle of apricot liqueur was being passed around. Its fiery trail burned Marthe's throat, and she had only managed a few tiny sips.

Arlette was speaking now. 'My father says there are those who want to believe it, that they welcome the invaders because they fear factions of our own people more – the radicals and the Communists. They are secretly pleased that the Germans are stamping out all the disorderly factions.'

'It always astonishes how many different views and interpretations of the same facts there can be,' commented her uncle bitterly.

A guttural sound of derision from Auguste. 'So we're all supposed to read this, and then roll over and let them walk all over us? We must all do what the Germans tell us to do because Pétain did the right thing once? It beggars belief! He and his stooges are just as fascist as the Germans. Have you seen the posters they've put up all over town? Smiling boys leaning out of train windows on their way to work in German factories. They make it look so benign! They're all in it together, and I can't stand it, I tell you.

'And actually, I want to talk about what the hell we are doing, still selling soap to those bastards who are stamping all over us. I mean—'

'I agree with all your political sentiments,' cut in M Musset. 'But we have to hold our noses and do what we have to do.'

'And sleep the sleep of the just and the ignorant each night?'

'We do it in order to survive. And it's not so black and white! Sometimes it's the "collaborators" who are keeping people safe – have you thought about that? The clerks working at the town hall who try to intervene on behalf of others, they are the ones to put themselves on the line, negotiating and trading with the regime.'

'Is that what we're doing?'

'Yes. The Distillerie Musset is open for business so that we and many others can eat.'

This measured response was met by another snort from Auguste. 'When my father planted the first lavender fields on the plateau after the last war, it was to build a better life, to safeguard the people and their livelihoods here. He was not doing it to surrender the fields of the south to the old enemy.'

'Your late father was a fine man, and a good friend to me. He was also a good negotiator. Don't forget the two of us were once in partnership, as we are now. He would have taken the practical line too.'

'He would turn in his grave at the thought of the way you appease Kommandant Baumann and his bully boys every time.'

'It's a good contract. And if we do not work, what are we?'

'You know they call us dirty collaborators, don't you?'

'They can call us what they like. We have our integrity and our ideals in this half-life of broken promises and self-interest from our politicians! We've worked hard to build up our business.'

'I don't disagree... How can I? But – ah! I get so angry!'

Auguste had changed. It was as if, with the occupation, he had found what he had wanted all along – a purpose. He sparked and fizzed with energy. His actions made clean, definite noises: a bang of his glass on the table, clipped footsteps, single swishes of newspaper. Not so long ago he had had a reputation of trying it on with girls who were too young for him, whether that was an issue of self-confidence or not. But now he was sure of himself, surer than ever. His time had come, and he was going to seize it.

'Pétain is eighty-seven years old! He won't be around to see the hell of what he's done! I don't care if he was the country's greatest hero of the Great War, he's turned against his own people.'

Mme Musset's soft voice changed the subject to less troubling matters. 'How is your girl, Auguste? Is that all still on?'

Auguste's girl worked in a dress shop in Céreste. Pretty, according to Monsieur and Madame. Vain and proud, according to Arlette, though she conceded that her clothes were always pretty, when most people rarely had anything new.

'Why would I not still be seeing Christine?'

'I'm only asking.'

'Well, I am. It's just that I've been so busy lately ... many things to be organised. She understands. You know how it is.'

'Of course, dear. Now, I expect you're hungry as usual, my dear idealist. There's hazelnut cake – surprisingly good, considering I've had to substitute grated nuts and carrot for flour and sugar. And Victor came back from Reillanne this afternoon with a rabbit, which I've stewed.'

Soon there was a soothing sizzle of courgettes frying in a pan.

Over dinner Auguste calmed down. When Marthe pictured him, he was the upright figure in the fields described by Bénédicte, sporting a dark waistcoat over a white shirt and baring the gold tooth that had commanded her sister's attention. Still a relatively young man who was not all he seemed, she had intimated. Marthe had always found him pleasant and sincere. You could tell a great deal by the tone of a voice, and while he was

144

undoubtedly impulsive at times, his usual state was cautiousness. He was determined, and he felt things deeply.

And Marthe too struggled to put aside what had happened to the country and not allow it to spoil the pictures she retained in her head. That was what she found unforgivable as news of the first atrocities swept across the villages with the malevolent force of the mistral. No longer did the vista of a single olive tree by a *borie*, or a stream above a rolling sea of purple, signify serenity; after old Pineau's death, they were execution scenes, just as the first white almond blossom of spring was now redolent of death. From across the valley the orchards were easily mistaken for drifts of white mist; a shroud for the farmer and his family shot in the back of the head for sheltering escaped prisoners of war.

The violence had come closer. Marthe could sense the disintegration of what had been passing for normality. Week after week as the year turned, the soothing choreography of feet on the floor tiles, the routines and rhythms of the family, the regular appearances of the workers, all was changing.

Marthe was disconcerted by unfamiliar footfalls and low voices. Heavy objects were moved around the farmhouse and the outbuildings. Swishing noises came from the entrance hall for which she could not find a source. Almost every day there was a new sound to be processed.

'What's going on?' Marthe asked Mme Musset. 'Nothing for you to concern yourself with, my petal. Here, take these peas to shell – that would be a help.'

Peas to shell. Soap to wrap. A knitted jumper to unravel and rewind the wool to use again. There was always a little job to keep her busy. To keep her quiet and away from whatever was happening. With trembling fingers Marthe bent to her task, alive to the faintest clue.

Arlette tried to lighten the mood. She had gone back to Lyon to visit her family at Christmas and came back with some gramophone records. M Musset put them on, and suddenly the house came alive with music, Arlette singing along. One recording was played over and over again: 'Douce France', sung by Charles Trenet. '*Douce France, cher pays de mon enfance... Je t'ai gardée dans mon coeur.*' Marthe realised she was not the only one whose childhood country belonged to a vanished world.

The other great favourite was 'Boum!' It was such a jolly song about the way the heart beat when you fell in love. '*Boum! La pendule fait tic-tac tic-tac ... et la jolie cloche din dan don ... mais Boum! Et c'est l'Amour qui s'eveille!*'

'Do you have a young man, Arlette?'

'No. I have several!'

'*...Quand notre coeurfait boum, tout avec lui dit boum...*'

'Are you in love with any of them?'

'Phooey, no! I just want to have some fun, and then when the war's over I shall concentrate on my career as an actress. I'm going to do it, you know, you just wait and see – I mean, sorry–'

'Nothing to be sorry about. I shall still see you

146

in my way, you know that. I shall be the first on my feet clapping and cheering as the curtain comes down.'

'You'll have to travel … to Nice and Paris and … Biarritz and beyond. Rome! London! New York! You won't see me for dust here after this war is over! But I shall always send you the money and tickets, don't worry.'

'It will be wonderful.'

It was easy to be positive with Arlette. She had even persuaded her uncle to allow her to help him recruit more workers. 'Why can't a girl do it? In fact, I shall make it my mission to improve sales despite all the obstacles. I might even have certain … advantages when it comes to persuading young men to stay here and work for us instead of getting on a train for Germany.'

Auguste seemed more cheerful too. Marthe heard Auguste and Arlette, chattering and joshing, setting off to town together. He gave her lifts sometimes in the old hayrick they used to pull the cut lavender to the copper still in the fields at harvest time.

'You're not in love with Auguste, are you?' asked Marthe shyly.

'No! Not in the least. Oh, he's nice enough, but he's a bit too old for me. He's more like a much older brother, one you can tease.'

It was just as well there could still be some light-heartedness.

Water coughed in the pipes. There were a couple of new workers in the lavender fields whom Madame had invited to have baths at the farmhouse. Marthe had heard the heavy tread of

147

their boots going up the tiled staircase.

'That reminds me,' said Arlette. 'Aunt Delphine asked if we would finish washing some sheets that have been soaking.'

They linked arms and went to the outhouse. They talked as they scrubbed sheets at the washboard. They worked until the tips of their fingers were cold and wrinkling like seaweed.

'There seem to be an awful lot of sheets.'

'You're not wrong there. It's hard work.'

'I don't mind,' said Marthe.

'I know you don't.'

'This reminds me of chores at home, helping Maman. I like it.'

For a while there was nothing but the sound of evening birds singing and the wind in the orchard trees. Then Marthe said: 'Please don't tell me I'm speaking out of turn, but I've sensed things lately ... sensed changes. Will *you* tell me what is happening here?'

She kept on working the cold sheet as if the steady rhythm would ward off her fears. Change frightened her. If the world changed completely, I wouldn't know it, she thought but did not say. In my head it will always be the world of my childhood, but the scenes will be obsolete, like the images frozen in woodblocks used to print pictures, or enamelled hard and shiny on old-fashioned ornaments.

'We have a few extra workers at the moment,' said Arlette. 'We have to billet them for now, that's all.'

'I know that. But–'

'Marthe ... dear, sweet Marthe, it's better you

148

don't know.'

'Please don't say that! That's what everyone says, and it just isn't true!'

But still Arlette would not tell her.

In the blending room at the Distillerie Musset in town, Marthe held a glass vial to her nose: a distillation of violet. She breathed in slowly until it seemed for those few moments the air was reduced to a powdery sweet-sharpness. This February, when the schoolchildren once again sold posies of wild violets on the street corners, Marthe asked them to bring all they had to the perfume factory and managed to extract a few drops of essence. Over the months since then she had experimented with other ingredients to intensify the fragrance, but now the addition of spicy acacia wood had deepened its distinctive sweetness (the scent that would always recall that first propitious visit to the Mussets) to capture its shaded woodland origins and the shy purple petals in the first shafts of spring sunshine.

Arlette clattered in. She had worn through her shoes with all the walking she did making deliveries in the towns and villages, and the cobbler had fitted wooden tips on the soles and heels. As ever, Arlette turned adversity to her advantage and announced her arrival with a little tap dance.

'Bravo! Monsieur Astaire of Hollywood will have you as his new partner yet!' Marthe giggled.

Arlette tap-tapped over to the tall wooden cupboards that lined the room. 'I thank you kindly, mademoiselle, and will perform an encore as soon as I collect some more of that new rose eau de toilette you mixed the other week.' Doors opened and closed as she helped herself.

'You're getting through that one,' said Marthe.

'It's proving very popular.'

'I'm glad.'

'What's so sublime is the way the true essence of the flower comes through so strongly and distinctly, and seems to grow as you wear it.'

'It's a soliflore. The simple essence of one flower, enhanced a little but absolutely itself.'

'That's right.'

'If you like that, come and smell this. Tell me what you think.'

Arlette sniffed at the glass vial Marthe held out. 'Mmm ... it's violet! Unmistakable.'

'Unmistakably itself, but deepened by using an extract from the leaves as well as the flower, and with acacia wood. Can you smell the cinnamon spiciness of the acacia? I've added a faint touch of orange and narcissus to sharpen it. Then a tiny hint of musky sandalwood too, which will help it develop on the skin and make it last.'

'It's just incredible. You know, we need a new, stronger fragrance ... another single flower–'

'Do we?'

'–and this could work very well, as it couldn't possibly be mistaken for anything else in our line.'

'It's an old-fashioned perfume really, but romantic. Girls used to say that violets stood for modesty and humility. Would it work today, though? You see, the reason I've been making this was ... well, it's silly and sentimental really ... but this was the scent I smelled out on the street that first day I came to–'

An excited *rat-a-tat* burst from Arlette's feet. 'I've got to go! Marthe, you are a genius!'

'Where–'

But Marthe was speaking to the air. Arlette had waltzed off, as lost in her own world as Marthe was in hers.

The violet perfume was good, though. It would be quite special when she had it exactly right.

But later that night at the farmhouse, long after she had gone to her room, Marthe overheard the Mussets talking. She stopped outside the kitchen, forgetting about the water she wanted.

'She is safe, though, isn't she?' asked Monsieur.

'Can we trust her, you mean?'

'We must all be careful.'

'I'm not sure. I want to – but it's hard to judge. There's certainly...'

'So what are we to do?' asked Monsieur. 'If we say anything–'

'I know.'

'We'll just have to watch and wait.'

Marthe felt sick. How could it be that the family did not trust her? And had they taken her in only out of charity, after all, a hopeless case to whom kindness should be shown? Worse, did they consider her a liability? But surely there could be no conceivable question about her trustworthiness and loyalty!

'It costs money to do all this,' went on Monsieur. 'Money that none of us have. Fuel for the truck, the working hours lost.'

A murmur from Madame.

'I thought about selling some books, but that

151

won't raise much. It will have to be my father's fob watch.'

'Take it to the pawnbroker, you mean?'

'No, that might be too obvious. It would have to be done on the quiet. I know someone who is willing to buy.'

'Who?'

'The Engineer. He's a wealthy man.'

Silence except for the ticking of the old clock.

'You can't sell that watch. But I could offer some bits and pieces from the jewellery my mother left me. I never wear the jade bracelet or that cameo brooch.'

'It's a kind thought, but that won't raise much.'

Another pause, then a light sigh. 'My pearl, then, as well. The setting, the chain – it's all good-quality gold.'

'But that was–'

'I know. But I don't need it any more to tell me you care. All the years since have told me that – my dearest, sweetest man.'

'Are you sure?'

'Of course. This way, we give it together to show we care.'

'But if Auguste can come up with a few things too–'

'We'll manage somehow. We have to.'

Marthe stood stock-still against the wall. The sense of elation at her achievement with the violet perfume had drained away.

In the days afterwards, as she tried and failed to decide what to do, the words went round in her head, humiliating her like a public slap. She was too frightened of what she might be told if she opened the subject herself with Madame, so she kept quiet, wanting to hold onto her job with the Mussets for as long as possible. There were many kinds of darkness, she realised then, and the most daunting was being cast off by those who had previously offered comfort. Marthe bore the secret knowledge as a fight she was not yet willing to concede, but nothing was the same. The water from the spring tasted bitter, where once it held flavours of thyme and mint. She ate sparingly, careful to take as little as possible at meals, and lay awake hungry, night after night.

The violet perfume was praised to the skies, but the Mussets allowed her to make only a very small quantity. Spring burst out and warmth returned, yet Marthe's world contracted tightly around her. She was more isolated than she had ever been before. Lonely too, in the most profound sense, as lonely as she had been when she first arrived at the school for the blind, but this was worse because once the Mussets had opened their magical world to her, she would always know what treasures were inside. She wanted to protest, but sensed that her only weapon was her pride. She would work harder than ever to prove herself.

Superficially, nothing had changed, but Monsieur was away on ever more frequent delivery trips, often taking Arlette with him. Auguste's role had changed to involve him much more in the product distribution, too. Madame often seemed preoccupied.

'Just the war, my petal,' she would say when

153

Marthe asked her if everything was all right.

When winter returned for a few weeks, frost killing any green shoots, it seemed a reflection of the mood at the Musset farmhouse. Dank mist over the orchard trees muffled bird-song and reduced voices to echoes in the gloom.

4

Thyme and Fig

April 1944

At the farm on the slopes above Manosque, the clock on the shelf ticked too loudly. It always ticked louder than usual and much too slowly on Thursday afternoons as they waited for Arlette to return from making deliveries in Céreste on the bus. Only when the latch rattled on the back door and Arlette's voice punctured the tension did it slip back to its normal volume and rhythm.

The hour sounded: five soft hits on the bell mechanism. Mme Musset opened a squeaky cupboard door and then closed it again, as if compelled to find some mundane business for her hands. The chink of a glass, water running. Monsieur padded over to the range and struck a match. The thin blue scent of a poor cigarette.

'She's normally back by now,' said Madame, unnecessarily.

Each week Arlette returned from Céreste with

tales of the lazy brutishness of the young blond soldiers who stood guard over Route Nationale 100 as it came through the village, of the *miliciens* kicking up the dust in the streets of the old quarter to harass the inhabitants of its narrow houses.

The Milice were a triumph of Vichy fascism, according to Monsieur. The French themselves had created this corruption of the military and the police, with the help of the Germans, as a paramilitary force to be unleashed against any dissent, in particular the growing influence of the Resistance. These *miliciens* soon became cruelly expert in executions and deportations. Some were criminals who were told their sentences would be commuted for this loyal government service. Some were the starving who joined for the regular pay and food. Many were locals recruited as parttimers, and all were more dangerous than the Germans because they knew the language and the terrain. After a year and a half, the vicious methods of the Milice were no better than the Nazis'. The old networks of families and neighbours had been corrupted. No one knew who to trust any more.

The quarter-hour *ting-tinged*.

Seconds later Arlette's chatter preceded her through the doorway. There was a clumsy thump as she brought the large woven basket down on the table. The scent of a fresh loaf of rationed bread. A rattle of cups and plates. Quick, light steps and flurries of air nudged the room back into its usual rhythms.

'How did it go?' asked Musset.

'Fine,' said Arlette. 'No need to be worried. I

155

did nothing, said nothing, out of the ordinary.'

She squeezed Marthe's hand in greeting. Rosewater softened the air as she drew close.

'What did you see? Did you notice any changes?' M Musset was already asking her. 'It's the smallest details that make the difference, even if you don't know what they mean yet.' He was here in the kitchen every Thursday when Arlette returned, eager to know what she had observed on her rounds. Needing to know that she was back safely.

'There are definitely more soldiers in uniform, going in and out of the Mairie and looking purposeful,' said Arlette. 'A couple of new ones in the café. Two young men I'd never seen before. One of them leered at me, like a pig with small eyes.'

'I hope you–'

'I smiled very sweetly, nothing more. The Milice were counting the passengers on and off the bus from Aix, but not ours.'

'They say there are more soldiers coming, German and those they're putting into uniform from the east of Europe, more every week – read the newspaper. Baumann is boasting of doubling the garrison.'

'May the saints preserve us!' Mme Musset interrupted. There was silence, broken finally by Arlette. 'That explains the next order. Here's the list, longer than ever.'

'Good girl. We will let them have what they need,' said Musset.

'They'll get what they need all right,' said Arlette defiantly. 'I hate them. Over at Castellet last week two families in the hamlet were shot outside the

156

church on Sunday just for supplying food to the Maquis. They say there are six hundred Maquis in the hills behind Céreste – all of them hungry and impatient.'

'Some of them are young hotheads. They don't think before they act, though I admire their spirit.' Monsieur sucked hard on his cigarette and then ground it out. A tarry bitterness hung over the table. Each week brought more tales of subordination and sabotage, followed by retaliations, swift and brutal.

'More and more are joining them, now they sense the tide has turned,' said Arlette.

'Make no mistake, the enemy is always most dangerous when it is pushed onto the back foot.'

No one said anything.

Madame began to investigate the contents of the basket, rustling paper wrappings. Since food rations had been cut, their coupons brought less and less back to the table. But they were better off by far than many, with their orchards of fruit and nuts and olives, chickens and land to grow vegetables. On market day in cities there was often little more to buy than swedes and turnips and tough plucked crows on the butcher's stall.

She sniffed. 'That cheese isn't too bad.'

'Exchanged for a bar of lavandin-rosemary soap,' said Arlette.

'You've done very well, my dear.'

'Tell me what the Engineer had to say,' said Musset.

Marthe felt the imprint of Arlette's hand on her shoulder and then a renewed sense of loss when her friend walked away into the garden with her uncle to continue their conversation.

A few days later Marthe was sitting alone on the terrace by the kitchen door, trying to separate the scents as they rode a warm breeze: thyme and lemon balm; the fig tree's spices, sweet as cinnamon milk in the drowsy afternoon heat. Madame had gone out to check on the chickens, hoping for eggs. A click sounded. It could have been the wind in the tree by the door. Marthe listened harder. Light footfalls came up the path and stopped in front of her.

'Who is it?'

'Christine.'

Auguste's girlfriend, who worked in the dress shop. Marthe tried to imagine what marvels of new clothing adorned her. All she could picture was a princess in an old book in a swirling puff of organza, and that could not have been right.

'Do you know where Auguste is?'

'I don't – I'm sorry,' said Marthe. 'In the fields, I would imagine. Either here or at one of the other farms.' Auguste had recently taken on a supervisory role at several other lavender farms, where workers were in short supply, linking them into a cooperative to keep supplies coming.

'And Arlette – where is she?'

'I'm not sure. Have you tried the shop?'

'She's not there.'

'She might be helping with the deliveries.'

'She might be. Or she might be with Auguste.'

'Well, I suppose she might. It's possible.'

'So are they somewhere together?'

'I've told you, I don't know.'

158

Christine reached across her. She picked up and set down various objects on the table: a candle lantern; a magazine; some papers under a weight.

Marthe stood up. 'I'm not sure how I can help you, Christine.'

'I am. You can answer my question: are they together?' Her tone was impatient, bordering on rudeness.

'I have no idea,' snapped Marthe.

A silence stretched between them. Then the other girl made a noise of furious frustration. She seemed to be focusing her anger on Marthe, but then swept past her and into the kitchen. The door slammed.

'Hey, you can't–'

She obviously had.

Marthe got up and stood in the doorway. Christine was opening drawers and cupboards. 'You won't find them in there!'

Without another word, the woman pushed past her. Marthe followed the movement to the wall of the terrace. Footsteps broke the path's crust once again, and the unsettling incident was over.

Marthe pressed her hands to her forehead and tried to recover her composure. She was trembling. She did not understand what had just occurred, sensed only that something untoward had taken place.

'Madame!' she called.

When there was no answer, she made her way down towards the chicken run, one hand on the wall that ran down to the stone barn. She knew every stone of the way. Lizards skittered. Sunlight seared her face and bare arms, then faded as if thick clouds had pushed in and absorbed all the heat.

A rustling noise caught her attention, then a low intermittent hum. She slowed, straining to hear, while creeping forward, keeping her steps soundless.

It was a voice, speaking in a low murmur.

She drew closer. At the edge of the barn she could hear male voices inside. She could not understand what was being said. Perhaps they were the foreigners who worked in the fields. Marthe had known for years that itinerant Spanish and Portuguese worked the lavender farms. But they should not be up here at the Musset farmhouse. They had their own large hut in the fields owned by Auguste's family.

Moving faster now, she worked her way round to the door. Already riled by Christine, she felt a rising anger that these men might have come to steal from the very people who were providing their work and shelter.

'What are you doing here?' she shouted into the space.

No answer.

'I know you're there. Answer me!'

Hay rustled. 'Caspian knows we are here,' came a whisper. A man's voice, oddly accented. So they were foreigners.

Her face was burning. 'Who's Caspian?'

'Keep your voice down! You know the rules. Caspian ... the Philosopher.'

'You're talking nonsense. I'll ask you again: what are you doing here?'

'Ssh! We're ... waiting for the moon...'

Waiting for the moon? It was as though she had stumbled into another farm, one in fairyland perhaps. They might be tiny sprites, another set of workers with an unknown purpose. Marthe shivered now, completely at sea.

'There's no Caspian here,' she repeated.

'Sometimes they just call him the Philosopher. You think I would say this to you if I hadn't seen you here for weeks, working, eating and riding the pony trap with the family?'

Marthe backed away.

'I'm going back now,' she said, edging her way out. He did not try to stop her.

Her forehead was tight; her head was beginning to hurt. This man was no Spaniard or Portuguese, she realised, feeling for the top of the stone wall under her outstretched hand.

She had to act quickly.

'Monsieur! Madame!' she called as she approached the farmhouse.

No answer.

Before she reached the door, someone caught hold of her and she jumped.

'Whatever's the matter?' asked Mme Musset.

'I'm not sure, but you need to know...' Marthe couldn't form the words fast enough. 'Strangers in the barn. Some men.'

'Stay here, I'll deal with this.'

But when Mme Musset returned, she said not a word about the men. 'Here, I've picked some courgettes and a nice fat aubergine. If you'll give me a hand, we'll make a start on supper.'

By now, Marthe knew better than to ask.

That night, as usual now, she pulled away from the voices in the kitchen and sat in the corner seat with her Braille stylus device and her slate, writing to a friend from school. If she had to earn the family's trust once again from the beginning, then she was determined to do so.

'What are you doing?' asked Arlette. Perhaps she had been so bound up in whatever was going on that she had only just noticed that Marthe was also behaving differently.

'I'm writing in Braille.'

There was a pause. 'Show me.'

Marthe offered up the slate and stylus. 'Once you know the patterns for each letter, you use these to make the dot from the back of the paper, writing in a mirror image.'

'Is it hard?'

'Well, not once you've learned how to do it.'

Arlette ran her fingers over the page.

'Did you know that Braille was once known as night writing? It was invented for Napoleon, so that soldiers could read messages in the dark with no need to use a light,' said Marthe.

There was no answer. Then Arlette clasped her so tightly around the shoulders that it hurt.

'Uncle Victor! Come here quick!' she cried.

M Musset drew up a chair next to her.

She knew what came next would not be easy for him, but this was it: he was going to tell her to leave, that they could no longer support her, and she began to prepare herself for the worst, to fling herself at him and beg him to reconsider.

'I am going to make a terrible demand of you, Marthe.'

She stood up to take the blow, however it fell, though she felt as though she were sinking through the floor. 'Please don't make me leave! You can trust me – you know you can!'

'Leave? Whoever said anything about leaving?'

'That's not what you wanted to tell me? I heard you talking, weeks ago – saying you didn't know whether I was safe or not, whether you could trust me,' she said.

'You heard that? We've never thought that! How could we?'

'But you said–'

There was a pause, during which she sensed silent communication.

'We weren't talking about you, my dear. Never.'

It was a struggle to contain her joy.

'Now listen, child ... I'm going to ask you something, Marthe. It is very serious. But before I do, you must know that you have a choice. You don't have to do it.'

Marthe wondered whether he realised that she could never refuse any request he made of her.

'What I have to ask you is–'

'Yes. I'll do it.'

'Yes? You don't even know what I'm going to ask!'

'If it's you who are asking, or Madame, then the answer's yes, whatever it is.'

'That's very loyal. I appreciate that, I really do. But some demands, some actions, are extremely serious. There are grave moral implications. There might be danger of the very worst kind,

163

my dear.'

'I don't care.'

Silence.

'All right. I hope what I say will not shock you.'
Marthe shook her head.

'Even now I cannot tell you too much. There
are aspects I know nothing about. No one knows
everything, except for the chiefs. Knowledge is a
dangerous commodity in these times. If we have
kept certain things from you, you must accept
that it was for the safety of all of us.'

They had begun by helping to repatriate Allied
airmen and escapees. For weeks, sometimes
months, the men were looked after at the lavender
farm, gathering their strength in sunlight by doing
light work in the fields, hiding in plain view while
they waited for the local guides who would take
them on to the port at Marseille. These British and
American men, sometimes a Pole or Czech who
flew for the RAF, were hidden among the Spanish
and Portuguese and the other refugee workers
who had moved south when this was still the *Zone
Libre*. If the Germans ever came to check, their
lack of good French could be explained away. But
thanks to Musset's tightrope walk playing the
collaborator, they were mostly left alone.

Over the past year, their links with the Resistance had strengthened. Auguste had drawn them
closer into active circles. At Céreste there lived a
man who in another life had been a poet; this
gentle but passionate man had built up cells of
resistance across the region, all playing their part,
all in contact with other cells, all links in the

chain. The idiosyncratic messages broadcast from London to friends and family in France on the BBC were coded instructions to the partisans.

'They confirm the imminent arrival of parachute drops and landings. The British send us weapons by air. Explosives. Clothes and shoes too, sometimes. Planes that land in the dead of night with no lights. We are all working together to regain our country. Now, I am only ever going to tell you only as much as you need to know.'

Marthe nodded eagerly, hardly able to believe what he was telling her.

'What we need is your expertise in communication.'

'My expertise?'

'After they got old Pineau, we knew we had to keep wireless communications to a minimum. The authorities can track the signals too easily. It's too dangerous to use radios between themselves – we have to keep our capacity to contact the British agents on the ground and for them to contact London. The fallback system has always been to leave messages in known locations, but many of these are now unsafe. There's no such thing as a safe house any more, and we can't put more people in danger.

'Anything written down, even in code, would be suspicious. But if we designed a wrapper for the soap, containing no additional note or markings – any visible markings–'

'Braille.'

'Yes, exactly so.'

'Just tell me what you want me to write, and I

165

will do it.'

'Good girl.'

'But what about a translator?'

'That's the other matter for which I need your help. Who can read Braille that you know you can trust absolutely?'

'Which area?'

'Over towards Apt, ideally. Aix. Sisteron.'

Her mind was already working through her old friends from school. Renee, of course. And Elise too. She could trust them.

'Renée lives in Apt now. She has a job in the music shop.'

'Good. That's a very good start. All the best drops have plenty of people legitimately going in and out.'

'There will be others... Elise is at Forcalquier now, and there's another girl, Jeanne, who comes from Aix. We will all work so diligently – we were taught well at the school!'

The prospect of the months to come was thrilling. Her tasks would be as absorbing as they were mysterious and exciting. But first there were other questions she needed to ask. 'The men in the barn...' she said.

'We decided to bring some of our ... foreign guests up here last week. It won't be long now until they can move on, and it's safer that they are here while the final arrangements are being made.'

'They said they were waiting for someone called Caspian who was a philosopher.'

There was a loaded pause. 'I am Caspian,' said M Musset. 'We don't use our real names, it's too dangerous. Also known as the Philosopher. I will

166

have to speak to them. We've made a narrow room for them behind tall stacks of hay, and they are supposed to stay completely quiet if they hear anything at all outside. But obviously they have not been as careful as they should be.'

At last she understood.

'It won't be long now,' said Monsieur. 'We're waiting for the full moon. When the moon is full, a plane is coming for them.'

Resistance. What was resistance but the will to survive? Like roots in the winter ground, they had been dormant, but when the sun warmed the soil, they would push up to emerge into the air again, every cell remembering the blueness of the sky, each tiny bud coiled tight and ready to burst out.

'I wore your violet perfume today,' said Arlette. 'Violet for modesty, to tell our people at Céreste that all is quiet but well. It sent a beautifully clear message. There were many compliments. Even our man Candide, pretending to be drunk as usual in the café, sniffed appreciatively.'

'I am learning so much,' said Marthe to Arlette as they said good night. 'But I'm not frightened.' That was not quite true. But she had been far more frightened of being cast adrift by the Mussets.

It was extraordinary, thought Marthe, how they had adapted to living in constant terror of discovery. At first it was exhausting. Then exhaustion and tension became normal, it seemed. It was extraordinary; yet another way the human body and mind adapted to circumstance.

There were two of them in the barn, and they were both Americans.

Arlette took Marthe with her when she brought food to the men. Arlette stood guard by the open door while they wolfed chickpea stew. It was the best they could offer that day.

Marthe sat on the straw. After a while they spoke to her. At first it was a conversation *in rondo*, one of those songs where the same tune and words are sung at different intervals. Their responses clashed and misfired. One of them could hardly speak French, just single words he had picked up. But the other could speak surprisingly well after months on the run through France.

His name was Kenton Attwater, and he was a twenty-three-year-old navigator in a plane called a Fortress that had been shot down somewhere close to Grenoble. He had managed to bail out, and his parachute brought him down uninjured but for a few gashes and bruises.

'I was lucky. It was a wild, remote place. There was no one watching me come down.'

He had buried the parachute and run into woodland where he hid until it was dark. At night he walked south. When he became so hungry that he had no choice but to take a chance on an isolated farmhouse, he was welcomed and fed.

'That was my second piece of luck. They let me rest in a barn, and the next day they brought a man to see me. I thought he must have been OK because he carried a British gun. He brought me that night to the next safe house.'

It took two months of resting and moving on at night, each time with a different guide, before he had arrived at Auguste's lavender fields.

'When we came over the hill there was a great cliff high in the sky but deep in shadow. It was a threatening place – the whole mountain was looming over us, purple and black. But in front of it was a smaller hilltop with a church on top and a very few houses, and this small hill was lit gold by the sun like a spotlight. I'll never forget it. I couldn't tell you why, but I felt safe.'

'You *are* safe,' said Marthe. 'There are so many complicated ways the mountains and valleys and plateaux link together here – that's our secret weapon. And you know, some of these farms and houses were built in the time of the Romans. The thick stone walls are defences, and the drystone walls that drop down the terraces provide secret enclosures. We can see who is coming up here, and we can be ready.'

'From a flying fortress to an old one,' the American said grimly.

'How long were you at Auguste's farm?'

'Almost a month. That's where I ran into Scotty.'

'Who's Scotty?'

'My friend here. Gunner Scotty Davis from Detroit. He's been in a prisoner-of-war camp. He managed to escape – that's quite something! He's lucky, too. He got a pack of playing cards in a food parcel. So he started a poker school. Two days later there's a letter telling them in code to drop the cards in a bucket of water. Turned out the cards were a fifty-two-part map of the route to Switzerland. So he started figuring out how he could use it.' He laughed. 'And would you look at that, there he goes again, taking his chances!'

'What do you mean?'

'He hasn't wasted much time with Arlette over there!'

'I can't look at that.'

'Sorry?'

'I can't see that. Or anything else.'

'You're blind? I didn't know. I mean, now you tell me, I can see it, but I – ah, no, I shouldn't have put it like that – I ... I'm sorry.'

'You mustn't feel sorry for me. I don't.'

In some ways they were all the same now. So many people stumbling around in the dark, just as she was. All across Europe there were secret roads along which men and women were moving, some towards safety, others farther into darkness. One false step. Lives in the balance. So much unknown.

Work at the perfume factory continued at a frenetic pace. Marthe spent hours each night at the farmhouse with her slate and stylus. The packages of soap with their embossed wrappers, different scents bearing different messages, were delivered to a hotel in Apt. The messages were transcribed and passed on verbally at the music shop a few narrow streets away. In Céreste, the Poet generously gave board and lodging to a blind refugee. He too was an eager recipient of soap, and wasted no time in organising his own distribution network.

The end was nearing, they could feel it. On 6 June millions of Allied soldiers had landed in Normandy and were breaking through from the north. But the dangers had increased. In Reillanne a medieval convent on the hill had been used for several years as a hostel for those who had fled the north, and other foreign workers. In an act of pure viciousness, fifty-four Jewish workers who had lived quietly among them were deported. In the nearby village of Saint-Michel the inhabitants were woken by pounding on their doors and ordered to gather in the square in front of the Mairie. A senior officer of the Milice stood on the steps and read out a transcript of Pétain's speech: 'People of France, do not worsen your unhappiness with acts that risk calling tragic reprisals upon yourselves...'

On 4 July a Gestapo officer was killed by a sniper in Aix, and only a matter of hours afterwards every one of the inhabitants – men, women and children – of the hamlet of Les Figuiers was either gunned down or burned alive in their homes.

There was despair among the resistants that the raid on the convent at Reillanne had taken place before they had any chance of stopping it. But there was also a terrible suspicion that factions within the Resistance, specifically the Communists, had their own political agenda; and that it suited their purposes to pick off German officers to provoke these cruel retaliations.

But there were successes, too. Thanks to the saboteurs, no more trains were running on the two main lines that reached down from the Alps, from Grenoble to Aix and from Briançon to Livron.

'And now we're winning control of the roads,' boasted Auguste. 'The Boches are only driving in

171

convoys now; you won't find a car venturing out singly. Neither do the motorcycle couriers roar around like they used to. Even the checkpoints are being drawn back to the outskirts of the towns where they have men stationed. The tide is turning, and they are practically prisoners where they're garrisoned.'

'You be careful. It won't be as easy as you make out,' said M Musset.

'It's true. They only go outside to get more supplies.'

'Or to effect some more reprisals.'

'When they go out, there's a fifty-fifty chance they're going to be attacked. The forces of the Maquis are being unleashed, and they're unstoppable. We're the ones who know the terrain and the back roads. Wherever they turn, there's a chance they'll be met by gunfire, hemmed in. They won't risk it now. I'm telling you, the roads are almost all ours.'

M Musset kept his counsel. His pauses and silences had always been eloquent, and now they held a restraint that gave Marthe goosebumps.

'You just be careful. Never assume. Never believe entirely what you haven't proved for yourself. We don't need dead heroes. And remember, if any one of us is caught, it will be the end for all of us.'

5

Citrus and Pine

July–August 1944

It was a Thursday, and Arlette had gone to Céreste as usual. A warm sirocco wind of the kind that sprinkled red dust like paprika and caught in the throat had strengthened throughout the afternoon. Now it sent dry leaves skittering across the ground and tugged at loose clothing.

By four the clock was already ticking ponderously. By five the faintest noise suggested Arlette's safe arrival home, and their hopes rose. Every sense was on the alert. Another *ting-ting* from the clock, the quarter-hour, made the temperature drop and stopped the heart for a few seconds. Musset's cigarette smoke.

Marthe's hands stopped moving on her book, fingertips resting on the raised patterns of the open page. She could all but feel the twitch of the minute hand on the clock. She sensed the wind stirring the valley, rolling like waves over the silence, gaining ascendancy over the hills, the almond and apricot orchards, ruffling the olive groves and meadows, over the road that should have brought the bus from Céreste.

She tried to imagine the bus on the road: Arlette in the clumsy vehicle as it climbed,

173

watching as the plain unfurled. I cannot see her, Marthe thought, but neither can any of us.

All those months when she had not understood why the Mussets worried so much about Arlette's trips to Céreste. Now, for all that the waiting for her to return was both terrible and frightening, it was shot through with a complicated, proud, painful happiness for Marthe: she was truly a part of life with the Mussets again, within the enchanted citadel where scent was the spell.

At six o'clock Arlette was still not back.

Monsieur reached for his jacket. Keys and coins jingled. 'I'm going to walk down to the village,' he said. 'Perhaps something has happened to the bus.' He kept his voice even, but a raw edge gave him away.

'You do that, my dear.'

He paused by the door to pat his pockets. Outside he whistled for the large black mongrel who usually accompanied him. His feet crunched on the gravel, and the dog's paws provided a lighter counterpoint.

'Best he goes to meet her. No use sitting around doing nothing useful,' said Mme Musset, though she too was unable to disguise the strain in her voice.

Marthe got up. 'What would you like me to do? I'll start peeling some vegetables for dinner, shall I?'

'That's the idea. They'll be bounding up the path before we've got the pans ready.'

They worked side by side, in silence.

The clock struck eight. The food, such as they could find, was ready. It waited, covered, on the stove. Mme Musset brewed a tisane. They sipped wordlessly.

When M Musset returned at almost ten, he was with Auguste.

'We're not sure what's happened–'

'She's been taken,' said Auguste.

Madame gave a cry, as if she was in pain.

'We don't know what's happened,' said Monsieur. 'There's every chance she is fine, that there's a simple explanation. We must not think the worst.'

'How? Why?' Madame was not convinced by her husband's attempt at calm.

'I'm not sure exactly what happened, but I cycled over to Pierrevert and telephoned the Woodcutter from there.'

'They have arrested Candide,' blurted out Auguste.

Monsieur lit a cigarette. 'No, we don't know for certain. It's only a rumour. Candide was in the café hunched over his newspaper as usual until five o'clock – the patron confirmed it. But Arlette wouldn't have spoken to him. That was the point. And he would never have made a mistake. They were both always careful...'

'Do you think she might have–'

Auguste was cut off by a knock at the door. They hadn't even heard an approach.

There was a tangible ripple of panic as they realised their conversation might have been over-heard. Then Musset flung open the door.

It was their neighbour Étienne, an elderly bee-keeper who lived one field down the hill. 'Have you heard anything?' He had a wheeze in his voice. He had followed them on the path up as quickly as he could.

'*Hélas*, no.'

'I'm going to Céreste in the morning with my honey, Victor. I will keep my eyes and ears open.'

'We would be most grateful.'

'Wouldn't have had her down as the running away sort.'

'No...'

An awkward moment passed, during which their neighbour would normally have been invited to take a drink and a bite to eat. Étienne hesitated, then seemed to understand that this was no time for social niceties, and bid them good night.

They waited until they were sure he had gone. 'How much does he know?' asked Madame.

'Nothing. Only that Arlette seemed to have missed the bus. I bumped into him on my way down to find Auguste. But he knew straight away from my face that something was up.'

'What now?' asked Madame.

'There's nothing we can do about Étienne.'

'I don't seriously doubt his intentions ... but–'

'No ... no ... I'm sure you're right. In the morning I'm going to go down to Céreste. Until we know what exactly has happened ... well, that's all we can do.'

Marthe lay awake on her iron bed. Only a few days earlier Arlette had come back to the distillery from a trip to Forcalquier where she had taken a

176

large order. Marthe had added a few drops of pine-needle essence to a citrus-peel infusion, and the pervading aromatic warmth made them both nostalgic for August evenings by the sea to the south.

'Pine for hope,' said Marthe. 'And I'm going to try amber for timelessness.'

'Hope,' said Arlette. 'Our instincts are always for hope. There's something rather mysterious but wonderful about that.'

'I'm not sure it is mysterious, actually. Surely instincts are the result of noticing tiny details that the body processes quickly.'

'So quickly that it seems you were anticipating all along ... an animal intuition... You're right, we do it all the time without thinking.'

'Exactly.'

Thinking about that conversation reassured Marthe a little. Arlette would be all right; she would read the signs and act accordingly. She *would*. She must not think of the other things she and Arlette had discussed. The only certainty was that others were watching.

She heard the cocks crow into an empty morning, and M Musset departing on his bicycle soon after sunrise. Her stomach contracted, but she knew she would not be able to eat.

Musset returned at midday. 'Cabot's finding out what he can. But Céreste stinks with informants, he says. Infested by Waffen-SS, too.'

Not all the gendarmes in Céreste were on the side of the Milice. Cabot was a living reminder of the fact that the police had once been trusted members of the community. Without a flicker of recognition, he had once pushed Auguste back onto the Digne bus just as a convoy of Waffen-SS and Milice were heard on the approach to the other side of the village. They rounded up five men that day, and only two returned.

Musset and Auguste had been to the village in the Woodcutter's van, the most reliable transport for underground business. 'We sent word with a small boy to the Poet in the old quarter, then met him casually by the water pump. He had no information, but they're putting the word out about a young woman, about so tall, with her hair up in a blue scarf and lavender-print apron, an innocent bystander. The last anyone seems to have seen of her, she was walking out of the café at about the time the bus was expected.'

Musset recounted the events in a voice so flat it seemed the life had been kicked out of him: a man in a three-piece tweed suit and round tortoiseshell glasses had seemed on the point of admitting to a sighting, but then quickly took his leave when a van sped past; shutters banged shut; a grey car the size of a boat had swayed to a stop outside the Mairie, and four German officers had gone in. Then nothing.

Then, as Musset and Auguste left the café, a man walked up behind them. '"The Milice arrested a man who was in the café the previous afternoon, a thickset man who played the drunk, pretending to read a newspaper," that's what he said. "Played the drunk", those were his exact words. Which is worrying–'

'You didn't ask him about a girl?'

'Too risky. The last thing I wanted to do was to come right out with it that they were connected – that I was connected too.'

'So you've no idea who this chap was you were talking to?' asked Madame.

'Never seen him before. He was about my age, dressed as a farmer. I didn't want to ask, and didn't want to give away more than I had to. According to him, anyway, the Milice had a busy day yesterday. They had a man held in the cells of the police station – the man who was taken from the café. That's all he knew.'

'What now?'

'There's nothing we can do. The Poet is getting a message to the Engineer, but after that, all we can do is sit tight.'

'If she's been arrested, they'll know that she's the girl from Distillerie Musset,' Marthe said.

'I expect so. All we can do is accept that she must have been taken, along with Candide – and try to find out what's going on.'

Which was exactly what the Milice would be doing, too. Everyone knew that they had their methods. Words that were not spoken.

'If they have Arlette, they will connect her to us.'

Arlette in Céreste with the deliveries. The messages in Braille wrapped around cakes of soap. The other blind girls waiting to act as translators, in Apt and Reillanne, Banon and Saint-Christol. A spider's mesh of tiny strands, only visible when the sun caught their beads of dew.

'Arlette will never break,' said Marthe. 'She wouldn't even tell me what she was doing, though

179

I begged her to explain. She never did – it was only when she saw how I might have the answer to the problem of how to send new messages.'

'She's young and pretty – she'll charm her way out of there,' said Auguste, with a confidence that no one believed, though they wanted to so badly.

They heard nothing.

The feeling of threat intensified. If Arlette did not return, then sooner or later the Milice would come in her place. There was only a week to go before the night flight, when the Americans would be taken north over the mountains to the clandestine landing strip.

Kenton and Scotty were moved out of the barn. Marthe's room on the ground floor had a trapdoor. A small room adjoining the Mussets' contained a staircase up to the low attic, which led to another route out of the house.

Kenton was the taller and the less agile; he would find the roof space harder to pass through. And Scotty had only the most rudimentary grasp of French, so it was better he be shielded by the Mussets. Kenton would sleep on Marthe's floor, ready to spring up if anyone arrived suddenly in the night. They had practised the drill. Marthe knew exactly how to close the trapdoor and pull the bed into the right position over it.

The first night before they all retired, Marthe advanced on the two boys with a scent bottle and sprayed.

'Hey! What's this?'

'A distillation made of pepper and lavender. It puts dogs off the scent. They might bring dogs.'

The American was solicitous, only knocking on her door when she assured him she was already in her little iron-framed bed. Then he came in, shut the door quietly and lay down on a mat and a padded bedspread. She heard his breathing, but she hardly dared to speak to him. Perhaps he was already sleeping, already on his way back to a country far away.

She lay awake, her head too full. When she finally dozed off, she dreamt of waiting for the full moon. First an evening when the western sky flamed, sending great fingers of rich red light up the slopes through the trees, then the rise of the great disc that silvered the night. Then Arlette lost in a forest. The Gestapo taking Candide to Forcalquier. If he talked, they were all as good as dead. Who had betrayed them, no one knew.

She was awake again, heart pounding. Across the floor, the airman was still breathing evenly.

The Milice came on the third night.

A movement on the gravel path alerted them. For the first time she understood why the approach had been covered in tiny stones. Then their own dogs barking. She reached out wordlessly for Kenton, felt urgently for his shoulder. He started. A soft shuffling, and he had left her side. He must have sprung like an athlete into the hole.

Marthe too played her part quickly and smoothly.

Her heart was pounding as she lay back in bed, now positioned over the trapdoor.

Fear pulled her skin tight. It was a hot night, but the sheet felt cold where her sweat-soaked nightdress stuck to her back.

A whistle blew. The dogs barked loudly, and there was an eruption of harsh shouts and boots stamping outside. Blows crashed down on the wood of the front door, then the kitchen door.

M Musset shouted back at them from the bedroom window. Whatever did they want? What was so important it couldn't wait for the morning?

'Open up! Open up!'

Leather boots on the tiled floors, drawing closer. Heavy footfalls on the stairs and along the corridor to Marthe's room.

When the man came to the door, she was already waiting for him, blinking with sleep.

'What's in here? Get out of the way!'

She turned her head away from his voice and said, 'What is happening, what is going on...?' A feeble voice, slightly stupid. 'Who are you?'

The first brush of his arm against her, as if he was about to push her aside. 'What does it look like is going on?' He smelled of rank garlic sausage.

Marthe put out her hands, feeling for the door frame but making an obvious, fumbling job of it.

'I'm blind... I don't know who you are.'

She sensed a momentary hesitation on his part. 'They keep me in here ... they don't want me to go outside. I can't see – have you come to help me? Please help me.' She patted the fabric of his uniform. 'Are you a gendarme? A nice gendarme?'

He slapped her hand away. 'We're searching the house.'

'Well, I have seen nothing – how could I?'

Shuffling feet on the stairs. More voices. Then

182

Musset, demanding that they speak to Kommandant Baumann and explain why they had come bursting into the home of a trusted businessman in the middle of the night. More noise in the corridor, and then her visitor was speaking.

'She can't possibly know anything. She's a halfwit farm girl, and blind to boot.'

'I know her, anyway,' said another. 'She's a mouse who sees no one.'

They retreated down the corridor. Voices were raised in the hall.

'What about the girl you had working for you, Musset?'

'Which girl? I keep lots of girls in employment!'

'The one who makes the deliveries in Céreste.'

'Oh, her... Look here, we're all just going about our business. I insist that you ask the *Kommandant*...' Musset was still complaining, demanding that they contact Baumann. Wake him, if necessary. Telling them of all the times the Distillerie Musset had supplied the Germans with scarce products, and lamenting the lack of gratitude. The voices died away.

Then Mme Musset's arms were around Marthe, and they were trembling as one.

No further sounds until the particular footfall that told them Monsieur was coming down the passage, and he was alone. Then he was holding them both.

When he did speak, it was in a low tone. 'It's all right. We're all still here and in one piece.'

'Thank the Lord.' Madame disentangled herself.

'Just wait a while longer, my dear. Just to be sure.'

183

'I thought I heard a car going away down the hill.'

'So did I, but...'

'You think they might come back?'

'They might.'

They waited an hour before they released Kenton and Scotty from their cubbyholes.

As if he could read her thoughts, Kenton reached out and touched her hand. The Mussets had left them, urging a few hours of sleep before morning broke. But how could they sleep now? They were sitting side by side on her bed.

Marthe pulled her hand away, unsure of herself. He said nothing, and she had no way of gauging his reaction. Why had she done that? She had felt the tremor in his hand.

Very slowly, she reached out for his face. She stroked his cheek, braver now. She felt his thick hair, how it slipped straight and smoothly through her fingers. She made his brow real – real to her – then the eyes, nose and chin. Finding the lines between imagination and reality, blurring the boundaries between sight and touch. Slowly, she moved one finger to his mouth and traced his lips. They were full and soft.

'Can I get into the bed with you?'

Marthe nodded.

She felt the shape of his shoulders and chest against her side. He was wearing a rough shirt and trousers. 'I'm sorry, I can't help it – after coming so far... I was scared.'

She found his lips and touched his mouth with her finger. 'Put your head on my shoulder and

184

close your eyes. Sleep here now.'

The comfort of another human body. Warm skin, limbs folding and fitting together. If he closed his eyes, there would be no difference between them.

The sun stroked the bed. Marthe was still half asleep. Then she started, realising. She had never woken up with a man before.

He was speaking to her, in a whisper, in his peculiar accent. She couldn't make out what he was saying.

'What do you look like?' asked Marthe.

'I have blond hair and blue eyes. Quite tall, quite broad. No strange distinguishing features.'

'Are you handsome?'

'I can't answer that.'

'Yes, you can. You just have. If you weren't, you would have laughed and said straight off that you weren't.'

He laughed then. 'OK. You win.'

'So do the girls call you handsome?'

'Of course.'

'Really?'

'Well, my mother does.'

'She'd be a poor mother if she didn't.'

'Very true.'

'Blond hair and blue eyes,' she repeated. 'The lavender fairy.'

'Now, hang on a minute!'

'Just *like* the lavender fairy has. There's an old story about the beautiful fairy called Lavandula who was born in the wild lavender of the Lure mountain. She grew up and began to wander

185

farther from the mountain, looking for somewhere special to make her home. One day she came across the stony, uncultivated landscapes of Haute Provence, and the pitiful sight made her so sad she cried hot tears – hot mauve tears that fell into the ground and stained it. And that is where, ever afterwards, the lavender of her birthplace began to grow.'

'Did you ever see it?'

'Not here, no. But I still remember the lavender fields near where my family lives. The fields there are much smaller, but I saw them when I was young.'

'That's awful. It's such–'

'If I hadn't lost my sight, I might never have come here, never have discovered my true vocation. I would have been just a farm girl, never knowing what I was missing, and then a farmer's wife like my mother, and set to repeat her life. Don't you see, it has opened my world, not closed it down, and I shall always be grateful for that.'

'So you haven't always been?'

'No. I could see until I was nearly eleven years old.'

'What happened?'

She liked his directness. So many people were curious but did not ask. 'It was very sudden. One day, one eye became blurred. I thought I had some dust in it, so I rubbed and blinked all day. Do you remember how simple life was at that age? I blinked and kept rubbing it, waiting for the eye to clear.'

'And it didn't.'

'No, it didn't. I told my mother, and she told me

186

I just had to wait patiently and all would be well. That was her remedy for all life's ills, and for a while I believed her. Then one day my younger brother Pierre pushed me off a windowsill where I was sitting. I can't even remember why he did it. I banged my head and sprained my wrist in the fall onto the cobblestones in the courtyard in front of the house. She took me to the doctor because she thought I might have broken my wrist, and I took my chance to tell him about my eye.'

'What did the doctor say?'

'He seemed to agree with Maman. All we could do was wait. For the next few months I concentrated hard on everything I could see with the right eye, all the while alive to the smallest variation in the left. Sometimes I seemed to make out more, but mostly I saw only fuzzy black and white, occasionally with a burst or tint of colour.

'Then one day I went to put on my red dress and found it had changed to a dull olive green in the cupboard.'

The American stroked her hair. Even now, the memory was disturbing.

'Something strange was happening to all the colours. The sky stopped being the blue I had always known and became a stormy grey-purple on even the brightest day. The pink oleander flowers were inexplicably light blue. I couldn't understand what was going on.'

'Sounds like you'd gone colour-blind.'

'Just for a while. Then, shade by shade, they all disappeared, even the mixed-up colours. Every day the world became a darker place.'

He held her tighter. 'It must have been awful.'

187

'I understand now, but then ... it was very frightening. It was always there in the cells of my body, the doctor said when I saw him again. He had to read a lot of books to find out, but when he did, it all made sense. I was born with it, so I should be pleased I saw as much of the world as I did. I was lucky in that it came on later in my childhood, and unlucky in that it was always much more likely it would happen to a boy than a girl.' Marthe sighed. 'But not in our family, it seems.'

'Do you see anything?'

'No. Though I am lucky because I have the pictures in my head. I still dream in pictures and colour, always the world of my childhood. I see the purple Judas trees at Easter lighting up the roadsides and terraces of the town. Ochre cliffs made of cinnamon powder. Autumn clouds rolling along the ground of the hills, and the patchwork of wet oak leaves on the grass. The shape of a rose petal. And my parents' faces, which will never grow any older.

'But it's strange how scent brings it all back, too. I only have to smell certain aromas, and I am back in a certain place with a certain feeling.'

The comforting past smelled of heliotrope and cherry and sweet almond biscuits: close-up smells, flowers you had to put your nose to as the sight faded from your eyes. The scents of that childhood past had already begun to slip away: Maman's apron with blotches of game stew; linen pressed with faded lavender; the sheep in the barn. The present, or what had so very recently been the present, was orange blossom infused with hope.

188

'I can understand that. For me, hot dogs are football games. Fairgrounds are oil and candy-floss. Paris is garlic, and Métro stations, that pungent—'

'You've been to Paris?'

'I came as a student before the war.'

'I have never been to Paris, but I'd like to. What did you study in Paris?'

'French, art ... literature. I thought I wanted to make my mark by trying to write, and Paris is where American romantic idealists come to do that. It was a year's exchange from my college. I didn't know a thing when I arrived. I was a baby, with baby opinions and ambitions. Pitiful, really. But now? I've never been so grateful for anything in my life as I am for that year. That I learned enough of the language to get by. Without that, I'd be dead for sure by now.'

'How did you come to be in the air force?'

He gave a short, bitter laugh. 'My father had connections ... and they put me on a training course, and the next thing I knew I was flying in a Fortress over Europe with a full payload.'

'A long way from home.'

'Yes.'

They were quiet for a while.

'You are special,' whispered Kenton. 'In more ways than one. What you did when the German came to the door—'

'There was no time to be afraid. I did what I had to do. It's normal. And he wasn't German. He was French. That is the most dreadful thing of all.'

'Maybe that was why he went away...'

'Maybe, but I don't think so. We fear our own people too.'

M Musset had explained it to her when he first asked for her help. Those who helped behind the lines took the greatest risks, because there was no uniform to protect them. The greatest risk was betrayal. And if you were betrayed, you were either shot or sent to a prison camp in Germany. They said it was better to be shot.

'You are the bravest of the brave. Never forget that.'

'M Musset says we are history as it is being formed.'

'He is a fine man. But Madame is unhappy,' said Kenton. 'Or rather, she is worried. You can't see the way she looks sometimes when she thinks no one is watching.'

'But she always sounds so relaxed and encouraging.'

'It's not how things seem, it's how they are, sweetheart.'

'I know.' Marthe swallowed hard. 'What would you be doing if there wasn't a war?'

He sighed. 'I can hardly imagine any more. I would have gone back to my studies. I might have graduated and then started more studies to work at the family firm. I might have been on my way to becoming a lawyer to please my father. The Attwaters of Boston – an old family.'

'My family is old too.'

'Old rich.'

'Oh. We are old poor. Becoming a lawyer – you mean that's not what you want?'

'I don't know what I want. No, wait – I do! I

want to get out of here alive. How's that for an ambition?'

'Very sensible.'

'And I'd like to come back here. It's such a beautiful place. I would love to see it again when the war is over.'

Marthe felt unaccountably pleased. 'You should. We will be better then.'

Despite what this extraordinary young man said about their bravery, it felt undeserved. So many people in this dark time were not what they should have been. Some were as closed as their shuttered houses. Too many seemed not to care about their own country. It was shaming. When the Gestapo started paying for denunciations, too many were only too happy to turn informant. Sometimes it seemed as if those who did care enough to fight back were akin to the boniest birds brought back from the shoot, the cold plucked skin that showed how very helpless they were against the hunters' guns.

Suddenly it was important to try to explain this.

'My family has lived here for as long as anyone could remember; it could be hundreds of years, because there was never any evidence that we came from anywhere else. We mark the years by vintages of walnut wine and fruit liqueurs, like the wines and olive oils of other farmsteads, and we keep our history in barrels and bottles laced with dusty cobwebs.

'If we don't stand fast now, we might be the last generation to live our lives like this.'

It was a while before he spoke.

'And when we win the war – as we will – what

191

will become of you, sweet Marthe?'

'I shall be a creator of fabulous perfumes – and I shall go to Paris!'

She would remember that sunlit hour for the rest of her life. Like a fragile fragment of a half-forgotten dream, it would rise to the surface of an ordinary morning. Kenton opened the windows wide, and she felt the lighter air come in, the silkiness of a light breeze on her face. His touch still shimmered on her skin. There was so much to discover, so many ways to communicate.

The Milice shot Arlette later that day.

6

Lavender

August 1944

Arlette's body was dumped at midday outside the police station in Forcalquier alongside Candide's, the two of them laid like bait. It was too dangerous to claim them, and in any case a sympathetic doctor protested that corpses should not be allowed to rot in the town square and arranged for their removal to the hospital mortuary.

But they could not go to fetch her. The moon was full.

On a plateau of lavender fields shielded by mountains near Saint-Christol, British planes dropped supplies at night to the Resistance. Carts tasselled with lavender drew up by each drop zone, and men went to work releasing the precious cargo from protective containers and hiding weapons and explosives under the sheaves of flowers.

The operations were urgent now. Partisan cells received parachuted agents on rocky terrain that was really only suitable for containers. They called the long, flat field Spitfire. It had been used before to land aircraft secretly, the length of the landing strip disguised with two hundred metres of lavender. Six hundred metres of grass, then the lavender, and then it became a potato field.

Each night the Mussets had watched the waxing of the moon and waited for confirmation. A courier arrived, but only to tell them to stay where they were: the flight was delayed. Contact with the organisers had been patchy. First they were on, then the flight was delayed in Italy, stuck on the ground in thick cloud. Then, at the beginning of the second week of August, when the moon had begun to wane, the message came at last. The plane was coming in the following night. The two Americans were expected, with the Actress as guide. With no method of further communication, Caspian and his group had no option but to follow their instructions. It was not possible to tell them that the Actress would not be coming.

'I shall be the Actress,' said Marthe.
'Don't be ridiculous!'
'They are expecting a young woman with the boys. You said so yourself.'
'I can't allow that.'

193

'But you need a girl. They don't know about Arlette, and there's no time to tell them.'

'Even so. You're not thinking straight – none of us is, with what's happened.' Musset's voice was tight with emotion.

'I want to do it. For Arlette. You have to let me. Kenton and Scotty will lead me. I just have to play my part. And think – who will suspect a poor blind girl?'

'They would never believe we would be so stupid as to try it.'

'All I have to do is let the organisers think I am Arlette. They will be looking for a young couple and their friend wandering into the field. That is the plan, and it cannot be changed now, since we are no longer in wireless contact. If anything does not tally with the agreed plan, if we don't arrive as arranged, they will suspect we are infiltrators – it will all have been for nothing!'

'We could ask Étienne's daughter.'

'And involve someone new? You can't do that. It goes against everything you have been so careful to set up. I want to do it – and I have to do it! I'm the obvious choice. The right size and age. The boys will steer me in the right direction.'

There was a long silence.

Then Monsieur began to describe the situation she must be prepared to enter. The men in peasant clothes, the baggy serge jackets, hunting bags slung across their chests. A gun with an end like a garden hose, designed by the Czechs and dropped by parachute by the British.

'The Army of the Night,' Marthe said to Kenton.

'And I'm going to be part of it.'

'You're sure, aren't you?'

'There is no other way. Arlette ... she would want me to do this.'

'I think – no, you're right. But–'

'Have you ever killed anyone?' she asked.

He did not answer. She was going to ask again, but before she could form the words, she decided against it. She did not need to know.

That night they slept in her room again; she in her bed, he on the floor. When they said good night, Marthe reached out and found Kenton's head, then snatched her hand away as if scalded. 'Your hair – where has it gone?'

'Shaved off. I gave myself what the army calls a number one. Too risky to travel with you, looking like an Aryan who isn't German.'

Neither of them had mentioned the time they slept in each other's arms for comfort. Courage was all now; and they had each decided, it seemed, that a need for comfort might be construed as weak. She bit her lip and tried to make no sound as hot tears rolled for Arlette.

The next evening, Madame prepared a meal they forced themselves to eat and drink. Toasts were made in cracked voices to valour and friendship. Auguste's cousin Thierry, the garagiste, had patched up the truck and agreed to come along in case running repairs were needed.

They would take the old roads over the mountains towards the peak of La Contadour. Boxes of soaps and more boxes containing bottles of eau de toilette, antiseptic and cleaning fluid were

195

lashed carefully to the back and sides of the truck's hold. When this was done, it was impossible to see the old wardrobe secured behind in which Kenton and Scotty were to stand.

Monsieur removed the unfilled boxes in front of the wardrobe door. It was an extraordinarily effective device. 'In you go, lads.'

Marthe felt a hand over hers briefly, then the Americans thanked Madame for all she had done before climbing up into the truck. Madame said a prayer first for the antique engine, and then for the souls it carried. 'Away with you,' she said. 'Good luck.'

The truck vibrated as Monsieur cranked the motor at the end of the bonnet. It spluttered and spat out the smell of burning charcoal from the gasogene appliance bolted on to produce the gas fuel that marked it as a non-military vehicle.

Two of the farm workers now began loading the back with implements of lavender harvesting: the bundles of twine, the ropes, the scythes, the tarpaulins. Then, more carefully, they lifted in the old alembic still that they would not miss if the expedition ended in disaster. Auguste jumped into the back and pulled down a wooden seat. It would be his job to ensure the cargo remained secure, and to provide the cover and first line of defence should they be stopped. He secured ropes around the brass belly of the still, then tapped his knife against his teeth. 'Newly sharpened,' he said. 'They say the crop's tough this year.'

Monsieur pulled Marthe up into the cab beside him; on the other side was Auguste's cousin Thierry's large, soft bulk. He was a man who spoke in bassoon tones and smelled of oil and gut-rot brandy. They rumbled off down the bumpy track.

Five minutes into the climb beyond Manosque, it was touch and go whether the old motor would keep ticking over. The jolts and wheezes became more and more pronounced. There were muffled protests from the back. Sitting shoulder to shoulder with Monsieur and Thierry, Marthe could feel the tension in their muscles as they swayed together.

There was a long wheeze and a sudden violent shudder. Then nothing. The engine stalled. Monsieur pulled sharply at the handbrake lever as they rolled backwards. His arm dug painfully into Marthe's ribs.

Before a word was said, Thierry jumped down and ran round to the crank. Not even a cough from the motor. Thierry cursed softly.

'Come on, beauty,' coaxed Monsieur, as he might to a favourite horse.

It felt like minutes before a spark caught. They were all holding their breath, willing the mechanical parts to revive. It seemed to die away, then abruptly there was a shake, and then another. Monsieur revved the engine, there were belches from the exhaust and Thierry threw himself against Marthe as the truck began to move.

They were climbing, Marthe's back pressing into the hard seat. At a stately pace, bends followed bends, the whine and grinding and rattling from the front of the vehicle rising and falling.

'We should sing a song,' said Thierry, with heavy sarcasm. No one replied.

197

'She was so full of life,' said Musset savagely. Arlette's death, the manner of it, was unbearable to him. Neither he nor Madame could speak of that. But they wanted to talk, to remember her as she was.

So they pushed on through the night as M Musset recounted his most vivid memories of Arlette as a child: when she had once stood on a table to sing to a family gathering, and then would not be stopped; when she put on a play using puppets she had made of paper and ribbon; the time she ate too many wild plums, unable to restrain herself because they were so delicious. 'I can't help it if I like them!' she cried, doubled over with a violent stomach ache. 'And I'd like some more as soon as I'm better!'

'You know,' confessed Marthe, 'I might once have been jealous of Arlette, when she first arrived to live with you, but as soon as I knew her better, I wasn't. Does that make sense? She was my friend, the best I ever had. She let me share her family. She never ever made me feel unwelcome, or as if I was taking too much of your attention away from her.'

'She was a truly good person. It's just so–'

'Roadblock,' said Thierry.

Musset slowed immediately, perhaps to give the men in the back time to ready themselves.

Dogs barked as they pulled up.

'Cut the engine.' The voice came from the left, through the open window. It was clearly an order.

'I'd rather not,' said Monsieur. 'It's a devil to restart, and I don't want to block the road.'

'Cut the engine.'

It shuddered and was silent. Its echoes continued to ring in Marthe's ears.

'Papers. It's after curfew. You had better have a good reason to be out.'

Monsieur reached into his jacket, jabbing his elbow into Marthe's side, and turned to hand them over.

'Where are you going?'

'To our suppliers in Sault.'

'Where have you come from?'

'Manosque.'

'Don't you have your own lavender growers over there?'

'We are in a cooperative with a few farms here. It's easier for us to take the distilling equipment there than try to transport the crop down the valley and up again. They grow lavandin here, and with our process we can extract four times the essence of traditional lavender.'

'What's in the back?'

'Deliveries. Products we made from last year's crop. That's part of the deal.'

There was a thump from the back, and renewed barking from the dogs. While one soldier was asking questions, others had come round to the rear and pulled the canvas back. From the bounces, it seemed that Auguste was on his feet.

'You'll find it all in order,' said Monsieur.

'You don't make deliveries at night.'

'No, of course not. But you cut lavender by moonlight. It's the best, the traditional time to cut, when the plants are full of juices. That's how we do it here. This is the way it's always been

199

done to extract the best-quality essences.'

The voices from the rear grew louder. It was impossible to hear what was being said.

'Papers for the vehicle. Why has it not been requisitioned?'

'It's so old no one would have it. It won't even start again for anyone who has not nursed it for thirty years or more. Perhaps not even then ... as for papers, unfortunately those I cannot help you with. That's like asking for papers for the rusted buckets at the farm, or the birds in the trees. It has never had any papers.'

A metallic sound as if a kick had been aimed at the side of the truck was followed by a heartfelt sigh from Monsieur.

'Tell you what,' he said. 'We're running late already, thanks to this heap of tin, missing the best hours for cutting. Let me come round to the back, and I'll see what I can offer you. One farmer won't be best pleased, but that's the price you pay for keeping going in these difficult times, eh? Some eau de toilette for your girl, perhaps?'

Before the soldier had a chance to think, Monsieur swung himself out of the cab, still speaking. 'Have you any idea how important this crop is to us? I don't care a fig about politics. You can do what you want as far as I'm concerned. Ask the *Kommandant*, if you care to – he will tell you. I have nothing to hide.'

Was it too brave a speech? Had his words been unable to contain the crack of emotion? The dogs sniffed. Then one sneezed.

Musset moved off round the side of the truck. The German soldier, grumbling in a token fash-

200

ion, followed.

Marthe pushed herself as far back on the bench as she could, straining to hear what was happening. Thierry stayed quiet. They ignored each other completely.

After what seemed an hour, but must only have been minutes, the door at the back slammed. The muffled voices sounded less unfriendly. Then Monsieur hoisted himself back in the cab.

'Thierry? The crank, please,' he said.

Thierry obliged. Marthe pressed her hands together in prayer on her lap. The first and second attempts failed. The third almost ignited. The fourth was hopeless. On the fifth effort, the engine shook itself like a wet animal and then roared.

The cab rocked as Monsieur took off as fast as the old crate would go.

'Where are we?' asked Marthe.

'On the road up to Simiane. Not far now to Saint-Christol.'

Their nerves had calmed after the stop at the checkpoint, but were starting to fire again now that their destination was closer. Marthe could only imagine the discomfort in the back, in the wardrobe. So close by. Kenton and Scotty were so close they must be only a hand's width away. Her heart was a hummingbird's wings – less beating than whirring.

The closer they came, the more she drew on what she held in her head. If they had used this field before, villagers must have heard the engines of the aircraft. They must have done. Whole farming villages apparently suffering from

201

communal deafness.

'All right, listen up,' said Musset. 'I'm going to tell you what I've been told. Marthe, you'll pass it on to the boys. The German Nineteenth Army Command has its headquarters at Avignon. There's also a detachment at Sault now. Last week some four hundred Germans carried out sporadic attacks on the road north of Apt. The Maquis took them on and sent them packing, but the Germans came back a few days ago, and this time they were too strong for the Maquis. They have control of the road from Apt to Sault, and the situation on the plateau is now more dangerous than it was before.'

'So why are we doing this?' Thierry asked.

'This plane is bringing in a large group of French military and politicians. They want to be on the ground when the Allies come ashore. It's a big plane, bigger than normal. They'll use it to get some of the escapees out.

'The landing field here is called Spitfire. The man in charge is the Engineer, also known as Xavier. He's the best of the best. You just do what he tells you.'

'How will we find him?'

'He'll be waiting under cover at the roadside edge of the field. Don't worry, he'll see you before any of you know he's there. Say nothing until you are spoken to. No names; you are the Actress.'

The truck whined and then bumped viciously as they turned. As Marthe was thrown across M Musset, she felt the wheel judder. A few more pitches, and they stopped. The engine died.

'What's wrong?'

'This is as far as we go.'

Marthe was helped down from the cab and stood, feeling disoriented. Her legs were cramped and she felt queasy, though it was hard to tell whether that was nerves or carsickness. She read the noises as the back of the truck was opened. There was a short burst of whispering and some indeterminate thumps.

The land around her was still and silent.

Then Monsieur's voice, close to her ear. 'It's this road here. Just turn left when you get to the top of the track. We'll be here, as though we've pulled in for the night, though it's so far off the main roads it would be unusual for anyone to come along. Marthe, you wait for me in the field afterwards. If it all goes wrong, then find your way to the lavender farm called Les Coulets on the road to Sault and tell them Caspian sent you to wait. Now go.'

They already knew the directions, had gone over them many times in the week since the first message came through.

Two strong arms caught hers, Kenton to the right, Scotty to the left. Whispered thanks and slaps on the back.

'Go!' urged Monsieur. He squeezed her arm to offer encouragement.

The three of them began to pick their way along the path.

'Is it easy to see?' asked Marthe.

'Moonlight,' said Kenton. 'Clear as anything. Don't you worry. We have open fields behind a hedge on each side. Then there's a tunnel of trees ahead.'

Armed with a lavender scythe, they advanced.

As they passed along the road, their footfalls were barely audible thanks to the rope-soled shoes Monsieur had insisted they wear. She thought about the way war had transformed her life. For the first time it struck her that there might be no going back, not to the blue curtain of mountains in the Luberon, nor to her family there. But she walked on, padding silently into the darkness.

The Engineer greeted them gruffly when they announced themselves as the Actress and her party. Marthe found herself bundled into a hollow under a tree and told to remain silent. It would all happen very quickly. They strained to make out the sound of the aircraft. When it finally arrived, men with torches hissed to one another to give the signal. It was returned from the plane. 'Light the red lamp on the boundary!' 'No, not there – get in line!' 'A white light – we need a white light over here!'

When the plane arrived overhead, it seemed to suck up the earth in ripples and press down the air. Marthe could feel the shadows of the great steel wings and the rush of wind. Loud vibrations shook the earth. Engines thrummed and throbbed, and then strained, changing pitch to a wail. The noise was terrifying. The immense bulk of machinery came over them so low it seemed sure to crush them. It shrank the fields and mountains. But the hoarse voices around her were telling a different story. 'Why is it not coming in?'

'What's wrong?'

'Signal, signal – have you given the right signal!'

For a moment it seemed the plane was flying on,

but then the noise intensified again. 'It's wheeling round – it's coming back!'

'They've put the plane's searchlight on,' said Kenton. He was holding her arm. 'It's coming in again.'

The roar intensified.

A voice rose. 'It's still not right – the strip's not long enough, it won't stop in time...'

'Ssh, keep it down!'

The scream of the engines cut through the night. Surely the whole area would hear it. Marthe tasted bile in her mouth.

'It's a Dakota! Would you believe that?' Kenton's whispered jubilation was reassuring. 'It's a huge plane! I never would have believed they could get one of those in here!' He pulled her to her feet.

Gusts of air cooled them as the plane came closer. It had a presence like a living thing. The engines were still running.

Sounds of movement across the grass began immediately. There was a shout from up high, something angry she didn't understand. 'That's the pilot. He says he doesn't believe that strip is twelve hundred metres,' said Kenton. 'And what the hell was in the field at the end?'

'Potatoes,' said another voice.

Now there were more people rushing forward.

Marthe felt his arms around her and a kiss on her forehead, 'Take care, angel.' Scotty too thanked her with a kiss. Then they were gone. She wrapped her arms around herself. Now she willed the plane to go quickly. How long would it be before the Germans and the Milice arrived? They must have heard it coming down. It would surely be impossible for it to take off again without them arriving.

She wanted to ask the person standing next to her what was happening, but knew she should not alert him to her blindness. If anyone knew that she had joined the operation, they would blame Caspian for compromising it.

The plane's engines spluttered louder, and then intensified into a great roar. Now there were competing noises and pitches, some smooth, some rattling. A bumping sound, the same as the wheels of the truck going over rough ground. Then an almighty vibration seemed to shake the very earth under the tree where she clung for safety, not daring to move. A mechanical squeal rose above the spitting and growling. Marthe's ears hurt.

Something was wrong. The engines were straining too much, like gigantic animals in distress. They couldn't go on like that, surely. There would be an explosion, and the aircraft would fall from the sky in flames.

There was no one to ask what was happening. The smell of burning oil was becoming stronger. The snarling noise gave way to a whine.

'It's coming back!' she heard someone shout.

'Too heavy. They'll have to let some of them off.'

'It's a risk – every extra minute the plane's on the ground–'

More ear-piercing engine noise and a rush of wind. The ground shook again, and men were running on either side of her.

Then Kenton was back by her side.

'What happened?'

206

'The plane was carrying too much weight. They tried to put too many of us on it, and we snagged on the band of lavender.'

'Just you and Scotty got off?'

'Eight men – all Americans. So close and yet so far,' he said. 'Everyone's been quite good-humoured about it.'

A Frenchman cursed at him and ordered him to keep his voice down.

'What now?' she whispered.

'They're coming back tomorrow night.'

Marthe groaned. She had no idea what they would do until then. But Kenton was upbeat. 'Think of it as good news. When it comes back for us, they can maybe get some more out too. It was close, though. We almost managed to get airborne.'

Then she could hear no more against the engines. The noise intensified and moved away. Kenton tensed. 'There they go again – it's bouncing around but picking up speed. Through the strip of lavender – Jesus ... nose-up position... It's not going to make it!'

All Marthe could think was that she was relieved Kenton and Scotty would not be in the crash.

'No ... wait a minute ... it's going through! The nose has gone up with the tail wheel still sticking in the damn potatoes – she's up!'

'Now that was a close call,' said Kenton as the engine noise grew fainter.

They had no choice but to return to Musset and the truck. Marthe's heart was beating fast as a machine gun. 'Monsieur will be coming to get me anyway,' she said. 'We'll meet him on his way here.'

They had hardly made it onto the road when shots echoed down the valley. A German patrol. More shots, closer now, and motors. Marthe was pulled into the undergrowth. 'Keep down,' hissed Kenton, shielding her head below his shoulder.

Minutes passed. 'Wait here,' said Kenton.

Marthe obeyed. She tried to orient herself by the sound of voices, but all had gone quiet. Then there was another volley of shots. They seemed to ricochet off the mountains. Then nothing but the sound of blood rushing in her ears. After a while she raised her head tentatively and listened. When she thought she heard whispering, she crawled towards the sounds.

She hit her leg against a sharp object, a rock perhaps. Involuntarily she let out the start of a cry before she managed to swallow it. Cursing her stupidity, she reached out her right hand and felt her way into the space.

Her foot struck something hard – it was the root of a tree. She followed its sinews and found a hollow. She curled herself inside and listened.

When she heard voices, they were none she recognised. 'Where's Xavier?'

'Gone already. They'll be on the road to the Armature.'

'Should we try to get there, to the area commander?'

'It's a hard mountain road–'

Marthe was about to speak, then stopped. The men were speaking French, certainly. But were they partisans or Milice? What if the Milice knew all about Xavier? She put her head down and pulled herself tighter into the tree trunk.

'Marthe!'

It was Kenton. He pulled her up onto her feet and put his arm around her waist. 'There's a farmhouse ahead. I think we should make our way there.'

'We need to go back the way we came, back to the truck.'

'Not possible. That's the direction the Germans moved off.'

Marthe swallowed. What of M Musset and Thierry? 'Where's Scotty, is he with you?'

'No. We got separated. Perhaps he's already on his way towards the farm up there. We have to go.'

Scotty. She couldn't bear it if anything had happened to him while he was supposed to be under her protection. 'We have to stay together.'

'We'll find him,' said Kenton grimly.

They set off at an urgent pace, ready at any moment to take cover in the ditch separating the road from the field. The possibility that Scotty might be dead or wounded, and would not be coming with them, was left unspoken.

'OK, it's not far to the house. Let's hope he's ahead of us.'

They covered the ground in silence.

'Almost there,' whispered Kenton at last.

'Tell me what the farm looks like.'

'Four buildings around a yard. There's a stone drinking trough. No lights on.'

'Does it look inhabited?'

'I can't tell. They're probably asleep inside.'

'There are no animal noises or smells. Any other signs of life?'

'No vehicles. Nothing.'

'Is there a barn? We could try hiding there.'

They walked on, as quietly as they could, up to the barn. No dogs barked; all was silent. The barn was locked. There was no sign of Scotty.

'We have to risk it and go to the door. If there is anyone there, I will speak to them,' said Marthe. The pitter-patter of water from the fountain feeding the trough matched the beat of her heart. She gripped his arm a little tighter. But this was why she had come with them in the first place. She was playing her part, as she had insisted. 'If, when they open the door, something doesn't seem right, then pinch my arm and I'll say what I can to get us out of there as quickly as we can. Do you understand?'

'Yes.'

They approached the door, braced for whatever would follow. Kenton knocked loudly. No one came. Knocked again, more urgently. Then there was scuffling inside the house.

'Who is it?'

'We were told there might be sanctuary here. We are farmers too, from Manosque.'

'Go away.'

'Please! Just for tonight–'

'Don't involve us – we don't want to be involved. I have a sick wife!'

'But we–'

'Go, just go!'

They had no choice but to walk on. They debated whether to head for the woods and wait out the night there or continue on into the village. They reached the outskirts of Saint-Christol before they decided to turn back. It would be harder to find safety in the narrow winding streets and close-packed houses, not knowing who might open the door only to denounce them. Just walking the alleys would be suspicious at this late hour.

'There's no chance of finding directions to Les Coulets tonight. We'll only draw attention to ourselves,' whispered Marthe.

They found a ditch in a wood nearby and tried to sleep for the few hours remaining until dawn.

The first warmth in the air brought Marthe round from her fretful half-slumber. She was floating in a deep black sea. The anxious feeling of being suspended in the unknown returned. For a moment she was falling down the stairs at school, half astonished at her own daring and the anger that had propelled her forward. What would Maman say if she could see what had become of her now?

Then she felt a hand on her arm, and heard her name whispered.

'Kenton?'

'It's all right, sweetheart. It's me.'

'I couldn't remember where I was for a moment!'

'It's all right. I'm here – and, good news, so is Scotty!'

Relief flooded through her. 'Thank God. How did he find us? Did you go looking for him?'

'I wouldn't leave you, you know that. No, he followed us out of the field last night. He said he thought that if another patrol came down the road, there was less chance we'd be stopped if we looked like a couple instead of a trio. Likewise when we went to the farm, it was safer for us to knock on the door as a pair.'

'Scotty?'

'I'm here.' He rubbed her arm.

Marthe sat up. 'We need food and water. I'll have to take a chance on the nearest house,' she said. 'I'm going to get a stick to walk with – find me one that's the right length – and when you see anywhere likely, I'm going to beg for some food.'

'I'm coming with you,' said Kenton.

'Me too.'

The boys spoke together.

'No, you mustn't. Best I go alone. We're much more likely to get something.'

They waited out the following day in the woods. Marthe's begging brought in a heel of stale potato bread and some plums. Scotty wanted to try to trap for food, but they could not have built a fire to cook it. 'Better hungry and safe, than fed and give ourselves away,' said Kenton. They ate the bread and plums and drank from a stream.

'If only the plane hadn't been so heavy, or the damn field had no potatoes and lavender,' said Scotty. Kenton translated.

'I know,' said Marthe gently.

Kenton retorted something in English.

'What did you say?'

'I told him you can't go through life thinking,

212

"If only.'"

'You're right,' said Marthe. 'That's what Arlette used to say.'

A terrible pause threatened to overwhelm them.

'Yet most people do,' said Kenton, forcing his voice to stay steady and not entirely succeeding. 'Even if just a little, if only regretting a very few paths not taken.'

'I don't want to live like that,' said Marthe. 'When something bad has happened, you have to use it to make yourself braver. Once you know that you will manage somehow, whatever happens, you have unlocked the secret of life.'

'I always—'

'Ssh!' said Scotty. 'Hear that?'

They listened.

A rustling noise was coming from behind them. It might have been human; it might have been some woodland creature. They froze, but the sound did not get any closer.

For the next few hours they stayed silent. The boys took turns trying to sleep. Marthe closed her eyes too, but could not rest. Her muscles twitched at the faintest sound. The scents drifting on the breeze grew stronger in the gusty heat, then faded. She told herself she had imagined it, but all day the dread rose. There were times when she was sure she could smell burning. Not the summer burning of the fields to stubble, but a vile mix of wood and fabric and perhaps worse.

She might be wrong, though she doubted it. Even so, there was always the possibility she could be wrong about the origin of the smell. The wind might have changed direction, or she might

213

be more disoriented than she thought.

Finally the moon rose.

'How much longer do we wait?' asked Marthe.

'An hour or so. We'll let it get higher in the sky, then I'll go ahead,' said Kenton.

'No, we go together,' said Marthe.

'But what if–'

'We go together like last night,' she insisted. 'But before we go, there's something I think you should know.'

All movement stopped. She could feel the power her words had over them.

'What?'

'I've been smelling burning – not all the time, but on and off all day. It may not mean anything ... but just so that you are prepared, I thought you should know.'

'Burning? You think the Dakota crashed last night?'

'No ... that didn't occur to me. I was more worried that the Germans had come back. That they were sending us a message in response to what happened last night.'

'Why didn't you say something before?'

'I didn't see what good it would do. I'm not sure that I'm right. What was the point in worrying you when we had no choice but to stay under cover and try to conserve our energy?'

'You should have told us before now,' insisted Kenton.

'I'm sorry, I–'

'Any information – even any *intuition* is valuable! It's all we have, you must understand that.

214

We would have had time to plan properly.'

'I'm sorry, I'm sorry! I thought I was acting for the best!' Marthe was close to tears.

When Kenton spoke it was to Scotty, in English. They seemed to be weighing up the information. All she understood was 'OK'.

Marthe chewed her fingernails. She hadn't done that since she first arrived in Manosque as a child.

'We have to go, and we have to be even more careful,' announced Kenton eventually. 'We have no choice.'

'Plane returns,' added Scotty emphatically. 'For us.'

'And Marthe?'

She nodded.

'I'm sorry too. I shouldn't have lost my temper with you.'

They walked towards Spitfire. Marthe held herself straight and stiff. Her back prickled with the anticipation of gunfire opening up on them; they were ready at any second to dive down at the side of the road and then run for their lives.

Then, a kilometre or so from the field, Marthe sniffed. 'There it is. The remains of a big fire. Still burning, I think. Can you see where it's coming from?'

There was no doubt at all that it was coming from the direction in which they were heading. The air held pockets of warm smoke and ash.

'Can't see anything yet,' said Kenton.

They walked on, hearts sinking as the smell grew stronger. Acrid fumes mingled with the

215

sickly sweetness of still-smouldering wood.

'Farmhouse,' cried Scotty, then spoke rapidly in English.

'It's the place that turned us away last night.'

Every step was further confirmation. The reek of scorched wood and plaster.

'My God ... it's completely destroyed! Burnt out ... those poor people!'

'The bastards – the filthy rotten bastards!' cried Marthe. 'Those people didn't even help us!' Hot rage called tears to her eyes, but she would not cry. If she started, she feared she would never stop.

'Perhaps they had helped others before.'

'Or perhaps all they did was close their ears to the sound of the plane.'

They hurried on. The time was long past when they could have done anything to help.

There was no reception committee in the field. Marthe's hopes had soared when she heard the first whispers, but were soon shattered. A couple of other Americans pulled themselves out of the darkness to stand with them in the shadow of a tree.

'Is there no one but us here?' asked Marthe faintly.

'No.' Kenton put a protective arm around her and pulled her into him so she could speak into his ear.

'But the plane will come.'

'It might. But we only have one torch, and without the official reception on the ground, we have no idea what the code letter is to signal that this is

216

the landing place.'

'Perhaps they are late – or we are early.'

'I hope you're right.'

They all knew it was hopeless, but they waited anyway. Conversation petered out as they sat on the ground with the two additional Americans. These escapees had spent the intervening day in a rocky cave in a cliff to the north. They too had smelled the burning. No one had any knowledge of what had happened to the missing four who should have been picked up when the plane returned.

Hours later, the big Dakota rumbled across the sky and flew on, oblivious to the distress signal flashed with the single torch by the Americans.

Low groans of frustration were countered by the possibility that the plane might be turning to come back, as it did before. They waited, listening intently.

The sound of the aircraft's engines faded into the night.

All around, the calm of loss.

Then the emptiness filled with furious voices arguing in English. Marthe could only presume what was being said. The prospect of another night in the woods and no food made her feel weak.

There was more urgent discussion, this time with someone speaking in French. Where had he come from – and the man who was replying?

'We're assuming these people can be trusted,' said the first.

'Our Americans say they're definitely Americans who were here last night.'

217

'Who's the girl? I don't think she's all there.'

'Simple but evidently trustworthy,' said the second. 'How else would these men have got themselves this far?'

'You never know who's playing which game these days. I trust no one. And if anyone recognises the van we'll be in trouble...'

'You have to help us,' said Marthe, breaking into the exchange, willing herself to sound as determined as she could. 'The van ... is there room for the three of us in the back?'

'Oh, so you do speak ... who are you?'

'We came with Caspian last night.'

It was clearly the best reply she could have made. 'All right. Where are you trying to get to?' replied someone.

'It's a lavender farm called Les Coulets on the Sault road. Do you know it?'

'I know it.'

'They're expecting us, if anything went wrong.'

'All right, this way. Get yourselves inside. Quickly!'

They were pushed in like animals crammed into a pen. In the back, Marthe found herself sitting on iron rods that rolled and trapped her fingers as she tried to stop herself moving with the vehicle. In the confined space they all stank of sweat and dirt.

The driver had a lead foot. They were thrown from side to side as the vehicle scaled the bends of the mountain road. When the men behind the driver cursed, he shouted at them, 'Count your blessings – you're alive, aren't you?'

'What's been going on?' asked Kenton.

218

'Ah – at least you speak French. They told us the Boches were marking time in Sault; that they weren't coming out of their hole. Couldn't have been more wrong, could they? They've been all through these roads, killing as they go. Want to leave their calling cards before they all get flushed out when your lot finally get here.'

'What happened to the reception committee tonight?'

'Some got it in the neck last night. Too dangerous for the rest.'

'So why did you come?'

The man gave a humourless laugh. 'Me? Perhaps I don't like being told what to do. Perhaps I thought the guy flying the Dakota might just be crazy or brave enough to keep to his word and come back.'

'You kept the two men here safe all day too.'

'So send me the medal when you're chief of staff.'

A high-pitched whistle was followed by a loud metal ping at the side of the van.

'Shit!' said the driver.

'Hold on tight,' shouted the other Frenchman. 'That was a bullet.'

Marthe was sent sprawling across knees and feet. The van swayed; they seemed to have veered off onto bumpy ground, still travelling at speed. She rubbed her head where it had hit something hard.

Kenton hauled her back into a sitting position, and kept hold of her. 'Are you all right?'

'Yes. What can you see?' she whispered.

'Nothing. There are no windows here in the

219

back. I can just about see through the windscreen between the driver and his mate. It's still dark, looks like we're back in the woods.'

The van pitched onwards. Another metallic ping.

Marthe gripped Kenton's hand. She thought of her family on the Luberon farmstead, her sister Bénédicte and brother Pierre. She prayed they would be safe where they were, that there would be a way to reassure them that she had died as part of something important and honourable. She would be brave, as brave as she could be.

Without warning, an urgent change of direction slammed them all against one side of the vehicle. When they landed, the bottom of the van scraped against the ground. Then they stopped.

'Quiet!' shouted the driver. 'Listen!'

Nothing.

A light wind in some trees.

Then the choking growl of another engine. It grew louder. There was a collective shudder as it passed and then went away.

'If they're still looking for us, they'll come back,' said the driver.

'I'm not so sure,' replied the other. 'That wasn't a serious chase. Those shots were all for show. Most of them want to get out of this alive as much as we do.'

They waited in near silence for some time. All Marthe could hear was breathing. After what could have been fifteen minutes, could have been an hour, the driver started the motor again and, carefully this time, edged them out of their place of sanctuary and back onto the road.

Then they drove as if the mistral was raging behind them.

They were dropped off at the end of a track and given directions. They were shaken, thirsty. Beyond hunger. When they began to walk again, it was on blistered feet that had swollen in their shoes. Lost in the maze of foreign paths and slopes, they stumbled upwards.

Praying they were heading towards the hamlet of Les Coulets, Marthe found herself quietly singing the old shepherds' songs. Songs of the fight to survive. A vision crystallised in her mind, almost as if she were hallucinating: a carpet of caper flowers. White flowers with unearthly pro-fusions of stamens like shooting stars. There had once been such a carpet at a property she had visited as a small child. She had seen the dust of dead stars there, or so she had thought, until she realised the glitter was broken glass and heard the flap of bird wings caught in the eaves of an empty barn. She was so tired she had to pinch herself back into the present.

'Any sign?' she asked weakly.

'There's another bend ahead.'

They trudged round it.

'Here! All OK!'

'Scotty's right...'

Marthe imagined the buildings huddled around a courtyard, small and modest perhaps, but generous in every way that mattered.

'It's here, outside!' Kenton swung her round suddenly.

'What?'

'The old truck. Monsieur's truck!'

They made it through an open door before her legs went out from under her. Through the relief, the sleeplessness and hunger, she felt Musset's arms around her and the taste of lavender dust from his jacket as she sobbed open-mouthed against his broad chest.

7

Orange Peel and Musk

August 1944

Back at Manosque, Kenton and Scotty were hidden again. The Mussets and Marthe showed them into the cellar at the factory. Wearily they climbed down and made a false wall with wooden packing crates.

Madame sat designing labels by the shop entrance in the room above. The girl behind the counter served the customers. Marthe stayed in the blending room, pretending to experiment with new fragrances. Wrapped in a large apron that concealed his loaded pistol, Auguste guarded the back of the premises: the storeroom where the cellar door was hidden, the distilling shed and the soap kitchen.

For four days and nights they hardly spoke, or even moved, except to take water to the Americans, and what little food they could find.

Marthe stood at the table combining orange peel and amber resin with shaking hands, unable to process any emotion except fear.

A hammering on the back door.

She heard Auguste cross the storeroom floor and ask tersely who it was, then the creak of the door that was deliberately kept unoiled. A woman's voice, and Auguste's remonstrance.

'I need your help. I work with Xavier.' She sounded desperate, repeating the name as if it were a password.

Instinctively responding to the exhaustion in that voice, all too familiar to her now, Marthe went through to the storeroom.

'Please help me,' said the woman. 'Do you know where Xavier is?'

'Who? I don't know who you're talking about,' said Auguste.

Marthe could smell the woman now. Fear was palpable in the sweat and dust that had dried on her clothes. This was no Milice trick. Marthe understood exactly how she could have come to be in this state.

'When did you last see this ... Xavier?' she asked, taking her lead from Auguste. The attempt to sound as if she had never heard of Xavier rang so false she was sure the woman must know it was a lie.

'More than a week ago. When the plane came in.'

'Why have you come here?' asked Auguste.

'The only clue I had. I know about the soap packaging.'

'I don't know what you're talking about.'

Marthe put her hand on his arm. 'I think–'

'I am British, a wireless operator,' said the woman slowly, despair ingrained in every word. 'I have been working with Xavier for months, organising operations throughout the South of France. I understand that you do not want to implicate yourselves in any activity, but I must know where he has gone.'

'I wish we could help you, but we can't,' said Marthe, kindly. 'But perhaps we can help in some other way. What do you need? Fresh clothes...'

'Can I stay with you?'

The prospect was horrifying.

'No! Absolutely not,' said Auguste. 'You've come to the wrong place. In fact, I want you to go right now.'

'Please! I daren't go back to where I've come from! I've tried sending messages asking for assistance, but my orders are always to sit tight and take instructions from Xavier. And to make matters worse – I think the Gestapo is onto me, they've tracked one of my frequencies.'

The stink of fear intensified, an animal musk, like the civet oil used in minuscule drops to add warmth to fragrance. It rose uncontrolled, over-poweringly unpleasant. Marthe could smell ammonia, too, and the iron tinge of menstrual blood.

They had to help her, somehow. 'Maybe we could–'

'Please! I'm begging you!'

Auguste was resolute. 'You have to go,' he said.

Marthe handed the woman a scrap of cheese she had been saving and a bar of soap. It was all

224

she had. 'We should have done more for her,' she said, after the back door clicked shut.

An odour of goat and salty dampness remained, mocking their actions.

'How could we have taken her in?' asked Auguste testily. 'If the Gestapo is tracking her, we had no choice. Every minute she was here put us in more danger. She may already have betrayed us just by coming here. And a transmitter on the premises? Are you crazy? We might as well shoot ourselves.'

Two more long days and nights passed. When she heard running feet outside, Marthe had been expecting the worst for so long she had forgotten what it felt like to react normally. She shouldn't have given the woman the new bar of soap, clearly stamped with the brand: Distillerie Musset. A stupid mistake. She had cursed herself for the implications every minute since.

The thinking part of her could only observe what the body was doing, detached and surprised. Raised voices outside the shop. A rattle of gunfire and more shouting. She tensed, primed for the attack. Could she throw the acidic liquid at the aggressors, or hurl herself at them to give Kenton and Scotty vital seconds to move?

But the sounds seemed to be coming from all directions. Shouts and running, and then – unbelievably – a cheer.

'They're coming! They're coming! The Allies have landed on the coast!'

By early morning of the twentieth of August, the

225

American advance divisions streamed down from the Valensole plateau, heading for Digne. In their wake came the ragged figures that had been fighting for so long in the fields and farms and the shadows of small villages. They descended on forgotten paths from the hills and walked the streets with their heads held high.

Arlette was buried that day in Manosque. In contrast to the many partisan funerals, where only the immediate family had dared to walk behind the coffin, officers of the Gestapo and the Milice watching hawk-eyed as the town pretended never to have known the deceased, hundreds of people turned out. Arlette's heartbroken parents led the mourners, with M and Mme Musset behind them.

It was touching, how many tributes there were. Even those Manosquins who had never known her now knew of her courage. 'There was a bunch of wildflowers and lavender in almost every window in the street leading to the cemetery,' Monsieur told Marthe. 'They honoured her.'

There was more bad news, though, when he made inquiries about the woman who had come to the Distillerie Musset claiming to be a British agent working with the Engineer. If it was the same woman, she had lasted only one night in Manosque. A defensive cordon of townsfolk had watched as she left the town; the Gestapo had swooped on her as she was risking one last transmission from a field on the road up to the plateau. She was last seen being bundled into a truck. Whether or not she was still alive, no one knew. The liberators came too late for her.

226

'We should have shown more courage,' said Marthe.

'No,' said Musset. 'You took the only course you could. It's hard to admit, but you did right, in the circumstances.'

'I smell her still – her terror,' said Marthe.

She would never be able to forget it.

In Céreste, too, the resistants emerged. They crossed themselves as they passed Christ on the cross framed in a fifteenth-century archway, giving thanks. There were women too, wearing short socks under leather lace-up shoes, raincoats over their shoulders, holding rifles as casually as handbags, and they gathered by the Mairie. A dirty tricolour hung from the flagpole in place of the swastika.

At the café, so the Mussets were told later, a large group of villagers listened openly on a radio set to the news coming in. The US Seventh Army was rapidly gaining ground, sweeping north through the Vaucluse.

Then there was screaming. They rushed out of the café to find that a young woman had been surrounded outside in the square. A crowd had pushed her until her back was to the railings, not far from the memorial for those lost in the Great War. Men and women were shouting, shouts that quickly turned to jeers. Through a cacophony of angry voices they insisted that she had betrayed resistants – they named Candide and the Actress, and others too. They spat the accusation that she was jealous of the Actress. She denied it, of course, but it was then that they recognised her as Chris-

227

tine, who had once been Auguste Baumel's sweetheart.

Christine tried to escape the mob, but was jostled back, cornered. She was screaming, begging for her life. Three shots were fired. There was a look of petrified disbelief on her face as she went down. Then the swarm melted away. Afterwards, no one remembered who had wielded the pistol.

A less bloodthirsty mob might have shaved Christine Lachasse's head, or tarred and feathered her, as happened in other towns and villages after the Liberation, when summary justice was handed out to women who had betrayed resistants or slept with the enemy. Apparently the Poet had tried to dissuade the villagers from violence of any kind – the political situation between the partisan factions was too finely balanced to upset – but even he had not prevailed.

'It was Christine, then?' Marthe still could not take it in. 'Christine who was responsible for Arlette being taken by the Milice?'

'I had my doubts about her, always,' said Madame. 'You once heard us asking if she was safe, and you thought we were talking about you, do you remember?'

Marthe did, with some shame that she had jumped to such self-centred conclusions. 'So was that why Auguste stopped seeing her?'

'Of course.'

Marthe gasped. 'She came to the farmhouse that day – when I heard Kenton and Scotty in the barn. Do you think–'

'I don't know.'

228

'But even so – shot in cold blood.'

'This is no time for taking high moral positions,' said Mme Musset.

The end of the fighting in Provence brought a bitter satisfaction. The settling of local scores began. The bludgeoning heat of high summer added to the unleashing of anger and resentment, which would continue for months and years. Others demanded patriotic celebrations. Kenton and Scotty made arrangements to leave.

On their last night, there was a victory dance in one of the tree-lined squares in Manosque. The townsfolk young and old linked arms and climbed the stones into the old town high above the plain, beckoned by the sound of a band whose players struggled, in their enthusiasm, to keep a coherent tempo. At the centre, the hubbub of excited talk, shrieks of laughter, drums and bass competed with the stamping of feet.

'Shall we dance?' Kenton asked Marthe as the band caught its stride. He grabbed her before she had time to reply.

And she was in Kenton's arms, letting him whirl her around. The night was still hot. Her forehead was damp around her hairline. She put her head back and felt the motion lift her. Round and round they went in time with the beat, in joy and sorrow for what had passed, and in hope for what was to come. The coloured lights would be moving around her, the other dancers, the plane trees around the square. She saw it all and more, in her imagination: the huge aircraft landing in the dark field. Kenton and Scotty walking on either side of

229

her along the moonlit road. And Arlette, so full of life, tap-dancing across the blending room, in the café, waiting at the bus stop at Céreste.

A tear trickled down her cheek.

Kenton slowed, and then stopped dancing. He touched her face so gently, it felt like a breeze at first. Then she felt softness on her lips, then warmth and tenderness. He was kissing her, and she kissed him back.

When they arrived back at the farm, the Mussets were already asleep. Kenton took Marthe's hand and led her to her bed.

He left early the next morning.

She refused to feel sad. It was a fine lesson in love, Marthe decided. In the darkness, they had all discovered what they truly were. There were those who had flown to the light, and those who had pulled back farther into the blackest corners. They had all had to learn the architecture of darkness, just as she had once learned to read the smells and sounds and textures of constant night.

After the war, she worked harder than ever to understand the language of scent, the best marriages of disparate aromas and strengths. She used the flowers and herbs that grew all around her, blending combinations into an intimate biography of her life.

One by one, the Musset factory put the scents into production. They sold well. Buyers responded to their sincerity and their relationship with the landscape. The old steam distillery evolved into the prestigious 'Parfumeur-Distillateur Musset', and Marthe Lincel became a creator of perfumes sold throughout Provence.

'A simple scent captures a moment in time,' she once said. 'A perfume tells a story on the skin.'

The letter from Kenton came several years later.

Somewhere, somehow, he had found someone to translate his thoughts twice over: into French and into Braille. The trouble he had taken spoke as much as the words themselves. 'I have still never met anyone like you,' he wrote. 'I think of you in your blue hills with your fragrances, as I hope that you think of me too, sometimes, in my land far away, and know that we are the same, that a part of us is together.

'I wanted to tell you that I am happy, and I am getting married. I hope you are happy too. You deserve it, dearest Marthe. I shall always be grateful to you for what you did for Scotty and me. Without you, I wouldn't be here today, and I shall always love you, in my way.'

With that letter came a notice from a bank in Paris and a lawyer's letter. The Attwaters of Boston had deposited a large sum of money to be used by the Musset distillery, with the stipulation that it was to allow Marthe Lincel to continue her work as a *parfumeuse*, and in time to open a perfume emporium in Paris.

When her parfumerie opened in the place Vendôme in Paris in 1950, Marthe sent a magazine article heralding the event to Boston. The photographs showed a slim, elegant woman with a beguiling expression. She was posed in front of a counter full of scent bottles and their fashionable striped boxes, smiling. Her dark hair was cut in a

231

short, fashionable style, and her dress was from Dior. Another captured her sitting on a gilded chair. It wasn't possible to tell from these skilful photographs that Marthe Lincel's lively eyes could not see.

The pictures she drew on were vibrant as ever, though. The crumbling stone farmstead overlooking the great Luberon valley where she was born. The blending room of the distillery in Manosque where she had experienced a kind of rebirth, beginning the transformation into the woman she was now. Scent was memory, and memory a complex blend of scent and emotion: the perfect flowers of the lavender hills, like millions of mauve butterflies fluttering on stalks; the violet; the heliotrope of home, with its heart of sweet almond and cherry vanilla. She mixed them all into her signature fragrance Lavande de Nuit, along with a breath of civet musk and a haunting trace of smoke.

BOOK III

A Shadow Life

1

Orchard Court

London, April 1943

The bath at Orchard Court was a deep black marble affair. This was unusual enough for a London flat (Iris was not the only one who looked at it longingly), but not as extraordinary as the onyx bidet by its side, the pair set off by striking black-and-white tiles. As there was nowhere else for visitors to sit as they waited, the bathroom had to serve.

Throughout March and April that year, an increasing flow of young men and women had arrived in the lobby of Orchard Court, a building on the corner of Portman Square and Orchard Street, and were shown up to this small flat, in which the sitting room and two small bedrooms were used as offices. The callers were never invited to Baker Street, but to this anonymous property a short walk away. 'Best they never set foot inside the Firm, that way there's no danger of anyone seeing or hearing something they shouldn't know,' said Miss Acton.

That day, two men and a woman were sitting on the edge of the black marble bath; another man was standing. Two partially open umbrellas were hooked over the taps, dripping.

235

The visitors had been greeted at the door of the second-floor flat by Iris Nightingale, newly promoted to intelligence assistant, and shown immediately into the bathroom, where they perched incongruously in their town clothes.

Colonel Tyndale had been unavoidably detained, and the reason was not good news, Iris surmised, judging from his expression a moment ago in the hall. His narrow face was not built for unnecessary argument; his brow flamed and the bags under his eyes grew pronounced whenever voices rose in anger or frustration. He had finally arrived at Orchard Court, in a hollow-cheeked fluster of raincoat and papers; he and Miss Acton were now closeted in the sitting room, where the interviews would take place.

At the door of the bathroom Iris produced a bottle of brandy and some unmatched glass tumblers. 'It won't be long now,' she said brightly. 'How about a drink?'

It really was the least she could do. Often the guests had very little idea why they had been invited to these odd gatherings. Their only qualification was that they had a French or Belgian parent, or spoke near-native French from years spent on the Continent. They came in batches after passing a selection interview in a small airless office consisting of two plain tables and some scuffed wooden chairs in the basement of the War Office, and were required to sign the Official Secrets Act.

These four were quiet ones, hardly speaking to Iris, let alone to each other. Not necessarily a bad thing. At this stage, it was merely a fact to note.

236

Iris gave a friendly smile as she committed certain obvious traits to memory. The man she guessed was the oldest, thirty-five perhaps, in a well-cut suit, gave the briefest grimace at the mention of Miss Acton's name. He tipped his drink back in one. The man next to him wore a suit that had crinkled and was damp on the shoulders, and his blond hair was slicked back – caught out in the rain shower. He leaned back against the tiles and looked up to the ceiling. The third man was very young. He met her eye, and a nervous tic jerked beneath his own, high on the left cheekbone. The woman sat calmly, answering when she was addressed but otherwise giving the impression that she was waiting for a doctor's appointment, absorbed in private thoughts. She was in her early twenties, pretty, though her dark hair looked as if she had cut it herself. She was the only one to refuse a drink. After a while, she got out some crochet work and bent her head over it.

'Sun and showers, what a day,' ventured Iris.

'Typical bloody England,' replied the man in the smart suit. He crossed his arms in front of his chest. Defensive, despite the air of sophistication.

'Better in here than out,' said the youngest, with an eagerness to please that only underscored his nervousness.

'I expect so,' said Iris.

The woman listened, now and then looking up from the hook and yarn to watch them in the mirror by the basin. Smart cookie, thought Iris. First impressions were vital. In some situations, that was all the chance they would have.

A low buzzer sounded.

'And we're off,' said Iris, nodding towards the nervous young man and deciding to put him out of his agony by giving him the first slot. 'If you'd like to come with me...'

It went without saying that Iris had no idea what she was getting into, though that was true one way or another, she suspected, of everyone who enlisted, was called up, or served their country in any capacity during the war. If anyone asked, Iris made a self-effacing reference to the 'little job' at which she was still plugging away. One of the other girls told her that she used to tell her friends she worked at Marks and Spencer's London head-quarters, whose building they had taken over, until the questions about the chances of obtaining good-quality clothes under the counter became too onerous. She had to pretend to leave and 'go into teaching'.

Iris had planned to join the Wrens when she left school, and might well have done so but for the intervention of her headmistress. Term was almost over when the jutting shelf of Miss Jeffery's bosom arrested any further progress down the library corridor.

'I understand you are contemplating your future in the Women's Royal Naval Service.'

'Yes, Miss Jeffery.'

'Have you considered playing to your strengths as a linguist and training as a secretary who can work in French and German? There is a bursary available, and I would be very pleased to recommend you.'

And so, because Miss Jeffery had almost always

been kind and well meaning, qualities all too rare in Iris's chequered experience of school life, the advice was taken. Iris enrolled in the three-month residential secretarial course in Bedford, gratefully accepting the bursary to pay her board and lodging, and assuming throughout that the language instruction in military and naval terms was required to enable her to enter the Wrens as a secretary or wireless telegraphist. The instruction was good, and Iris, always meticulous in her work, came top of her class of twenty-five in the final exams. She emerged with a certificate in typing, shorthand and French and German translation. Her tutoring in Morse code did not seem to be certified on paper.

A few days after she'd completed the course, a letter came to her aunt's flat in Battersea from the Inter Services Research Bureau, giving no details but asking Iris to contact them to arrange an interview for a job. She telephoned the number she was given and was asked to present herself at a small hotel in Victoria the next day.

'Could you tell me a little more about the position, please?'

'Why don't you come along, and then it will be easier to explain,' said the woman's voice, clipped and authoritative, on the other end of the line.

'I will, but could you tell me please how you came to know I was looking for a job? It seems a bit–'

'You have been recommended. We'll see you tomorrow then, at ten. Goodbye.'

The next day the bus from Battersea dropped her at Victoria Station in plenty of time to walk to

239

her appointment. October leaves had collected on the sandbags that lined the streets north of the river. The hotel was a soot-streaked commercial establishment behind Ebury Street. She was directed at the reception desk to a small room on the first floor, facing the street. She had hardly raised her knuckles from a tentative knock under the metal number 4 before a young woman wearing pearls and a grey serge suit pulled the door open. Twin beds had been pushed against opposite walls to provide seating. Between the beds, a wooden table took up most of the space.

A wide-shouldered woman with a gravelly voice stood up, held out her hand and introduced herself as Miss Allott.

'Do take a seat.'

Iris took the bed on the other side of the table.

Miss Allott stared intently at a flimsy sheet of paper for a few moments.

'Born 1922, and you've just turned nineteen.'

'Yes, that's right,' said Iris.

'Lived in Hove, but in 1931 you were sent to a boarding school in Switzerland for six years. What were the circumstances of this move?'

Iris was taken aback, but found herself answering politely as ever, the natural result of years spent under the control of Miss Jeffery and her ilk. This Miss Allott, with her carefully sculpted hair and severe expression, was undoubtedly one of them.

'My father died. My mother remarried and went to live in Berne with her new husband.'

'There follow various boarding schools in Sussex and Wiltshire ... would you care to elaborate

240

on the reasons?'

'My mother ... felt she was unable to cope. She was having difficulties in her second marriage. We returned to England. She couldn't settle in Sussex, so she tried Wiltshire. I think she wanted me close by but not actually at home.'

'And where is she now?'

'She lives just outside Salisbury.'

'Other family?'

'An aunt, my mother's sister. I'm currently staying with her.'

'So...' Miss Allott did not pursue the investigation. 'Languages – you speak French and German well, and some Italian too?'

'I speak them well enough. French with fluency, German adequately. Some Italian, but only enough to get by.'

Miss Allott crossed her arms and leaned forward across the table. '*Que pensez-vous de la situation politique en France actuellement?*'

Iris replied that it was an impossible situation politically for the French. Was their government for or against the old France and its people; were the members of the Vichy regime motivated by political expediency or personal power? And all the while the ordinary citizens were surely only trying to get by as best they could.

After a few more questions about her unsatisfactory background, Iris was abruptly dismissed from the twin-bedded interview room. She was making for the door when Miss Allott tossed one last ball.

'Would you say you were imaginative, Miss Nightingale?'

241

What an odd thing to ask.

Iris hesitated. 'I don't consider that I am, particularly. I'm not a dreamer, if that's what you mean. I would say that I was rather straightforward ... sensible. I've rather had to be, with a mother like mine.'

Miss Allott frowned. She said nothing more, and a moment later Iris was out in the corridor again. She had said too much about her personal difficulties. It seemed she had failed to satisfy her interlocutor, just as she always did her mother. But the next day a letter arrived inviting Iris to present herself for work the following Monday at 64 Baker Street.

It would be a few months before Iris realised that Mavis Acton (not Allott at all) made up her mind almost immediately as to the suitability of a candidate, and very rarely revised that opinion.

Iris signed the Official Secrets Act on her first morning at 64 Baker Street. It was an elegant light-grey stone building, six windows wide; a brass plate by the door offered the anodyne misinformation that these were the offices of the Inter Services Research Bureau. She was introduced, with perfunctory politeness, to Colonel Hugh Tyndale, head of F Section. His harassed manner implied that Iris had arrived at a tricky juncture, but it was not long before it became apparent that this was his normal demeanour. He looked down on her – he was a tall, thin man with a stoop – and blinked through round tortoiseshell glasses before nodding his dismissal and hurrying past.

It was clear too that Miss Acton was the lynchpin of the operation. She may have had a commanding manner and expectation of total obeisance, but Miss Acton carried herself in the certain knowledge that men still found her attractive despite the weight of years; she must have been in her mid-forties. Her dark hair was immaculate, waved and pinned. Her signature scent of fern whispered of Paris before the war. Her excellent legs marched in high heels. Clip-on earrings made of silver and mother-of-pearl caught the attention, as if a single butterfly wing had alighted on each earlobe. The high-necked blouses in soft fabrics were chosen to drape and flatter. Mavis Acton was calm and reserved at all times, her edicts issued in low tones that both asserted absolute authority and attested to the strength of the Senior Service cigarettes she smoked with such fervent pleasure.

It struck Iris that in many ways she had swapped a world run by schoolmistresses for an uncomfortably similar set-up run by another version of the type, lacking only the bushy eyebrows and corridor-blocking chest.

For the first few months, Iris's duties consisted of typing reports and translating from both French and German. She was part of a team gathering intelligence about all aspects of occupied France. Some of the information was very basic: the travel network, the way food coupons worked, the latest coins in the occupation currency minted by the Germans. Most of this came from newspapers provided by businessmen from neutral countries who were still permitted to travel into France, or who met their French

243

counterparts in Lisbon or Geneva.

There were strict office rules. In the evenings, it was considered a serious breach of security to leave out any papers. Every book, every newspaper clipping, every single written word, had to be locked in steel filing cabinets.

Before they left the office in the evening, a night-duty officer would come round with one of the twenty-four-hour guard to collect all waste paper. Then they went through the room testing locks on cupboards and the steel cabinets, and checking that nothing of value was sitting in an unsecured drawer.

'A word please, Miss Nightingale.'

Iris followed Miss Acton into her office.

'You realise, don't you, that any slip-up could put the lives of our people at risk?' said Miss Acton. She did not wait for a reply. 'Blotting paper, Miss Nightingale. I am extremely displeased that you have been so careless. If you had been here longer, leaving out blotting paper would have been utterly unforgivable.'

'I'm sor–'

'It's quite possible to work out what was blotted. Do you think that we are simply playing at war here, Miss Nightingale?'

Mavis Acton raised her hand for silence as she began a tirade that rapidly increased in volume and fury: anything Iris saw or heard in the department was strictly confidential; she knew that she should speak of it to no one, should deflect any inquiries about her line of work; and yet what was the purpose of any of that if she was leaving

244

matters of the highest national security out in full view for anyone to see?

Iris could think of nothing to say in her defence. She was sent to collect a file from the Firm's offices at Norgeby House, across the road. ('I suppose you can manage that?') In the ladies' cloakroom on the half-landing there, Iris splashed cold water on her blotchy face and tried to calm herself. She was furious to find that she was still trembling.

'It's Iris, isn't it?'

A face bobbed up behind hers in the mirror. Auburn hair and wide eyes.

Iris nodded.

'Nancy. Nancy Bateman. I'd only been here a couple of days when you arrived.'

'In the big room ... yes, I recognise you.'

'That's right. I was moved over here a few days later. How are you finding it?'

'Well, it's certainly an interesting "little job"...'

'You don't want to get on the wrong side of Miss Acton, though,' said Nancy Bateman, twisting and repinning her hair in two large combs.

Iris finished washing her hands, wondering how much it was possible to say. 'Is it that obvious?'

'Let's say you're not the first to have to come in here to repair her face. What did you do?'

'I left out some blotting paper last night.' A few inky marks on which two lines of reverse writing were barely visible.

'Heinous crime.'

'I wasn't thinking. She was right. I was utterly boneheaded. But no one told me – no one says anything!' Iris looked up and met Nancy's eyes in

245

the mirror. 'No one talks to anyone else. It's all little bits of paper with typed messages and brown envelopes and never quite explaining what's going on.'

'Talking would be far too sensible. Though of course Miss Acton is right. She's always right. But it's not the end of the world. You do know that she's known to be hardest on those she thinks have most potential?'

'Is that true? Or are you simply saying it to make me feel better?'

'Both.'

There was a firmness in Nancy's tone that made them both laugh suddenly.

'Oh, well – thank you. You *have* made me feel better.'

'Everyone's frightened of Miss Acton, even the men, though most of them have developed a manner with her that they imagine covers it up.'

Nancy was right. Iris had seen the way men stood in the presence of that husky yet clipped voice. Madam, they called her, to her face.

'What are you doing for lunch?' asked Nancy.

They had tea and toast at the Lyon's Corner House. Nancy was twenty-one, from Lincolnshire, and had a fiancé in the RAF. She was a slip of a girl, with a determined look in those big eyes, a striking mixture of blue and green. She chatted easily about her training as a teleprinter and her previous posting to RAF Duxford near Cambridge, a Spitfire base and Fighter Command.

'When I told my mother I was off to Duxford, she kicked up a dreadful fuss. "Think of all those men!" she said, and did everything she could to persuade me not to go,' said Nancy.

'Sounds like she was right to worry.'

Nancy grinned. 'She certainly was.'

It was a great relief to make a friend. With her old school chums, even the girls she had met on the course in Bedford, Iris felt uncomfortable lying about what she was doing. Some seemed to look down on her for not joining the Wrens to do her bit. One by one they had dropped away. You were only ever completely at ease with others in the same position, and even then you needed to be certain exactly which spot on the same side they occupied.

In the capacity of a secretary at Baker Street, Iris had typed reports and kept files on the men and women who were sent undercover to France, but had never met them. Two years later at Orchard Court, she came face to face with them all, from the admired veterans to the new recruits.

As she was tall and slim with dark blond hair falling in natural waves to her shoulders, the men would invariably flirt with her; men who were confident and, if not good-looking in too striking a way, then invariably charming, with a certain allure. Miss Acton always called them 'our friends', never anything else. The 'girls', too, were lovely. Iris once overheard someone else remarking on that undeniable fact, followed by Miss Acton's response: 'Yes, because that gives them self-confidence.' Perhaps she hoped that their charms might prove protective, and in this, as in other matters, she was often proved right.

For some who returned to Orchard Court, having passed their training at various secret northern locations, it would be the last visit to London before being sent to France. Others would never make it past initial training and assessment at Wanborough Manor near Guildford; for them, the drink in the bathroom followed by a chat with some strangers who asked personal questions would be relegated to a memory of another odd episode during the war.

When the last of the potential new agents had gone, packed off with instructions to present themselves at Wanborough, Iris took out the small notebook she always kept in her pocket and studied the scribbles she had made. At a rickety table in the minuscule kitchen, she pulled the typewriter towards her, rolled up paper and carbon and made sense of her shorthand. On separate papers for the files, she noted idiosyncrasies of speech and phrase, the cadence and tone of each recruit's words, in French and English. What she wrote now might never be needed, but in certain circumstances it could prove vital, and it was never too early to start. When the only means of communication with the agents on the ground was by coded wireless messages, there had to be safety checks in place to guarantee their authenticity.

Miss Acton put her head round the door. 'Would you type up Thérèse's debrief before you go?'

'Just about to.'

'Any thoughts?'

She meant about that afternoon's four new faces. 'The girl seemed a cool customer,' said

248

Iris. 'I rather liked her. First man in was very young – a bit twitchy.'

Miss Acton nodded, and left her to it.

Iris made brisk work of the first job and inserted a fresh sheet of paper. After five months in France, Thérèse had brought back a substantial amount of information: details of changes to identity documents and travel permits; current living conditions; the most frequently voiced complaints; snippets of news that provoked the most comment; alterations to train timetables. Noting changes was crucial. The French magazines and newspapers she brought back would be scoured for nonsense about the latest fashions as well as the papers French citizens were expected to carry, the hours of curfew and how often ration cards were now being issued.

The first time Iris met Thérèse at Orchard Court she had put her age at about twenty. She had taken her wisp-slim figure, timid manner and perennial concern for her parents to indicate a girl way out of her depth. She was a private seamstress from the East End by trade, which seemed the perfect gentle occupation for her. Wrong on almost every count, it transpired. Thérèse (real name Lucienne Jarvis) was almost thirty and adept at self-effacement, at stepping back and observing. A Belgian mother had passed on a perfect command of the French language, and the accent had been refined by a number of years at a Parisian couture house; her father's background as a merchant seaman from the Mile End Road provided a tough resourcefulness.

She was friendly and funny, though never overplaying either quality. Not far beneath the surface was a nervousness that was considered more good than bad: the nerves would keep her alert to danger. There was no doubting her courage and determination.

Iris was not sure she could have done what Thérèse and the others did. It was suggested at one time that her name be put forward for consideration, but nothing came of it. She would have gone, thought Iris, but she wouldn't have rated her chances of coming back. She had never regretted not being chosen. Miss Acton said she was of more use where she was; she shared with her boss a sharp memory and an instinctive grasp of detail. So London was where Iris stayed, her relief the secret she kept most securely of all.

2

The Making of an Agent

London, June 1943

The self-contained girl in the bathroom made the grade at Wanborough Manor. She was sent on to the Western Highlands to learn how to handle guns and explosives and commit acts of sabotage. There, she had confounded expectations, hitting more targets with her quiet accuracy than quite a few of the men. She had emerged unscathed, apart from a sprained ankle from parachute training. She arrived back at Orchard Court in the uniform of the First Aid Nursing Yeomanry, the usual cover, newly purchased from Lillywhites department store in Piccadilly.

She was no longer Rita Williams; she had a code name now: Rose.

The physical exercise had trimmed a few pounds from her face and waist, and the hacked-about hair was greatly improved, cut short by the French hairdresser working from one of Thérèse's magazines. It was tinted a rich chestnut shade that complemented her shrewd brown eyes, and gave her an undeniably Parisian look.

'It suits you,' said Iris. '*Vraiment très chic.*'

'*Je vous remercie, mademoiselle.*'

Rose's accent was impeccable, with an easy roll of the r.

'You've lived in France, haven't you?' said Iris conversationally.

'Yes.'

'Whereabouts?'

'Paris. I spent time in Nice, too.'

She was a year older than Iris, and she had been a companion to a wealthy elderly woman. Not the kind of job Iris would have relished, but you never knew what circumstances dictated choice. The girl's quiet composure radiated patience. No doubt she had learned to be resourceful in attending to the whims of her employer. According to the file, Rita Williams had spent her childhood in Camberwell, south London. She had left school at sixteen and spent two years in France before the outbreak of war. Her widowed mother was killed when a bomb struck the house in Camberwell in

251

the Blitz of 1940.

Rose sat with her hands resting on her hand-bag, a delicate cobweb of black crochet work.

'That's an awfully pretty little bag,' Iris per-sisted. 'Did you make it yourself?'

'As a matter of fact, I did.'

She didn't ask Iris how she'd guessed, though. She was friendly and polite in response to Iris's questions but did not chatter. Miss Acton rated her very highly. Self-containment and concise answers were always a plus with Miss Acton.

A click-clack of heels sounded on the polished floor of the corridor, and Rose was borne off in a waft of tobacco and steely purpose.

All the preparations seemed easier than normal with Rose.

Before the agents were sent to France, a tailor skilled in the Continental style made clothes for them: suits, jackets, skirts, appropriate to their cover story. The men's suits carried forged trade tapes, indicating in which town the clothes had been made, to fit these fictions. Shirts, underwear, socks, shoes – all these too were carefully assembled. But Rose already had a substantial and authentic French wardrobe of her own, dresses she had made herself from French fabrics and patterns, though not nearly to Thérèse's standard. The odd stretched or puckered seam gave the impression, quite usefully, of stoic vulnerability. Other authentic items of clothes had been altered and refitted from her employer's cast-offs. There would be no need to change her profession once she arrived. The backstory would be that her pre-

252

vious employer had only recently died; it was vague enough, and she would be kept well away from Nice to avoid any chance of being recognised. Easily confirmable facts were overlaid with fantasy, but it worked best to leave in an element of truth.

'What do you think of these specs?'

'I thought you didn't need glasses?' Iris had a jolt of panic. One of the very first criteria when the agents were recruited in London was 20/20 vision. In the rough and tumble of their work in the field, the last worry they needed was keeping their glasses safe.

'I don't – these are plain glass. But if I do this' – Rose squinted – 'I can look really quite the shrinking violet, can't I? And ... oops, just a bit clumsy.' She caught some papers on the desk with her elbow.

'Very convincing.'

It was true. The old wire spectacles gave her a disconcertingly timid and ineffectual look, yet seemed to relax her at the same time. It made all the difference to her to play a part. She was almost ready to go to France as a wireless operator for the Swagman circuit operating between Paris and Tours. The wireless set was hidden in a small leather suitcase. False identity papers had been prepared for her, and fake German-stamped passes of various kinds, food cards and bread coupons, a Carte de Vêtements et d'Articles Textiles, all of which had to be up to date.

For weeks now she had been rehearsing her story with Miss Acton as well as Iris, immersing herself in every aspect of her fictional back-

253

ground until it seemed real, coming out perfectly naturally if she were challenged, however tired she was, or if taken by surprise.

'How did you meet your "fiancé"?'

'In the Parc Zoologique in Lille, where I had my first job. I was out strolling by myself, and so was Hubert. He does sound suitably boring.' Rose pulled a deadpan face and then laughed, showing pretty teeth.

As the preparations went on, she was becoming less reserved, more confident about showing a bit of personality within the Firm. Iris was pleased about that. 'The point is that it doesn't involve anyone else or any awkward details except for the layout of the park. Where is Hubert now?'

'He's working in a factory in Germany. He's a model citizen who answered the call. And if I absolutely have to give his name, it is authentic?'

'It will be there in the official files. When you get to France you will have to immerse yourself in being this character, this Rose Mielhan, originally from Paris, from the area that you know well, who worked for a time in Lille for an elderly widow who died. Her name is also in the official records, with a headstone in the cemetery there.'

'I know. I've done nothing else for the past week but memorise my dull life there with her and Hubert.'

The life expectancy of a wireless operator in a French city was put at six months. Iris was uncertain whether Colonel Tyndale or Miss Acton had passed on that information.

Iris thanked God she could talk to Nancy. Not all

254

the time, nor about every detail, but the pressure was eased by not having to pretend when they were finally off duty. By the end of 1942, Iris and Nancy had taken a small flat together. They were putting in longer and longer hours, and if the bombing had been bad, it could take hours for the bus to cross the river and grind into town from Battersea, and Nancy's tram to come up from New Cross, where she had dismal digs. It was just too far every day, and Iris's Aunt Etty (whom, in truth, she hardly knew) had not bargained on Iris staying for longer than it took to get herself set up with a job.

Nancy and Iris sublet an attic flat off Tavistock Square from a friend of a friend. The two bedrooms were tiny, but they could walk to work. With Nancy's fiancé Phil serving abroad with his squadron, it seemed the ideal solution.

They rarely brought other friends back, not through a lack of them but because they each understood implicitly that this was their sanctuary from watching what they said outside the Firm, from speaking about cyanide pills sewn into shirt hems, and explosives, and keeping up morale. Sometimes they spent the whole weekend in companionable silence. Nancy wrote long letters to Phil, while Iris composed bland little missives to her mother in Salisbury, saddened by the realisation that they had no secret language forged in closeness.

Other times, they went out to clubs and pubs with the crowd. There were always invitations on offer to the Café Royale, to the Dorchester bar and to the shows. As the agents passed through

Orchard Court and Iris got to know them, flirting a little with the men and befriending the women (though always alert to their behavioral quirks and speech patterns), some of them would be asked along. As often as not, it was a means of eating, as one of the many wealthy men who had taken what was known as 'special employment' in the secret services would settle the bill before anyone had a chance to offer to pay a share.

When they were left to their own devices, meals seemed to consist of tea and toast. They were almost always too tired to cook after work, and usually too late for the shops. Once they tried to cook a pigeon on the kitchen fire. It was not an experiment they repeated.

Iris had no shortage of admirers. There was John from the War Office, older and wiser than the others, and a full deck of servicemen: Alan, who was in the navy; Peter from the Royal Engineers; RAF pilots Jack and Rory, when they were in town. None of them was special.

'Your trouble is, you've too many to choose from,' Nancy said.

'So how did you know Phil was the one?'

'I just did.'

'No help at all! But listen, I won't be back tonight.'

Nancy raised an eyebrow.

'Nothing like that. Full moon – I'm going down to Sussex.'

3

Tangmere

Chichester, July 1943

Rose was going to France.

One afternoon, a car pulled up outside Orchard Court. Rose took a rear seat alongside Iris. Miss Acton, who usually made airfield trips, had important meetings in London. They headed south out of the embattled city, its streets made foreign by jagged grey bomb craters and ruined buildings, and into countryside that offered reassurance that life did still exist as it had before.

Cow parsley frothed from the verges of the country roads. Dog roses fluttered in a warm breeze. Birdsong and brightness imitated peacetime, if only for a few hours. Iris and Rose hardly spoke. In the green fields east of Chichester the village of Tangmere was sleepy, marked only by the shingle-clad spire on the church roof. Trees and bushes formed a green screen on either side of the road.

'Here we are,' said Iris as they drove up a short gravel pathway. 'The Cottage. The gates over there are the main entrance to the airfield.'

Rose nodded.

She looked terribly young and vulnerable, thought Iris. In the dark gabardine suit chosen to blend in to the crowd, she was so slim as to be childlike. Rose's cheekbones had become more prominent and her eyes huge. It was all too easy to believe that she was making her way in the world as best she could on her own – that part was true, after all, since the loss of her mother – while her fiancé was away. The cheap garnet ring on her finger was noticeably looser than it had been a month earlier.

'All right?' asked Iris.

'Yes.'

Rose was doing a good job covering it, but she was scared. It was only natural. Iris would have to keep a keen watch on her, perhaps make a difficult decision, when the time came.

They got out of the car. Tangmere Cottage was a low redbrick house, about a hundred years old. The brickwork was almost entirely covered with ivy, through which small-paned windows managed to assert themselves. There was one upstairs floor and a thick chimney stack on the end. The property and garden were protected from sight by a Sussex stone wall and dense hedges.

'Come on inside,' said Iris. 'They do a lovely cup of tea here.'

That got a smile. Rose gathered her bag and gloves and followed.

Inside, the cottage – a requisition, naturally – was still more domestic than military, extended over the years to produce a useful muddle of rooms, none of them very large.

'Hello, Stephen,' called Iris as they entered the back door to the kitchen.

Her cheery greeting was returned by a tall,

thickset man in uniform, one of the two flight sergeants of the RAF police service who governed the Cottage.

'This is Stephen. He's cook and security all in one, which makes this the most comforting guard-room in the country. Nothing and no one gets past Stephen.'

'Hello, miss,' he said, nodding at Rose. She was not introduced, not even by her new name. 'Kettle's on, make yourselves at home.'

'Thanks! Come through to the ops room.'

Keen to keep the mood upbeat, Iris led the way into what had once been a sitting room with a simple brick fireplace, now full of heavy brown furniture. Dark wooden beams made the ceiling seem lower. On the wall hung a large map of France. A table and a selection of unmatched chairs gave the room a relaxed air. The remains of a coal fire were unlit. On a small wooden desk were a black telephone and a green telephone.

A couple of young men stood smoking by the window. Iris grinned. 'You two again! Rose, I'm delighted to be able to introduce two of our finest – Jack and Rory. One of these renegades will be taking you up tonight, and you couldn't be in better hands.'

'Unless you get Verity, of course,' said Jack, as they shook hands. He was tall and fair, with an angular frame. 'Though I fear you are indeed stuck with one of us. Heigh ho.'

He pushed back his floppy mop of blond hair. He reminded Iris of the earnest young men who worked for the BBC after graduating from Cambridge. But there the similarity ended. If he looked will-o'-the-wisp, Jack Wallace was a particularly steady pilot, a meticulous checker of everything from the wind to the instruments in the cockpit to the quality of the fuel to the political situation. He was a careful navigator, with a near-photographic memory for the routes learned from maps, and a tendency to worry masked his methodical approach and fierce determination.

'It's quite all right. We've been practising,' said Rory to Rose, who tried to smile. Rory was shorter, with a mop of dark curly hair and wide brown eyes that always reminded Iris of her childhood teddy bear. 'In fact, I'm beginning to wonder whether I wouldn't find it a shock to the system to fly in daylight now.'

'And we've been eating our carrots,' said Jack cheerfully. 'I've got the night vision of a rabbit!'

'How many of these trips have you made?' Rose asked.

'This will be my tenth sortie for Special Ops.'

Rory took a final deep drag on his cigarette and stubbed it out. 'Eight for me.'

Iris rubbed goosebumps from her bare arms, and hoped the girl hadn't noticed. All summer, agents from both F Section and the other intelligence services had been dropped into France by Lysanders, planes that were short-winged and light, able to land in restricted spaces like small fields. With so much activity, there had been many times when Miss Acton could not make the trip, and it had fallen to Iris to accompany the agents from London to the airfield during the full moon. It still seemed incredible that men like Jack Wallace and Rory Fitzgerald brought down

260

planes deep inside enemy territory, flying by moonlight, navigating across France by picking out silvered strips of river and other memorised landmarks; when they landed it was in darkness, guided only by hand torches.

'How long do you stay on the ground?' asked Rose.

'As little time as possible. If we can turn around in less than ten minutes, that's all right. Any longer, and we risk being rumbled.'

'Well, I am very grateful indeed not to have to drop out on a parachute.'

'Any bloody fool can drop joes over France and come back without touching down, but it takes skill to land a Lizzie and take off again,' said Jack.

Rory stubbed out his cigarette and immediately lit another. 'All part of the service. Ah, tea – jolly good.'

Over tea and more cigarettes they swapped off-duty gossip: Iris telling them who had been in the crowd at the Dorchester and the 400 Club, the pilots giving the latest updates on their twin passions. In Jack's case this was an old black motorcycle he called the Beauty, which he would strip down and tend with oil cadged from the mechanics at the airfield; Rory had Sam, a collie dog he had rescued in his native Yorkshire after the death of an old hill farmer.

'We had a soppy Airedale at home, so sweet-natured,' said Rose. 'I miss her dreadfully.'

The house that was bombed out, thought Iris. It took the dog as well as her mother. She was struck yet again by the girl's composure, her ability to master her emotions. Rose would be fine, quietly

261

resourceful and reliable.

'I was desperate to keep Sam at camp, but they wouldn't let me,' said Rory. 'It was thanks to Jack, and one of the Beauty's not infrequent break-downs, that we found a farmer close to Tempsford who would look after her.'

'Is that near here?' Rose asked.

'Not really. But closer than Yorkshire.'

'And he writes Sam lovely letters when he's away,' teased Iris.

She did not explain that 161 Squadron (Special Ops) was based at RAF Tempsford in Bedford-shire. During the full moon they came down to Tangmere because it made for a shorter journey into the heart of France, when the range of the aircraft was crucial. From the Sussex coast they could penetrate as far as central France and re-turn. The pilots were normally at Tangmere Cot-tage for a week before the full moon and a week after.

'You couldn't bring him here? Why, there's even a garden!' said Rose.

'And conditions like a cheap Turkish hotel up-stairs,' said Jack. 'So many camp beds up there ... sometimes you can't even see the landing floor. The idea of that hound howling outside all night ... no, thank you.'

'And what about your noisy lump of metal, eh?'

'You wouldn't know it, but these two really are great friends,' said Iris. 'Except where dogs, motorcycles and women are concerned.'

'Where women are concerned, that's good-natured competition,' said Jack, sitting up straight and pretending to adjust his collar. 'Go on, Iris,

262

You've had long enough to decide – which one of us is it to be?'

'Oh, you know I could never come between you boys. That would be treachery.'

Dusk was falling. Cooking smells drifted from the kitchen, where the mess sergeants were busy bringing a game pie to perfection: assorted meat (mainly rabbit) and vegetables (mostly carrots) under a crust of mashed potato. They had become used to rationing, but were still obsessed with food. Two trestle tables were laid for supper in the plain whitewashed dining room next door.

More young men arrived through the kitchen as the comforting aroma grew stronger. One of them cranked up a gramophone in the corner. The room grew misty with cigarette smoke, pierced by notes of exquisite pain from a saxophone. 'Give it a rest, Richie,' someone grumbled. 'Leave the torture to the Gestapo.'

The atmosphere was lively as they sat down to eat. Nervous energy was countered by banter. A young man in civilian clothes was ushered in late. He was not introduced by name, so he must have been an agent from one of the other special services. Rose remained quiet at Iris's side. She was outwardly calm, but Iris wondered how she really felt, now it was almost time to go. They were joined by squadron leader Hugh Verity, the genial, unassuming and much-respected head of Special Duties operations. Like all the pilots, he wore a mixture of uniform and civilian clothes; if he was shot down and managed to survive bailing out, he would lose or burn his battle blouse and

263

pass for any other slightly scruffy young man.

'We had a dreadful night. The flak came at us for miles over northern France on the way back. Two joes in the back, we're well off track ... but everyone's keeping their cool magnificently ... then the underside takes a hit just before we cross the Channel. Somehow or other we splutter over the finishing line in low cloud and on the last gasp of fuel. We all stagger out, and the only event that provokes a reaction from the French is getting in the car on arrival and being driven off on the wrong side of the road!'

'...it's not stunt aerobatics, you know. Though some of them seem to think we can land on a franc coin on the edge of a cliff, some of the places they've been finding for us...'

'...remember Stamper landing in thick fog on the stumps of the Lizzie's legs? He'd taken the wheels off on a cliff, and there was telegraph wire wrapped around the tail wheel, and a hole in the undercarriage, and the supplementary fuel tank only hanging on by a couple of twisted screws...'

Iris felt dizzy with the effort of trying to follow as many stories as she could, but Rose was emotionless, as composed as she had been the first time Iris had met her.

After they had eaten, Hugh Verity led them back into the ops room and gave the briefing. It was a double Lysander operation. Standing in front of the map of France, he pointed out the two flight paths and shared reconnaissance photos of the landing fields. The weather forecast came in from the Met Office: mainly clear with scattered cloud.

264

On the green telephone, fitted with a scrambler for confidential conversation, he took a call from air ops on London confirming that the BBC message had gone out, and the reception groups would be assembling on the ground in France.

Final checks were being made on the airfield. The pilots went outside to accustom their eyes to the dark. At the Cottage, Iris handed over the wireless set disguised as a small leather suitcase and went through Rose's pockets one last time to make sure no bus tickets remained, no receipts or stray coins to give away where they had been recently.

'Let me see the labels in your coat and jacket. Blouse? You've checked any labels on your underclothing – nothing British at all?'

'I've gone over everything a hundred times.'

The only sign of nerves was a slight tremble.

'Right ... French identity card, money, food cards and bread coupons?'

They went through her handbag together.

'Photograph of the fiancé?'

'In the side pocket.'

'It's always the smallest things that give us away.'

Everything the agents took back to France with them had to be authentic. English soap, for example, lathered too well, so the poor dry stuff most widely available on the Continent had to be made specially. Imitation Gauloises cigarettes had been given up as a bad idea – the British gum used on the packets was too strong and would not disintegrate in the same way as the real ones. All the everyday items like string and matches, safety pins and hairpins, scissors, razors, pencils, had to be unmarked, with no 'Made in England' cut into them to give the game away. Best of all was to use those items that had been recently brought back by other agents.

One of Miss Acton's rules was that she would always give the agents a chance to see her alone before they went out to the plane. 'If they have any doubts, best let them confess,' she said. Iris touched Rose on the arm. 'I'm popping upstairs to the bathroom, if you want to come too,' she said.

On the landing Iris turned and asked, 'All ready? Speak now or for ever hold your peace.'

'I'm all right.'

'Completely?'

Rose took an audible breath and composed herself. 'That's a very pretty pin you have in your hair, Iris. Such a clever design.'

Iris clicked it open and took out the silver and paste clip in the shape of a rosebud. She checked it under the landing light and handed it over.

'Oh no, I didn't mean–'

'I know. But I want you to have it anyway. And–'

'Yes?'

Iris hesitated. Then she leaned forward and gave her a spontaneous hug.

'Good luck.'

When they walked downstairs, Iris had the uncomfortable feeling that she might be sending a friend to her demise.

At 10.30 p.m. a large Ford estate car arrived at the Cottage to take them to the plane waiting on the tarmac. The luggage was loaded. They stepped

266

into the vehicle. Minutes later, they were standing underneath one of the two Lysanders flying that night.

It was stubby, with non-retractable under-carriage legs, high wings on a V-strut. The plane looked like an awkward, stunted insect, but in the right hands it was an astonishing machine, capable of landing and taking off in exceptionally small spaces. The wings were positioned at eye level either side of the pilot, who sat high in the cockpit under the greenhouse roof that allowed such good visibility.

'In case no one tells you, there's a half-bottle of whisky in front of the passenger seat,' Iris whispered to Rose.

The unnamed man arrived with an officer in another car. He and Rose climbed the ladder. Iris could see them in silhouette, stowing bags under the wooden seats. Heavier luggage, like the wireless set, was harder to manage, but they did.

Iris watched the plane move off, its wings lit silver by the moon.

Back at the Cottage, Iris gathered up any items left behind. Books and magazines in English, cigarettes, matches and sweet wrappers were the usual haul, but this time Rose and the unknown man had been completely clean on arrival. That was always a good sign. It showed they were already in character.

'Go and get some sleep upstairs, why don't you?' suggested Stephen. Her driver had already done so.

Iris shook her head. Tonight she was waiting for

the return flight. She was tired, but she knew she wouldn't be able to sleep properly. Where were the planes now? Were they safely over the Channel yet? She looked at her watch. It was gone 11.30 p.m. They should be. A round trip lasted between four and six hours. Iris settled into an armchair and reached for her coat to put over her legs. Hours passed. She dozed, all the while alert for a dull engine drone overhead.

When she finally heard footsteps outside, the clock read four fifteen.

The door opened noisily. A group of men entered, Jack among them, stamping mud from their shoes, flinging off jackets and dropping bags. The drinks tray was raided and glasses clinked. Triple brandies all round. The release of tension was palpable. From the kitchen, like a well-oiled machine, came the smell of coffee and frying bacon.

'Now I know I'm in England,' said an exceptionally handsome man with a French accent and a world-weary air. He turned to Iris and winked. 'No more ersatz!'

Iris clambered to her feet, feeling dazed.

'Real coffee, mademoiselle – no more acorns and chicory, at least for now,' he said, in excellent but extravagantly accented English. He raised his glass of brandy. 'To freedom!'

'To freedom,' she replied.

He slept in the back of the car all the way up to London. A British man with him slumped against the window, staring out with bloodshot eyes while the grey light over the trees turned pale yellow with the dawn.

4

Xavier

London, July 1943

So that was Xavier Descours.

Until then, Iris had only seen his name in the files and heard accounts of his apparently fearless command of the air operations landing in France. Before the war he had been the manager of an electronics company, specializing in the manufacture and shipping of wireless components. He had been recruited in France to organise the supply of these to the British SOE and the Resistance, while still, ostensibly, running his business for the Vichy government. He was thirty-eight years old and had a reputation for being a cat with nine lives, a charmer who ran terrible risks; in the past year he had become more deeply involved in liaison missions for F Section and was now indispensable to the secret air service.

Two days later he turned up at Orchard Court. He spent a long time in the large room with Colonel Tyndale and Miss Acton. The murmur of voices rose and fell, though it was not possible to hear what was being said.

Iris served tea to two young men, undergraduate types – at least, one of them was wearing a college scarf – who were being prepped to fly into

269

France at the next full moon. With only the six of them in the flat, there was no need to press the bathroom into service as a reception area. They drank the weak brew with little enthusiasm in the smallest bedroom office. When they were summoned into the main meeting, Iris was left alone.

She typed up some notes while they were fresh in her mind, fragments of information she had picked up while their guard was down: the Yorkshire public school and holidays in Scarborough of one of them, and his support of Leeds United football club; the admiration for the novels of Émile Zola of the other.

The atmosphere was depressing, with the dank cold, the cigarette smoke and fog rubbing up against the building like a wet dog. She stood up and moved around to try to get a little warmer, was hardly thinking when she delved into the pockets of the coats that had been thrown over the back of an armchair. It was a reflex action that brought up nothing more exciting than a book of matches, some crumpled bits of paper and a selection of bus and tube tickets that would have to be disposed of before the men went over to France.

'What are you doing?'

He had come up behind her soundlessly. She turned round and found she was looking directly into Xavier's deep brown eyes. His olive skin was smooth, and he was so close she could smell honeyed tobacco, so deliciously different from the acrid tar of Senior Service.

'Sorry, I–'

'That is my coat.'

'I get so used to doing it.'

He seemed to be weighing up the possibility that she was being disingenuous. Straight eyebrows lowered; then he pulled the coat out of her hands and folded it over his arm. He walked over to the window with a confident swagger and turned. 'We are supposed to trust each other.'

'Well, of course–'

'Do I have to prove myself to you?'

She felt herself blushing. Then the eyes crinkled, and he laughed gently at her discomfiture. He really was an extremely handsome man, she thought, well aware of his own reputation and used to getting his own way; she would do well to watch herself.

The two young men saved her from having to find an answer by emerging from the other room, visibly more relaxed as they talked cricket. Even so, she recognised the forced nonchalance of the chatter, and the shot of excitement and purpose that sharpened their features. Iris handed them their coats with a smile and showed them out. Xavier remained standing by the window.

When she returned, he sniffed in distaste at the cold remains of the tea she had still not cleared away. Then he looked up with another smile that lit up his face.

'I am going to take you out for dinner,' he said. It was not an invitation, it was a statement. 'I want to walk up past Trafalgar Square to the Coquille in St Martin's Lane with a pretty young woman.'

She ignored the compliment. 'You know it then, the Coquille?'

'I used to go there before the war.'

Iris had heard of it, but never been.

'And the Wellington pub in the Strand,' he went on, 'is that still there?'

'I think so.'

'It's short notice, I know – but do you accept my invitation?'

'I'm not sure why you're asking me.'

'Oh, come now. Don't think I haven't noticed the way you look at me!'

'But I – what–' She had to look away, fearful of giving him any more encouragement.

'No need to be embarrassed. I am flattered.'

'I'm sorry, you really have made a mistake.'

'Please, as I say, there is no need for dissembling among us here – surely?'

Iris felt herself reddening.

'So. Let us start again. Would you care to have dinner with me, mademoiselle?'

As he spoke, Miss Acton appeared behind him in the doorway. She stopped, clearly having heard.

Iris felt as if she had been caught doing something she shouldn't, but Miss Acton nodded her approval.

'All right,' said Iris. 'Give me ten minutes to tidy up here.' She scooped up the tea tray and dumped it in the kitchenette, then grabbed her bag, straightened her skirt and stockings and attended to her make-up as best she could in the black-tiled bathroom mirror.

In Trafalgar Square, the fountains were empty of water. A huge hoarding advertising 'War Savings' was wrapped around the base of Nelson's Column. It was not yet dusk, but there was already a queue outside the Duke of York's Theatre in St Martin's Lane, not long reopened after suffering bomb damage in 1940. The title of the play on the billboards was *Shadow and Substance.*

'Perhaps we should see it. It might offer us some help,' said Xavier.

'It might. I think the subject is faith – though the story is about Ireland and the Catholic Church.'

'Faith, ah – faith is what we must all keep.'

Iris, feeling unaccountably ill at ease, did not respond. She never felt like this with any of the other men she went out with. But with this man ... she did not know quite what she was doing here with him. He was not a stranger exactly, but someone she knew only by reputation. Perhaps that was what was making her feel uncomfortable, unable to ask questions and provide the light chatter that would normally come naturally on an evening out.

Xavier, on the other hand, showed a hawk-like curiosity about the streets she took for granted, wanting to know about everything they passed: the sheet music hanging in a shop window, the words and music for 'Mexicali Rose', 'Hurry Home', 'If I Didn't Care'; the poster that read 'Let Music Lighten the Black-out'. What music did she like; did she play an instrument?

The glass in the shop window was taped into criss-cross squares. Sandbags, nine or ten deep, were propped against the walls. She was used to the sight now, like the barrage balloons that floated in the sky above central London, but what did he make of it all, this Frenchman who worked behind the lines in Nazi-occupied France?

At the Coquille they were whisked into another world of starched white linen and battalions of silver cutlery. The atmosphere was womb-like, cocooned from reality. 'It hasn't changed!' he exclaimed, visibly gratified. 'There's no need to be unsure of yourself, you know,' he said. Was it his experience living on the edge that gave him the ability to read her so accurately?

'Oh, I'm fine.'

'I hope you're hungry.'

'I'm always hungry. It's hard not to be.'

It was out of the question to discuss anything to do with work in a place where they might be overheard. Presumably, anyone who heard his French accent would infer that he was one of the numerous Free French who had pitched up in the capital. He took charge of the menu, expressing delight at the prospect of quail. A good claret was ordered after discussion of the selection on offer.

When the waiter left, he was silent for a few seconds. She was caught in another of his disconcerting stares. Sitting so close to him felt heady, even though he was doing everything to put her at her ease.

'What do you want out of life, Miss Nightingale?'

'Well ... that's a very big question.'

It was one Iris was not sure she had ever been asked, and perhaps she had never even asked herself.

'Too big, perhaps. I understand.'

He crossed his hands on the table. Lightly tanned hands that looked strong and weathered

274

by an outdoor life despite his elegant city clothes. He leaned forward, smiling.

'In that case, tell me about your favourite place.'

His voice was low. His full attention made her feel dull in comparison, but she had to say something. Then she shook herself. Why shouldn't she have some enjoyment? How was this so different from being out with the pilots and chattering away to them? What was it about him that made it so much harder?

'There's a spot down by the river on the Embankment where I go to think. I should probably give you a much more exciting answer, but if you want an honest answer that's the best I can give. Now, you tell me yours.' It still wasn't a question, but she was making some progress.

He smiled, as if the thought alone of his favourite place was enough to fill him with pleasure. His teeth were straight and white, with a tiny imperfection at the front, where the bottom row had started to cross.

'When I was a boy I had a boat, just a small rowing boat, but to me it was a magic carpet. I used to take it out with my friends, and we would jump into the sea off the side and swim. But I also loved to go out by myself to a bay enclosed by rocks. I had a device my father made for me, a wooden box with a glass bottom that I could press into the water over the side of the boat and see what was under the water so sharply it was like a cinema screen. The precision of it amazed me. I would spend hours leaning over the side of the boat, my back becoming deep brown as oiled wood in the sun, just watching the shoals of fish.

There are fish there that you would not believe – all painted in exotic colours, darting here and there among the rocks.'

He seemed far away as he spoke. The pictures he made were of a place teeming with vibrant life: first the fish, then the birds, against a backdrop of fruit stolen from orchards, flowers and pines and, everywhere, the sea. She had never seen anything like the scenes he described. The years she had spent abroad had been in the white mountains of Switzerland and its grim, forbidding valleys, brown and industrial. Lausanne and Montreux. The ordered grey streets of Zurich. And now the fog and grime and smoke of London, bleached of colour by the war.

The food arrived, and he told her about his boyhood wish to become a fisherman, to spend whole days on the sea all year round.

'But alas, real life made its unreasonable demands. I had to wake from my dream. So I went to university in Lyon, and became an electronics engineer. The rest I am sure you know.'

He was serious suddenly, and checked his watch.

'Will you excuse me for a few minutes? I have to make a telephone call.'

He was gone for much longer.

She sat at the table in a happy daze, sipping the good wine. The restaurant was packed, and the hum of conversation rose. She thought of the risks he had run and shivered involuntarily.

'Did you get through?' she asked when he reappeared.

'Eventually.'

He poured some more wine, and she noticed

276

that his hand was shaking. Whatever he had been attending to had upset his natural ebullience. She would not ask.

They ate a dessert of cheese and some apple slices while he asked her about her family and Switzerland, and her social life in London, though she sensed she had lost his full attention.

Xavier turned to gesture for the bill.

He offered her a cigarette and lit it. They smoked in silence. Mostly he looked at her, until she dropped her eyes, as if he was trying to communicate something without words that she was unable to understand.

'What is it?' she asked eventually.

'I want to ask you a favour.'

'I see.'

'You are resilient, aren't you? As resilient as you are beautiful.'

She didn't know what to say. He was making her nervous again. 'I'm wondering what you are buttering me up for.'

He hesitated, seemed about to say something, then held back. He stubbed out his cigarette in the china ashtray shaped like a shell and asked brightly, perhaps too brightly, 'So what do we do now, Miss Nightingale?'

She took a last sip of her wine. 'I believe there's a rather fascinating series of lectures on at the School of Art in the Charing Cross Road – "The Continuity of the English Town". Daily lecture, free to the public. Just the kind of improving programme we recommend to all our visitors.'

He laughed.

'Do you dance, Miss Nightingale?'

277

'I love to dance. But only in appropriate circumstances.'

'And where would be an appropriate place close by?'

'Well ... the Opera House at Covent Garden is a dance hall now. They took out all the seats. It's rather spectacular, with the band up on the stage.'

'I would like to see it,' he said casually.

'It's not far to walk. I can tell you how to get there.'

'You could show me, surely.'

'I could.'

'You could then accompany me inside.'

'Just to look, with no dancing?'

'It would be a shame not to dance.'

'But would it be appropriate, given ... our positions?'

'Perhaps not. But shall we throw caution to the wind?'

The place was thronged. He bought her gin and orange that made her light-headed and reckless after the wine. It seemed too good to be true, the light touch of his hand on the small of her back, the warmth of his hand in hers. Hard to tell if he was a good dancer or not: the place was packed with crowds as rough and temporary as the floor, the men in uniform, the giggling girls and the loudness of the band in a place designed to carry sound. They shuffled around, awkwardly, bumped into other couples.

'It's no good, I like to talk,' he said. He caught her hand as they came off the dance floor and did not let it go. 'Let's walk.'

278

London during the blackout was a ghostly place. At Piccadilly Circus the statue of Eros had been removed into storage. Ultraviolet head-lamps from a single car picked out white dashes painted on the kerb to delineate it in the darkness. Black buildings towered unlit like a set in a dark theatre. They walked on towards Green Park.

'I have to leave London tomorrow,' he said.

She knew better than to ask where he was going.

In the park, he pulled her into the shadows. He brushed a strand of hair away from her temple. 'I wish I could stay.'

He dipped his head. His kiss was a gentle brush of her lips.

Then, when she did not pull away, he kissed her again, and this time it was electrifying, tender yet surprising, generous and impulsive.

'I will take you home.'

He found a cab outside the Ritz, and put his arm around her shoulders for the short ride. She wondered what she would do if he insisted on coming upstairs, but he said good night gallantly on the pavement of Tavistock Square.

What was she supposed to make of the evening? It was hard enough to decide what you thought of someone you'd only just met, when you had only spent one evening together. But Xavier Descours? She thought of the way the women at F Section talked about him, the photographs in the file that had piqued their interest. Of all of them, he had chosen her. If they knew, they would all want to know where they had gone, what they had talked about, what it was like to be near to him, the focus of his attention. But she wouldn't tell them.

She wasn't sure she would even tell Nancy, not the important parts anyway. The light touch of his fingers on hers as he lit her cigarette. The way his eyes had seemed to soften in the low lamplight at their dinner table. His perfect height for her, not too tall, not too short. The easy gallantry with which he had helped her with her coat and guided her out of the restaurant into the darkness outside.

The experience had already assumed a dream-like quality. It was like a date with a film star manufactured for the newspapers by the studios: one lucky woman reader will have the honour... She could not shake off the uneasy feeling that all was not quite as it seemed. And what was the favour he had changed his mind about asking?

5

Bignor Manor

Sussex, November 1943

It was everywhere, the sense of being trapped. Trenches dug in parks, railings uprooted, air-raid shelters and sandbags at the end of streets – brick and concrete shelters held fifty people, with two-tiered wooden bunks crammed along the length of the walls. In tube stations, the terrible smell of people pressed so closely together without adequate ventilation was worse than being smothered inside the vile rubber of a gas mask. The Anderson shelters sunk in gardens were not much better: dark and cold holes where damp permeated the wooden benches inside and left a thin cushion of moss.

When a bomb hit the road in Balham, it left a crater like the top of a volcano into which a bus had tipped nose first, its rear upended. Tramlines twisted and hung over the hole in the ground as if the route were being diverted to the centre of the earth. Shops and houses were ripped open by the blast; papers and boxes were blown off shelves and valuable stock smashed; in private rooms, flowered wallpaper was exposed and curtains flapped like flags of surrender.

Grey days and months passed and were clumped together in her mind, losing any brightness and elasticity, while the memory of that one evening glowed, assuming more import, taking up ever more space, pushing all else aside. Now all she saw were the streets of grime and smoke-dirt, little improved around London Bridge from the Southwark of Charles Dickens. Prisons, and tramps, and the smut of steam trains. And in quiet streets nearby families lived in houses that no longer had glass in the windows.

For weeks afterwards, she saw the city through Xavier's eyes. She felt the soft mohair of his coat, walking by her side, one hand in his trouser pocket, hat pulled down almost to his eyes, as she walked past the queue outside the Whitehall Canteen, beside the National Gallery on Trafalgar Square, where society ladies served coffee to war workers under murals by Duncan Grant, and up St Martin's Lane to the Coquille, now imbued with a magical association. She tried to picture what he was doing in France, wondered again about the unasked favour, and relived the kiss.

In November the weather closed in. The full moon was on the wane, and so far only one Lysander had made it out of Tangmere and back. Miss Acton had spent two evenings at the airfield and gone back to London. Iris had orders to stay down at Tangmere for a few more nights on the off chance that they could make the run that month and deliver three joes as scheduled from France.

In the Cottage, a radio was tuned to a music station. Iris read and chatted to Rory and Jack and other pilots who dropped by. A ping-pong table was rigged up and in constant use for a complex knockout tournament. There were fast and frantic darts matches (behind the plywood surround that fielded stray shots was a secret cupboard containing maps of France on silk scarves and compasses). The mess sergeants gave permission for the drivers to take anyone who wanted to go to the Unicorn pub at Chichester; the landlord was particularly welcoming to the RAF, for whom he kept special bottles of claret and burgundy and never charged the full price. On the walls of the bar were pictures of pilots from the Tangmere squadrons and their aircraft, though the collection did not include a Lysander.

The fog thickened. When it was clear there would be no flights that night either, the call came through: party at Bignor.

Tucked under the rolling hills of the South Downs, Bignor Manor was less than half an hour's drive from the airfield. It was the home of Major Anthony Bertram, one of the escorting officers who met the flights at Tangmere, and his wife, Barbara. The major was attached to MI6, but down in the Sussex countryside at the sharp end of the special air operations, interservice rivalries were sensibly forgotten, or so it seemed. The couple had two young sons, and Bignor Manor was a happy family home where – or so they told any villagers who inquired – they occasionally put up convalescent French officers. The cheery and indefatigable Mrs Bertram would let the maid and the gardeners go and continue without help at night, but there was no apparent subterfuge in what she was doing.

Despite the grand name, the heavy stone and Elizabethan origins, the manor was not a particularly large house; it had only four bedrooms and was approached from a typical farm-track entrance, on which it stood discreetly, well back from the rest of the small village.

'Come on, Iris, I'll give you a lift on the back of my bike if you promise not to scream,' offered Jack.

'I'll certainly come, but not on that thing. Last time my legs were completely black with soot when I got off!'

'She's coming with me, aren't you, Iris?' interrupted Rory. 'In a nice safe car from the ministry.'

'Only if Denise is driving.'

Barbara Bertram was pretty and bright, much loved by all. She made her job seem effortless, caring for so many in conditions of great secrecy, attending to her menagerie of farm animals – the hens, rabbits and goat, the hives of bees, the dog, the cat. She was last to bed and first up in the morning, yet always had time to sit and talk, to make up a four at bridge or to play darts with the party. She would cook bacon and eggs with a smile for the new arrivals at four in the morning. The young Bertram boys called the French 'Hulla-baloos' on account of the strange and guttural sounds they made when speaking to each other; neither of them yet understood the language.

But always underlying the calm exterior was the strain of the danger faced by the visitors, agents working in occupied France and members of the Resistance. The anxiety often became irritability, especially if the weather reports continued to be dismal and flights were postponed. That was where Mrs Bertram's perception proved invaluable. She'd call in new blood and a sense of fun to lift the mood, and 'Party at Bignor!' was always a popular shout. There would be supper, and the men might dance with the girl drivers like Denise, a popular redhead with dimples and a wide smile who knew all the latest steps. Thank God for those other girls, thought Iris; they made those evenings fun when all might have been too tense.

She got in the car with Denise, Rory and another pilot known as Stamper on account of some idiosyncrasy he had in preparation for a flight; the girls knew the nickname could apply equally to his two left feet on the dance floor. Iris had never asked his real name. They drove over in convoy, the spitting hellfire of Jack's motorcycle within constant earshot.

'Worse than ack-ack, that bike,' said Rory cheerfully. His faithful collie Sam was along for the ride too, at his feet in the back of the car next to Iris.

Everyone was in high spirits. 'Kindly remove your hand from my knee, Flight Lieutenant Fitzgerald,' said Iris.

'Spoilsport.'

Iris smiled to herself.

'Hope there's a decent feed,' said Stamper.

Rory scratched the dog's head. 'Always is at Bignor. Eh, Sam? Might even be a scrap for you.'

Mrs Bertram worked hard on a fine vegetable garden to keep all the visitors fed. No windfall from the fruit trees went uncollected, and every edible paring was judiciously used in the kitchen. Some of the French enjoyed gardening, and they would mow lawns and weed, or help to milk Caroline the goat – anything to keep active while they waited to fly. The manor's potager was a model of international cooperation.

A couple of men came through, carrying a stack of cracked plates and chipped saucers and a handful of glasses to the dining room.

'Hello, dears. As you can see, no chance of any new crockery.' Mrs Bertram sighed. 'But I'm pleased to announce that we have pheasant pie on the menu tonight – well, pheasant and rabbit.'

'Though it was only supposed to be rabbit,' interjected Tony Bertram. 'Lord Mersey expressly said rabbit only if you were to shoot on the estate.'

'But the pheasant – it flew in the way between

the gun and the rabbit,' said a man with a French accent who was cheerfully laying knives and forks on the long table, his back to them.

'Oh, bad luck!' said Rory.

'Yes, awfully, wasn't it?' said Mrs Bertram brightly. 'We had to make the best of things though.' As was customary, she did not introduce the Frenchman even when he turned round.

Iris stepped back in delighted surprise. It was Xavier. The effect of his unexpected presence was electrifying. She stood, smiling stupidly, but he looked away.

'A bottle of whisky and a bottle of gin from the mess,' said Rory, reaching into his flying jacket and handing them over.

'I'll get some glasses. Why don't you go through to the sitting room? A few of our visitors are already having a drink there. The rest are still at the White Horse – there's a darts match against the village team. They did very well against them last time. As it's so important to make everything seem above board, one of the French put one arm in a sling, pretending it was his throwing arm, of course. None of the villagers could quite believe how well he played with his "wrong arm"!'

Iris was taken aback to see in the flesh the man she had spent so long building up in her imagination; it was almost an embarrassment, as if he'd know, just by looking at her, what'd been passing through her mind in the intervening months.

'I'll let you introduce yourselves,' said Mrs Bertram. 'I need to check on the food.'

'We have already had the pleasure of meeting,' said Iris, aware of Rory's interest as she extended her hand to Xavier.

He shook it, neutrally. '*Ma chère mademoiselle*, I am enchanted – but I think you must be mistaken.'

Jack was in the sitting room, handing round cigarettes and drinking beer. Through the open glass doors to the garden, Sam's excited barks indicated that he had found someone to play with. Iris smiled and shook hands with three men, all strangers to her.

The pilots were discussing the night the Windmill Theatre came to put on a show at the camp cinema, and the fan dancer Phyllis Dixie had delighted and amazed the men when she held both feather fans out at arm's length at the end of her act. 'The place went wild!' said Stamper. He sounded the same as ever, but Iris noticed that his eyes seemed dull and his face drawn as he told the story Iris had heard several times. He took a large glass of whisky from the tray Mrs Bertram brought round.

One of the Frenchmen, a jowly man with a moustache, watched puppy-like as Barbara Bertram turned for the kitchen. 'A wonderful woman.' He sighed. 'The first morning I arrived, she asked me to take the mud off my boots on the metal outside the back door. Madame Barbara – you know what she did? She put all this mud in a container, and she grows little salad leaves ... yes, now I know the name, mustard and cress ... on it, so that when I arrive last week to make my return to France, knowing that my heart is heavy, she offers the cress salad to us, the French: salad grown on French soil!'

No wonder they loved her.

Iris listened politely, her mind churning, as another man began to tell her, in French, how a darts match had been convened at Mrs Bertram's instigation when the discussion between rival political persuasions had become too lively. Darts was a perfect diffuser of tension, he averred; when the war was over, he was going to get himself a board.

Perhaps, thought Iris, she should ask for a game to calm her nerves. Xavier stood talking to a man she had never seen before, giving no indication that he was aware of her. Was it possible that he did not even remember her? She had never felt such disappointment.

They were joined by two more men and another young woman driver who knew Denise. Iris saw Xavier give the girl an appreciative glance, then continue his intense discussion.

After dinner the men all helped with the washing-up, throwing the plates from one to another, while Barbara Bertram averted her eyes. 'Do be careful, boys. Oh, I simply can't look! Have you any idea how hard it is to get enough crockery for everyone here? I didn't have nearly enough in the first place!'

Upstairs in one of the bedrooms there was a wooden mirror on the wall – no room for a dressing table with all the single camp beds for the visitors – by which the girls brushed their hair and pencilled their eyebrows. Denise applied some powder, chatting about the French. Iris rolled her hair high over the front of her head and pinned it back to show off her earrings. She was wearing her favourite dress, of thick brushed cotton with a cherry print. Normally it brought her luck, but its talismanic properties had clearly failed this evening.

The other girl introduced herself to Iris. 'I'm Aster. Two blooms together!' She was jolly in an obvious way, the kind of girl Iris was on the whole glad to have left behind at school, but it was hard not to offer some friendliness in return.

'That's a pretty lipstick shade,' said Iris.

'Thank you. A present from Paris, best not to say who from, I suppose. I say, that French joe down there ... he's an absolute dream, isn't he?' Iris could not have failed to notice that Aster had been seated next to him at dinner. The giggles and touching of his arm had made her want to throw cold water over them.

Iris wondered whether it was worth asking which one she meant, but it was so obvious that to say anything would only draw attention to her feelings.

'He certainly is.'

'Any idea who he is?'

'Not a clue,' said Iris.

They went downstairs to find Stamper trying to explain to Xavier in very bad French how to fly a Lysander – 'et alors vous poussez ça, et vous tirez là – et Robert est votre oncle!'

'Are you planning on helping yourself to one of our planes, monsieur?' asked Iris neutrally.

'He used to be a pilot,' explained Stamper.

'Did he indeed?' Iris cocked her head.

'I most certainly was, mademoiselle. I fear it is no longer valid since I have been otherwise engaged these past few years, but I achieved a private pilot's licence before the war.'

She was about to ask him where he had learned to fly when Rory marched up with Aster, both of them distinctly put out to find Iris so intent on listening to the handsome Frenchman.

Stamper helped himself to more whisky and started telling another of his stories: '...It was a lone raider, and he didn't stand a chance against our guns – took a direct hit. Flew on for a mile, then made a terrible sound as it smacked into the ground. We jumped into a car and raced over. It was a Dornier, great big crate of a thing, broke up on impact into at least five pieces. Three bodies in the wreckage, and three live bombs. Flames shooting over the fuselage. My revolver was loaded and I was mustard keen to use it to arrest some live Germans ... sadly, not to be.'

Music rose louder from the gramophone. The singer warbled about the spell of Paris and an April dawn. Iris, sitting on the sofa, closed her eyes and clenched her hands together to dig her fingernails deep into the flesh of her palms.

'Are you praying, mademoiselle?' asked Xavier, coming to stand in front of her. 'If so, what for?'

She said nothing.

'I'll be looking at the moon ... but I'll be seeing you...' sang the gramophone.

She would not ask him.

For a second she thought he was looking at her in the same way he had in the Coquille restaurant. But then Barbara Bertram passed with a tray of glasses. He caught her hand and brought it up to his lips. *'Chère* Madame Barbara,' he said

290

fondly, taking the tray and placing it deftly on a sideboard. 'Would you do me the honour of allowing me this dance?'

His high spirits were infectious. Soon all the girls were dancing. 'He's quite something, isn't he?' whispered Aster as she finished a turn round the floor with Xavier. Her colour was high, flushed from the dancing in the too-confined space in his arms.

'Quite something,' agreed Iris, the edge of sarcasm in her voice lost as Aster was swept away again, this time by the jowly Frenchman with the moustache.

Mercurial – that was Xavier, the one all eyes were drawn to, with his olive-skinned good looks, the easy manner and appreciative story-swapping with the men, the chivalrous manners with a dash of flirtation to disarm the women. Even Sam the collie was charmed, returning again and again to his side for Xavier to rub his head and stomach until the poor creature rolled over in ecstasy.

At one point, Xavier went out through the glass doors to the garden. She half heard an argument in French outside, but Iris could not see who it involved. When he returned, his expression was closed; then, in an instant, he seemed to don a mantle of social gaiety, and the petulance lingering about his mouth was gone.

He came straight over to her. 'Is it our turn to dance at last?'

Iris accepted his hand and his arm around her. His fingertips on her back were light, barely touching the material of her dress, but she felt every connection as they began to move. In his warm hand, hers was secure. It was an odd conjunction of intimacy and awkwardness. He looked into her eyes, saying nothing. When she responded in kind, he pulled her closer. She concentrated on the present: she was in his arms again; Xavier Descours was flesh and blood. How much of our lives are spent wholly immersed in the present moment? It seemed to Iris that it was not very much at all. Not nearly enough.

Was this silence a mark of their complicity – or did he really not remember her? They danced on, to all intents as strangers.

Then she was whirled away by Rory and Jack, then Stamper, and Rory again. And they drank and laughed until she felt like crying.

The following night the moon rose early like a beacon, then was smothered by clouds and rain. The operation was forced to stand down. There would be no more November flights.

Xavier's appearance at a gathering at the 400 Club on Leicester Square a few nights later was noted in the ladies' cloakroom on the half-landing at Norgeby House.

Iris listened, downcast, as a new girl from Colonel Tyndale's office described him as 'that ravishing Frenchman' who made her dance so often her feet were aching. All morning at Orchard Court Tyndale had been in a foul mood. And now Iris knew why: according to his chatty new typist (perhaps a mite too chatty?) there had been a run-in with RF Section – République Française, the Free French. Ever since General de Gaulle set up his government in exile in June 1940, they had operated their own secret-service department from a house in Duke Street. They brooked no interference from anyone, least of all the British, as they dropped their own agents and formed their own circuits in France.

With his innate sense of fair play, Colonel Tyndale could not comprehend why de Gaulle was so often hostile to his country of exile, so mistrustful. They were supposed to be working together for the greater good.

It was a trying day, and apparently endless, too. It was after nine o'clock when Iris walked round the corner of Tavistock Square, feeling for her keys in the pocket of her handbag, and almost stumbled into him in the darkness. He was leaning against the wall of the entrance portico.

'Iris?'

'Who's that?' she said, though there was only one person who spoke like that, who would have presumed like that.

'Are you on your own?'

'How did you know where to find me?'

'I took you home in a taxi, remember?'

'I remember. I thought it was you who couldn't.'

'Can I come in?'

She left him waiting for a short while in silence before she opened the door and led the way up the winding stairs to the top floor.

The flat was cold. Iris went over to the eaves window of the main room and checked the blackout curtain before clicking on a lamp. Xavier stood at the door.

'Do you live here alone?' he asked.

'No. My friend Nancy shares with me.'

'Will she be back soon?'

Nancy had taken leave to be with Phil in Lincolnshire, but she wasn't sure he should know that. 'She might.'

Iris took a box of matches and knelt on the rug to ignite the gas fire. Xavier was so quiet that she thought for a desperate few seconds that he was not there – that he'd slipped away from her again, or perhaps had never even been there at all. It was four days since he had blanked her at Bignor.

'What can I do to help you?' she asked, trying to keep her tone neutral.

He shook off his coat and dropped down at her side on the tatty rug.

'You can forgive me ... for the other night.'

'Pretending we had never met? I'm sure you had your reasons.'

'It would not have been wise to show it,' he said.

In any other circumstances she would have asked him to explain himself. If he had been any man but Xavier Descours – if he had not been such a respected key player in the network, far senior to her. As it was, they sat and watched the sputter of the blue flames and listened to the hiss and murmur of the gas. Then, very slowly, he turned to her.

'Would you rather I left?' he asked.

'No.'

He seemed nervous, which surprised her. She still had no idea what he was doing here, whether it was in contravention of some official rules, whether he was here because of her job or whether it was personal.

'Is everything all right?' she asked.

294

'Of course it is.'

'It's just–'

'*Qui s'excuse, s'accuse.* Talk to me.'

'What about?'

'Anything. Anything that is not about the war.'

The room warmed. She found a bottle of brandy. The first glass blunted their mutual nervousness, and the second made them laugh too readily and talk nonsense. They ignored the old armchairs and the divan draped in the Moroccan blanket and remained on the floor.

'We ought to eat something,' said Iris. 'Though Lord knows what.'

'Madame Barbara is right,' he said. 'We should allow ourselves to find enjoyment where we can. Pretend to ourselves that we live only in the present, where there is no war, no inhumanity, no terror.'

Iris raised her glass. 'To the present.'

She began to talk about a play she had seen, but was disconcerted by the way he studied her, curious and alert to every movement. After a while they simply watched each other, taking in every detail. For the longest time, nothing was said.

'It's the little things that give you away,' he said.

'What do you mean by that?' she asked.

'You are clearly a dedicated follower of the rules.'

'Whereas you are not?'

'Let's say I don't dwell on the rules, the possibility of failure, of disaster. I try to find the positive wherever I can.'

His expression was serious, without a hint of a smile or the amused twist at the corner of his mouth.

There was no contact between them, but her skin was tingling. It took her by surprise; she felt naked, even through the fabric of her clothes. She wondered whether she should stop this now.

The rug seemed rougher under her hand as she shifted on its woollen ridges. 'Where are you staying?' she asked.

'I was hoping to stay here.'

Still the silence between them pressed in. He was in no hurry to break it. The gas flame hissed. A door slammed below, and footsteps receded on the stairs. A vehicle passed on the road.

She thought about the bar near the office where the men and women of F Section and other special employments mingled; the 'bedtime stories' that were common currency. There was no reason for him not to presume she was the same as all the other young women who lived fast in these uncertain times.

'I've never done this before,' she said.

A small smile reached his eyes. Was he mocking her? Anxiety rose in a wave, and then fell back as he – finally – reached out. He touched the side of her cheek very lightly with a fingertip. The gesture was so tender that she assumed it was an apology.

She pulled away. What had come over her? He was so different from other men; it was his difference and experience that she wanted.

The shapes of the room seemed to shift. The tiles on the fireplace caught the change in the light as he moved to pull her closer. She felt his warm hand on her arm, then it moved to stroke her leg, her ankle. She shifted her position, more afraid now that he would stop than she was of

296

doing the wrong thing. Gently, he reached for one shoe and eased it off, then the other.

She felt no shame, only innocence.

She arrived at Baker Street the next morning with the warmth of his body still on her. In her bed under the eaves, he slept on. The way he felt had surprised her – so soft and yet strong, his muscles and ribs and the velvet touch of his skin; his sea and herbs scent. The gentle touches that had produced sensations she had never experienced before. The surprise that it was actually happening, the thrill of her own audacity, the impulsive wonder of it all.

It was hard to concentrate. She was light-headed, raw but elated. Don't think about what happens next, she thought, whether he will be there when I return. None of that mattered, only that she had acted on instinct and been rewarded.

He was there when she returned. In the mirror, her reflection glowed and her eyes sparkled. He stayed for the next four nights.

The only person Iris told was Nancy, when she returned from leave.

'It was pretty obvious, as soon as I walked in,' said Nancy. 'There's a look that tells the world. You're lit up from the inside.'

They were toasting crumpets she had brought back from Lincolnshire, holding them out on forks to the fire.

'Xavier Descours ... my goodness, Iris, you *are* a dark horse.'

'Nancy, you can't breathe a word.'

'I know. You know I won't. Where is he now –

am I going to meet him?'

'He's away for a few days. Tempsford, I think.'

Long afterwards, when Iris came to question her own judgement, the one thing she never questioned was the extraordinary joy of her intimate relationship with Xavier. She had wanted it as much as he had.

The troubling complexities of his character and their situation were still dormant. She did not know his real name, but she called him *chéri* – darling – rather than risk his safety by asking; it was of no importance. She knew he was capable of betrayal, though. He was married, for one thing, though he claimed it was unhappily, and there were no children. 'The worst part of marriage is the compromising. Everyone says it doesn't work without compromise, but what if that is the very death to the spirit?' She would remember that, too, long afterwards when the words were given weight by her own experience.

'Does your wife not love you?'

'She cares for me all right. That is not the problem.'

'Then what?'

'Children – I always wanted children, a family. But it has never happened.'

Even so, Iris arranged, on Nancy's earnest advice, a consultation at the Marie Stopes clinic to be fitted with a diaphragm. He was right. There could be no disappointment in the present. Who knew what might happen next week? It was war. Different standards applied.

They seized the moment, together. When he let

down his guard, he was surprisingly vulnerable. 'I live my life in disguise, yet all I want is for you to know me as I really am, love me as I am – and forgive me for it,' he told her.

Love. She was amazed that he spoke so quickly of love; she had not expected that. Even in her new reckless, awakened state, she was not so lost as to be unaware that a man like Xavier Descours was used to having affairs, that he would give women only as much as he wanted. She would not press him to define his feelings; she was not even sure of her own. Was it love she felt, or exhilaration, or just plain lust?

It was not a normal relationship, and never could be. Under the eaves of the attic flat it unfolded unseen, in another secret compartment of a secret life, yet always threatening to burst the confines of this small place of safety. What was it he saw in her? Iris wondered. She held onto remarks he made unprompted but did not ask outright, fearing to break the spell.

'I have a restless spirit,' he said as they lay in bed during the second week. 'But you give me calm. You are pure spring water on a day when the sun bites.'

She took that to mean that she was uncomplicated, while he burned with nervous energy.

'But you want me, don't you?' he pressed.

'I want you, *chéri*.' More than any man she had ever met.

'I need to be wanted,' he said.

'None of the other men managed to persuade me into bed. I'm not that sort of girl, did you know that?'

'Rory told me.'

'What? Well, he shouldn't have.'

'I made him very drunk.'

'Some people would say you were not to be trusted,' she said idly, teasing.

'People say the most disagreeable things about me.'

'Do they – really?'

'I trust no one,' he said, though the implication was that he trusted her. 'Though the kindness of others touches me greatly.'

'That first evening at the Coquille. You said you were going to ask me a favour – what was it?'

'Did I?'

'You know you did.'

'I can't remember. Probably something very silly. Like iron a shirt for me. Or give me a map of London with your flat marked in red.'

It was hard to know when to take him seriously, sometimes.

He went away for several days and returned, a pattern that was repeated throughout the month. Soon it was December, and she tried not to think that he would soon be leaving.

One evening they joined a crowd at the Dorchester bar, a rumbustious mix of pilots, their girlfriends and assorted faces from the Firm. Jack Wallace was there, and Iris recognised some of the men as Free French agents she had met at Tangmere.

She spent most of her time chatting with Jack, flirting a little in the usual way, though she was uncomfortably aware that she was doing it only so no one would suspect she was with Xavier. For his part, he seemed to be exchanging terse words with one of the Free French.

'You find something you can do, and it seems to work, so you do it again,' Xavier was saying as she went past to say hello to Denise, who had just arrived. Iris slowed her pace and let Denise approach.

'I work hard. It was how I was brought up, to do my best, and in doing so to help others,' she heard Xavier say, shoulders squared, chin tilted upwards.

'No question of money?'

'Not in this case.'

'You are the most cynical person I've ever met.'

'I can assure you that I am not.'

They left it there, with Xavier striding to the bar. But after that, Iris noticed, his natural vitality was held in check. He seemed remote when they got back to Tavistock Square at about ten o'clock. Nancy had taken to staying with another friend while Xavier was in town.

Iris made a pot of tea, to which he raised none of his usual objections. He said little and smoked, each cigarette lit from the previous one.

'My life has been ripped apart these past few years,' he said at last. He spoke angrily in French, as if he was thinking aloud. 'I've always refused absolutely to admit defeat. But other people are not, as I always imagined, unanimously blessed with the same dedication – or quickness of mind.'

Iris listened without comment.

'How can you understand the effort of climbing a mountain if you yourself do not climb? The

301

greater the number of people who know anything, the greater the danger.' He dragged on his cigarette. *'Je suis entre deux feux.'*

Between a rock and a hard place.

Iris lit a cigarette for herself, was shaking the match out, when Xavier sprang up like a cat. He was halfway to the bedroom door a second later when a key rattled in the latch of the door. Nancy walked in, full of apologies for startling them – it was no go for her at Eileen's that night, as family had turned up unexpectedly.

Xavier quickly recovered his calm, pouring Nancy a cup of tea and asking about her day. If he was tense, he worked hard not to show it. A door opening – such a simple act, but he'd not been expecting it. It was an insight into his life in France. He was embarrassed afterwards, tried to make a joke of it, but Iris could tell he'd been truly frightened. That was the only incident she could recall when he was not in total control of his emotions.

Five days later, they were back at Tangmere.

It was another double Lysander operation: Miss Acton and Iris were seeing off the capable Thérèse, seamstress and collector of magazines, for a second mission, along with another agent, Yves; Xavier and a Free French agent were also leaving.

The BBC message had gone out, referencing Caroline, the goat at Bignor Manor: 'Caroline's milk is making very good cheese this year.' The weather was cold and cheerless, but the forecast was for a clear night.

Over dinner Xavier was in blustering good form, though. He told stories that implied his eagerness to return to his people in France: about the farmer who was told to build a haystack in the middle of a field because the Germans had realised that it was long enough for a plane to land on – he did what they wanted, but he built it on a wooden platform with wheels so that it could be moved by the reception committee and then put back into place after the plane had left.

Somewhere else, the reception committee for the incoming plane arrived to check out a landing field and discovered that a group of farm workers had been ordered to build a wall across a large field. The workers were persuaded to go very slowly, as an operation was imminent. That night they helped dismantle the wall, and build it up again the next morning as if nothing'd happened.

'The hardest part is finding these fields in the beginning,' said Xavier. 'They have to be at least six hundred metres long, but you cannot go around the country pacing up and down fields to find out how long they are and how flat, and whether they flood in winter. That would surely draw attention. No, the best ones are found by our people who put on peasant clothes and go out pretending to be mushroom and truffle hunters. Or country people who know the land well, of course.'

The Free French agent and Thérèse listened attentively but said little.

Thérèse was ready. If knowing exactly what she faced on a second trip was worse than the blind optimism and courage of the first, she did not show it.

'Don't forget to send my Christmas cards next week,' she said to Iris.

'They're all in my desk drawer.'

'And here's a birthday card for Mother – January the twelfth. You do have a note, don't you?'

Iris took it. 'Don't worry. I'll take care of everything.'

'Thanks, Iris – you're a pal.'

Iris gave her a sympathetic squeeze of the hand.

Away from the others, Xavier gathered Iris into his arms for the last time. She closed her eyes and imagined they were back once again on the rug in front of the gas fire at Tavistock Square. Was it only their special circumstances, or did other love affairs run the course from delightful surprise to infatuation to commitment and cold reality in the space of a month?

'I will get a message to you,' he said.

She nodded, kissing him again rather than wasting time on words.

He released himself gently, then gathered her up again. 'I want you to know, Iris, I have never loved as I have loved you. You have been my light in this darkness.'

There was no goodbye. Minutes later the cars were taking them onto the airfield where the planes were ready. Iris watched as Jack climbed into the cockpit and gave a wave. The two F Section agents squashed themselves into the rear passenger seat, but both Yves and Thérèse were carrying two pieces of luggage, including a wireless transmitter set into the usual small suitcase for Thérèse. It was not going to work. Urgent decisions had to be made. With the weather closing in, and the missed opportunities of the previous month's moon flight, there were no other options.

'Thérèse will come with me to Châteaudun,' said Xavier. I can easily make new arrangements when we get there.'

She swapped with the Free French agent, and followed Xavier with her suitcases.

The smoke of last cigarettes lingered in the night air as the plane rose. For the first time Iris felt she wanted to stop the operation, to bring the passengers back to the ground. A tear prickled and slid down her cheek as she returned to the Cottage and picked up the stray belongings: an English book and a magazine, a box of Swan Vestas matches and a couple of theatre ticket stubs from a West End show she had seen with Xavier two nights before. She slipped the stubs into her pocket and put the rest in the hidden cupboard in the sitting room to await collection when the owners returned.

6

Messages

London, January 1944

They heard nothing at first from Thérèse, but Rose was doing well with her wireless transmissions from Paris. Right from the start she had proved as reliable as they had hoped. In France, the Firm's focus was moving to the north and the south. The order came from Churchill himself that the arming of the resistance fighters of the Maquis inland from the Mediterranean and the northern resistants behind the beaches of Normandy, in preparation for Allied invasion, was now the priority.

At last a message from Thérèse came through the secure teleprinter link at Baker Street.

Miss Acton handed Iris the deciphered page. 'What's your first thought?'

Iris took the paper. In the large room next door the sound of typewriters rose and fell in rolling waves of metallic clatter. Thérèse had 'a doctor's appointment on Thursday'. It was what they had been waiting to receive, confirmation that Thérèse was in Lyon, awaiting news of her contact.

'It was a "dental appointment" she was supposed to write,' said Miss Acton crossly.

'She's left out her security checks,' said Iris.

Miss Acton fiddled with her pen, the only form of agitation she allowed herself. Slapdash ways had been creeping in among the agents in France, and a new rule had been introduced: 'Adios' or 'Salut' to sign off if all was well. If the wireless was being operated under duress, then 'Love and Kisses'. And Thérèse had ignored it, giving no sign-off.

'What else?'

Iris stared hard at the message. Apart from the lack of checks, it was all as rehearsed, or almost.

Miss Acton went away and returned with Tyndale.

'Send a message back,' he said tersely. 'You

306

have forgotten both checks.'

'But that's–' Iris didn't want to say it. How could she criticise the boss for making an elementary mistake? She looked across at Miss Acton, wanting her to be the one to contradict him.

'Silly girl,' said Miss Acton. 'I'd hoped for better from her.'

'It's very bad, this lack of attention to detail,' said Tyndale, petulance creeping into his tone. His eye bags were starting to puff and his complexion redden. 'I thought you'd drummed it into them all.'

'But Thérèse *is* careful, she always has been,' interjected Iris.

Miss Acton bristled. 'Not always, if I remember rightly. There were a couple of times when she was in Tours last time that she forgot the exact form of words we'd agreed.'

'With respect, that's not quite the same as missing the sign-off.'

'Send the message back,' instructed Tyndale. 'Get her to reply correctly. She never would concentrate properly.'

'What if she hasn't forgotten?' asked Iris.

Miss Acton's pen tapped furiously. 'Well, she has forgotten – she gives neither sign-off. She can't have been caught. She's been with Xavier Descours, and they haven't had time to do anything.'

'Please send again with security check. Be more careful,' Iris was told to signal back.

Minutes later the check was produced. 'Adios.' After that Thérèse's messages were scrupulously free from mistakes.

The next time it happened, in a message from

307

Rose, Iris knew without doubt that something was wrong. With the first flawed radio messages it had been only a woman's instinct, and there was nothing she could say, given Tyndale's conviction that it was a simple slip-up. But in view of Rose's composure and efficiency, it seemed ever more unlikely that she had transmitted in a slapdash manner.

'The fist is right,' said Miss Acton.

Iris pulled out Rose's card from a new flip-flop wheel file system she had made of each agent's individual quirks – the spaces and natural rhythm – while sending Morse code. The 'fist' could be read like an electronic fingerprint.

It did seem right.

'But you said yourself that we should at least consider the possibility that the lack of checks was deliberate,' said Iris. 'The fist could be right because it is Rose sending the message, but under duress.'

Miss Acton hesitated.

'I know it's not my place to suggest this, but I think we should send a message back asking something personal,' Iris went on. Tyndale was out of the office, and she felt more comfortable over-reaching.

'You may be right.'

But when Tyndale returned, he ignored all reason and unleashed a volley of invective, at least some of which made it across the Channel in his furious reply to Rose.

A couple of days later a Canadian F Section agent code-named Roland sent a message in French.

308

Tyndale sent a pithy reply: 'Why have you changed your language? Do not do this.' Roland began again in English, omitting both his bluff check and true check, again provoking fury at Baker Street.

'We agreed that he was always to transmit in English – how are we to deal with these idiots who won't take instruction?' raged Tyndale. Miss Acton made sympathetic noises.

Iris remembered Roland from a long afternoon in Orchard Court when they had chattered for hours about the theatre. He was a big country lad from the Québécois mountains who had a talent for mimicry and liked to laugh. She had accompanied him to the Playhouse one evening to see a mindless farce, and then taken him on to meet Rory and Jack, who were in town. The evening had been a grand success, not least due to his introduction to the Bag O'Nails nightclub after Iris had left them to it.

'Tell him the bag is still full of nails,' said Iris.

When there was no personal response, just a thank you, Iris was certain. The Roland she knew would have come back with a witty retort.

'This isn't right,' she told them. She showed them the notes she had taken at Orchard Court, the quirks of his conversation and his sense of fun. 'If everything was all right, he wouldn't just have said thank you politely.'

'Signalling is dangerous. He's being sensible, keeping it to the minimum,' said Tyndale. She was trying his patience, it seemed.

Tyndale was determined to believe the agents were all safe, because any other outcome was unthinkable. He could not lose face, and Miss

Acton supported him, equally unwilling to be proved wrong. Plans continued to be made over the radio. Cheerful messages were received at Christmas from Thérèse, Rose, Yves and Roland, as well as from most of the others in France.

One afternoon in the ladies' cloakroom on the half-landing at Norgeby House, Iris overheard some girls who worked for the Dutch and Belgian sections whispering in a cubicle. They were worried about anomalies in radio messages to D and B Sections too, and they didn't know what to do about it. They were scared they might lose their jobs, and if that happened, then the background knowledge they had built up would go with them, to no one's benefit.

'You heard what happened to Penelope, didn't you?' said one.

Iris strained to hear, holding her breath.

'A transmission came back saying that Anders had broken his skull on landing north of Antwerp, then there were messages about doctors' reports, and then that he had died of meningitis. Penelope kept asking questions about this. Her brother is a doctor and she asked him, and it all seemed unlikely, very unusual for a landing accident. She was certain that something wasn't right, but no one in authority would listen. Last week she was sacked for "letting sentiment override her duty".'

'But perhaps if we all–'

'Not a chance.'

Iris knew the woman was right.

She was at Waterloo Station, seeing a promising new girl off to Guildford, the night the bomb fell.

Air-raid sirens had sounded, followed by distant explosions and then the all-clear. The glass roof of the station was blacked out, lamps shaded, leaving eerie silhouettes of policemen and soldiers; music played over the loudspeakers in a vain attempt to lighten the gloom. Glowing cigarette ends moving towards her. Iris and the new girl watched the clock and the empty platform. Ten minutes after the train's scheduled departure, there was no sign of it. Groups of people scurried past in earnest discussion. Announcements over the concourse loudspeaker cancelled one service after another. Iris mentally logged the way the girl's composure had quickly slipped in the confusion. That was disappointing.

The train did not arrive. It was pinned down on the track by debris when the bombs targeting Battersea Power Station failed to hit their mark. They exploded with a deafening, earthshaking force. The wail of the sirens was too late; the streets around were filled with a hail of devastation and choking clouds of dust. One hit the mansion block where Iris's aunt Etty lived. She was pulled out of the rubble alive but badly injured.

In the weeks that followed – her aunt's fight for life; the ruins and the smoke; the difficulties with the agents in France and intransigence in Baker Street – Iris heard nothing from Xavier. In a further devastating blow, Jack Wallace was lost, presumed dead, after a night sortie from Tempsford.

I have never loved as I have loved you. Now, when she ran the words through her head, as she did countless times every day, her joy was blunted by that invidious past tense. Attuned as she was to

311

every shade of verbal communication, she clung to this interpretation: it was not his love for her that was in question, but the possibility of not returning.

Rose's wireless messages continued, though. She was doing exceptionally well, keeping information flowing to the network of Resistance cells in Paris. Occasionally there were anomalies in her transmissions that might have been caused by atmospheric interference, but in the circumstances that was hardly surprising; she had to try to broadcast at a certain time, no matter what.

Then, during the February moon, at past four o'clock in the morning, a Lysander arrived back at Tangmere with an unofficial extra passenger. It was Thérèse. She was thin and bruised, and spitting with anger as she stumbled through the back door of the Cottage.

'You have no idea, do you? Not the faintest clue about what's really going on in France!'

Exhausted as she clearly was, Thérèse was running on shot nerves and rage. At Orchard Court, she was debriefed by Colonel Tyndale and Miss Acton. Iris sat in, writing detailed notes.

'When we got to France, the first thing Xavier was told was that his wireless operator in Provence had been betrayed and executed by the Germans. It was all a mess. I was already dependent on him to get me down to Lyon to join up with Charles, but the heat was on. So Xavier decided to take me with him to the south as his replacement operator. Only we didn't get that far. I was arrested, taken to Paris, and I tried to warn you, but you ignored all the signs ... dead as mutton in London.'

'When were you arrested?' asked Tyndale, his tone cold.

'Only a few days after we landed near Châteaudun. Xavier told me to wait for him at a small commercial hotel while he attended to some business in the area.'

'What business – his legitimate business, or liaison with the Resistance?'

'He didn't say. Does it matter? He didn't show up at the hotel where he sent me, but the Gestapo did. They took me – made me bring my luggage, including the radio transmitter. The owner of the hotel was shot on the spot as we went out. They pushed me into a car and took me to some kind of SS headquarters in the town. I spent the night in a cell and was driven to Paris the next day.'

'Where in Paris?'

'The avenue Foch. A beautiful building, very luxurious – the Gestapo are enjoying themselves there, I must say. A most charming German officer by the name of Kieffer received me with great politeness,' said Thérèse. Her bitterness was palpable. 'He asked after you, Colonel Tyndale, and whether you were pleased with the progress of F Section agents.'

'Don't be ridiculous! How would any of them know my name and that of the Firm?'

'Oh, they know all right. Kieffer asked me specifically about the wireless messages: was everyone pleased with their quality?'

Iris's blood turned to ice. She glanced at Miss Acton and saw her close her eyes, as if to steady herself.

313

'They know everything about our activities in France. On the wall of his office, lest anyone be in any doubt how much the Gestapo knows, is what looks like a large family tree. It's us. It shows how everything links up, who knows who, when and where agents arrived. How the branches intersect.'

'Not possible,' said Tyndale, but the bluster was faltering.

'They have a number of our intelligence agents under their thumb just in avenue Foch. There's not much they don't know. They offered me a choice: either I could play along and pretend I was still at liberty by sending messages under German control, or I would be tortured and imprisoned. It was all very civilised. The whole Prosper circuit has been dismantled, and a substantial number seem to have been turned by Kieffer! I believe the SS is now in command, via our radio transmitters, of our operations in Lyon.'

Miss Acton lit a cigarette with visibly trembling fingers. Senior Service smoke, harsh and tarry, fogged the room.

'And rather obligingly,' Thérèse went on, 'the British kept sending more agents to the agreed landing fields! You do realise they now have Roland – the Canadian – and Yves? And they had Rose, too.'

It was far worse than they could have imagined.

'There was no point in lying to them – they already knew almost everything. It was there on the wall. All any of us could do was appear to cooperate while giving away nothing they didn't already know.'

Tyndale had deflated in front of them.

314

'But even so, I tried my best to tell you. What I cannot understand is how you repeatedly ignored my radio warnings! You put the checks in place, and then you seemed to forget they had ever been agreed! What was the point?'

What could they say? That Tyndale had taken the view that she was a silly girl who was sloppy with her checks? That the signs had been ignored because they did not sit well with their high hopes for the operation?

'And you–' She turned on Iris. 'You've always been so careful – why didn't you spot what was happening?'

'Well, actually, I did–' Iris couldn't finish. She felt deeply ashamed.

'What, you *did* realise? Then why in hell's name–'

Thérèse's contempt was clear to see. She let fly then, calling her every name under the sun, accusing them and Xavier of betrayal.

'Calm down now. You've had a rotten time, but you're out now,' said Tyndale uncomfortably.

True to form, Miss Acton was the cool head. 'What we have to do now is work out exactly what happened, and who has been compromised.'

When it was clear that Thérèse could not or would not add to the Gestapo's understanding of F Section operations, she was beaten and transferred to the place des États-Unis. There she was held in a small room at the top of a building used as a holding pen for captives who might yet be useful to the Gestapo.

'After the avenue Foch it was much more like a prison. The rooms at the top were cell-like, and there were women on either side of me. We were not allowed to see each other, but we communicated by tapping Morse code on the water pipes. One morning, the girl on the right-hand side was replaced by someone whose situation was uncomfortably similar to mine. It was Rose.'

Iris felt sick. She kept her head down over her notepad, intent on taking down every word accurately.

'For two weeks we tapped our messages as we tried to work out what had happened and whether there was any way out. The windows did not have bars, but it was a long way down. Even so, with drainpipes and places where the carved plaster made tiny ledges, we decided it might be possible to climb down into the garden.

'We could both see a gardener in the grounds. He would stare up at us, and we would stare back. That was our first plan, but actually what happened was much simpler. Rose asked if we could take turns walking around the garden, even if only for half an hour, and the guards agreed.

'So that was what we did, very gratefully and humbly over the course of the next few weeks. When the guard saw that we were no trouble, he didn't mind when we began to walk together, Rose and I, doubling our exercise time. He started courting one of the maids, and they enjoyed a stroll themselves when she broke for lunch. One day they took themselves off under some trees.

'The gardener stopped us for a word, and then we all strolled along together. He was pushing a wheelbarrow full of leaves. We fell in step beside him. The wall of the garden was overgrown with

316

bushes. Suddenly he pushed us both into these bushes, warning us not to make a sound. We'd no idea what was happening, it was so quick. But behind the foliage, hidden from the garden, was a small wooden door. He kicked it open and pushed us through – along with the barrow. Suddenly we were outside on a quiet street. He reached into the pile of leaves and pulled out a large bag, then told us: "Now we walk, fast, but don't run. Xavier is waiting. If we get separated, go to the Chat Noir on rue de Montreuil in the eleventh."'

Iris's heart lurched at the mention of Xavier's name.

To thick silence in the room, Thérèse went on with the account of her escape. 'We made it down one street and then another. With every step I expected someone to shout at us to stop, or to hear the screech of car tyres or gunshots. But there was nothing. When we reached a main street, we slackened our pace and walked along with all the other people on the pavement. I have never felt more grateful for city crowds.'

Xavier was waiting for them at the rear of the Chat Noir café. For a month Thérèse stayed in a safe house, and he organised her return.

'He judged you had had too much of a close shave to carry on?' asked Tyndale. 'He gave up on the plan to take you down south?'

Thérèse stared at him with something close to contempt. 'I'd had enough. My mission went wrong, right from the start. I couldn't do it – my nerves were in shreds, I'd have been a liability. In the end, it was best for me to come back and tell you in person what's going on, as you won't believe it any other way!'

'But the messages we received from you, all through last month?'

'From the avenue Foch. I had long gone.'

No one needed to mention the information that had been transmitted in return.

'Where's Rose now?' asked Miss Acton.

'She is the one who has gone south with Xavier.'

If Iris expected them to praise Xavier's actions in facilitating their almost miraculous escape, she was mistaken.

'Xavier Descours takes a lot on himself,' said Tyndale with a note of grim sarcasm.

Neither did Thérèse seem grateful. 'He was cavalier about my safety. He just left me in the hotel at Châteaudun. If you ask me, there's something not right about him.'

From their reactions, it was evident that Tyndale and Mavis Acton considered this escapade typical of Xavier, his high-handed assumption of responsibility as well as his daring. In these risky endeavours it was essential to make pragmatic decisions at crucial moments, though some would say he acted without regard for others. Iris took a deep breath and concentrated on note taking.

Two weeks later, a message was sent to London from a wireless that was now on the suspect list. Signed off 'Geheime Staatspolitzei' – the Gestapo – it thanked them for the extremely useful information, supplies and pleasant, talkative agents. 'Some of them, most regrettably, have had to be shot, but others are being far more cooperative.'

318

7

What was Left

London, spring 1944

The clock at Piccadilly Circus was the centrepiece of the 'Guinness Time' advertisement. 'Guinness is good for you. Gives you strength'. Iris tried a glass, but a few sips made her feel sick.

On rainy streets the smell of wet wool and sweat-soaked uniforms of all kinds was unpleasantly overwhelming; travel by tube was unbearable. Even the air in the office at Baker Street was thick with a dusty ink-and-old-paper stench that turned Iris's stomach. It was as if her sense of smell had suddenly intensified. Was this what it was like to be a dog?

She was pregnant.

When Xavier next came to London, she would tell him. Their situation was unconventional, but even so, she knew he would be pleased. Tyndale had already sent word to France that Xavier was being recalled for an urgent update on the situation in France, and to explain himself. Though Xavier would be the one setting out certain bleak facts to Baker Street, of that Iris was certain. He was the one who knew the brutality and the hazards at the sharp end of the operation – the action, the roar of engines and rattle of gunfire –

319

while London drowned in the quiet intensity of paper and secrecy.

'Evil is like a snake,' Xavier had told her, his bare feet rooted in the pile of her bedroom rug. 'If you flap at it or try to stamp on its tail, it will switch round and strike you. You have to aim for the head.'

She had no doubt who would prevail. But Iris's defining quality had always been determination. 'You just don't give up, do you?' her mother used to say, usually more in exasperation than wonder. She would need to draw on all her reserves for the coming months and years. She had no claim on Xavier, but that did not mean she could not hope for the future.

More immediately, she would have to think how on earth to frame the information for her mother. She would have to tell Miss Acton, too, and sooner rather than later. She dreaded doing so, but she had taken out her clothes as far as they would go. There was no longer any disguising it.

But Xavier ignored the exhortations from London and did not return to England. Since Rose's escape he had relinquished his role as air movement officer in the north and centre of France and moved south, where the Resistance was strongest.

At Tangmere the operations continued doggedly, though Iris was not often sent now. The stuffing had been knocked out of F Section – the Dutch and Belgian sections had suffered similarly at the hands of the Gestapo in what they called the Radio Game – and the traffic was predominantly MI6 intelligence and Free French.

It was one of the Free French, newly arrived by

the April moon, who delivered the parcel to Orch-ard Court. The doorman brought up the unex-pected gift with an expression of some distaste, for the paper was tatty and ripped, a Francs-Tireurs propaganda sheet on which Iris's name was scrawled.

Iris pulled off the wrapping. It was a bottle of perfume: a voluptuous lavender scent with the label 'Distillerie Musset, Manosque'.

'Was there a message?' she asked, desperately trying to damp down her hopes.

'No card, miss. But the gentleman who brought it did say something.'

'Yes?'

'This is from Xavier.'

'Nothing else?'

'No, miss.'

He had not forgotten her. She ran her hands over the bottle.

'Careful, miss.'

'I'm sorry?'

The doorman bent over and picked something up from the floor. 'This fell out of the packaging. You didn't even notice.'

It was soft, an envelope of black velvet two inches long, hand-stitched. No wonder she hadn't heard it fall.

'Thank you,' she said.

Iris returned to her desk before opening the flap of the velvet pouch. She pulled out a neck-lace: a single pearl on a fragile gold chain. She sat transfixed by the lustre of the tiny globe. Through her tears, it glowed against the velvet like a minia-ture moon in the night sky.

She undid the clasp and put it on.

After that, nothing.

At the end of May 1944, rockets charged with high explosive thrummed across the London sky before their engines cut out. In the ominous silence as they began their descent, the souls on the ground could only pray to avoid a direct hit, that the device would remain airborne for a few seconds longer. On impact, houses caved in like matchwood. As if to defy the destruction, allotments sprang up everywhere on the cleared spaces between smoke-streaked buildings, but there was no security or certainty anywhere.

Iris was let go from F Section. She would not – could not – wish the baby away, though she wondered how on earth she would manage. Then she stopped herself. How many other women were in the same position? How many were young widows? She would only be one of many. It wouldn't be easy, of course, but she would manage. What else could she do? A letter to her mother resulted in four pages of disappointment and invective by return post, leaving it clear that she could expect no support from that quarter.

'I know there's no hope of marrying Xavier, or any kind of relationship in all probability,' she told Nancy, 'but I do want to tell him.'

So much death – what else to do but balance it with life where it took hold?

'Is there really no chance of a relationship?' asked Nancy.

Iris touched the pearl at her throat for re-assurance. 'I have no idea – but who knows? Who knows anything any more?'

When France was liberated that August, and with the baby due any day, Iris steeled herself and telephoned Miss Acton to ask for news but was given short shrift by one of the secretaries who had always previously been polite. Iris felt the moral superiority down the line; she was told she could leave a message, but she should be aware it was unlikely to elicit a response.

The child was born at the beginning of September, and named Suzanne. Iris and Nancy moved into the bottom half of a bomb-damaged house in Chester Row, near Sloane Square. The house was solid enough, but the wooden fittings had skewed with the force of a nearby explosion, so that the stairs mounted at a disconcerting angle and few of the doors closed properly. They didn't mind; the rent was cheap in consequence, and they would never otherwise have been able to afford such a pleasant location.

An early visitor was Rory Fitzgerald. Iris was well aware that her situation had been much discussed among her former colleagues: most were surprised, to say the least; almost all felt quietly sorry that she had ruined her chances of a decent marriage; several publicly expressed the view that she was an utter fool. Not Rory. He arrived with a bunch of red dahlias from Yorkshire, a teddy bear for Suzanne and a soppy grin on his face. She was so delighted to see him that she almost accepted impetuously when he asked her to marry him; but then reason prevailed, and she let him down as gently as she could. He was too bound up in the events that had brought her into Xavier's world, and she knew she would never be able to dissociate the man she loved from the man she would have to make herself love.

She tried again to contact Mavis Acton, with no more luck than before. She wrote her a letter, addressed to Baker Street and marked 'Private', reiterating her wish to help in any way she could and giving her new address. She received no reply.

Iris cradled the warm, plump weight of the child, feeling the slub of her daughter's flannel nightdress and the softness of her feet. She cupped the shrimp toes in her hand, and the child moved and settled deeper into her arms with a small breath of contentment.

Sometimes it seemed the baby was the only part of her life that was still in colour, while the rest had receded into the monochrome of her wartime memories and present losses. All she had left of Xavier.

Now that it was over, the great, momentous events of the war seemed insignificant compared to the powerful, painful, small personal experiences that had given her this new life. The first kiss in the blackout at Green Park occupied more space than the repetitive work at Baker Street; their nights under the eaves at Tavistock Square glowed more brightly than the flames above bomb-blasted London. Her mind lacked all sense of perspective. The birth of their child was made bearable by the liberation of France and the hope that Xavier would return.

Loud knocks on the door made them jump.

324

It was the week before Christmas. They were not expecting visitors.

'I'll go,' said Nancy. 'You look far too comfortable to move.'

'Another pack of carol singers, I expect,' said Iris. 'Not that you can blame the poor children for trying anything to earn pennies.' But even as she said it, she could hear there was no feeble rendition of 'Away in a Manger'.

Nancy returned with Mavis Acton.

Iris got to her feet with the baby.

Miss Acton glanced at Suzanne, made no acknowledgement and spoke as if Iris had never left Baker Street. 'I got your letter. It's not good news, I'm afraid,' she said.

Iris swallowed, feeling grateful for the matter-of-factness. The less emotion, the better. She could deal with Mavis Acton's brand of compassion.

Her former boss accepted a cup of tea, and Nancy slipped away to make it.

She took off her elegant coat and sat by the fire, getting straight to the point.

'In September, Colonel Tyndale and I went to Paris to set up a meeting point at the Hotel Cecil where our people could come in. We had about a hundred F Section agents still missing, sixteen of them women. At first there was a steady stream of returning agents. Over the following months almost half did turn up, most of them with harrowing tales to tell.

'We did a tour of the F Section circuits, gathering information and offering congratulations, rather in defiance of General de Gaulle, who is now railing against the presence of any British

325

intelligence in the country, denigrating any part we played. He seems determined to peddle the myth that the French people rose up and liberated themselves without help from anyone. It's shameless, it really is.'

Iris had the disloyal thought that perhaps Tyndale had gone to make sure all traces of F Section's failure in London were covered over.

'Gradually the trickle of new arrivals in Paris dried up. We began issuing the names of our missing to all the agencies that were piling in, especially the Red Cross. Captured German officers and agents were being interrogated by the Allied military. We started going through the transcripts of these interviews, checking their versions of events with what we knew from our own sources, looking for clues, trying to build up the picture.'

Miss Acton looked at the baby, still unable to bring herself to speak of the child's connection to the story.

'Most of the men involved – in MI6, the SIS, the Foreign Office – are convinced that those agents who have still not made it will get home at some stage. I think otherwise. My responsibility is to remain in place until all are accounted for, especially the women agents. There is some ... disparagement of my continuing efforts.'

Her use of the pronoun *my* was telling. Tyndale had slid from the scene. Iris understood immediately the opportunity she was being offered.

You will need some help,' said Iris.

'I have informed the War Office, such as it remains, that I require an office and an assistant until further notice.'

'I accept.'

'How will you manage?' Miss Acton, nodding towards Suzanne.

'I don't know yet, but I will.'

Nancy stepped in. Not for the first time, Iris realised she would never have been able to do what she did without her friend. It was the best chance she had to find out about Xavier, and they both knew it. And Rose, who had gone south with him. Rose was also among the missing.

Good intentions had gone wrong, mistakes had been made. Mavis Acton was big enough to admit as much, which was more than some of the men would do. There was an embarrassed lack of will to go in search of those who had not returned. It was as though they knew they ought to do it, but would or could not. But they could save face by permitting the women to follow their sentimental instincts, even while they disparaged their efforts. To her immense credit, Miss Acton carried on, past caring who thought her unconventional.

That winter, the atmosphere turned as dark as the days. Accusations of treachery and collaboration were made. Information was hard to assess. The French security police took control of German records and limited British access. They were told repeatedly to keep away, to stop requesting records pertaining to the actions of years past. The more obstacles thrown in their path, the more dogged their search became. Only now had the Firm begun to be referred to as SOE, the Special Operations Executive, as conceived by Churchill himself.

Iris left Suzanne with Nancy and went to Paris, where she and Miss Acton (there had been no invitation to call her Mavis) went with a former SIS agent to 31a, place des États-Unis, the building used as a Gestapo prison, where Rose and Thérèse had been held and from where they had escaped. They were shown blood on the walls, some from SOE agents who were last seen alive there.

The SIS agent survived thanks to being held back at 3a place des États-Unis for further interrogation. He managed to escape by befriending the guards, and made a run for it through the same garden gate. One of the guards, a Russian conscripted from Georgia on the Eastern Front, had been bribed to leave it unlocked. The agent had remained in hiding in Paris until the city was liberated.

The Poles had most of the up-to-date information. It was through colleagues in the Polish Section that they first heard of Ravensbrück. 'Before, I thought the worst thing I ever had to do was to sew a tablet of poison into the shirt cuffs of men who knew they would be tortured if captured. Now I know that was a mercy,' Iris told Nancy on her return.

It was becoming clearer what had happened to the prisoners held as spies. More and more reports were emerging that many of these missing men and women had been 'transferred to Germany'. They had been taken to the concentration camps.

In Paris, more than four hundred people linked to the Prosper network built up by SOE had been killed – and leads to Xavier abounded, though the information was often contradictory.

One overcast afternoon, in a private room above a nondescript café close to the Gare du Nord, Miss Acton and Iris interviewed a former resistant from the Swagman circuit based in Tours. He was an elderly gentleman, a watchmaker by trade who often had business in Paris. His white hair, round cheeks and veined nose gave him a harmless, avuncular look. He had last seen Rose in the summer of 1943, shortly after she arrived in France; he had known Xavier too.

'Descours appeared just at the time when the secret air operations were beginning in 1942. The landing grounds in France, chosen by Resistance members who were not pilots, were most unsatisfactory. But Descours had been a private pilot, and he knew what was required. He said he would arrange it, and he did. He was impressive.

'There had always been rumours that he had certain links to the Gestapo. But we looked at his record in France. All we saw was that the fellow did more good than harm. More than a hundred agents transported with no losses. Yes, he was ... what you call, a chancer, but at that stage we took a line of pragmatism. To operate successfully, it was part of the thin line one walked.

'But he was quite an operator.'

The watchmaker lit his pipe.

'Some people didn't like him. They wondered if he could be trusted.'

'Why was that?' asked Miss Acton evenly.

'The Gestapo in Paris knew too much. There must have been a double agent somewhere.

Someone who knew exactly when and where the agents were meeting.'

'Do you have any theories about who that was?'

'Personally, no.'

'But some people were suspicious that it might be Descours?'

The old man spread his neat, steady hands. 'Circumstantially, it could have looked that way. They asked themselves how aircraft could fly secretly over an occupied country without incident – how was it that there were so few shot down? They deduced that it was because the Germans knew all along, and allowed the planes to land.'

'Suppose that was the case,' said Iris. 'If they had stopped to think properly, they would have seen that any contact with the German authorities was a necessary evil. Perhaps the Germans were the ones being used.'

'That's true. We all knew about a high-ranking German officer here who smuggled gold back to Germany every leave. He had it welded behind his teeth by a French dentist. The dentist had had no choice but to give him this gold service treatment, but he was no collaborator. The German thought so highly of him that he was often invited to dine at the officers' mess, where he was privy to all kinds of information, which he naturally passed on to our network.'

Iris nodded, heart pounding. Xavier had told her that very story. 'Where did this gold come from?' she asked, remembering her lover's disgust at the presumed source, the molten remains of jewellery stolen from Jewish deportees.

'Better not to ask,' said the watchmaker. 'But

330

then, perhaps there was a bigger game.'

'What do you mean?'

'Only that. There were rumours that Xavier Descours was seen at the avenue Foch, and he was no prisoner of the Gestapo. On the contrary, he was on very good terms with the SS man there, Kieffer.'

Once a person had a first twinge of suspicion, there could be no recovery of complete trust. When Iris thought back to the times she'd spent with Xavier, and examined what happened in the light of what she knew to be true, she was forced to admit that there was plenty of cause for suspicion. The more she found out, the harder it was to see the man she thought she knew; he was as evasive in absence as he had been ruthless in action.

But then she remembered his self-reliance and energy, his ability to withstand pressure. The secretive nature of all that they did. His underlying sadness, too: the way he would not speak of his family; the tightly closed emotions whenever he spoke of home, wherever that was.

Iris always thought Xavier loved the danger every bit as much as he loved her. He was an egocentric, a marauder, a diehard. Perhaps that was exactly what had attracted her.

'*Qui s'excuse, s'accuse,*' he once told her. Whoever makes excuses accuses himself.

And also: 'People say the most disagreeable things about me.'

Back in London, they were thanked for their efforts and advised to confine themselves to 'welfare work'. The head of the security directorate had asked for the F Section files, a hand-over that Miss Acton staunchly resisted. Time was running out to find what they needed.

'Rules will have to be broken,' Miss Acton decreed.

The rules had been broken in the first place to get the SOE agents, especially the women, to France. The women were issued with First Aid Nursing Yeomanry suits as a cover story while in Britain, but they had none of the internationally agreed protection conferred by a uniform; in France they wore civilian clothes, which meant they were spies and likely to be executed if caught.

It was a fight every step of the way. It took six months before the Security Directorate sanctioned the names of SOE agents being published in prisoner-of-war casualty lists. While they waited for any news, they worked their way through the thousands upon thousands of pages of testimony that was spilling out of commissions in Germany and territories that had been under Nazi control.

Unspoken was the mutual agreement between Miss Acton and Iris that they would not countenance these agents remaining in limbo with 'Missing Presumed Dead' stamped on their files; they would uncover their fates, no matter how terrible. Meanwhile, they parcelled personal effects that had been brought back from the Cottage at Tangmere and sent them back to the families of the agents with a brief note: 'Unfortunately we are still without further news.' Knowing that the Baker Street office was likely to be closed at any time, they gave out the address of the Special

Forces Club, with a polite request that all inquiries should be made through F Section and no other agency, so as not to complicate matters.

Iris worked on the files, checking and cross-referencing in the sitting room of the house she still shared with Nancy, as Suzanne slept or watched her from the rug on the floor. A telephone was installed (negotiated by Mavis Acton to facilitate the suggested welfare work) that enabled their investigations to continue.

Among the last letters forwarded to 64 Baker Street was one from 'Fabienne Descours' asking if the SOE had any news of her husband, using his code name so there could be no misunderstanding. Iris knew then, in her bones, that he was not coming back.

Over the months, pieces of the picture began to fit together. Iris was physically sick the first time she read part of a concentration-camp file: there had been nothing to prepare her.

The British were finally allowed to interrogate the French collaborators who had worked in these death camps, testimonies taken before the collaborators were executed. Some of them recalled agents by description, men and women of British and many other nationalities, including French. The trail led to other camps where the staff who had given useful witness statements, and might have been able to provide further clues, had already been executed, confessions unheard.

By the summer of 1945 there was additional pressure on the search. Relations were deteriorating fast between the Allies and the Russians, and if they wanted access to camps in the east, there was little time to waste.

The public was not even supposed to know that women had been sent into occupied Europe as spies. Even after the war, when so many were telling their astonishing stories publicly for the first time, as many others were seeking to cover their traces. The father of Violette Szabo, the SOE agent executed at Ravensbrück and later to receive a posthumous George Cross for her heroism behind the lines, was making waves as the War Office dithered about admitting what was considered an unpalatable truth.

Quietly, it came to be generally accepted that anyone in Europe who had not returned home by August 1945 was not coming back.

Never one to give up, Mavis Acton travelled to Germany in January 1946 with a list of fifty-two SOE agents who were still missing, twelve of whom were women.

In London, Iris read the newspapers avidly. Miss Acton telephoned with descriptions of the destruction in Berlin: the jagged walls of bombed buildings, the dust and desolation. Long queues snaked from water pumps in rubble-strewn streets. And the quietness. Defeat manifested as a heavy, silent state of shock.

From Berlin, Miss Acton travelled to Bad Oeynhausen, headquarters of the British zone, having been promoted to the rank of squadron officer both to facilitate access to the documents she needed to see and, more importantly, to interview key German personnel awaiting trial for war crimes. In particular she wanted to speak to the camp *Kommandants* of Sachenhausen and Ravensbrück, where she knew several of her 'girls' had been transported.

She compiled a roller index of card files, of names and places where they were last seen alive.

'Colette and Francine were in Dachau by November 1943, executed two months later,' she said, businesslike. 'However, not all our girls were sent over the German border. There was another camp, in the Alsace, tucked into the Vosges mountains: Natzweiler. A small camp. Not many people knew about it. That was how it was supposed to be. It was for resistants, spies and political dissidents, where they were to vanish without trace. *"Nacht und Nebel"*, they called it, Night and Fog, into which prisoners would disappear. Very few records, no hard evidence of who lived or died there.

'There are reports that at least one British woman was taken there. Two Frenchwomen and one Englishwoman arrived at the camp in June 1944.'

Iris braced herself.

'According to the evidence I've seen, that woman was Rose. We can't be absolutely certain. We are reliant on witness testimony and description, some from surviving prisoners.'

'What points to Rose?'

'The description fits – height and build, hair, all correspond. A fellow prisoner saw her arrive. He particularly remembered her calm bearing, was astonished by it, in fact. The most important account comes from a German who worked at the camp' – Miss Acton hesitated uncharacteristically – 'as a stoker in the newly built crematorium. He has stated that these three women were given injections, gassed and then burned. There were no remains.'

'But Rose went south with Xavier ... how did she end up in Alsace?'

'The women were held first in a prison in Karlsruhe. They could have been sent there from anywhere in France. One of the Frenchwomen left a message scratched on an enamel cup there, of their three names and the date they were moved out. Two names mean nothing to us, but the third was Rosa Williams. Rose's real name–'

'–was Rita Williams.'

Iris took the news like a blow to the chest. She should have acted more decisively on her instincts when the agents' wireless messages came in with their embedded warnings. She should have made Tyndale take her seriously. As it was, the story was growing that the British had known exactly what was going on but decided to play the game themselves, though it involved the sacrifice of their own people. As a face-saving story, it was not convincing in the slightest, thought Iris.

But it seemed Miss Acton had not discounted the possibility of truth in the watchmaker's reference to a bigger game. As far as she was concerned now, Xavier Descours was a traitor, a double agent embroiled with the SS in Paris.

Could that have been the case? He had been recruited in France, and so had never passed through the F Section training and vetting. His cover story was that he worked closely with the

Vichy government, and by extension, the Germans, providing electronics equipment, at least in the beginning. Was that a blind to his true loyalty? After most of the members of his circuit were betrayed, he insisted on going back to find out what had happened and to alert other cells to the disaster – or was he returning to betray more himself?

He had still not been traced.

The office in Baker Street closed. Iris continued to work from home and to speak on the telephone with Mavis Acton. Over tea at Fortnum and Mason, Miss Acton's preferred venue to meet face to face, Iris tried one last time.

'If Xavier was in contact with the Gestapo, you could say that he was playing them for all he was worth – far from betraying his circuit when he disappeared, leaving Thérèse at Châteaudun, he was trying to protect her. Don't forget he organised the escape for her and Rose.'

'In the end, he was not one of ours,' said Miss Acton.

'But we were all in it together, weren't we?'

'That's a rather *romantic* view of things, wouldn't you say?'

There was no doubting her meaning. She closed the subject, with an imperious wave to the waiter.

Mavis Acton was now convinced of Xavier's guilt, and there was no persuading her otherwise. In the long weeks afterwards Iris felt as if she might have been used – it was just possible Miss Acton had been keeping an eye on her all the time they had been working together, waiting to

337

see whether she was still in contact with Xavier.

But no contact was ever made, and somehow Iris had to live with the ambiguity of their intimacy and promises, and the knowledge that he and she had been complicit in at least one betrayal – that of his wife.

On the strength of a fine reference from Miss Acton – she was always fair, which made her conclusions about Xavier that much harder to take – Iris secured a part-time secretarial job at the Home Office. Her minuscule salary went almost entirely into the pot at Chester Row, where the top two storeys of the bomb-damaged house had become available.

Iris lived here with Suzanne and a young mother's help called Jane, who had lost her family and all her possessions in the Luftwaffe's firestorms over the capital. Nancy and Phil, who had married as soon as Phil came home from the Far East, had the lower maisonette. When Nancy and Phil's first child was born ten months after the wedding, Jane worked for them all. She came to be treated as part of the extended family, and the arrangement proved a boon all round.

8

Never Give Up

Provence, May 1948

After the war, Xavier was sometimes mentioned in the many books about SOE that began to appear. But a man who is no longer there cannot defend his reputation. He was a convenient scapegoat. Many years later, when more authoritative histories were written with the benefit of newly opened archive material, there were still more questions than answers about Xavier Descours.

Those who knew him and worked with him always expressed surprise that he was the one who had betrayed them. He was a good man, a moral man, they said. If he had been in cahoots with the Germans, he must have been doing so for the greater good. How had so many of his people escaped capture? How had his flights never been intercepted? During the moon periods, the Luftwaffe was active all along the north coast of France, and although other flights had been intercepted or shot down, the Descours flights had achieved an astonishing record of success. Had he been blamed for others' failures? Did he take German money? Many claimed he did. But the truth was harder to call.

It transpired that he had indeed been to the

339

avenue Foch, on more than one occasion. The first time he was called in to be interviewed by the Gestapo's Kieffer, but he walked free afterwards. Had Xavier managed to persuade the Germans that he should be allowed to go about his business, while keeping them informed? Did he, like the German officer's dentist, intend to get more out of the arrangement than the Nazis did?

His fury when he realised how inept London had been in handling messages from the captured radios was real enough. The Germans had everything, from the codes to the timetables when the signals were due. Some ventured that he was so angry, he didn't care any more, because to him it was clear that he had been working for idiots. Others remained convinced that the setback had spurred him to work ever harder, but more independently from the British, away from his dangerous game with the Gestapo in Paris.

Was he dead – or had he begun a new life far away from all the complexities of his wartime tightrope? *'Heureux sont ceux qui ont beaucoup peché, il leur sera beaucoup pardonné'* – Happy are those who have sinned greatly, for a great deal will be forgiven them – he had once told her. For years she had pulled that aphorism apart, wondering if it held an answer.

As the years went by, it was not hope of finding Xavier alive that drove Iris, but the desire to know what to tell Suzanne about her father.

Time and again, Iris came back to the last known sighting of him.

On the night of 10 August, 1944, Xavier

340

Descours was the flight liaison officer for a joint British-American operation in Provence. The RAF flew a Dakota in from Cecina in northern Italy to a secret landing strip known as Spitfire, close to Saint-Christol in the Sault lavender area. The mission that night was not a complete success. On board were fifteen men, including returning French politicians and agents, and seven hundred and fifty kilos of freight. The disembarking French and the freight – mainly weapons and explosives – vanished into the night without incident. But the turnabout and takeoff with a total of thirty men, most of whom were escaping US Fortress aircrew, was more problematic. The Dakota – the largest aircraft to set down at Spitfire – ran out of runway at the end of the field, snagging on a band of lavender growing across the strip to disguise its length from the Germans. The only solution was to let down eight of the US escapees to lighten the load, with promises to return for them the next night. Even then, the plane struggled to get airborne again, though it eventually lifted off at the very limit of its capacity, thanks to the skill and nerve of the pilot.

But by then the repeated bursts of aircraft noise had alerted a German patrol – or had the Germans been expecting the operation? As the reception committee and their charges scattered, shots were fired. Reprisals were swift and cruel.

After that, nothing. Had Xavier been killed, or captured, then executed? Or had he melted away into a night and fog of his own devising, having played a double game all along, as some were convinced?

Through the Libre Résistance, a society formed by what was left of the old networks, Iris was put in touch with some of the old *maquisards* in the south. They exchanged letters, and she used her fortnight's leave in the late spring of 1948 to go to France. She crossed the Channel and travelled by train to Paris, on to Avignon and then Sault. She was met at the railway station by Gaston Durand and his young wife Émilie.

Gaston took her suitcase and led her to a van that looked like corrugated cardboard on wheels. 'We'll go to Saint-Christol, but before I show you the field, we'll all have lunch,' he said.

The van lurched through a rocky landscape of twisty roads and fields. In the village of Saint-Christol they parked in a narrow street of cracked houses. A cold wind gusted, and a clock struck twelve with a thin, tinny sound. Chickens scurried across their path as M and Mme Durand led her into a café that was surprisingly full, and over to a table where a man was already seated.

'May I introduce Thierry LeChêne? He was there at Spitfire that night.'

He rose to shake her hand.

'So you want to know about the last Spitfire operation?' he opened directly. He had a broad Provençal accent that took a moment or two to understand.

'Yes – and one participant in particular,' said Iris.

'We will do what we can to help you, but as I'm sure you know, these things were complicated.'

'I realise that. I'm very grateful–'

Gaston Durand waved that away. 'We are the

342

ones who are grateful. We won't forget what was done here by the RAF.'

Iris smiled. 'That's ... rather refreshing to hear. General de Gaulle has not been so generous-spirited since the end of the war.'

It was undoubtedly for the best that any further discussion of the president's aggressive nation-alism was interrupted by the arrival of a waitress bringing plates of pâté and salad.

'The centre for our cell was Céreste,' said Thierry. 'Each person in the group knew only the participants closest to themselves, and everyone else by a pseudonym only. A knock at the wrong door might be a death sentence. You were never sure of other people's loyalties, even those you had known all your life.'

'We knew of Xavier Descours, but only by his first name. More often he was referred to as the Engineer,' explained Gaston.

'And he was ... well respected?'

'Very well respected. He was one of the best.'

'What do you think happened to him?'

They exchanged glances and shrugged expres-sively. 'You have to understand. Xavier was not a local. He came in like the British and the Ameri-cans came in, and then he left. We never saw him afterwards, and he didn't turn up for any of the honours ceremonies, but there could be many reasons for that.'

'Do you have any reason to think that ... he didn't make it to the end?'

He shook his head. 'We have been putting the word out, as you asked. But no one has come up with any new information.'

343

'What about a young woman code-named Rose, his wireless operator? Was she there that night?'

Again, they looked blankly at each other.

'You never came across her at all?'

'No. But that was as it should be. There had been problems keeping our wireless operators safe. The first one was shot. Maybe too many people knew what he was doing. If the Engineer was doing his job right, he would have kept his operator well out of it.'

As they ate, Thierry showed her photographs: grainy pictures of men in peasant clothes, posing in groups in the fields. Some carried a gun with a rose at the end like a garden hose.

'Dropped by parachute by the RAF, those,' said Thierry.

'Designed by the Czechs,' added Iris acerbically.

Afterwards, at the field they called Spitfire, they stood in contemplation.

'Is that the strip of lavender that proved such a hazard to the plane?' she asked Thierry.

'More has been planted since then. There wasn't that much during the war, but we had to disguise the length of the fields somehow.'

'The people living on the farms out here must have heard the engines,' said Iris.

'They knew,' said Émilie.

'They say now,' said Gaston, 'that five per cent of the French population actively collaborated with the Germans, five per cent were active in the Resistance and ninety per cent did nothing. But here, one has to revise that to take account of all the small acts of resistance. The farmers who gave their land to allow the planes to come down and the drops of equipment to be made, which meant that at a time of hunger they couldn't use it to grow crops, and also implicated themselves and their families. They had to count on the loyalty of villages close to the landing fields – all the people who closed their eyes and ears to what was going on. It was a complicity of the many.'

They looked out at the lavender field, its neat corduroy rows and the plants still in the process of waking from grey to purple. Hills rose on three sides.

'Hell of a place to land a plane as big as a Dakota,' said Thierry.

'How did you get here that night?' Iris asked him. She was trying to picture it: the full moon, the night noises, shadows moving.

'I came in the lavender van with the man they called the Philosopher – Victor Musset. He ran a soap and scent factory at Manosque. My cousin Auguste was a committed resistant, but in his other life he was a lavender farmer, a big supplier to Musset's. That was how the connection was made.'

The bottle of scent.

'Musset ... is he still alive?'

'Certainly.'

'Might it be possible for me to meet him?'

The Durands put her up on their farmstead in the hills above the town of Apt. Émilie told her how she had been the network's courier, usually on her bicycle.

Two days later Iris was shown into a bar in the medieval heart of the town by the cathedral. It was a dark and undistinguished room with a vaulted ceiling, made to seem lower by Victor Musset's height. He was a large man; judging by his girth, he enjoyed his food. He did not generally talk about the war, he told her. Too many bad memories.

M Musset had a small glass of cloudy pastis in front of him, from which he hardly drank.

'It is a long time past,' he said, in a kind voice, sadness in his spaniel eyes. 'People change their stories. Sometimes they don't even know they are doing it. They hear more of the background in later years and assume they knew those facts at the time. But they did not. None of us could see the whole picture, or foresee the outcome. All I know is what I saw, but even then I cannot be certain I am not overlaying that with knowledge acquired subsequently.

'What you must never forget is that the Resistance was diverse, made up of all kinds of people with all kinds of allegiances. We wanted to emerge from the war into a different country from before, a different political landscape. By August 1944 an active member of the Resistance had a life expectancy of three months, yet many young men felt it was worth the risk.'

'According to the RAF records,' said Iris, 'the Dakota did return the next night for the Americans stranded near Spitfire, but there were no lights on the ground at the coordinates.'

'The reception committee decided it was too dangerous to try again.'

'Were the Germans watching the field?'

'They might well have been. The morning after

the Dakota landed, they shot an elderly couple who worked the nearest farm, no doubt after torturing them for whatever information they had, and burned the farmhouse to the ground. Terrible, simply terrible – and so pointless, you know? The war was nearly over – why did they have to do that?'

Iris shook her head.

'That was the first time one of Xavier's operations had gone wrong,' he said. 'They used to say he was the best of the best.'

'Is he still alive?'

'Who can say? Many people grabbed what they could at the end of the war, especially those who had been striving for a new France, a better France. It was a time when scores were settled, and sometimes not everything was as it seemed. He may be someone else now, or he may be the person he was before the war that we never knew. From what we now understand, it was not just the South of France that he covered, but right up to Paris. He was a wealthy man, we knew that. He could have come from anywhere, and returned anywhere. Or his body might be in a mass grave.'

'He was a successful businessman, I can tell you that. Before the war, and during it, he ran an electronics company. We made inquiries all over France, but he is not involved now in any similar business,' said Iris.

'He was usually known to our cells as the Engineer. That makes sense.'

'What do you think happened to him, monsieur?'

'In the absence of any further information, if

347

you ask me what I believe, then I have to tell you that he is probably dead.'

'But there is no evidence of that?'

'None that I know of.'

Iris nodded slowly, not willing to speak.

'I have made some inquiries,' Musset went on, 'but no one here knows what happened to him after the night the Dakota landed. I remember there was an incident at the time because not even his wireless operator knew where he'd gone. I've even asked the Poet.'

'The Poet?'

'The leader of our cell. A man who would never have been passed fit for any army – too shambling, too apparently disorganised. He had two safe houses in Céreste, each with two exits, just like the fields we used. It was quiet in this region, but strategically important, between Lyon – a hotbed of intrigue, denunciations and Gestapo terror – and the coast.

'Tough decisions had to be made. When we heard that a woman who worked at the pharmacy here in Apt where messages were dropped had threatened to denounce the network, one of us had to take action. Our man was on a bicycle. He shot her while she was outside the station, did it very quietly, and cycled back to Céreste.'

'Was that one of the stories that had to be changed?' Iris said.

'Maybe. Ah – you can rouge the corpse, but it remains dead,' said the Philosopher. 'There were times when grave sacrifices had to be made. The Poet had a protégé, a young man of twenty-two who was as courageous as he was talented as a

348

writer. The Poet himself had supplied his false papers – and one terrible afternoon, not very far from a village, he saw this young man taken by the Germans.

'The Poet could have saved him; he was out of view; he had the Germans in his gunsight; he could have squeezed the trigger, but he did not. He had to make the decision not to fire, to save the village from the ferocious reprisals this would have unleashed. Afterwards he wrote the most moving words I have ever read; he called it "an ordinary village, an extraordinary place". It was a time that marked us for life.'

'I understand that,' said Iris.

Musset gave her a sad smile. 'Yes, I think you do, mademoiselle.'

9

Almost Happy

Sussex, 1950 onwards

Miles Corbin was a good man, apparently without a secret life. For many years after she met him Iris was almost happy. A civil servant like Iris, he rose to a senior position in Customs and Excise; he was as scrupulously honest at home as he was at work. He once told Iris that he had never cheated at golf, though he was once sorely tempted at Sandwich and never quite forgave himself. It might have been that confession that persuaded her to marry him.

If not quite handsome, with his wispy sandy hair and hollowed cheeks, Miles had a certain dash. During the war he had served as a navigator in the RAF's Coastal Command, from which he developed a serious interest in marine cartography; he also had a passionate interest in Greece, its history and poetry. He clearly adored her, was amusing and kind to Suzanne, and he loved to travel – though it went without saying that not even the smallest bottle of cognac or perfume from Paris went undeclared at Dover on their return.

When Iris fell pregnant with their daughter Betsy, she gave up work and became a full-time housewife. When Suzanne was old enough to understand, she was told that her father had died in the war, like so many brave men.

Iris could not easily forget Xavier. At the smallest provocation he insinuated himself into her thoughts. In Paris in the 1950s, she smelled a distinctive lavender fragrance on a woman who passed her in the street. She almost ran after her to ask what it was, but then held herself in check. The familiar scent lingered in the air, leaving a musky trail and an inexplicable sense of danger. She stood in the rue Saint-Honoré, feeling both trapped and euphoric – or had the perfume only triggered these sensations in her brain?

It wasn't quite the same fragrance. This was a deeper, warmer, more complex distillation than the scent she knew so well: the perfume he had sent her, eked out drop by careful drop; the scent of hope that had diminished by the day, month, year. She still wore the pearl he sent her, symbol of the moons that brought them together and took him away. What a fool she was.

Sporadically over the years, Iris was approached – usually by letter – by the writers and researchers of various books on the clandestine operations of the Second World War. Invariably she turned down their respectful requests to meet. Some of those who had been involved, especially the agents who had faced the greatest dangers, were eager to tell their stories and enjoyed the recognition. Others, like Thérèse, preferred to remain in the shadows. Iris never heard a word from Thérèse after her last furious outburst at Orchard Court, and respected her all the more for it.

When she succeeded in banishing him from her waking hours, Xavier shook Iris awake from dreams that began with the night sky, clumps of cloud, moonlight. The small plane waiting.

He was there, even if she could not see him. She only had to glimpse the silvered darkness to know what would happen. Sometimes she was in the seat next to him, so close she could feel the wool of his coat and the brush of his hand.

For so many years, Iris found him in transcendent dreams; he lived with her, still speaking and dancing and tangling in absurdities with her as she slept. In endless variations of the same dream, Xavier climbed into planes and flew into the night, nights so vivid she felt what he felt: the rush and lift of the headwind under the wings; the chill of the glass beyond which gleamed the moon. Ahead, storm citadels and skies planted with forests of electric trees. High in a sea of cloud, the small aircraft hardly moved across gusting waves, hanging like a spider on a thread.

Always the same ending: the sky convulsing, throwing up ridges and folds that might be walls of cloud, or hills, or rising waves. Sea or sky? No difference; no place of safety. The pilot knows when his plane passes the point of no return. The crash is imminent. The black night is still beautiful, clouds lit by moonlight. Time slows. It is all so simple now. No more decisions. What to say? What to do? There are only minutes left, only seconds. There is no time left, only the beginning of time.

The plane is carried onwards, blown by the wind into emptiness.

Long, long after he slid up into the night sky away from her, Iris held him in her sights.

After Miles died in 1990, Iris embraced widowhood. She moved to The Beeches, an ample Edwardian cottage on the edge of a village near Chichester, happily relinquishing along the way the slavery of the lunch and dinner service, the boredom of making conversation with a decent man with whom she had no spiritual connection. Not that she was heartless, far from it: she had made an honest mistake in imagining she could make a successful marriage to a man she had once respected but never loved. It had always been a contract of companionship, and she thought he knew that. Did that make her a bad woman, or simply a pragmatic one? It was all she was able to be. After the war and its aftermath, there were too many damaged souls; she was yet another. For all those years she had been the perfect wife and mother to Suzie and Betsy while Miles commuted up to London from their home in Surrey, to his government desk; Miles with his ever more solid demeanour, his golfing friends, his increasing dependence on whisky, his outbursts of frustration.

Iris did not tell him that in one of the thick folders she kept in a bedroom trunk was the note she had scribbled the night she had seen Tyndale on *Panorama*, admitting that he knew there were double agents, and intimating that London had sanctioned them, though without telling any of the other agents. The sacrifices, in other words. There were other notes and references. One, a photocopied page from Hansard, answered the questions in Parliament that arose after the first books had appeared, with their notions of conspiracy: 'Penetration (by German agents) was deliberately concealed.'

The only person she ever spoke about the war with was Nancy. They both enjoyed their long exchanges by letter and occasionally on the telephone when any genuinely new information surfaced. It had become a touchstone of their long friendship, more than an expectation of a final resolution.

10

Vapour Trail

Sussex, September 2013

The telephone rang. Iris moved so slowly in the early mornings – frustratingly slowly, as if she were no longer in complete command of her own limbs – that she was sure whoever it was would give up long before she arrived in the hall to pick it up. If it was yet another cold call about solar panels, she would tell them that no meant no, and if they bothered her again she would report them for harassment.

'Hello, is it possible to speak to Iris Corbin, please?'

'Speaking.'

'Mrs Corbin, this is Anna Lester from the *Daily Telegraph*. I'm not sure whether you remember, but I wrote a piece a couple of years ago about the National Memorial Arboretum in Staffordshire and the Mavis Acton memorial, and you very kindly gave me some background details.'

Iris sat down carefully on the chair next to the telephone table.

'I remember.' The one time she had relented and agreed to speak, and then only to make sure the facts were correct.

'Do you think I could come and see you? I'm

working on a related story, and sometimes it's easier face to face.'

'I'm very sorry, but I'm not sure I can help you.'

'The thing is–'

'The answer's no, I'm afraid. I – I am not myself at the moment, a family bereavement.'

'I am sincerely sorry for your loss, Mrs Corbin. But you see, the – the way – sorry, I–' Anna Lester was struggling to find the right words, 'There's no easy way to say this. I had no idea that Ellie Brooke was your granddaughter until I started researching an in-depth piece about ... about her death. And I've found something ... that I think you would want to know about.'

'When would you want to come?'

'As soon as possible, whenever suits you best.'

Waiting was always so much worse than facing news head-on. 'Come this afternoon, then,' said Iris.

Through the open kitchen window, the pumping of a tractor engine from a field below echoed Iris's heartbeat. Here on the outskirts of the village, it was quiet and secluded. Cars passed on the road, but not too many. The hedge was kept high on that side. From the rear of the property were sweeping views of the Sussex countryside and farmland beyond a sloping lawn.

'Shall we go for our walk, Marion?'

The housekeeper glanced at her watch. 'Right now? It's early. Might be a bit dewy – why not give it an hour?'

Marion had been at The Beeches so long, she was a vital fixture of the house, like the stairs or the roof. Every elderly person should have a Marion, and it was a crying shame that most couldn't.

'I just have the feeling I have to get on,' said Iris. 'Silly, really.'

'Well, all right. We'll go now if you like, Mrs C.'

The trick of it was never to stop. Walking, in this case, but the same dictum might apply equally to anything in life, thought Iris. Never stop, no matter how much you might want to give in. She worked on the principle that if a person walked every day, there would never come a day when she couldn't. It was stopping that would cause the muscles to weaken and the joints to complain.

Marion dried her hands as she slotted the last breakfast plate in the drainer. She was a large, motherly woman with a soft voice. Her hair had turned grey over the past year, which had saddened Iris. For so long, Marion had been the young woman who 'did', the young pair of legs up and down the stairs.

'Not necessary to go far, but necessary to go,' said Iris.

Marion smiled. 'Quite right. Breath of fresh air never hurt anyone, neither.'

The only concession Iris had made to her daily walking routine was to allow Marion to accompany her. A fall, at her age, would put her out of action for too long.

('Slippery slope,' said Iris. 'In all senses.')

A bridlepath led down one side of The Beeches, meandering to a large pond and a cluster of agricultural buildings and a holiday let. It was a gentle English landscape, of flowing fields and winding paths under trees. The kind of landscape

356

that made one feel safe – that was what he had once told her, wasn't it?

A lively wind threaded grass into silver patterns. A chintz of cow parsley danced on the breeze, and a vapour trail smoked high in a blue sky.

'You're very quiet, Mrs C.'

'Just thinking.'

'There hasn't been any more news ... from the island, has there?'

They made a slow but steady footfall on the stony path. In a wooded hollow, the pond water was a dusty antique mirror, reflecting oak and beech.

'I may be about to find out.'

The death of Suzie's daughter Ellie on the island of Porquerolles had been a loss more terrible than any other. The random nature of the tragedy, the circumstances so unforeseen; that was what had been so shocking.

When Ellie did not turn up to take the return flight she had booked from Hyères to London Stansted, there had been days of worry. Her partner in the garden design business, Sarah, raised the alarm when Ellie failed to contact her. It was three agonising days before the body was found washed up on the south-western rocks of the island. From the start, it was deemed most likely to be a dreadful accident, or perhaps what was termed inconclusively 'misadventure'. Various sightings of Ellie the day before her flight put her close to the Fort de l'Alycastre, the harbour and the hotel where she was staying – then nothing. It was suggested that she had gone swimming alone and run into difficulties when the weather changed. The sea had done its worst to the body. She was identified by a ring on her finger and the necklace she always wore.

That was the salt in the wound for Iris: the necklace. Ellie had been wearing the wartime 'moon' pearl, Iris's one superstition, and it had failed to protect her. It had been given to Suzanne when she was eighteen, and she had passed it on to Ellie. The pearl pendant had come back to them, but Ellie had not.

The accounts carried by the newspapers had been respectful, by and large, but still painfully speculative. But it was a poignant story: the young woman making a name for herself as a designer of gardens, the evocative Mediterranean location, the dream job and the tragic outcome. Iris and her daughters understood why some of the journalists had made much of the details, but could not forgive them for the intrusion on their grief.

Even now, Iris had difficulty in accepting what had happened. It had been bad enough when Ellie had lost her young man in Afghanistan, an act of war that had brought granddaughter and grandmother closer than ever. But for Ellie to be taken in this way still seemed perverse.

All the young men and women she knew who had died young had died in war. They had signed up to carry out acts of exceptional bravery; all of them were daring, motivated and reckless and knew the risks. Some of them had themselves killed.

Different times.

It hardly mattered. Ellie was dead.

Anna Lester was slightly older than her voice on the telephone had intimated, with dark shoulder-length hair and clever brown eyes. A pleasant smile reached her eyes, and her handshake was firm. She wore minimal make-up, if indeed any, and her short linen jacket and trousers seemed to wrinkle more with every movement, an outfit that gave the impression more of a harassed off-duty school-teacher than a cut-throat reporter on a national broadsheet. There was a resolutely self-deprecating air about her that did not fool Iris for a second: she had been extremely well informed the last time they had spoken, her questions informed by a genuine interest in wartime history.

'Do you mind?' A small recording device came out of a large bag.

Iris shook her head.

'I find it easier. I make notes too, but...' She pressed a button and set it on the side table by Iris; then, perched on the edge of her seat with a notebook, she stared around the sitting room. Duck-egg-blue walls, hung with fine prints and watercolours. A walnut display cabinet. A magnifying glass poised on a side table on top of the morning newspapers, the *Times* and the *Daily Telegraph*.

Marion brought in tea, served in the decent porcelain cups, then left them to it.

'Best get straight to the point,' said Iris. She smoothed down her skirt and swallowed hard.

'Last week I went to Porquerolles,' said Anna Lester. 'We had a tip-off that the police had taken Ellie's client Laurent de Fayols in for further ques-

tioning. By the time I got there, he had been released without charge. I was hoping I might get an
interview with him, but – understandably, I suppose – he refused to meet me. I decided to retrace
your granddaughter's journey and visit the locations where she was known to have been, trying to
build up a fuller picture of what happened, looking
for details, descriptions that went beyond the
police reports. I'm sorry, this must be hard for you
to hear.'

'Go on.'

'I stayed at the hotel where she stayed, and
spoke about her with the assistant manager. He
was friendly and helpful, and remembered her
very well. She had arrived looking distressed but
said nothing about the suicide on the ferry that
delayed her – it was only later he found out why
her trip to the island had started so badly.

'She went out every day and often seemed dis-
tracted when she returned in the evenings.
Though there was one night when she did not
come back.'

'Is that significant?'

'Possibly.'

The journalist opened a notepad at a marked
page and ran a finger down a column of writing
mixed with shorthand squiggles. 'I gather Ellie's
client sent someone over to collect her luggage in
order that she could stay over at the Domaine de
Fayols. But the next day she was back at the
hotel. On the Friday evening, the last night she
was booked to stay at the hotel, she came back
much happier. Jean-Luc Martin – the assistant
manager – passed on a couple of messages, and

she went out again, using a bicycle he lent her. But before she went, she gave him something to put in the hotel safe. Jean-Luc had forgotten about it until I came along, asking questions.'

'What was it?'

'A notebook containing sketches, ideas and plans for the garden she'd been working on.'

'He must have remembered to show it to the police, surely?'

'Of course. He said he did show it to them in the days after she died, but they looked through it and dismissed it as unimportant. After that, well, I think the truth is that it got lost for a while when it didn't go back into the safe. The Oustaou des Palmiers is a charming little hotel, but the reception and office are extremely cramped and, frankly, a bit of a mess.'

Anna Lester cleared her throat and flushed. 'I'm afraid I have a confession to make. I may have let him believe I was rather better acquainted with the family than our conversation a couple of years ago would warrant. But as it turned out–'

'A very old reporter's trick. Spare me the justification.'

'Well, you may not be entirely displeased when I tell you that' – she bent over the capacious leather bag at the side of her chair and fished out a black book – 'I have the notebook here. Jean-Luc let me have it, on condition that I handed it over to Ellie's family.'

She held it out.

'I think he was pleased to have it taken back to its rightful owners. They hadn't known quite what to do with it. It wasn't much of a gamble that I would bring it to you. I was upfront about being a journalist, and he was astute enough to realise that I would get a better story by handing it over in person.'

Iris took the bulging, stained book. Minutes passed as she flipped through the pages filled with drawings and notes, measurements and perspectives.

She looked up. 'You have read it right through, haven't you?'

'Yes.'

'I thought so. There must be more than planting schemes and topiary designs to bring you here with it. What is it?'

The journalist indicated the book. 'May I?'

Iris handed it back. Anna Lester turned the pages carefully.

'Here. Can you read this?'

'I'll need my glasses ... where did I put them? Read it aloud for now.'

'It says: "A message for Iris." Your name is underlined twice. Then it reads: "Thy word is a lantern unto my feet: and a light unto my path."'

Iris composed herself, determined not to react. 'Anything else?'

'Yes. There's an account of a Second World War operation involving a French Resistance agent and the lighthouse on Porquerolles.'

'Read it.'

The journalist did so.

Iris tipped her head back on the high-winged chair and closed her eyes to listen. Trembling, she was actually trembling.

In August 1944, a plan was made to disable the lighthouse beam in order to confuse the German night defences as the Allies landed at Saint-Tropez in August 1944. British and Americans working with the Resistance in southern France had originally wanted to bomb the lighthouse, but Xavier (a French liaison agent) refused to sanction the destruction of the Porquerolles lighthouse, arguing that it could be more effectively and subtly disabled. He was born on the island – he had known Rousset the lighthouse keeper since he was a boy. How could he allow him to be killed in an explosion? He volunteered to go to Porquerolles himself.

The island was ringed with barbed wire and mines. Xavier was a native of the island, knew every rock and cove, but realised it would be impossible to come by sea. Time was not on his side. He was already running late after waiting an extra day for a repeat landing on the Saint-Christol plateau that had been called off. He begged the use of a Firefly aircraft hidden near Rians in Provence, and piloted the plane himself on the night of August the thirteenth, the last possible night. Allied bombardment prior to invasion was due to start on the fourteenth.

Landing on flat ground by the cliffs at the Domaine de Fayols, he ran to the lighthouse. The lighthouse keeper Rousset was astonished to see him but agreed to what Xavier asked. He would disable the beam on the night of August the fourteenth – and claim there was a mechanical fault.

It was highly dangerous for Xavier to be on the ground. He ran back to the plane and took off as quickly as possible from a field on the cliff where the wind lifted the wings. The take-off was risky, but he

363

made it. Then the German guns opened. The plane was hit but flew on. Halfway to Marseille, it began its final descent into the sea.

'There are a few notes at the end,' said Anna. '"Are there any records in London regarding that night? Any records at all of Xavier? Why has the wreck of the plane never been found before now on the seabed? (This must be G's big discovery...)" Are you all right, Mrs Corbin? This obviously means something to you.'

'Yes.'

'Can I ask what that is?'

Iris pulled herself together. 'Is it possible that this has a bearing on ... what happened to Ellie?'

'I honestly don't know.'

'Can we verify this story – can it be true? Where would Ellie have found this account?'

'Iris? What on earth are you doing?'

Iris, on her knees in front of the old travelling trunk in her bedroom, started at Marion's admonishment but was relieved to see her. She wasn't entirely sure she would be able to get up again. The lid of the trunk was open. Piles of photograph albums and papers were banked around her.

'I'm looking for something.'

'I can see that,' said Marion, indulgently. She was a big woman, tall and strong; she nearly filled the doorway. 'You said you were having a rest once your visitor had gone.'

'It must be here...'

'What? What are you after? If you tell me, perhaps I could help.'

364

Iris raised her head, straightening painfully. 'You can help me up, in a minute.'

Marion nodded. They had come to an understanding, many years ago. Marion never mentioned age or its limitations.

It had been so long since Iris had last seen what she was searching for. Could it somehow have disappeared? How could it not be there? But it was. Among the most private papers, letters, and mementos was the file marked with his name and enclosing the pitifully few photographs. The papers too sensitive to have a place in the bulging filing cabinet she kept in her, admittedly, rather untidy study downstairs. The cabinet had been exclusively her domain for decades, ever since Miles passed away, but even so she had these items under separate guard. This trunk, leather-bound, scuffed and dented, was the cradle of her older, frailer possessions.

Iris reached farther into the trunk, finally exhuming a small parcel of tissue paper. She peeled back the crackling layers. Inside was a glass bottle, five inches tall. The perfume it had once held was nothing more than a brown stain on the base. She fumbled with the stopper, twisting it off with some effort; it seemed to have stuck. Or was it the shaking in her fingers? She put her nose to the lip of the glass and inhaled. She sat and waited for a moment, concentrating before she took another breath. But it was no good. The scent had finally evaporated. There had been times when she had seemed able to catch a remnant of it, but now nothing came. If she smelled anything, it was the dust and cold hard glass of the present.

Downstairs, in Ellie's notebook, lay what might be the final chapter of the story, and yet it was impossible. How could Ellie have heard it, or stumbled across it? She knew she should contact Suzie, but she felt too exhausted. If Nancy had still been alive, she could have picked up the phone right then. She missed her, too.

A week later the telephone rang. It was around the time Suzie or Betsy usually called, and Iris picked up the phone in full expectation that it was one of her daughters.

'Mrs Corbin, this is Anna Lester.'

'Anna.'

'Look, I know we agreed you would call me when you were ready, but something has happened. Trust me, you will want to know about this. Laurent de Fayols has told the police that he has some more information, but he wants to meet you first.'

11

Le Train Bleu

Paris, September 2013

Naturally, Suzie and Betsy had counselled against travelling, ridiculously overprotective as they were. Betsy, in particular. Slighter, blonder, more cerebral than her sister, she was her father's daughter: risk-averse to a fault. Iris had rather enjoyed the heated exchange that ensued, in which her daughters' opinion that she was too old to charge off to Paris had been countered by Anna Lester's reassurances that she would send a car to bring her up to London and remain at her side every minute of the first-class rail journey on the Eurostar. A five-star hotel would be booked for the night, and the meeting over lunch would take place the next day. Even Marion had been drawn into the argument, finally asserting that Iris really was not your average ninety-one-year-old lady, had never been average at any age and still had plenty of the old get-up-and-go.

Whatever anyone else thought, it was immaterial. Iris was resolute. If Laurent de Fayols had asked to see her, with Anna there as part of the deal, nothing was going to stop her from granting his request that she join them.

'Why can't he come to London?' asked Suzie.

'I don't know. We didn't ask.'

'I want to come with you. I should be there.'

Iris put her hand on her daughter's shoulder, almost the same height as her own. The calm determination on Suzie's face reminded her of Xavier every time she saw that expression. 'I know. I did ask, but he specifically said he wanted to speak to me alone – if I could do it without Anna, I would.'

'It's very odd.'

'It will be fine. You want me to find out what he has to say, don't you?'

The high-speed train across northern France

367

seemed to fly over fields stretched wide and flat under white skies. It was mid-morning, and the carriage was quiet except for a middle-aged couple at the other end and a group of businessmen intent on their own discussion, conducted over four open computers. Even so, they kept their voices down.

'Has he intimated anything about what he has to tell us?' asked Iris.

'No. I got the impression he was not going to say anything until you were there.'

'I see.'

'The police have spoken to him several times, which is as you would expect. He was the reason Ellie went to the island, and she ... her body ... was found quite close to his estate. He didn't want to speak to me when I was there, but I left my card in case he changed his mind.'

Iris put her chin on one hand. 'You asked when you came to see me whether the message and the story in Ellie's notebook could be connected to her death. It seems incredible that it could be.'

'But not impossible?'

She had decided that there was no point in obfuscating any longer. 'If it is, then it is a long and complex story, and one that – I have to warn you – I have never managed to unravel myself. Frankly, I had come to terms with not knowing.'

'Either Laurent de Fayols has something to confess – or he too needs to understand something that only you can explain.'

'We'll find out soon enough. It's a question of trust, Miss Lester, isn't it?'

'Please call me Anna. So ... if this story goes

368

back to the war, it must include your days with SOE. There is currently a great deal of interest in those operations. More and more information is becoming available–'

'With every obituary published in the newspapers.'

'Also being released from archive files.'

'This story may not *be* in the archive files, despite the notes that indicate Ellie's intention to try to find some corroboration there,' said Iris. 'It may involve the unthinkable, perhaps for me, perhaps even for you.'

'I don't understand.'

'How cynical are you, Anna?'

'Not much surprises me.'

'About people, their passions and self-interest, about political movements and government agencies?'

'Very cynical.'

'Good.' Iris reached out and picked up the recording device. 'Condition one. I may be old, but I am still wary. Please turn this off. Now put it where I can see that the red light has gone. You may make notes, of course. Condition two is that you publish nothing without my approval. Is that agreed?'

'That's exactly how I would want to do it.'

'All right. Now I will do everything I can to help you.'

'The story about Xavier in Ellie's notes,' said Anna. 'Am I right in thinking that this must refer to Xavier Descours?'

'I think you must be.'

'You knew him, I take it?'

369

'Yes,' said Iris. 'I knew him. Clearly, you are familiar with Xavier Descours from the many accounts of the SOE in France. Some of those accounts are admirably perceptive; others bear no relation to reality. There again, elements of them seemed like complete fantasy, until I found out later they were true.' She smiled. 'I was in love with him – but even at the time I only knew a part of him. I accepted that. It was necessary to what we were doing that only certain aspects of one's life were known. But later on, of course, the deceptions and disguises we had used made it doubly hard to discover the truth.'

Anna nodded, made some rapid notes.

'After the war, Xavier did not turn up in Paris with the other agents who survived. Neither did he surface in the south. It had to be assumed that he had either been captured or killed. I did my best to trace him, without success.'

'Surely others were searching for him too?'

'If they were, they kept me in the dark. But you're right, other people were looking for him, and I should imagine some were mightily relieved when he would not be found.'

'Explain exactly who you mean.'

Iris sighed. 'The intelligence services, all of them: British, French and what remained of the German. I'm not sure how much you know about the wider picture of the intelligence services, the petty internecine spats between them, what was really going on.'

Anna nodded. 'I've read enough to know that SOE was considered a liability by other services, SIS and MI6. There was little sharing of information. It was possible they were undermined from within the establishment.'

'We all deal in lies – that is the only truth.' That was what he had told her. Perhaps the time had come to put it all on the record.

'I think now,' said Iris carefully, 'that Xavier was not only working for SOE as air movements officer – but that he was working for the British Secret Intelligence Service, and that his real boss was there. I once ran into him unexpectedly, at a Tangmere fog party over at Bignor. He pretended we had never met, and I couldn't understand at the time. But it was clear he knew Bignor Manor and the Bertrams well. The Bertrams were MI6, not SOE.'

She cleared her throat.

'This sounds outrageous, but it is just possible that the whole of F Section was being used as a blind while the real intelligence work went on at SIS or MI6 – and that the decision to sacrifice the Paris agents and the Prosper network was made at the highest level.'

Anna stopped writing. 'I've heard that theory, of course, but consigned it to the conspiracy file.'

'I said, "just possible". SIS ran a network of deniable agents – expatriate businessmen, mostly, who had been operating on the Continent for years before the war. Xavier's profile – the wireless component company, the international contacts – it all fits much better with SIS than SOE.'

'Where does that leave you?'

'A very good question,' said Iris. 'If it's true, then he was probably using me to keep tabs on what was going on inside SOE.'

It was not a happy thought, and the first time she had ever admitted it to anyone but Nancy.

'Don't imagine I was completely naive,' said Iris. 'I was young, but I had become involved in matters of national security – I was pragmatic. I thought his interest in me was probably motivated by some ... favour I could do for him. Either that or the simple fact that it was easier for him to be with me than to find another woman who might complicate further an already complex life. Apart from everything else, he was a married man.'

'But you did try to find out the truth about him, after the war.'

'The powers that were didn't take me seriously,' said Iris. 'Miss Acton thought that because I was in love with him, my judgement was impaired. Why was it so hard for them to accept that I needed to know the end of the story, precisely because I had been in love with him? I wanted to know the truth, not to bend it, as those who were covering their backs were doing. And I had to be so careful, not only out of consideration for Miles, but for Xavier's wife as well. He would never have wanted me to upset her, nor would I have wanted to. That would have been cruel, and I never intended to be unkind. I was very lonely, for a long time.'

Laurent de Fayols was waiting for them at Le Train Bleu. How had he known it was one restaurant in Paris that always reminded her of the war and its networks? Above the jostling concourse of the Gare de Lyon, it was a time capsule, pure belle époque: all gilded mirrors, brass fittings

372

and white linen, a vast cathedral to the glories of rail travel and dining a hundred years ago; above were the wall and ceiling paintings of Mediterranean destinations depicted in sun-drenched, flower-strewn whimsy: Toulon, Marseille, Nice, Montpellier, Perpignan, Cassis, Hyères.

Iris thought of all those meetings with Mavis Acton and their French contacts after the war, the leads that seemed to promise solutions, then went nowhere. All those names, all those places.

Laurent was a dapper little man, dressed in a dark suit and tie; his hair was suspiciously brown for a man in his sixties, and the tan could not disguise the shadows under his eyes. A bottle of white burgundy was cooling in a silver bucket on the table.

Introductions over (gracious but awkward), orders efficiently taken (memorised, not written down, by the waiter), Laurent de Fayols seemed nervous as he turned his attention fully to Iris. 'I understand you knew Xavier Descours, madame?'

'I did.'

'How much did you know about his background?' It could have sounded like a brutal question, but his voice was low and sympathetic.

Iris attempted a wry laugh. 'Only what he told me – what he told any of us. That he ran a company making radio and electric components.'

'That's true,' said Laurent. 'It was in Toulon. He made a lot of money out of it before the war. He was known as the Engineer by the Resistance in the south, even though that was not quite right. As for the rest, it seems he did an admirable job of covering his tracks.' He turned to Iris. 'Did you

373

ever know his real name?' he asked gently.

'I did not. If he had been recruited by F Section, I would have known, but not otherwise. We never asked. You have to understand–'

'You could never have asked. I do understand.'

There was a long pause.

'His name was Gabriel de Fayols.'

Iris brought her hand up to her face.

'He was the son of the doctor on Porquerolles. My father's cousin.'

The island boyhood, the deep blue waters he had described to her. It was all falling into place.

'Gabriel?' Anna pulled out a pencil sketch from inside her notepad. 'Is this him?'

Laurent narrowed his eyes, too vain perhaps to find his reading glasses. Iris took the paper from him.

'That's Xavier ... as I knew him,' said Iris, her glasses already in place. She traced his lovely face with a finger that, like her unreliable legs, no longer seemed to belong to her but to the elderly stranger who had usurped her body. 'Where did you get this?' she asked the journalist, irritated that this was the first time she was seeing it.

'It's a photocopy,' said Anna. 'The original is in Ellie's notebook. Didn't you see it?'

Iris had not.

'The sketch was in there,' said Anna. 'In the blank pages at the back, as if she opened the book at random and made the drawing. She wrote the name Gabriel underneath and dated it June the seventh.'

'I don't understand.'

Anna was sharp, you had to credit her. 'It

374

implies that Ellie found out about Xavier – and exactly who he was – only three days before ... she was found dead. The last day she was seen alive, the seventh of June,' she said, turning to Laurent. 'Remind me where Ellie was that day – in the garden on your estate?'

'No, she wasn't there – that is, not during the day. She came to the Domaine in the early evening.'

'So how did she find out about Xavier?' cut in Iris.

Laurent looked distinctly uncomfortable. For the first time the suave exterior cracked. 'It must have been from my mother. I believe you knew her too, a long time ago, Mrs Corbin.'

The waiter brought tiny rounds of foie gras with quince jelly and thin curls of toast. Iris was not sure she would be able to eat any of it.

'Your mother? Who is your mother, monsieur?'

'*Was* my mother–' He checked himself. 'I regret to say she died two weeks ago.'

None of them seemed able to eat. Anna seemed flushed with excitement at the unravelling tale, though perhaps it was the wine; Iris was uneasy, sensing that more was about to be revealed. Anna had brought her notepad to the dining table, a lack of manners that Iris overlooked in the interests of accuracy. Her mind seemed incapable of concentration, sliding dangerously between the present and past fears.

Laurent de Fayols was intent on establishing certain events.

'Mrs Corbin, I understand that you worked for

SOE during the war,' he said. 'And that a woman called Mavis Acton was ruthlessly protective of the young women sent secretly to France.'

'Many people admired her,' said Iris, gauging from his tone that he was not one of them.

'My mother despised her.'

'Mavis Acton was not universally liked,' said Iris. 'She recruited women into the SOE as agents in France, when no women had ever been to war in quite this way before. She coordinated their missions and worked tirelessly after the war to trace the final movements of those who did not return. She pursued this with great determination – against much opposition from those who were equally determined to wrap the recent past in convenient silence.'

The speech came out pat; she had used it before. There was much to admire about Miss Acton, and Iris would always defend her if she was asked her opinion of her former boss, having learned to keep her real thoughts to herself. 'Strong meat, that was Miss Acton,' she would say. 'A powerful personality. Well, one had to be, didn't one?' Mavis Acton could have done no more; after the war she traced all her girls; it was a great pity that Iris never managed to persuade her to keep going on the men.

'You kept in touch with her when the war was over, though?'

'Yes. I was her assistant.'

'You were good friends?'

'I wouldn't go that far. We worked well together.'

Iris had seen Miss Acton only once more after their tea at Fortnum and Mason. The occasion

376

was Colonel Tyndale's funeral in London. It wasn't so much respects Iris was paying as hoping to run into one last chance, among the assembled signatories of the Official Secrets Act, of finishing what she had started all those years before. But Miss Acton appraised her beadily, as she always did, and made it clear that her inquiries had met a dead end a long time ago. She lit one of her strong cigarettes and dismissed her with the same hand that tossed the match.

That had angered Iris. If anyone should have understood how she felt, it should have been Mavis Acton, but the woman displayed a perplexing lack of empathy. She showed no heart, though clearly she had one.

'I have not been successful in finding many declassified papers about the SOE women,' Laurent was saying.

'I gather there are very few actual SOE papers that survive,' said Anna. 'They were due to be handed over to the Foreign Office, but there was a fire.'

'A most convenient fire.'

He straightened his cutlery, smoothed his napkin. This was a man who would have loved to light up a cigarette as he always used to in restaurants, thought Iris. He caught her gaze.

'How did you feel when you first found out that the real agents were being held and manipulated by the Gestapo, and that SOE was unknowingly making arrangements directly with the Nazis?' he asked Iris.

How do we feel? Always the same question, so lazily emotive. It was invariably asked on the radio and television, when it was facts that were required. It wasn't possible to begin to express how they felt, and certainly not for public consumption. Iris pushed away the hundred thoughts that threatened to engulf her. Had she made a mistake in coming? But she of all people knew that if you never took the risk, you might never find what you were seeking.

'I was furious. It was the first time I realised that those in charge were not taking women like me seriously.'

They had known – or rather some of them had known. The women who would gather to gossip in the ladies' cloakroom on the half-landing at Norgeby House knew, but they spoke only among themselves and said nothing to their superiors, because they were not supposed to know.

'It seems astonishing, but the position of women in society has changed so radically from those times that it barely seems possible now,' said Iris. 'But back then, that was the way it was.'

'And it was left to two women to track down what had happened to the SOE women who never returned.'

'That's right. It was important to know what happened, for the families of those who never came back, even if the conclusion of the story was harrowing... For some it was many years spent not knowing, and in some ways that was worse...'

'But you were satisfied that you managed to find out exactly what happened to each of them?' asked Laurent.

'Yes.'

Anna said nothing, but listened intently.

'Does the name Rose mean anything to you?'

Iris straightened her back and gave up the pretence of eating. She put down her knife and fork. 'It was a code name.'

'What happened to Rose after you sent her over here?'

'She was arrested while working as a wireless operator in Paris. She spent some months being held by the Gestapo, before being helped to escape, along with another woman agent.' It was strange, thought Iris, how readily these facts came to her, when the details of other, far more recent memories remained frustratingly elusive. 'The other woman, Thérèse, was flown back to London. Rose went south with Xavier. It was he who had organised the escape. We had only sporadic contact with her after that.'

'Why was that?'

'By 1944 the RAF and the American Air Force had bases in North Africa, Corsica and Italy – most of the Resistance communications from the South of France would have been to those bases. It seems that she was arrested again. There is circumstantial evidence, unproven, that she was sent to Natzweiler, a concentration camp in Alsace. She died there, executed as a spy.'

They were silent for a few moments.

'No,' said Laurent. 'Rose didn't die in a concentration camp.'

Iris frowned. 'What are you saying – that you knew her?'

'Rose was my mother.'

Laurent summoned the waiter to pour more

379

wine, and said, 'Rose was still working as a wireless operator for the man known as Xavier Descours in August 1944. He was the man who habitually took enormous risks ... and she kept pace with him. But he abandoned her, left her to fend for herself after a big air operation up-country in Provence went wrong. She was told to lie low and wait for him, but Xavier never came.

'She was arrested by the Gestapo as she was making for the plateau above Manosque where the lavender grows. She had a transmitter – she would have been shot as a spy immediately at any other time – but the Germans knew the tide was turning. It was only days before the Liberation began. They took her north to Digne, threatened her, trying to get as much information as they could, but they didn't kill her. That night, a young German officer helped her get away. Maybe he just wanted to save his own skin at the end, but he saved her too.'

'Why did she never make contact with us in London?' asked Iris. Too many disconcerting thoughts were chasing themselves. Too many questions.

'She felt she had been badly let down. Perhaps she had no reason to go back. She took the chance to make another life for herself here.'

'Many people did, after the war. For a long time, I thought that was what Xavier must have done.'

'It always comes back to Xavier. Do you know, Mrs Corbin, that it was because of Xavier that my mother met my father? Charles de Fayols – code name Maurice – was one of those who had helped her escape the first time in Paris.

'Rose met Charles again sometime after she fled Digne. She must have gone south, possibly still looking for Xavier. Anyway, she married Charles in 1946 and became chatelaine of the Domaine de Fayols. I was born two years later. She kept the name Rose, by the way – she liked it. Rose was who she had become.'

Iris pressed her fingers into the linen tablecloth. Her ears buzzed, and too many competing memories derailed her train of thought. Rose and her neat crochet work in the bathroom at Orchard Court, her silence and self-possession, the history that was still being rewritten.

'She must have told Ellie the story in the notebook,' said Iris eventually. 'But ... how did Rose know who Ellie was, her connection to me?'

'A newspaper article, I gather.'

'It would explain the "message for Iris",' pointed out Anna.

'I suppose so.'

Iris tried to stay calm. Too many different strands of thought still coiled in her head. When had Xavier given Rose the message intended for her? Just before he had disappeared? She had never conveyed it to Iris, so was it possible that she had only recently passed it on via Ellie? It seemed absurd, but it was the only logical explanation.

Laurent twisted the stem of his wineglass. 'It was my mother who persuaded me to try an English designer for the memorial garden – one designer in particular. Ellie Brooke. She was most insistent. I thought it was a good idea, something that would make her happy. She was not well, had not been

381

well for many years ... she was unpredictable ... there were episodes of mania...'

Unexpectedly, Laurent reached over the table for Iris's hand. 'I will tell you now what I think happened to your granddaughter – including what I did not tell the police while Rose was still alive.'

Time slipped as she looked into his eyes, so like Xavier's brown eyes.

'On that last evening, my mother was very unwell. All day she had been in the grip of a manic episode. She was convinced that she was seeing Xavier, that he had come for her at last. She was screaming and shouting that she was in greater danger than before, and that Jeanne and I were the ones who had to help her now.

'She was so disturbed, gibbering about evil spirits, cowering in her chair and crying that we did as she demanded, and called a priest who agreed to come and bless the house. Whether it was a real exorcism or not, the incense and the chanting calmed her for a while. She slept that afternoon, a relief to all of us.

'Not long after six o'clock, Ellie arrived to collect her phone. I'm sorry to say that my mother had picked it up and kept it when Ellie left it in the library where she had been working on plans for the garden. We were having an aperitif, Ellie and I, when Rose appeared. She seemed improved at first, but then her mood reverted. She pulled out an old pistol. I had no idea she possessed such a weapon. Perhaps it had been my father's. Even when she took it out, I thought it was not real, that it could not possibly be loaded, or even if she pulled the trigger, it would never fire. But it did. I was moving carefully behind her, intending to take it from her, but then the gun went off. She fired twice. One bullet hit the floor and the other hit a case of butterfly specimens. The glass shattered, but no real damage was done. Ellie ran. Not just for cover, but out the doors and down the terrace steps into the garden.

'I have to tell you, she was nervous, agitated that evening. Different from the confident young woman I first met. I tried to go after her, to re-assure her that she was in no danger. My mother dropped the gun as soon as it went off – she was in shock, and Jeanne was calming her.

'But Ellie – she ran fast. A storm was breaking. It was raining. It is steep on the path down to the *calanque*, and slippery underfoot. You can trip over stones. It's hard enough to walk down in daylight, but on a wet night ... to fall...'

Iris stared up at the murals of coastal scenes set high on the walls, at the painted ceiling, hearing the noise of the lunch service and the conversations over white-clad tables, holding her emotions in check. Carefully, she brought her eyes back to Laurent. It was only then that she became aware of the men sitting at the next table. She recognised the way they held themselves as they sat, alert and quietly powerful. Laurent de Fayols had not come alone to tell her; he had been escorted by the police.

'There is one last thing you need to know. As I say, Rose was aggressive as well as unbalanced, and it was difficult. It was only after she died that we found out why. The myrtle liqueur she drank was contaminated with datura – a spectacular but highly toxic plant. The effects can be hallucinogenic. Perhaps her illness as well as her behaviour that night can be partly attributed to her regular consumption of it.

'It was analysed after she died, and was found to contain an alarming quantity of datura poison. I don't believe she added it deliberately, or at least, I don't want to believe that. That part of the garden had been neglected over the years, and the datura had spread in an extraordinary way alongside the myrtle hedge, threading itself through the place where she always picked the berries. The liqueur killed her, in the end. I'm sorry to say that it's possible that Ellie drank some too.'

Laurent looked ashamed. 'I am so very sorry. Until my mother told me exactly who Ellie was, I knew nothing of these old connections. Rose was hardly making sense by the end, but when she was lucid, it was all about the past. When she was dying, she kept repeating the name Xavier, and that I should tell you she was sorry. I gave her my word.'

There was a long pause, then he turned to the men at the next table. 'Lieutenant Meunier? Thank you. It is done.'

Suzie was waiting when the Eurostar came in at Ebbsfleet. Nearly seventy years old now – unbelievable! – but she looked younger. The family resemblance was strong, particularly the height and the dark blond hair, now artificially ash blond, but she had her father's perceptive brown eyes and olive skin. Even now, her face was not lined as deeply as that of most English women her age, but Ellie's death had snatched away the natural exuberance and self-confidence.

She drove Iris home, concentrating on the road, changing lanes in her usual deft manner, asking no questions, aware of the undercurrents as ever; waiting until the time was right, insisting that Iris rest for a few hours when they arrived back at The Beeches.

Late in the afternoon they shared a pot of tea in companionable silence, Iris both marvelling at her daughter's composure and concerned by it.

'Come with me,' said Iris. 'Let's take a turn round the garden.'

They went on patrol among the leaves and petals, dealing with any unwanted developments, the sooner the better. In the kitchen garden a few tomatoes had ripened, and Iris pulled them off the vine for Marion to serve with supper. Waste not, want not.

Iris told Suzie all she could, choosing her words carefully, about Rose de Fayols, and how Ellie had died. How Laurent and his loyal house-keeper had initially covered up his mother's part in the story that night, reasoning that the firing of the gun could have been construed as attempted murder, that nothing could have been changed by the admission except for further deterioration of her mental state. After the old lady died, how the pathology examination had led to an investigation of the chemical content of the liqueur she had always made.

'Datura can have dangerous effects. Anna did some research on her computer while we were waiting for the train.

385

It can be a soporific as well as a hallucinogen. In certain circumstances, it can induce drug trips that recur for as long as a week after taking it. Sometimes it's enough to smell it, or even to think about it, to prompt the brain to return to an altered state. It's not the physical effects like a racing heart that can kill, it's the illusion that a path goes straight ahead – or that the sea is a garden where you can lie down for a little sleep...'

They sat on a bench by the apple tree, noticing the dry leaves and the first copper curls on the grass. They would never know exactly what had happened to Ellie on that last night. So they talked of her vitality and the enormity of the space she had left; her drive and determination.

'What she wrote about Xavier in her notebook,' said Suzie. Too late now to call him by any other name. 'Do you think that could have been what happened to him – that his plane went down over the sea?'

So many years, so many variations of the dream: the aircraft beating through the dark, the climb into the night sky. The seas of cloud, the controls that did not respond, the start of the strangest journey the pilot has ever made. The horror that habitually jolted her awake: the plane rushing onwards into the emptiness; no time left, only the beginning of time; then, afterwards, the closeness she felt to him as she lay there in the dark. Once, she felt a tender kiss on her cheek that was so warm and real she felt his presence there at her bedside. A long time ago, but vividly recalled despite having convinced herself that she must still have been on the cusp of dreaming and waking.

'I have the feeling it is.'

'And the sketch of Gabriel – what was that, a copy of a photograph?'

'Laurent swore he'd never seen one like that, and there was nothing even similar in his mother's effects.'

'From a book, maybe.'

'The policeman Meunier said something odd,' said Iris. 'Ellie had consistently claimed there was another witness to the suicide on the ferry, but this man could not be traced. The sketch matched the description she gave of him.'

'Perhaps she was trying to be helpful, getting it down on paper the way she knew best.'

'She wrote the name Gabriel underneath,' persisted Iris.

Suzie stared out over the fields. 'You understood the message, didn't you?'

'I understood.'

'Will you tell me what it means?'

Iris considered. *Thy word is a lantern unto my feet: and a light unto my path.* She could not explain the miracle by which the message had been delivered, nor the picture; it was no stranger than the dreams but equally unthinkable to articulate. *I have never loved as I have loved you. You have been my light in this darkness.* Those were Xavier's words in their final seconds together before he flew back to France. She had never been sure, and now she was.

'He did love me,' said Iris to their daughter. 'And he would have loved you, too.'

Epilogue

In the early hours of 4 November, 2013, a small fishing boat working the waters south-east of Marseille caught a twisted piece of metal the size and shape of a shark. The boat pitched in heavy rain and darkness as the two fishermen cursed the rips in the net caused by the object's sharp teeth, and were about to cast it overboard when one of them noticed a flash of silver as he eased away the torn netting and removed knots of weed.

Closer inspection revealed a band of steel imprinted with a serial number. They took a GPS reading of the exact location. The metal shark returned to the harbour with the catch of *rascasse, girelle* and snapper.

The barnacled metal was identified as part of the engine casing of a Caudron C270 Luciole, a light aircraft built in the 1930s and known as a Firefly. The remains of the plane were recovered by marine archaeologists from a deep shelf in the seabed between the Golden Isles and Marseille, where it had landed, presumably sometime during the Second World War, to judge from the explosive damage to the undercarriage.

Author's Note

The area of Provence I know well was a stronghold of the French Resistance during the Second World War. It's the kind of country place where people are proud of their past and stories are passed down in everyday conversation. The Resistance years are spoken about – to British, American and Canadian visitors in particular – with considerable pride and a sense of shared history.

I have long been intrigued by the stories of clandestine wartime airdrops of arms and agents by the RAF, and the secret landings of planes while France was under Nazi occupation. When I began research into these air operations, I discovered a poignant detail in the memoir *We Landed by Moonlight* written by one of the RAF's finest Special Operations pilots, Group Captain Hugh Verity. On the makeshift landing strip known as 'Spitfire', close to the great lavender fields of Sault, a Dakota was flown in carrying key French personnel just before the Allied landings on the south coast in August 1944. The plan was to land, drop the passengers and collect a group of escaping American airmen who had been on the run. But the Dakota was too heavy, and the makeshift runway too short. On the run-up to take-off, the undercarriage snagged on a wide strip of lavender that had been planted to disguise the length of the field from the ever-vigilant occupying authorities. Before another attempt could be made, some of the US airmen had to disembark. Promises were made to come back for them the following night, but it was too late. The botched operation had taken too long, the Nazis and their Vichy enforcers, the Milice, were now aware of it and took brutal reprisals. The next night, the Dakota returned but there was no Resistance reception team waiting to signal it down.

That strip of lavender was the spark behind *The Lavender Field*, the first section to be written. It features the blind perfume maker Marthe Lincel, who appears in *The Lantern*, and tells the story of what really happened to her during the war when she began her apprenticeship with the perfume factory in Manosque. I should say here that the main characters and stories in my book are all fictional, even if they are underpinned by real events.

For the historical aspects of the book, visits to the Musée de la Résistance at Fontaine de Vaucluse, the Musée de la Lavande, Coustellet and the working lavender distilleries at Les Coulets in Rustrel and Les Agnels at Buoux were invaluable.

More insights came from the work of the French poet René Char. In his secret wartime life, Char was a highly respected and successful Resistance leader, code-named Alexandre, based in the village of Céreste at the eastern end of the Luberon valley. The account by his friend Georges-Louis Roux, *La Nuit d'Alexandre*, is full of local detail. It might have seemed, to eagle-eyed readers who notice these things, that my mention of the trustworthy local policeman Cabot in the story was another thank you to my literary agent Stephanie Cabot (as indeed it was), but the good gendarme Cabot did exist in real life; he was instrumental in recovering some jewels which had been stolen on their way to being sold to buy food supplies, not only for Char and his host family, but for the army of resistants hiding out in the hills for whom 'Capitaine Alexandre' was responsible.

In *A Shadow Life*, another young woman experiences a different aspect of the war. In bomb-blasted, monochrome London, Iris Nightingale works for the SOE, Churchill's Special Operations Executive, formed to sabotage and disrupt behind the lines in occupied France. Iris works behind the scenes, recruiting and preparing the agents for their missions in France, and evaluating their wireless messages from enemy territory.

The starting point for this story was the real-life figure of Vera Atkins, the senior woman officer at SOE's French Section in London (Mavis Acton in this novel). A strong woman who provoked strong reactions, Vera Atkins proved her mettle by her resolute determination to discover what had happened to those SOE agents who did not return after the end of the war, especially the women she had personally recruited. In this, I am indebted to Sarah Helm's brilliant and gripping book, *A Life in Secrets: The Story of Vera Atkins and the Lost Agents of SOE*.

The character of Xavier Descours was suggested by the real Henri Déricourt, a pilot (in civilian life) and wartime flight liaison officer between the RAF and the French Resistance. After the war, there were many questions about his true motives, and whether he was a double agent for the Nazis, or triple agent working for the Allies. It is a question that remains unresolved.

Quite by chance, I acquired another source of information and background when I was asked to join a charity fundraiser, Authors for Autistica, an auction in which authors pledge to include the name of the winning bidder in a new book – or a name of the winner's choice. I was invited to talk about the auction on BBC Radio Kent, which I duly did, mentioning that I was researching the RAF/SOE 'Moondrop' flights taking special agents into France. I didn't give any details or character names. I had only just begun writing, though the synopsis was complete at that stage. I already had a character called Nancy, a young woman who was working for the RAF. How strange, then, that the request of the winning bidder was to give a character the name of Nancy Bateman, his mother, who was ninety-one and had worked in the wartime RAF... I spoke with the family, and was sent a photo of their Nancy. I have woven some of her experiences into the novel.

The air museum at what was once RAF Tangmere in Sussex was a fascinating source of information. The clandestine flights carrying passengers into and out of occupied France operated from this airfield, and there is a large collection of artefacts from the era. The curator David Coxon and his staff took evident pleasure in telling me of ghostly sightings at quiet times, especially around the doomed Battle of Britain plane that has been reassembled from fragments dug out of its crash site. They also told me a tale of the disembodied arm clad in wartime RAF uniform that politely opens doors for the cleaners early in the morning...

The late Barbara Bertram is another real-life character, the indefatigable hostess at Bignor Manor. I have not changed her name, and drew on many of the details in her memoir, *French Resistance in Sussex*.

The island of Porquerolles, off the southern French coast, is the setting for the first story, *The Sea Garden*. Early in the summer season, before the main crowds have arrived, the diving by the cliffs and *calanques* is spectacular, and there are shipwrecks on the seabed that are now home to fish and corals.

Some of the wrecks date from the Second World War, when the island was occupied first by the Italians and then by the Germans. The only Frenchmen allowed to remain were the lighthouse keeper, Monsieur Pellegrino, and his assistant. In 1944, Pellegrino saved the lighthouse from destruction by the Germans, an act of heroism for which he earned the French Cross of the Legion of Honour. Although I proceeded to take liberties with the historical facts in this story, this was the starting point for this section.

What links these stories is the theme of communication, or the lack of it: coded wireless messages; torch signals; lighthouse beams; Braille; the human senses, especially that of smell; information withheld; misinformation; differences in language; symbols. The novel's structure mirrors the oblique connections between underground cells, where security is paramount and the best defence is limited knowledge of the activities of others in the organisation.

Of the very many books I read while researching this one, these are the ones I found most illuminating, and recommend without hesitation to anyone who would like to know more about the true stories that lie behind the fiction.

We Landed by Moonlight, Hugh Verity (revised edition, Crécy Publishing, 2000)

Wartime Writings 1939–1944, Antoine de Saint-Exupéry (translation: Harcourt, 1986)

The Resistance, Matthew Cobb (Pocket Books, 2009)

A Life in Secrets: The Story of Vera Atkins and the Lost Agents of SOE, Sarah Helm (Little, Brown, 2005)

Déricourt, The Chequered Spy, Jean Overton Fuller (Michael Russell, 1989)

French Resistance in Sussex, Barbara Bertram (Barnworks Publishing, 1995)

Black Lysander, John Nesbitt-Dufort (Whydown Books, 2002)

Moondrop to Gascony, Anne-Marie Walters (revised edition, Moho Books, 2009)

Résistance et Occupation (1940–44), Midi Rouge, ombres et lumières.3, Robert Mencherini, (Editions Syllepse, 2011)

The Death of Jean Moulin, Biography of a Ghost, Patrick Marnham (John Murray, 2000)

La nuit d'Alexandre: René Char, l'Ami et le résistant, Georges-Louis Roux (Grasset, 2003)

Feuillets d'Hypnos, René Char (Folioplus, 2007)

René Char, Selected Poems, edited by Mary Ann Caws and Tina Jolas (New Directions, 1992)

Acknowledgements

My sincere thanks go to my literary agent Araminta Whitley, assisted by Sophie Hughes at Lucas Alexander Whitley in London, and the dream Orion team of Kate Mills, Susan Lamb and Juliet Ewers, along with Candace Blakely, Rachel Eley, Gaby Young, Alex Young and cover artist Sarah Perkins; my US literary agent Stephanie Cabot, and Will Roberts, Rebecca Gardner, Anna Worrall and Ellen Goodson at The Gernert Company in New York; and to my wonderful editor Jennifer Barth, David Watson, Miranda Ottewell and Katherine Beitner at HarperCollins, New York.

Louise Cummins, garden designer at the award-winning Garden Makers in London and Surrey, generously gave me the inside track on design and landscaping projects for a private client and the Chelsea Flower Show.

Peter Coxon, curator of Tangmere military aircraft museum, and the magnificent group of enthusiasts there could not have been more helpful. I would also like to thank Philippa Stannard and Authors for Autistica for the introduction to her mother, Nancy Bateman, and the use of her name along with some of her RAF memories.

My own mother, Joy Lawrenson, was, as ever, my valued first reader, along with Robert Rees.

The publishers hope that this book has given you enjoyable reading. Large Print Books are especially designed to be as easy to see and hold as possible. If you wish a complete list of our books please ask at your local library or write directly to:

Magna Large Print Books
Magna House, Long Preston,
Skipton, North Yorkshire.
BD23 4ND

This Large Print Book for the partially sighted, who cannot read normal print, is published under the auspices of

THE ULVERSCROFT FOUNDATION

THE ULVERSCROFT FOUNDATION

... we hope that you have enjoyed this Large Print Book. Please think for a moment about those people who have worse eyesight problems than you ... and are unable to even read or enjoy Large Print, without great difficulty.

You can help them by sending a donation, large or small to:

**The Ulverscroft Foundation,
1, The Green, Bradgate Road,
Anstey, Leicestershire, LE7 7FU,
England.**
or request a copy of our brochure for more details.

The Foundation will use all your help to assist those people who are handicapped by various sight problems and need special attention.

Thank you very much for your help.